T0149550

Fields under Heaven

BOOK 1:
Insurrection

DG PALMER

iUniverse, Inc.
Bloomington

Fields under Heaven
Book 1: Insurrection

This is a work of fiction. All of the characters, names, incidents, organizations, and dialogue in this novel are either the products of the author's imagination or are used fictitiously.

iUniverse books may be ordered through booksellers or by contacting:

iUniverse
1663 Liberty Drive
Bloomington, IN 47403
www.iuniverse.com
1-800-Authors (1-800-288-4677)

ISBN: 978-1-4759-5390-9 (sc)
ISBN: 978-1-4759-5389-3 (hc)
ISBN: 978-1-4759-5388-6 (e)

Library of Congress Control Number: 2012922262

Printed in the United States of America

iUniverse rev. date:11/26/2012

PROLOGUE

Pearl, capital city of the Celestial Empire

Admiral Christie of the Imperial Navy entered the base gym. Tall and generously proportioned, he would be a difficult man to overlook in a crowd. He arrived at a counter where an older man, his back to him, was writing upcoming events on a bulletin board. As the door closed behind the admiral, the man turned around. On his shirt was a simple tag identifying him as the manager.

"Admiral," he greeted the visitor. "How may I help you?"

The gym manager was of retirement age; his dark hair was shot through with gray, commonly known as "salt and pepper." From his athletic build and present employment on the naval base, Christie decided the man was likely a former marine.

Christie normally did not come to the gym. His preferred sport was bowling. For conferring with his peers, he played golf. With its slow play, it was more conducive to uninterrupted talk, and the wide-open playing fields kept most distractions at bay. However, the person he had come to meet at the gym was a practitioner of neither bowling nor golf.

"I am here to see Inspector-Major Genda," Christie announced.

The manager looked uncomfortable, which was understandable. The inspector-major had a reputation for fierceness. As the manager opened his mouth to forestall the officer, the admiral continued. "I'm expected."

"Ah," the manager recovered. "I'll take you there, sir." His manner showed it was rare that anyone purposely sought out this member of the Celestial Guard.

Christie followed the manager to a doorway that led to a large gymnasium. Inside, bleachers rose on either side of the large area. On the mat that spanned the floor between the bleachers, a group of men and women were engaged in martial arts training. Their attire varied—shorts and tank tops, sweat suits, as well as the more traditional gi. Of them all, one person stood out.

Dressed in a black gi and belt, a middle-aged woman with short black hair faced a large man who was wearing a sweat suit. At the admiral's entrance her head turned to him. Christie divined nothing from her enigmatic expression. At that moment, the man she was sparring with took her distraction as an opportunity to attack. She collapsed before his onslaught, almost too quick for the eye to follow. The other personnel on the mat paused in their activity to observe what was happening as the man followed her down to immobilize her. In that position, the man obstructed Christie's view of the woman.

No sooner had the man knelt over her, however, than he suddenly stiffened and then fell sideways clutching his middle. With surprising nimbleness, the woman rolled over and effortlessly rose to her feet.

"You left yourself open." Even though Genda aimed her comment down at her opponent, her voice carried easily across the gym.

In answer, the man groaned as he pushed himself up into a sitting position. She held his shoulder to steady him and offered her hand. Accepting her assistance, the man permitted himself to be pulled to his feet.

"Walk it off," she advised him. "Think about what happened. We'll try it again next time."

The man nodded and began his walk. The woman turned toward the admiral and approached him. A few potential opponents attempted to make advances against the woman, but she raised one hand up to decline further training bouts.

She stopped an arm's length from the admiral. Her dark, almond-shaped eyes regarded him from a face that glowed with the sheen of perspiration.

"Thank you for seeing me, Inspector-Major," he greeted her. His deferential treatment of Genda was not meant to be patronizing. Celestial Guard ranks did not equate to those of the imperial military services. The highest rank in the Celestial Guard was that of commander, held by the supreme commander of the service. The next senior rank was inspector-major. With a mandate derived directly from the imperial throne, that authority was equivalent to that of admirals and generals.

"Of course, Admiral Christie," she replied.

"May we talk privately?" He gestured toward a section of bleachers that was unoccupied.

"Yes." The two walked a short distance until Genda stopped and faced him.

Christie spoke first. "I was recently contacted by an official from Holland. He wants our help in the surveillance of his planet."

The inspector was silent, but the impatient look on her face made it clear she did not comprehend what was expected from her.

Christie continued. "I've got most everything laid on for the mission, but I was told you are the one I need to talk to about an undercover security detail."

"Undercover." Genda repeated the term tonelessly.

"This is not an overt governmental operation," Christie explained. "The envoy is not an officially recognized representative. We do not have any treaties with Holland, so there will be no diplomatic status."

"And you were told that I am the one to talk to." Genda conveyed reluctance within her deduction.

"Normally, the marines would be tasked with their security, but this is a special case."

"You asked them and they refused," Genda guessed cynically. "My people are not mercenaries."

"Excuse me?"

"You wish my people to pull security for someone not in our government."

"What? No! I didn't mean to imply that!" Christie held his hands up as if to placate the inspector-major. "The envoy is from our foreign office. She is not a diplomat. She is just a courier. I can send you all of the information I have."

Genda looked at the admiral, nonplussed.

Christie continued. "What I meant is that we do not want her to appear as a representative of our government."

"A spy," Genda speculated.

"No, we're not gathering information on them for us. We will be providing information about them to them."

"I fail to see the difference. Espionage is espionage. Imperial citizens apprehended performing covert subversive activities against a foreign state can be shot as spies. On the other hand, diplomats are immune from execution."

"The empire has never recognized Holland. We have no diplomatic treaty with them."

"Then it would seem to me that the foreign office should go there and negotiate that treaty."

"I was warned that you could be difficult." He sighed. Genda said nothing. "Establishing that treaty first would be for the best all round," he agreed, "but there are political concerns on the ground there that make that action impractical."

"Then why bother dealing with these people?"

"In a nutshell, this place is a backwater with limited defenses. The planet provides all the necessary natural resources to provide sanctuary for unaligned hostile ships. Our long-range patrols are the only naval presence in that area of deep space. It would not be in anyone's best interests—least of all ours—if Holland were to become an outlaw state."

"Spying on them for them," Genda said slowly. "Doing this will help them how?"

"He has concerns about elements in his own government," Christie explained. "He was very forthcoming about sharing his information."

"He? Who is *he?*"

"Oh, I'm sorry. I've talked to so many people about this that I forgot you haven't been briefed," Christie apologized. "I'm speaking of Colonel Stuaart of the Holland Constabulary."

"And of course he's not one of the insurrectionists."

Christie cocked his head at Genda's tart comment. "That's where I was thinking you could help," he replied. "I'll share all of the information I have. He gave us the planet's history as well as a roster of everyone of importance, past and present. With personnel on the ground to investigate, we can confirm his records. For a country with no navy, they seem to have given a good account of themselves against ship-borne raiders."

In her black gi, Genda looked forbidding as she silently contemplated what he wanted from her. "Send the information to my office," she said after a long moment. "I will review it and get back to you."

"Thank you, Inspector-Major ..." Christie said. But Genda had turned around while he was still speaking and strode purposely back onto the mat. Lifting her arm, she held up three fingers. Two men and a woman took up her challenge.

She met the first man, dispatching him in such a way that propelled Genda herself toward the woman. Surprised, the woman braced for the attack. Genda almost flew into her, seizing her forearm and pivoting the hapless attacker into the second man. The two fell to the mat in a heap.

The entire bout had taken less than ten seconds.

"She's as tough as the Wicked Witch," Christie commented in an undertone to no one in particular.

"They're both fearsome."

Christie turned in surprise to see the gym manager standing nearby. The man had remained, after escorting the admiral to the gymnasium, and the admiral had forgotten all about him.

"She comes here about every week," the manager continued. "She works out and polishes their skills at the same time. That sergeant in the gray sweats that she sucker punched before—he'll be back next week for a rematch. It's like that for all of them. She gets through their defenses and makes them figure out what they're supposed to do."

The two men continued to watch the man sheepishly untangle himself from the woman who had been thrown at him. The woman was laughing unabashedly as she explained that the older woman's assault had foiled their plan of attack.

"Show me what you were trying to do." Genda backed away and gestured for them to get up. Her attitude toward her sparring partners was fairly tolerant; she had taken a more obstinate tone with Christie.

Christie gave a noncommittal noise as the participants squared off again. "Laughing in the inspector-major's face seems a rather unwise tactic," he commented.

"It's not about rank out there," the gym manager explained. "Even though she's Celestial Guard, these young people are able to approach her. They respect her skill. "We all serve the same emperor. Strong training makes a strong empire."

"That sounds like a quotation," Christie observed.

The manager nodded in affirmation.

❖❖❖

Office Q, Celestial Headquarters, Pearl

Genda sat at the desk in her office. She was clad in her dark charcoal–colored Celestial Guard uniform with the distinctive tan leather Sam Browne belt over the jacket. Though she was entitled to wear the red blood tab on the button on her right cuff, she kept it in a box located in her personal living quarters. It had been awarded to her after her brief stint as the captain of the guard to the emperor.

As Admiral Christie had promised, the files had been delivered to her office. It was clear from the content that Colonel Stuaart, retired, was a shrewd man. Understanding the reception his request would receive, he had included everything that a discerning intelligence investigator would require.

Given her druthers, she would have nothing to do with this mission. Under the circumstances, what was required was a trained covert observation team. Save for the protection detail, this was not under the purview of her special operations, much less that of the Celestial Guard.

It all began with Holland. Until today, Genda had never heard of the planet. It was not surprising. The inhabitants had not originated from the Celestial Empire.

It took the planet Holland 709 local days to orbit its primary star. Given that the planetary cycle was exceedingly long, it was divided into two years, which were each divided into twelve twenty-nine-day months. Two dividing periods separated the years: seven days at the summer solstice and six days at the winter solstice. These were listed on the Holland calendar along with the months.

It had first been settled as a mining charter almost four hundred years before. Two companies had entered into a partnership: Maitland Conglomerated and Holland Mining. The term of the charter was for a standard ninety-nine years. At that time, the planet had been named Katarina after the daughter of a senior Maitland shareholder. During the years the mining industry thrived, an entrepreneurial economy grew around it to offer a variety of services and needs.

In a span of barely sixty years, Holland Mining had managed to excavate and process the more easily obtained ores. In time, the miners had to go deeper and farther to produce. The process required more effort to maintain quota, a process that became more expensive and time consuming.

The shipping partner, Maitland Conglomerated, chose to cut their losses before the charter ran out and permitted Holland to buy them out. Lacking sufficient funds for an outright buyout, Holland was forced to pay periodic fees to Maitland. Lacking shipping resources, Holland found it difficult to continue commerce, much less make payments. The loss of contact with interstellar consumers spelled the end of the mining enterprise. The company of Holland ceased to exist.

The remaining denizens had already seen the abandonment by Maitland as betrayal. During the social upheaval that came with the collapse of Holland Mining, in spite, the residents replaced the suddenly unpopular name of the planet—Katarina—with Holland, the name of the defunct company. The choice was decidedly nostalgic ... reminiscent of better times.

Despite the name change, no amount of nostalgia could reverse the fact that Holland had become a grape dying on the vine.

The currency of Holland was not recognized on the interstellar market. Holland had originally used the Royal League kroner, known as RLK. In singular form, it was referred to as krona. Also called crowns, the money had been the primary financial medium. The lack of a merchant fleet, much less any shipping at all, had made Holland primarily dependent on trade with the home country. Very few ships made stops there; and a fair portion of the ones that did stop were surveyors for the purpose of provisioning. Apart from such necessities, very few of its citizens had anything of worth to trade. Most everything on Holland could be found on other planets for less effort and cost.

As isolation set in, the Bank of Holland was given additional responsibility. Originally used to dispense pay from the chartering companies, it became an institution to hold savings and expense accounts. It also provided loans for business and personal activities. To make up for the lack of off-planet trade, the bank was tasked with printing local currency to support the planetary economy. Based on the RL kroner, the popular nomenclature for the new money was the Holland crown (HC), but the traditional terms also survived to the present day. The savings and expense accounts were immediately converted to HC. In order to address the currency still in circulation, the citizens were given a short deadline to trade in their RLK for the new currency at a rate of one for one. After that deadline, it would take ten RLK to receive one HC. In the face of a devalued RLK, many Hollanders were quick to take advantage of the offer. The Council of Bremen, having oversight over the Bank of Holland, profited from the collection of RLK. Collecting the universally recognized currency had provided the ruling council a monopoly over what little trade actually arrived on planet. Since the HC was worthless off-planet, the average citizen was unable to buy off-world goods. Conversely, off-world currency was equally worthless, discouraging those same citizens from selling Holland products. Trade was permitted only through the council-approved conduit of Holland Commerce Company, locally known as HCC.

Now something was happening to make the power brokers of Holland seek to consolidate their dominance over Holland. Making a profit did not seem to be enough. Attempts were being made to enthrall the population itself. The competent authority that protected the citizens under their care, the Constabulary General Staff, was being replaced with individuals whose loyalty was to the Council of Bremen. It was this activity that had caused Colonel Stuaart to contact the Celestial Empire.

"What benefit does Holland offer to the empire?" Genda asked aloud to herself. She swiveled her chair around and reached over to the bookshelf that was behind her desk. Within easy reach was a framed picture. The lacquer on the frame was worn where she had picked it up countless times. In the picture were the emperor and his first consort. Genda had taken the picture herself at the Imperial Memorial Garden at the palace. She looked fondly at the picture for a moment then put it back on the shelf.

Returning her attention to the files set before her, she resumed her reading. Like other worlds, Holland supported her population with agriculture. The surplus from harvesting had to be large to last the long winters. Winters on Holland were brutal, lasting approximately ten months. Luxury culinary delicacies, if they existed, were obviously out of the question. The mining industry was a mere shadow compared to what had existed centuries before, but ships did leave with Holland commodities. The primary export was forestry products. Especially prized was an exotic wood known as iron crown. The tree was so named for the rust-gray color the leaves took on in the autumn. The lumber was unusual enough to be sought after for use off-planet. Even so, the economy did not appear to be very lucrative.

The mission as described offered nothing to the empire. Away from regular shipping traffic, the planet would make a logical stopover for patrol ships. Since it was not the Holland government requesting help, it was unlikely that permission would be granted to establish a base of operations. Colonel Stuaart lacked the influence to change that.

For his part, Admiral Christie had been able to sell the mission to the Foreign Office, albeit to a low-level functionary named Hampton Lewellen. It was not lost on Genda that the other foreign office representative was also a Lewellen. This was not unusual since nepotism was common practice in the Celestial Empire.

Additionally, Admiral Christie had managed to get a destroyer squadron allocated to support the mission as well as a company of marines. At face value, such a force would be more than adequate to rescue the small delegation. In a coordinated attack, four ships could systematically spike the guns and land with impunity. Lacking a navy to supplement the guns, Holland would be unable to prevent extraction.

However, of utmost concern was the safety of the population. That underlying nature of the mission dictated that the guns remain intact. Vital for their protection, the defensive infrastructure was placed off limits to attack. Leaving the inhabitants vulnerable was out of the question.

With the planetary defenses intact, it would take more than a company of marines to extract the envoy should the visit turn sour. Those defenses were localized around the capital city and the vast plain surrounding it, making any such recovery suicidal at best. In the face of such overwhelming firepower, even the celebrated Witch could not hope to carry off such a restrictive mission with only one flight of destroyers.

The mountain ranges encircling the flatlands on Holland formed a natural defensive barrier, which the people of Holland had been inspired to name "the bowl." It was on these heights that snipers were emplaced; sniper being the accepted nomenclature for planet-based, anti-ship weapon systems. Since their installation two hundred fifty years before, no raider had successfully landed within the bowl.

The rest of the planet was another story.

The stationary defenses were augmented by a paramilitary police force, referred to as the Holland Constabulary. It was actually one of two armed services, the other being a conventional police force. The police were employed within Bremen, the capital city of Holland and the single largest population center. Outside of city limits, the Constabulary staked out patrol zones. Division East was responsible for the mountains and the portion of the flatlands to the east of Bremen. Division West was assigned to cover the vast remainder of the flatland area to the ridges that bordered the land. It was here that most of the known civilization of Holland resided.

Settlements outside of the bowl were the exception, not the rule. The mines and energy processing sites proved to be relatively undefended targets for preying attackers. The Constabulary maintained a roving patrol, not only to guard against piracy, but to discourage locals from becoming renegades. The history of the planet was punctuated by the struggles against both foreign and domestic enemies.

In addition to the roving truck convoys, the Holland Constabulary maintained a fast-reaction force that used light lifters to not only to carry troops but also provide gunfire support once those troops were on the ground. The Constabulary provisions had proven more than adequate in the defense of the area around the bowl.

An example provided in the files made a case in point. A raiding force of merchant armed ships had attempted to establish a base in an uninhabited hemisphere on Holland. A Constabulary observation outpost located atop the rim of the bowl reported radio signals of unknown origin. In response, the Constabulary assembled an expedition with units from both Division East and West. Division Central supplied the lighters that transported the expedition. In addition to providing intelligence about the composition of the raiders, advance scouts confirmed the presence of slave pens. With only one invading ship destroyed on the ground, the resulting surprise attack was not entirely successful. The other ships escaped, but prisoners were taken and their victims released from captivity. Evidence of piracy and slavery supported the conviction and execution of the offenders after trial. Consisting of a dozen crewmembers and passengers of pirated ships, the rescued prisoners were given passage on one of the rare freighters that called on Holland. Lacking the capability to return them to their homes, Holland officials paid for their passage to a port that enjoyed more interstellar traffic.

Holland was much more than a potential secret base for raiders. It was also a target to be exploited. For years, the population had been fending off raids by unscrupulous trespassers. A battle report underscoring the significance of the threat was included in the dossier. In it the colonel had placed particular emphasis on one of the men.

Lieutenant Michael Wilfz had commanded a patrol during an interdiction mission. His was one of three patrols that had been dispatched against a grounded converted freighter turned raider. Each patrol had been transported in a separate lighter. The attack transports approached at night from high altitude. To avoid detection on the ground, the aerial vehicles shut down their engines and went into unpowered descent. A risky maneuver at any time, it was highly dangerous over mountainous terrain in darkness. One of the lighters crashed, and many casualties were sustained, among them the company commander. By maintaining communications silence, the rest of the assault force was able to preserve the element of surprise.

When Wilfz's lighter landing in the perimeter, he led his patrol with lightning speed through the camp. Although a few of his men fell along the way, the rest of the patrol maintained the assault and entered the ship. The vessel's crew had barricaded themselves in the engine room and bridge, the rest of the hull remaining open to the atmosphere. The crew intended to launch their ship and fly up into the airless void of space, causing the patrol to expire from lack of oxygen.

This was not the first time transgressing ships had employed this tactic. Holland had lost many men this way. It was a tragic waste of manpower. Christie had included a handwritten note suggesting that the patrol might benefit from environmental suits, which should be supplied by the empire.

In the case of this attack, Wilfz broke his patrol into troops to attack the two occupied areas of the ship. His leading sergeant led one troop against the engineering space while the lieutenant attacked the bridge in company with the other sergeant and the remaining twelve men. Despite breaching the door with a satchel charge, the defenders were neither caught off guard by the blast nor unprepared to counter the Constabulary charge. One of Wilfz's men intentionally leaped in front of the lieutenant when the troop came under fire. He was killed immediately, his sacrifice saving his officer. The troop overwhelmed the bridge defenders with superior, accurate firepower. It could be argued that shooting within the enclosed area of a ship made target acquisition elementary. In reality it was a difficult feat to dispense any kind of accuracy while resisting the overwhelming urge to duck incoming hostile fire.

The report gave a pale reflection of the kind of a leader Wilfz was. He obviously had the loyalty of selfless subordinates. It was a rare kind of man who could get others to follow into what was potentially a suicide mission.

Genda sat back in her chair and stared at the closed door that led out of her office. The same observation could be made concerning the kind of men and women serving in the Celestial Guard. They were prepared to defend those assigned to their safekeeping—to the death, if necessary. The report did not end there.

Once the ship had been taken, communication was established with the downed lifter. It had crashed in isolated mountain wilderness, and many of the men were lying broken and bleeding in darkness. They required immediate medical attention but had maintained radio silence for the good of the company, fearing that a call for help could alert the enemy and endanger the other men. As a demonstration of their faith in their comrades, they were willing to wait in the hope that the other two lighters had not crashed and would be successful in the attack. In dire circumstance, they had been confident with the knowledge that they would not be left behind and forgotten. Such esprit de corps was difficult to ignore when taken in that context.

As soon as he was able, Lieutenant Wilfz embarked on a lifter with the surviving members of his patrol to recover their injured comrades. The few able-bodied crash survivors had extracted the injured from the wreckage, and were tending to them as best they could until help arrived. Wilfz loaded the most critically hurt onto his lifter, and sent them to Bremen for hospitalization. Remaining behind with the rest of his men, he supervised the establishment of a camp where they could await their own recovery. That selfless devotion typified the fighting men of Holland.

With his company commander badly injured, Wilfz served as acting captain for months after the battle until a new commanding officer was assigned. It wasn't long before he earned his own company.

Despite the empathy that she felt for the members of the Constabulary, Genda could not completely accept the necessity of the mission requested by Admiral Christie. She did not wish to use her specially trained covert personnel in what was by definition an overt protection assignment. Her people were trained to blend in and not be noticed. The people Christie wanted in his mission could not hope to remain unobserved, especially if they were to contact members of Holland government. By the time she had finished reading the dossier, she had decided on a different option altogether.

❖❖❖

"You will be escorting a foreign office delegate named Monique Lewellen," Genda briefed the Celestial Guard officer seated at the opposite side of her desk.

"Would that be the actress?" Lieutenant Cameron inquired.

"The actress?" Genda paused with a frown then spoke peevishly. "Is she *that* actress? Damn." The two shared a look, and the lieutenant opened his mouth to speak. Genda frowned at him. Squeezing his lips together, Cameron said nothing.

Monique had been a popular starlet, able to write her own ticket in the entertainment industry. Having a reputation as a prima donna, she had participated in a drama production that portrayed the Celestial Guard less than favorably. At the height of her popularity, she had chosen to drop out of the limelight, after which she had apparently disappeared into the obscurity of government service.

"What leap of logic assigned her to this cockamamie mission?" Genda asked rhetorically. "They must have faith in her abilities or believe the mission so simple that anybody could do it. What are these people thinking?" She smiled at Cameron's shocked look. "If I can believe their curious logic, the actress is a decoy." Genda spoke her thoughts aloud. "Holland has a cultural bias toward the *gentler* gender of the human species. In their culture, it would be inconceivable for a woman to be placed in a risky situation. Her famous personality could be the cover story for all of the men in her retinue … men who could provide her with security and attend to her every need."

Cameron gave a nod of comprehension.

"I fear that the foreign office may have over thought their plan," Genda went on. "I wonder if they realize what it means to be isolated. The rest of the universe has abandoned Holland. They lack all but the most basic of everyday conveniences. In fact, it's so technologically backward, it's unlikely that anyone would know who Monique Lewellen is."

Genda went on to explain the mission, the ultimate objective being to enable a foreign nation to continue denying sanctuary to marauding ships. Lieutenant Cameron listened with an uneasy look on his face. Though this new assignment was not in his field of responsibility, as a good officer he did not voice his objection. The mission: establish contact, confirm authenticity of the information, set up communication, withdraw by commercial or military means, and most importantly avoid war.

"You will receive all the information that I have been given, but let me give you a brief synopsis of the situation. Not that the Celestial Guard is supposed to do anything about it, but it would seem that the government of Holland is engineering a coup d'état against itself." He nodded, indicating that her words confirmed his thoughts. "It sounds preposterous, I know, but that's the simplest way to explain it. They are going to use their own police force to take over their own world by first replacing the officers in charge of it."

She watched the lieutenant nod as he absorbed the information.

"The officers will not be in charge of the government, as in a junta, but will act to administer the authority of the Council of Bremen itself."

"Sounds like a dictatorship to me," Cameron surmised.

"Yes," Genda agreed. "Now, here we come to your part in this mission. As I said, you will be escorting Monique Lewellen. As a representative of the foreign office, she will be our envoy. In place of a proper ambassador, she is empowered to provide information to Colonel Stuaart, the man in charge of their Constabulary Intelligence."

"What benefit can we possibly be to him?"

"Off hand, I imagine it is our ability to gather intelligence," Genda guessed. "Our destroyers make excellent surveillance platforms. The good colonel wishes for us to spy on his planet for him and provide him with the data."

"Why do we need to do this?"

"The foreign office wants to create a dialogue with a member of Holland's government," Genda explained. "Eventually I think they are hoping to install an embassy there."

"Shouldn't the marines be escorting the envoy?"

"We don't have a treaty to allow our armed military forces on their sovereign soil," Genda said. "This is splitting hairs, but giving her a team of covert armed escorts will limit the risk of political ramifications. Miss Lewellen will be visiting Holland as a private citizen of the empire. Your team will be employed as part of her delegation."

"Wouldn't our uniforms bring political attention to the mission?"

"No, you will be in civilian guise," Genda clarified. "To help you blend into the local population, your team will consist only of men."

She noted his puzzled look.

"There is an extreme disparity in the ratio of genders there. Men outnumber women five to one." Genda gestured, first holding up all five digits of one hand and then making a fist and holding up her thumb. "Though it probably wouldn't be unusual, it would be best not to attract too much attention by having an overabundance of females in your company."

"A woman like Monique Lewellen is going to attract a lot of attention," Cameron said unnecessarily.

Genda made two attempts to reply. Cameron kept a straight face, his eyes bright with suppressed amusement. She gave him a stern look before continuing. "I know. This assignment is strictly voluntary. You and your men have the choice to decline." Genda gave a humorless smile. "You are not to perform espionage, but since you will be a conduit for the communication of information, there is a risk that you could be charged and prosecuted for that offense anyway."

"So basically this is an internal dispute within a foreign nation. We do not have official dialogue with them. We will effectively be taking sides."

Cameron's synopsis demonstrated his understanding of the situation.

"The difference is that the original authorities have established their credibility through their deeds. The new regime is cleaning house. We have only Colonel Stuaart's files to go by right now. Once we begin surveillance, we'll be able to see the facts for ourselves."

Cameron looked away as he thought about it. "I'll do it," he said finally. "I'll go ask my team and let you know who will accompany us."

"Thank you, Lieutenant."

CHAPTER ONE

Gold Borough, Bremen, Capital of Holland

The chilling bite in the brisk autumn wind seemed to confirm the meteorological forecast of a fierce winter to come. Major Michael Wilfz shrugged his shoulders inside his overcoat, trying to find a warm spot. The coat had been tailored to make the wearer look good, not to provide comfort. He preferred the practical comfort of his field jacket. Since he had been promoted to major prior to his release from the hospital, he had been allowed no opportunity to wear that overgarment, much less his field brown uniform. In his opinion, office greens were the most unattractive uniform of his required issue. The only redeeming feature was the narrow red stripe that ran down the outer seam of his trousers. The stripe designated his affiliation within a specialized branch of the Constabulary.

Two Constabulary officers dressed in blue coats and tan trousers stepped out of the Bremen Central Plaza Hotel. He watched as one of them glanced in his direction and then murmured to the other. Hunching down from the chilling wind, they diverted their heads from him. The bold silver insignia on their shoulder straps proclaimed them to be lieutenants. The two junior officers passed close by as Wilfz approached the door they had just exited. Recognized decorum dictated that they render a salute to him. Using the weather as a pretense not to notice him, they failed to give him that sign of respect.

It was not an unexpected snub. The blue-coated officers believed themselves to be superior to the regular officer corps. Had these men outranked him, undoubtedly they would have called him up short. They would have demanded that he salute if he had failed to respect them as they had just done to him. Even though they did not look at him, he felt no such compunction not to look back at them. The officer who had noticed him first was smirking.

As a superior ranking officer, Wilfz was remiss in not correcting their misconduct. The twinge of pain in his leg, an ever-present companion since he left the hospital, was a constant reminder of the accident. Rather than object, he felt an odd pleasure not having to return the honor. Due to the manner in which he had lost command of his company, he had no problem in not recognizing them as comrades.

It had been one of these self-glorifying blue-coated officers—a pilot—who had inadvertently strafed his forward observation post during a live fire exercise. Rather than follow the attack coordinates, the pilot of the strike lifter had homed in on the radio that transmitted them.

"Amateurs," Wilfz muttered at the memory. The man who had smirked jerked his head up suddenly, obviously thinking this comment was directed at him. He came to a stop, but the other officer gripped his biceps, and the two men kept walking.

The major continued into the hotel, perversely satisfied by the reaction to his unintended slight. As he walked through the door, the heat of the lobby washed over him.

There was little activity in the reception area. A concierge and two desk clerks were behind the counter. Knowing the suite number, Wilfz did not need to speak to the desk help and went straight toward the elevator. The concierge, however, seemed to take exception to this. He raised a finger to get the attention of a hotel employee on the floor. Wilfz saw the concierge point to him, and this put him on the defensive.

As Wilfz reached the elevator, the employee joined him. "May I help you, sir?"

Wilfz eyed the employee, sensing that the man was more than just an attendant. Even though he wore the prevalent hotel uniform jacket, Wilfz assumed he was member of hotel security. The suspicion that colored the man's polite inquiry confirmed his assessment.

"I have an appointment with the delegation in suite two-one-six," Wilfz announced, not a little bit insulted by the apparent lack of trust. In the field, his uniform never failed to inspire confidence in the civilian population. It was understood that he was there as their protector, not their adversary.

"Allow me to escort you, sir," the attendant offered.

"Thank you," Wilfz accepted stiffly. He was unaccustomed to the insular attitude he encountered in Bremen. The capital had its own police force. This escort was a subtle reminder that Constabulary officers had no authority here. Since Wilfz was not a guest at the hotel, his presence was naturally all the more suspicious, if not unwelcome.

Major Wilfz had come to the hotel at the behest of Colonel Stuaart, his new commanding officer. After he had been discharged from the hospital, he'd been assigned to the Office of Constabulary Intelligence. It was not the usual duty assignment for someone on medical light duty. The colonel utilized him as his personal assistant, relying on his experience and knowledge from his years in the brigades. Wilfz knew nothing of intelligence matters. In fact, he felt more like a glorified courier. Because he had no real security clearance, it was not uncommon for him to be sent out for a walk whenever the colonel had a meeting. And this was a curious circumstance, given that the enlisted men who worked the office held higher clearances than he did.

Yet, the colonel had sent him to meet with the Celestial delegation at the hotel, ordering him not to write anything down. He was to commit everything he was told to memory and then not tell anyone but the colonel himself. A very unusual order, again given that Wilfz had no security clearance.

The two men rode the elevator to the second floor in silence. When the doors opened, the attendant gestured courteously for the major to leave the elevator first. Wilfz stepped out, stopping in amazement after crossing the threshold.

The spacious room outside of the elevator did not look like an interior room. What he was looking at was a park. Trees and flower gardens were interspersed among carpeted pathways. The far wall rose up in a gradual curve overhead, providing a believable impression of a bright sunlit sky. The walls on either side extended several stories, and he looked up at the balconies that marked the individual rooms. He was now standing in a beautiful courtyard. Several tables and chairs were arranged for comfort and privacy. On the upper floor balconies, Wilfz saw hotel guests relaxing at tables. It was much more comfortable in this faux summer environment than it was outside where the air was tinged with the cool temperatures of autumn. The warmth of the hotel was beginning to drive out the chill from his overcoat.

"Sir, this way." The attendant brought him back from his reverie.

"Yes." The major nodded. "This is a wonderful room."

"We like it," the attendant said in a conversational manner. "In the evening, the display turns to twilight."

After a short walk down a side corridor, the two men arrived at the suite. The attendant knocked three times on the door. After seeing the spectacular park, Wilfz had expected a door chime. Several moments passed before a swarthy Asiatic man opened the door. As the attendant announced him, Wilfz examined the man in the doorway. Although he wore a simple suit, his trimmed hair, clean-shaven face, and alert bearing marked him as a serving member of a military service. His youthful age precluded retirement, but it was possible that he had been discharged.

"Yes, thank you," the man acknowledged. "The major is expected. Please come in." He stepped back to permit Wilfz to enter.

Nodding his thanks to the attendant, Wilfz stepped past the doorman. As he shifted his stance, a pulse of pain shot up his leg. He made an involuntary guttural noise in his throat.

"Sir?" the doorman inquired.

"Nothing," the major shook his head.

Closing the door behind them, the man escorted Wilfz around a partition and into the spacious front room. Befitting a suite in such a grand hotel as this one, there were six doors leading to bedrooms. Along one wall was a counter and a wet bar. In the far corner was a dining table. At the center of the room was a grouping of chairs arrayed around a low table. Directly across from the dining table, near a corner of the room, two couches were arranged in an *L* pattern. Standing in the room on either side of the couches were two men, attired and groomed much like the man behind him. From Wilfz's observations, he assumed the men were serving as security escorts. Where the swarthy doorman was close to his height, the other men were noticeably taller. They returned his notice with what he would estimate to be professional interest. There was no aggression in their mood; rather, a cool competent self-control exuding confidence.

He had not been made privy to the identities of these people, and he had assumed that they would be entirely male. Seated on one of the couches were a man and a woman. The man wore a luxurious dining jacket over slacks and a silk shirt. Wilfz assumed this was the delegate he'd been sent to see. As for his companion, she provided a very provocative appearance, and Wilfz did not attempt to conceal his surprise. Staring unabashedly at Wilfz, she leaned into the man and hugged his arm. He appeared uncomfortable and annoyed with the woman's proximity.

She was a beautiful woman. Her auburn, shoulder-length hair gleamed, and there was a narrow hint of dark shading surrounding her eyes. Rouge accentuated her narrow cheekbones. A red satin gown clung to her svelte figure. A short string of pearlescent stones suspended from silver earrings dangled against her elegant neck. A matching ring sparkled on her right hand, and another ring graced a toe of her bare left foot.

Of average appearance, Major Wilfz had long ago accepted that his looks would not unduly attract women, never mind a woman such as this one. Her blatant staring made him feel uncomfortable. The women of his nation were not known for their boldness. Given the ratio of at least five males to one female, it was the women who had their pick of life partners. With that disparity in numbers there was no need to resort to attracting men. He turned his eyes from her and fixed his attention on the man he had come to meet. The man looked back expectantly.

Wilfz attempted to introduce himself when the woman interrupted him. "You must be warm in that coat," she said.

Wilfz could not miss seeing the delight sparkling in her eyes. As he paused, the man looked at the woman. For the first time, the woman took her eyes from the major. Leaning her head onto the man's shoulder, she smiled up at him.

Wilfz could see that the woman was proving to be a distraction. Whatever the reason the colonel had sent him, he was certain the woman need not be privy to the discussion.

The man looked away from the woman and spoke to the major. "I'm Cameron." He motioned to the other couch. "Please, take your coat off and have a seat."

As he unbuckled the belt and unfastened the buttons on the coat, Wilfz was immediately aware of heightened alertness from the other men around him. He wasn't sure what type of weapon they expected him to have hidden under the coat. The tight fit of the overgarment would have revealed any concealed weapon.

Having shrugged the coat off, he draped it over the back of a chair and sat down on the couch. With the tailored coat off, his trim physique was more apparent. The woman gave the colored ribbons on his chest a cursory glance, quickly returning her attention to his face. On the other hand, Cameron looked at the display of awards with what seemed to be serious consideration.

Wilfz doubted that off-worlders would know the actual significance of the colored ribbon awards. Most of them represented recognition in leadership and efficiency. In the universe at large, the planet of Holland was only a backwater. War and other interstellar conflict were extremely rare. The only test of courage came from dealing with the occasional pirate or raider, which the uppermost ribbon could attest to. A dazzling display of diagonal black and white stripes, it was the second-highest decoration that could be awarded for gallantry. As a lieutenant, Wilfz had received it after the Third Assault Company had overrun a raider landing zone.

"Those are pretty adornments." Since the woman had initially disregarded the decorations, it was ironic that she would bring the subject up now.

"We don't see the battles that the Celestial Empire finds itself engaged in. That's why our armed forces aren't an army. We have only police and the Constabulary," Wilfz replied in a less-than-candid manner. In reality, Wilfz had led his patrol in a boarding action against a ship. Although the attack had caught the defenders by surprise, the ship's crew had managed to rally and put up a stiff defense. In the end it had been Wilfz's patrol that carried the day. "Here we have found other ways to distinguish ourselves. Administration and organizational efficiency isn't glamorous, but we do our part." He observed her sharp eyes become dull with disinterest. He felt relieved when she turned back to the man she'd been fawning over. Wilfz almost didn't notice Cameron's frown as he took a second look at the ribbons.

"You are a staff officer," the woman presumed.

"I'm newly assigned," Wilfz said with a nod. "Just waiting for an opportunity to prove myself." Most men would try to impress a woman like the one lounging before him. As a younger man he would have been tempted to make himself appear indispensable in his proclaimed area of expertise. Rather than endeavor to look good in her eyes, Wilfz went out of his way to make himself uninteresting.

"I'm sure you will succeed," she remarked in a bored tone.

It looked as if he were succeeding.

"I was instructed to meet with you," Wilfz prompted in an attempt to get to the heart of the matter. Colonel Stuaart had not sent him to this suite to discuss the awards on his chest.

"Messenger boy." The woman uttered the comment in a very low breath. "Major messenger ..."

Wilfz squeezed his lips closed, surprised that the woman's casually expressed words had stung. He withheld himself from responding. It was not in his cultural upbringing to bring a woman to task, even a woman from off-world.

Cameron demonstrated that he was under no such compunction. He quickly turned to her, the anger clear on his face. The woman twitched, startled at his sudden reaction. Then she looked back to Wilfz and saw his pinched expression. Her face lost color. "Did I say that out loud?" Her tone was apologetic as she raised a finger to her lips in a tentative manner. "*Choe song hamnida.*" She leaned forward in a bow, her hair veiling her lap.

Wilfz did not understand the foreign phrase, having never heard that spoken language before. There was no way he could know that she was speaking Korean, the court language of the Celestial Empire.

"Perhaps if we spoke in private," he suggested to Cameron.

Sitting back up, the woman slid one arm behind Cameron, and he suddenly jolted as if pinched. She leaned her head onto his shoulder, never taking her eyes from the major. The situation seemed unthinkably unrealistic, and Wilfz wondered what was going on.

Cameron cleared his throat, his face tinged with embarrassment. Out of the corner of his eye, the major could see that one of the other men briefly grinned.

The major was feeling increasingly uncomfortable, and it was not just the insensitive comment. The other men in the room were no doubt bodyguards. Cameron had admitted to being the contact that Wilfz had been sent to meet, but who was the woman? Her flimsy clothing seemed to indicate that she was a casual companion of some sort. If not his wife, perhaps she was his mistress. Despite the occasional expressions of displeasure, Cameron had for the most part treated her in a deferential manner.

Is this a trick? The major wondered if he was doing anything illegal by meeting this delegation. Based on the behavior he had witnessed so far, he instinctively felt an impulse to leave the suite.

Which begs the question, he thought wryly, *How do I explain this when I report back to the colonel?*

"Major Wilfz." Cameron leaned forward, causing the woman to relinquish her grip on him in the process. "We can talk here."

At that moment, another man entered the room. In his hands was a small electronic device. On seeing him, Cameron held up a hand to Wilfz; then he signaled silence by holding a finger upright before his closed lips. The man waved the device out before him, keeping his focus on what Wilfz assumed was some kind of readout on the top. Taking a bearing, the man followed the signal toward the three seated occupants of the room. He stopped at the table, looked up from the device, and stared at Wilfz. Cameron also looked at him, his eyes narrowed with suspicion.

The man with the device stepped around the table and pointed the unit in Wilfz's direction, but before he was within a pace of him, he paused and puzzled at the device. Then he aimed the device at the table and knelt down, affording Wilfz a quick glance at the meter gauges on the device. A needle flickered along numbered ticks and then flat-lined to rest position. The man stood and extended the device over the tabletop. Then he drew back. Slowly waving the box up and down, he finally centered the device on the rim of the table. He repeated the process by following the table edge from corner to corner, maintaining his scrutiny of the readout.

The man looked at his companions, pointing at the strip of decorative trim that extended around all four edges of the table. Wilfz understood that it was the trim that had registered on the meter. Given the silent attention it had received, he concluded that the trim was apparently some sort of surveillance device.

Wilfz imagined that the delegation had previously swept their suite on a regular basis, looking for subversive electronic activity. They had obviously been monitoring for any intrusions during his visit. He did not believe that it was a coincidence that the table device had become activated while he was there.

The colonel had not provided him with any guidance. His only order was not to write anything down, just to memorize what he was told and then report back. The cautious nature of the order implied that there was an element of risk. Now Wilfz realized that he could be in danger. *I'm out of my depth. What am I doing here?* Wilfz wondered. As an experienced company commander, he was accustomed to exercising independent action. Whatever his mission was, it had become compromised.

Wilfz pushed himself up off of the couch and stood in place. The counter surveillance technician recoiled, smoothly stepping away. The man to his left reached reflexively into his jacket; there was no doubt that he intended to draw a weapon. Saying nothing, Wilfz locked eyes with him. He remained motionless, waiting for the other to make the next move. They stared at each other until the man relaxed, withdrawing his empty hand from his coat.

"Then maybe we can talk again ..." He nodded to Cameron and picked up his coat. As he turned to leave, he felt the pain lance up his leg again. He grimaced as he walked toward the door. The doorman stood in front of the door, giving him an inquisitive look and blocking the exit. He made no move to get out of Wilfz's way at his approach. Wilfz stopped a few paces away, staring the young man down just as he had with the bodyguard a moment previously.

"I am leaving now," he announced in a no-nonsense voice. The doorman's eyes flicked toward Cameron. "Don't look at him. I don't require his permission to leave." *Or yours*, he added speechlessly. He was angered by the suspicious regard displayed first by the hotel employees and now by these people.

The doorman returned his attention to the major. After a perceptible pause, he gave a curt nod and stepped aside. Tipping his head in acknowledgement, Wilfz moved past him. The man followed him to the partition. As the door closed behind him, Wilfz heard an exasperated sigh from the woman.

Stopping in the hall, Wilfz shrugged into his overcoat. With the sigh still fresh in his mind, he thought about her. He had never seen a woman like her before. She had displayed herself so shamelessly. On this world where men outnumbered women, why would a beautiful woman like her bring unnecessary attention to herself?

The twinge in his leg had not diminished. He limped through the hallway to the park and sat at one of the tables so he could massage the muscle pain. If it hadn't been for the accident, he would still be a captain—actually the senior-most captain on active duty. He would still rather be out in the field, doing what he had been trained to do. Instead, he was a junior major on a mysterious errand. *Major messenger* indeed!

❧✻❧

Monique Lewellen had been genuinely contrite when she apologized to the major. Her utterance of the verbal slight had truly been inadvertent. As soon as the Hollander had departed the suite, she went to her room to change her clothing. Lieutenant Cameron followed, clearly displeased with the charge under his protection. She could understand his ire, but it wasn't as if she had meant to be offensive.

"I knew this was a bad idea," Cameron pronounced.

"I remember," Monique admitted.

"And then you had to say that to him," Cameron continued.

"I was playing the empty-headed travel companion."

"Good work!"

"I didn't expect him to get *that* angry!" Seated on the bed with her back to him, she glared over her shoulder at him in response to his left-handed compliment. Discarded across the foot of the bed was her gown. Her pale silk blouse was open in front, and she was in the process of pulling on form-fitting pants.

The two had retired to her bedroom away from the surveillance device, where she could change her clothes. She had chosen this venue to have their conversation, a choice that she found herself regretting.

"It's not as if he claimed to have any special ability," she defended herself, remembering Wilfz's self-abasement. She also recalled that Cameron had said nothing to refute it at the time.

"He did not have to," Cameron countered. "I thought you had read his dossier."

"I did," the woman said.

"Not very tall, is he?" He mimicked her voice. As Monique snapped another angry look at him, she noticed that the two of them were not alone. Sergeant Van, the doorman who had earlier admitted the major into the suite, had joined them. He was holding his superior's overcoat while Cameron shrugged into his shoulder holster. The sergeant's eyes were wide in shock at the irreverent familiarity his lieutenant showed their ward.

She was not bothered by the additional presence of the sergeant. Her lack of modesty was the result of a life previously spent in show business. She was accustomed to sharing dressing rooms with other entertainment professionals as well as the plethora of attendants that entailed. Compared to that, she felt relatively private with only two men in her room.

"Well, people here *are* short," she replied lamely. Neither man looked at her.

"You might want to wear something less provocative," Cameron suggested.

"I have to wear these pants with these boots. They show off my legs to the best effect, and they keep me warm," the woman explained. It was only common sense.

Cameron shook his head.

"If you had bothered to read his dossier, you would have known his appointment to staff duty was recent." With his dogged determination to remain on topic, Cameron had once again proven resistant to her charm.

"We don't have an army. We're just the Constabulary." Monique impersonated Wilfz.

"I'm starting to believe that you have no idea why you are here."

The woman opened her mouth to retort, but Cameron continued. "Major Wilfz spent most of his career in the brigades, much of that as company commander. One of his ribbons attests to his courage in battle. He wasn't kidding about the lack of war, but …"

"My, you *are* angry." Standing up to pull the pants up over her hips, she looked over her shoulder at him. "He's the one who made light of his staff duty. I merely spoke in concurrence."

"As I said, if you had read his dossier, you would have realized that he was unhappy with his promotion."

"Look. I know you don't respect me. I'm not royalty …"

"If I had been assigned to accompany the crown princess," Cameron interrupted her, "and if she were acting as you have been, I would still speak this way."

"As if!" she taunted, still facing the wall in front of her. *If you were really that good, you would not be my escort.*

Buttoning up her blouse, Monique turned to face the two men. She noticed that Sergeant Van had turned his eyes toward the ceiling. Cameron, his face taut with anger at her spiteful comment, did not give her further opportunity to speak. "We are here as representatives of the emperor. We have come to render assistance to a friendly nation. Our navy intercepts raiders such as the one Major Wilfz captured. Their planet may be backward in culture and technology; the people may be smaller in stature, but it has been soldiers like Major Wilfz who have prevented these raiders from establishing bases." He paused briefly, but not long enough for her to speak. "Ma'am ..."

Her eyebrows arched in surprise as he addressed her with respect.

"...given that we are visiting a male-dominated society, you were discreet in pretending that I be the head of this delegation. That being said, it was a mistake for you to choose to be my mistress. It would have been more socially acceptable if you had posed as my personal assistant."

"You've said that before," the woman snapped. "I could never pass as a personal assistant to anyone. You know that."

"You have a point, but I thought you were an actress," Cameron continued. "You take this assignment much too lightly. Your brother may have sent you here to keep you busy ..."

"Uh, sir?" Sergeant Van ventured. Cameron stopped speaking and looked at him with a nod. "I might remind the Lieutenant that if we wish to catch the major before he gets on the train ..."

Cameron took the coat that Van offered and donned it. The garment had been carefully tailored to conceal the fact that the officer was carrying a pistol. Monique admired the fit. She knew the rest of his team was similarly attired.

"Thank you, Sergeant." Monique was truly thankful for the sergeant's cautious interjection, taking it as a reprieve. She did not appreciate the way Lieutenant Cameron had taken her to task. She sat back on the bed and began pulling on her boots.

Monique was not completely callous in regard to the mission. She understood the point that Cameron was making; she had not been taking her assignment seriously. No matter how true, she was reluctant to listen to the criticism.

CHAPTER TWO

Bremen, Capital City of Holland

Major Wilfz stood on the Gold Borough boarding platform. The walk to the train station from the Central Plaza Hotel had restored the chill to him. The station name was boldly painted on the wall behind him for the benefit of arriving passengers. Before him, below the platform, two pairs of rails ran parallel through the station on a bed of gravel. An express train was just passing on the set of rails farthest from the platform, the rush of air causing him to involuntarily shiver. According to the posted schedule, the three-quarter-hour shuttle would soon arrive.

At the moment, he could see downhill into the business district for which the station was named. As he took in the vista of Gold Borough, his mind wandered back to his recent encounter. Memories of the woman's outrageous behavior vied with his thoughts about the suspicious reception he'd encountered in the hotel lobby. Both instances were foreign experiences to him. Preoccupied in his thoughts, he only gradually became aware of the train's arrival when it obstructed his view

The doors were standing open to the coaches in front of him. He followed an older woman into one of the cars. They were the only two passengers in the coach, and she sat in a seat by the door. He walked past her to one end of the car, choosing the bench-style seat facing the platform. The air inside seemed relatively warm compared to the cold draft from the door.

As he settled back in preparation for the ride, he looked outside at the people still on the platform and observed a familiar face. The man reminded him of the doorman back at the suite. Walking swiftly alongside the train, the man was peering in the windows in obvious search. He stopped when he noticed Wilfz. He looked back the way he had come and signaled toward the coach. A moment later, Cameron and the woman appeared, followed by two other men from the suite, one of them the bodyguard who had almost drawn a weapon on Wilfz.

It was the woman, though, that drew his attention. He had never seen any female dressed the way she was. Her fur hat was the only sensible attire she wore, her glossy hair swept up into it. Her gray jacket was edged with fur accents at the collar and hem. Hugging her svelte figure, it fit like a very short dress. Her dark pants revealed the definition of her legs as she strode along in knee-length boots with impractically high heels.

Enthralled as he was by the feminine image before him, he almost didn't see the doorman hold a hand up. The motion caught his attention and he watched the doorman prevent a passenger from following Cameron and the woman onto the train car. The man resumed his duty, now serving as doorman to the train as he had done at the suite for the delegation.

Wilfz returned his attention to the woman, who had entered the coach and was now walking the length of the aisle. As she took a seat opposite him, he couldn't help looking at her legs. Seeing her smile, he realized that he had been caught ogling and suddenly looked away.

Wilfz was discomfited, and he felt his face warm in blush. No woman in his memory had ever worn anything as revealing as what adorned this woman who was seated before him. The dress-like coat was much too short in his opinion, and even though she wore long pants, they were tight and clung to every muscle and curve. No, women on Holland would never dare to dress so indecently.

"Ma'am, could I ask you to sit in another coach?"

Cameron's respectful voice caught Wilfz's attention. Curious, he turned his head and saw that Cameron was addressing the older woman who had preceded him onto the train. The woman looked indignant. "No, you may not," she said.

Without thinking, Wilfz spoke up in her defense. "If mother wishes, she may remain as she pleases."

Cameron took a step back, clearly nonplussed. The woman looked to Wilfz and inclined her head in thanks. Wilfz nodded back.

Cameron looked over at the woman sitting across from Wilfz and then at Wilfz himself. As if making up his mind about something, he turned back to the older woman. He gave a short bow. "I apologize," he offered. "It was not my intention to offend."

"Please think no more about it," she replied with a tolerant smile, graciously responding to Cameron's display of good manners.

"When we last spoke," said the young woman, turning her attention to Wilfz, "you failed to mention that you were the Wolf of Red River, Major Wilfz."

The older woman looked toward the major in surprise, but Wilfz did not spare her another thought. Swiveling his head back to the younger woman, he could see that she regarded him with a quirky smile. She was sitting back now, with one leg crossed over the other, providing Wilfz with an unobstructed view underneath one fabric-sheathed leg. It took an effort for him to not look away again. Ignoring her tightly clad figure, he concentrated on her face.

"Do not call me Wolf," he instructed her in a level voice. Wolf was a nickname that he did not like at all. The woman did not even blink at his effort to correct her.

"You told me that you were 'just' a staff officer," she said in a mocking accusatory tone. "You told me that those decorations on your chest were just recognition for ordinary achievements."

"Well, in the Constabulary, superior performance is ordinarily considered the norm," Wilfz declared. *I almost believe that myself.* He saw that she stared at him in disbelief, as if she knew better.

A bell rang, and the door slid shut. Within moments the train began moving. Cameron sat next to the woman while the doorman and two bodyguards remained standing. The three men kept an eye on the doors at either end of the train coach.

The woman opened her mouth to speak, but paused when Cameron leaned over and whispered something in her ear. Looking over at the other woman, she nodded to him. Seeing her resolve to remain silent, Wilfz took the opportunity to examine the other men. As they were attired, these men could pass themselves off as well-dressed office workers. The doorman shared the relatively modest stature of the men of his planet, whereas his companions were of greater than average height. With their short hair, cleanly groomed faces, and attentive stances the men looked as if they belonged in uniform. Without exchanging a word, they demonstrated the competence of men who were accustomed to working together as a team.

Wilfz decided from the way Cameron carried himself that he was likely an officer. If he were the dignitary of the delegation as Wilfz had been led to believe, he would not have asked the older woman to leave the train car. One of the other men—probably the doorman—would have done that.

Having observed the conduct of the remaining men, he guessed that the doorman could be a senior enlisted man. He had seen how the other bodyguards had shown deference to him.

For a moment, Wilfz remembered the meter operator in the suite. That individual had not accompanied these people here.

That left the woman who accompanied them. From her apparent irreverence, he was uncertain what her purpose was. That she was present on the train did not seem to bode well with this encounter; nevertheless, they had followed him onto the train. It seemed they had unfinished business, and it was apparent that he would not be leaving their company empty handed as he had previously assumed.

Wilfz continued to avoid looking at the woman. It was not lost on him that he was still disturbed by her. The gown she had worn when he first me her had been provocative. Even weighed against that outfit, it was unimaginable to refer to her present manner of dress as demure. There should be some standards, even if she was from a different culture. While he thought about that, he continued to observe the men of her delegation. The doorman seemed to sense his scrutiny and looked at him curiously.

Wilfz shrugged and looked away, only to find that the woman was still watching him. No matter how he tried to resist, she constantly attracted his attention. *I should probably be flattered by her attention. If I were only ten years younger …* He stopped thinking what he would do and amended his thought. *If I were ten years younger, I would not be here and she would have no reason to be talking to me. I wish she would stop staring like that.*

The train began to slow as it approached the next station. This was a residential district; one- and two-level homes dominated the panoramic view. Many were of wood construction, and some were of brick. Above the homes, dark electrical power lines spanned the skyline between towering concrete poles. The train came to a complete stop. As the door opened, a voice from a speaker mounted in the ceiling announced their arrival at Copper Borough. The older woman stood, but rather than immediately leaving the coach, she approached Wilfz. She extended the back of her hand, fingers down, toward him. "Thank you for what you have done on our behalf," she said to him.

Taking her hand in his, he held it to his forehead. He was touched by her appreciation and not a little bit embarrassed.

"We appreciate the sacrifice made by the heroes of Red River," she continued.

"On behalf of those I served with, I accept …" Wilfz couldn't finish the sentence, and his voice choked off suddenly. Many of the men with him that day had not survived to see the dusk. He did not think of himself as a hero. The heroes were the ones who had fallen in service for Holland.

She stroked his cheek in a maternal manner.

"I understand," she said. "My cousin was with the Free Scouts. There is no need to explain."

Wilfz nodded. The woman looked across the train then leaned down until her face was by his ear.

"Beware of salacious women," she said in a low voice. The doorman turned his face away, hiding his smile. To judge by his amused reaction, he had been close enough to hear.

As for Wilfz, he felt no such compulsion to conceal his response. He let himself smile, permitting his teeth to show. The woman seated by Cameron narrowed her eyes in realization that she had been the subject of commentary.

The older woman straightened up, favoring Wilfz with a kind glance. She then presented a look of disapproval to the young woman. With no further word, she departed the train.

In the meantime, the bodyguard had been discouraging new passengers from boarding. The mystified people on the platform looked searchingly at the almost-empty coach before going to another coach.

"What did she say to you?" the woman asked.

Had she been a man, Wilfz would not have hesitated to tell her. However, as she was a woman, he was reluctant to satisfy her curiosity. Even though she was not from his world, his cultural upbringing prevented him from saying something even remotely disrespectful to her. He chose to ignore her question as if she had not spoken at all. Perhaps the manner in which he exercised discretion could be considered a little rude, but at least it would not cause overt insult.

His grin faded to a distracted smile as he took note of her boots. The buff-colored leather had been stitched rough side out. She was already a tall woman, and the heels added perceptively to her height. Having never seen footwear like that before, Wilfz wondered why she felt the need to become ever taller. The leather uppers molded firmly around her ankles and calves, and went all the way up to cover her knees. He could only imagine the struggle she had pulling them on.

The warning bell rang, and the door closed. Once the train had departed the station, Cameron stood up. "We can talk now," he announced. "We don't have much time. Your stop is next, correct?"

Wilfz looked from the woman to Cameron. He gave a curt nod.

"I am the emissary," the woman explained. A moment later she laughed at the look of open-mouth surprise that appeared on his face. "Oh my, you really *are* uptight!"

Unaccustomed to the forward manner in which she delivered her delighted accusation, Wilfz kept his silence. He dared not criticize her unconventional behavior. On Holland, women did not act so rashly, much less hold positions of responsibility outside of the home. That was especially true concerning women of childbearing age. Sending such a woman to another world was unheard of, given the inherent hazards of interstellar travel. With women being essential for the continued survival of their population, it was an unacceptable risk.

Wilfz thought about what he knew of the Celestial Empire. Admittedly, much of it was hearsay. Even though Holland was cut off from the rest of the universe, Hollanders did hear things from visitors. Anything remotely interesting was passed around, often growing or becoming more outrageous with each telling. He felt that was the case here.

The marriage of the monarch to his consort was not recognized. For reasons he did not understand, the consort could not become empress because the two of them lacked an heir. He was also prohibited from appointing her his successor. The ruling line had to remain "in family." That seemed to be a bold and unconventional way to rule a nation. That concept of government seemed unbelievable, but this outrageous woman was giving credence to what he had heard.

"Lady," Cameron warned her in a low voice. Wilfz realized that her team, or at least Cameron, was unhappy with her conduct. She waved absently at him, nodding in acknowledgement before speaking again.

"I am with the Foreign Office," she said.

"You're not supposed to say that," Cameron interrupted her.

"It's not as if nobody knows we're here already, Lieutenant. The surveillance device proves that."

"It's called plausible deniability."

The woman gave Cameron an exasperated glance then looked back to Wilfz. "The Celestial Empire does not have an ambassador here. That is why I have been sent."

Wilfz shrugged at her candor. "We are not a very big nation when it comes to interstellar relations," he said, resorting back to his self-effacing manner.

"After you left, I was reminded of the importance your nation has to my nation," she replied. "I have been authorized to inform you that …" She stopped speaking and looked to Cameron. "You are sure it is safe to speak here. Is it not so?" she asked.

"Now you ask?" Cameron responded caustically. "Unless we are being observed, we are reasonably secure for the moment."

"The electric motors underneath us are interfering with my scanner," the bodyguard at their end of the train coach announced. Wilfz then noticed that the man held a small device surreptitiously in the palm of his hand. "If there is something here, I cannot detect it. If there is long-range surveillance watching us from outside, it won't show up on this anyway."

Looking at Wilfz, the lady pursed her lips in thought. Uncrossing her legs, she rose smoothly and crossed over to his side of the train. She sat down very close to him. He tried to shift away, but she prevented him by placing one arm over the backrest behind him and gripping the lapel of his coat with her other hand. Leaning toward him, she placed her lips close to his ear. "The asset is in place." She breathed the words out in an airy whisper. "All you have to do is ask."

Looking at her from the corner of his eye, he could not help but be aware of her proximity … her light-green eyes staring. His face once again grew warm in discomfort. *I'm getting too old for this,* he thought. He carefully removed her hand from his coat and then stood and took a few steps over to the other side of the car. The woman leaned back and crossed her legs again.

"Don't forget," she said with a small smile. Wilfz gave a nod. The memory of her warm breath in his ear was unforgettable. There was no question in his mind that the experience, not to mention the words, would stay with him for a long time.

※

Monique could feel the train begin to decelerate. The coach rattled as the motors on the wheels acted as brakes. She watched Wilfz stand up and go toward the door in readiness for the train to stop. According to the voice over the loudspeaker, the upcoming station was Iron Borough.

As the door opened, Wilfz gestured to Sergeant Van. "If you get off here, you can catch the uptown train in ten minutes," he explained as he tilted his head toward the door.

Curious, Monique glanced in the same direction as Van. There was a train schedule posted on the station wall. She perceived that a train would be headed in the opposite direction soon. Two passengers stood next to the sign. They had begun to walk toward the train, but paused when the major spoke. Thinking nothing of their cautious behavior, she followed when the rest of the delegation stood, having heard Wilfz's advice to the sergeant.

Cameron came to her side, his eyes on the sergeant. She looked, noticing that Van kept one hand behind his back, out of sight of the men by the sign. She failed to put any significance to that. She watched as he followed the major off the train, his hand twitching. She assumed that the sergeant had hurt himself and was trying to shake off the pain without anyone noticing.

"Stay with me, Lady."

Reacting to Cameron's murmur, she automatically started to ask for the reason when he silenced her with a quick "shh!" When she turned to him, she noticed that Cameron was still observing his sergeant. It dawned on her that Van was trailing the major.

She was conscious of the lieutenant's firm hand holding her elbow as he guided her onto the train platform. Reacting to his urgent manner, she was now fully alert.

She saw Wilfz, hunched in his overcoat, walking toward a kiosk selling hot beverages. He appeared oblivious to the activity of the team behind him. The thought of drinking something warm was most welcome to Monique, now that she was thinking about it. She took fresh notice of the two strange men as they altered their direction toward Wilfz. Van followed after the major as his men took up positions near the lieutenant and their lady.

"Down, Major!"

Monique watched as Van clapped a hand down on Wilfz's shoulder and forced him down to the platform. The Constabulary officer was clearly startled by the sergeant's sudden intervention.

She saw him look around, but with the bench between him and the two men she couldn't tell if he had seen them before he was dropped to his stomach. Feeling a sense of surrealism, she observed one of the men pull a pistol from beneath his jacket. She could not believe this was happening.

"Stay down, Major." Van was sitting on the major's back and, having drawn his own pistol, used the solid bulk of the bench as a shooting rest.

Monique thought that was an unnecessary order.

"You're the one shooting," Wilfz responded. The man seemed remarkably docile considering the rough manhandling he had just received from Sergeant Van.

As for Monique, she resisted Cameron's direction, and she felt him use both hands to force her down onto the platform. She struggled fretfully, impatient to see what was going to happen next. The trash receptacle that Cameron had chosen for cover was blocking her view. The unexpected display of firearms did not frighten her. Rather than feeling terror, she was frustrated that Cameron would not let her up. She reached back to push at him while he drew his weapon, but her struggling proved ineffectual. Cameron held her down all too easily while he aimed his pistol over the trash container.

"Get *off* me!" she hissed. Cameron gave no sign that he was listening to her.

The only place Monique could see was the area where Van protected Wilfz. Looking in their direction, she caught the major staring at her. As their eyes locked, he slowly grinned. *What does he find so funny? He's stuck too.*

Disconcerted by his illogical expression, Monique found herself relaxing.

A woman screamed suddenly. Other voices rose in dismay. The armed men had been noticed.

"Call the police!" someone cried out.

Monique looked toward the train, seeing passengers duck back in. She watched a woman with a small boy crouch down, using her body to shield the child. There was a scuffling of rapid footsteps as others ran for safety. In her mind's eye, she could imagine the people fleeing in terror.

As for the two strangers and her own escort, she could hear nothing. There was no talking and, more importantly, no shooting. There were only two gunmen facing her four armed Celestial Guardsmen.

The two men had obviously been waiting for the major to get off the train. They obviously had not expected him to have protectors.

What's happening?

She watched Van shift himself and pat the major on the shoulder.

"They're gone," he reported in a low voice. "You can get up."

Monique failed to get the same careful consideration from Cameron. The lieutenant gripped her under one arm and wordlessly pulled her to her feet. His impersonal disrespect for her dignity piqued her displeasure.

As the guardsmen put their handguns away, she watched the woman with the boy rise to her feet and hurry the child away. The action of Wilfz brushing himself off attracted her attention back to the Holland officer.

"So, who are you people? Are you spies?" he asked as he looked around.

"No, sir," Sergeant Van gave him a tolerant look. "Celestial Guard."

Monique saw the surprise on the major's face.

"Well, most of us, anyway," Van corrected himself, glancing toward Monique. Wilfz followed his look, and once again Monique met him eye to eye. From his puzzled look, she felt that he was trying to get a read on her.

She watched the two men rejoin the rest of the team. Wilfz's attention lingered on her, and she thought she could detect a sense of awe as he regarded her.

"We have to get out of here before the police respond," Cameron declared.

"Is there any reason for running from the police?" Wilfz asked quietly.

Monique belatedly realized that the Constabulary and the police were brother services. The primary difference was the location of their jurisdiction.

"We have no diplomatic status here. It would be in our best interests not to get caught here. We don't have your government's blessing to possess firearms. I'm sure you do not wish to answer questions about being in the company of illegally armed men." Cameron turned to the doorman. "Sergeant Van, get back to Perez. We're moving."

"Sir," Van acknowledged.

"The rest of us will escort the major home and join you later." Cameron turned to Wilfz. "How far are we from your office?"

"Just five minutes by tram."

"Tram?" Monique repeated in an inquiring tone.

"Bus," Cameron replied impatiently.

"Mine car," Wilfz corrected, visibly displeased. Cameron raised his eyebrows at the major's disapproval. Somehow Monique felt it was not the subject matter that had raised the Hollander's ire, but his inappropriately curt response to her.

"We're going to travel in a mine?" Monique injected a tone of amusement into her voice. Her use of subtle vocal manipulation was rewarded when Wilfz's posture relaxed in response.

"The trams are modified mine cars," Wilfz explained. "The manufacturer used to build and maintain mining vehicles back in the day when we were a charter of Maitland and Holland."

"Quaint," she commented. "I can't wait to see this." She was rewarded with a small smile from Wilfz and an exasperated groan from Cameron.

At that moment, a train headed back toward Gold Borough arrived at the station. Van took his leave from his team and boarded the train.

"Okay, Major, let's get you home," Cameron said. He did not relay any orders to his remaining men. The two guards automatically took up positions at either side of the trio, keeping a wary eye in all directions.

Wilfz guided the group to the station exit. Not far from the exit was a waiting area for the tram. A sign identified the thoroughfare that ran next to the station as Broadway. The street was paved with brick and bordered by wide walkways that surrounded mortar-crafted buildings.

The waiting area for the tram was immediately outside of the station. A bench faced the street, a sign posted next to it. Monique saw the major read the schedule on the sign and then look at the timepiece on his wrist. "Is that analog?" she asked.

Wilfz looked at her in surprise. In answer, he turned his wrist to give her a better look at the wristwatch. There were raised tick marks in place of numerals. Representing the hours of the day, they seemed oddly spaced to her. The positioning was not symmetrical as she had been accustomed to seeing. Given the peculiar time structure of the planet, her delegation had synchronized their digital watches to match.

"It was a farewell gift from my first patrol."

"Patrol," Monique repeated. "Your first patrol—that's like an initiation?"

"I imagine that your armed forces would call it a platoon." Wilfz turned his attention to Cameron. "Just two minutes until the next one."

The vehicle arrived on schedule. Typical of vehicles derived from heavy mining equipment, the driver sat forward and to the left, his seat positioned over the front axle. Since all road transportation traveled on the left side of the road, the driver sat curbside. The passenger compartment was placed between the front and back wheels, so the floor was level to the walkway. The internal combustion engine that powered the tram was over the rear axle. Against the far wall of the vehicle was a long bench.

Inside the door the conductor sat in a seat with his back to the driver. Wilfz handed him a paper bill of currency. "It's for all of us," he said, nodding to the man. The conductor nodded in return.

The conductor looked up from examining the money he had been paid and looked directly at Monique as the group boarded the tram. She could see the attention he was giving her knee-high boots and skin-tight pants. As he made eye contact with her, she gave him a dazzling smile. He twitched, smiling in return before looking away to her companions. *The major isn't the only one who is uptight around here*, she observed.

Cameron guided Wilfz by the arm toward the rear of the tram. Apart from the driver and conductor, their group was the only occupants on board.

"Sit down against the engine. We'll form a human shield around you," Cameron bade the major. As Wilfz complied, the lieutenant directed the woman over. "Sit by him here and …"

As she sat, Wilfz suddenly stood up. "I do not hide behind women," he quietly declared.

"It offends your manhood, right?" Monique found that she was surprised by her own sense of indignation.

"Women should never be put in peril," he patiently explained to her, and then he faced Cameron, his anger surfacing. "Your conduct is irresponsible and dangerous. I find your casual disregard for her safety and welfare disturbing."

Wilfz's voice was low, barely carrying beyond the men surrounding him. Monique looked to the employees operating the tram, but they gave no indication that they had heard any of the conversation.

"Sir, we are just concealing you."

As Wilfz looked to the bodyguard who spoke, Monique remembered his name. He was Guardsman Gray. It was an easy enough name to remember. She didn't need her eidetic memory to do that, but the ability to retain information was what had made her a quick study, and that had contributed to her success as an actress.

Gray slipped his overcoat off. "Here, put this over your coat. I'm bigger than you are, so it should fit." Monique could now see the pistol holstered high on his left hip, the butt pointed toward his right. It took a moment for her to imagine the practicality of being able to reach into his overcoat with his right hand and cross draw the pistol. Given her former dramatic career, she'd witnessed her costars costumed the same way. He held to coat to Wilfz. "Nobody will see your uniform if you're wearing this."

Giving a noncommittal grunt, Wilfz accepted the coat and shrugged it over his shoulders. At the same time, Gray unclipped the holstered weapon from his belt and surreptitiously handed it to Cameron who stuffed it into his own coat. Monique understood that, if anyone else joined them on the tram, no one would realize that there were armed men present.

The tram moved away from the curb and smoothly accelerated along the street. Compared to other road conveyances, it was a relatively slow vehicle, but still about four times faster than a person walking. Monique observed Wilfz. With Gray's coat draped over him, he looked comfortably warm. Ever since the encounter at the station, he was keeping an alert eye on everything he saw around him, examining each person in view. He had since ceased feigning disinterest where she was concerned. He had to be aware of the attention that Monique was giving him from the furtive glances he was sending her way.

I can play, too. Monique settled back on the seat, crossed her right leg over her left, and clasped her hands primly on one thigh. Looking up at Wilfz, she noticed he was looking at her hands. A moment later, he lowered his eyes to her booted foot. He must have noticed that she still wore the ring on her finger. Had he noticed that toe ring as well? Had he wondered about it?

She tilted her head to the side to catch his attention. When he looked at her face, she parted her lips slightly as if asking, "yes?" She was gratified to see his eyes widen.

For a moment, Monique thought he might smile again. Instead he looked over her head with a faraway look in his eyes. It was as if he were ignoring her.

With a little bit of disappointment, she turned her attention to the passing buildings that lined the street. Unlike the lighter architecture of her planet, Pearl, which used concrete and composite construction materials, the architecture of Holland relied on the ancient art of layered brick and mortar. Many of the buildings were constructed of bricks that had been applied by hand. A few other buildings were pieced together using carefully carved blocks that had been put in place with the use of heavy equipment.

In the midst of the stone built structures was one that was made completely of wood. Noticeably smaller than the other buildings, it was enough of an anomaly to make her swivel back to get a second look.

Wooden buildings were not uncommon on Pearl. In fact, wood was often used in the construction of temporary movie sets. During her career in show business, she had spent months acting in simulated residences and other artificial locations.

Monique remembered the housing in Copper Borough, where Wilfz's admirer had left the train. The majority of the buildings there were made from wood. It was surprisingly rustic for a city serving as planetary capital.

Bremen was the only city of Holland. Monique remembered that much from the brief that had been given to the delegation. Despite Lieutenant Cameron's accusations to the contrary, she had actually perused the report. She refused to give him credence that she had not shown the proper attention to the brief. She remembered everything that she had read about Major Wilfz.

As the house disappeared behind the tram, Monique looked forward again. The major had been looking at her, possibly because of her reaction to seeing the distinctly different house. As she returned his gaze, he looked away.

She smiled at his renewed discomfiture. *We are back to playing tag*, she thought.

The tram eventually reached Wilfz's destination, a tram stop across the street from the Constabulary Management Office. The CMO was a sturdy building surrounded by a two-meter-high brick wall which in turn was topped by a series of one-meter-high wrought iron spikes. A narrow gate stood open providing access to a broad stone stairway, three steps high. At the top were located the main doors to the building.

"I think you can make it from here, sir." Cameron nodded toward the CMO building.

"I think you're right," Wilfz acknowledged dryly. Doffing Gray's overcoat, he handed it back to the guardsman with a word of thanks. He then gave directions to a tram stop where they could catch the tram back to the train station.

"Don't worry about us," Cameron spoke quietly. "Just let the colonel know that we're moving."

Wilfz nodded. After raising a finger to his forehead in salute to the rest of Cameron's team, he turned and stepped into the street and turned toward the CMO compound.

"It was a pleasure to see you again," Monique called softly. Wilfz gave no sign of hearing her facetious farewell, but she caught Cameron's expression. He was quietly infuriated.

"We're in trouble and you're flirting with the major," he muttered into her ear. Before Monique could respond, he turned to his men. "All right, let's get out of here. We aren't going rejoin Van and Perez directly. I want to make sure no one is following us. We'll do a little sight seeing around the capital." He spared Monique another glance of displeasure.

Monique remained unrepentant in the face of his anger.

❖❖❖

On either side of the entrance to the Constabulary Management Office building stood two Constabulary troopers, a sergeant and a corporal. They watched as Major Wilfz stepped lightly up to the doors. In contrast to the major's office uniform, these men wore parade dress. Light tan field jackets topped matching trousers that were bloused into saddle-soaped brown leather boots. Along the outer seams of the pants were two narrow green stripes, indicating that they were regular troopers of the Constabulary. Black leather duty gun belts were buckled around their jackets. Completing their ensemble were wide-brimmed hats, the left brim pinned up with the silver Constabulary emblem. Apart from their rank insignia, the only other difference in their uniforms were the blue cuffs on the corporal's jacket. The uniforms were flamboyant, but due to the comfort of wear they were very popular throughout the ranks.

The two sentries pulled the doors open to admit Wilfz. Using the back of one shoulder to hold the door, the sergeant assumed the erect stance of attention and brought a stiff hand up to his hat brim in salute. Wilfz's lips quirked up in a surprised smile. Without hesitation, he returned the gesture of respect.

◄❄►

As the sentries let the doors close behind the major, the corporal spoke up. "We're not required to salute while on guard duty," he said.

"That's okay. He's one of the good officers," the sergeant replied.

The corporal gave him a skeptical look. "What kind of good officer walks in scuffed shoes?"

"Mind your own rank, Corporal."

"By saying that major is 'one of the good ones,' you're saying that the other officers we let in are bad," the corporal argued. "What's so spectacular about that major anyway?"

The sergeant contemptuously looked at the corporal's blue cuffs, declining to answer.

◄❄►

Wilfz mulled over his thoughts as he left the team and the woman. He could not understand the lady's behavior. He had indeed heard the woman's farewell remark, her bold manner implying some kind of intimate relationship. Not knowing how to answer, he had chosen not to react.

Back at the station, when they were disembarking, he had not noticed the two men until the doorman pulled him down to the ground. It had not previously occurred to him that he would be in danger … that he would be the target of persons unknown. Living in the relative safety of Bremen had lulled him into docility. His folly was compounded by his overconfidence as a Constabulary officer. As a law enforcement officer in his own right, what would he have to fear from local peaceful-mannered denizens?

He had been helpless to defend himself from the strange men. The timely action of his new acquaintances had prevented whatever had been planned, and their response had indicated their care not to initiate a firefight in the crowded public place. They had acted together wordlessly, displaying a deliberate competence that he admired.

As for the attackers, in his opinion the encounter could have ended only one way for them. Not having cover for their protection, they had chosen discretion over defeat. After all, they must have been as surprised as he was to discover that he had backup support.

What puzzled him was the reason for the attack. Though he did not understand Colonel Stuaart's secrecy, it would appear that he did have reason. The men at the station had not worn uniforms. Were they affiliated with law enforcement? Were they even representatives of the government of Holland? He suspected not. That they had chosen to depart rather than communicate their intention seemed to indicate a lack of legitimacy. Something was definitely not right.

He thought back to the permanently mounted surveillance device on the table in the suite. It had activated while he was present in the suite, a sign that someone was interested in his activity with these people. From the encounter at the station, it would seem that the interlopers had been unable to eavesdrop on the lady's whisper. He remembered her words, breathed warmly into his ear: "The asset is in place. All you have to do is ask."

What was the "asset"? Who wanted to know about it? If he were to be interrogated, what little information he knew would be of questionable value. *They're not going back to the hotel. How do we contact them to ask? Hmm, they did not say how we go about doing that.* Wilfz hoped that the colonel would know.

With so little to work with, his mind shifted from the mystery of his errand to the people he'd just met. The Celestial Guard was the premiere protection service for the royal family of the Celestial Empire. They were famous for their motto, which stated that as long as their ward was within their sight, they had jurisdiction. Did the fact that they accompanied the auburn-haired woman mean she was a member of the imperial family? He had believed that all of the royals were of Asiatic heritage, just like the doorman. Perhaps this woman was the world-famous first consort to the emperor. As soon as that thought came to mind, it immediately seemed unlikely. A world leader surely would not send a personal acquaintance into a potentially perilous situation. But, with the Celestial Guard as her protectors, she was apparently of some import.

That would explain her haughty attitude, Wilfz decided.

Back on the tram when she had caught him looking at the ring on her hand, he had almost asked about her connection to the royal family. In spite of the inviting smile she had given him, he had decided not to satisfy her curiosity with such a personal question. Her blatantly provocative behavior was quite unlike anything he had ever experienced before. Even now, after he had left her company, she still preyed on his mind. He could not stop thinking about her. With the gender disparity on Holland, it was unthinkable that a woman would tease a man. On a planet where only one man in five could hope for marriage, Wilfz had long resigned himself to a life alone. In his family, he had three brothers and no sister. Not being the eldest, he could expect little in the way of inheritance. His older brother worked for their father and would take over the family business one day. In spite of being middle aged, his prospects of marriage were considered good due to the affluence of the family. Wilfz's two younger brothers had also become involved in the family businesses, one having worked his way up to running the ranch while the other had gone into forestry to manage the orchards and lumber.

As for Wilfz, his talent lay in tracking and hunting, a solitary pursuit his father had tried to discourage. Mentored by his uncle on his mother's side, Wilfz found himself estranged from his family simply because of a skill he had developed.

Wilfz followed the hallway leading from the grand vestibule. After the first few days, he had become a familiar enough figure in the CMO that he was no longer stopped. The officer in charge merely noted his arrival in the logbook at the main desk. At the end of the hallway was a staircase that led down to the basement. Wilfz took the stairs. When the steps reversed course at a landing, he did not continue downward. Instead, he stopped and faced a door to his right that was heavily barricaded and fitted with a small, shuttered observation window at face level. He pounded on the heavy metal with a closed fist. His assault barely rattled the door within the jamb. Locked in place, the door was as sturdy as the cement wall. The shutter opened and a sentry peered out.

"It's me." Wilfz held up his identification card for the man to see. His manner seemed irreverent to the security process, but in his opinion it seemed redundant to speak his name when the sentry could read it clearly.

Raising the crossbar that held the door closed from within, the sentry swung the door back and admitted him.

"Lang is with the colonel," the sentry said in a carefully low voice. "I think he is looking for you."

Wilfz gave a noncommittal grunt. Director Lang was the council-appointed civilian head of the Constabulary. *Why would the headman of the Constabulary be concerned with* this *lowly major?*

The passage was darker than the stairwell he had just come down. There were fewer lighting fixtures down here than in the rest of the building. The closed doors he passed were widely spaced, implying large rooms beyond. At the end of the hall was an open door. The room within was much brighter. As he entered, he could hear an indistinct angry voice coming from beyond another closed door within. He knew the room was Colonel Stuaart's office.

"Thank goodness you're here." This was from Lieutenant Holloway, who was seated behind a desk in the corner of the room. On the other side of the room were several file cabinets. Two sergeants were, as far as Wilfz could see, pretending to work. The men were carefully fingering through the file folders stored in the upper drawers. There was a closed door across from the one that Wilfz had just entered that led, he knew, to a storeroom. Another door was located between the filing cabinets. It too was closed, and that was where the sound of the voice came from.

The lieutenant left his desk and crossed the room. He knocked twice on the door and opened it part way. The voice suddenly stopped in midsentence as Wilfz was announced.

"Send him in," the angry speaker snapped.

"We'll see him now." The colonel's voice sounded calm and polite in contrast.

Wilfz stepped past the lieutenant and into the colonel's office. As the door was closed behind him, he wondered if the men in the outer office would remain in place or find other matters to occupy themselves elsewhere.

"Major, where the hell have you been?"

This demand was from Constabulary Director Lang. His expensively tailored suit fit well over his broad shoulders and revealed a man who had previously worked his way up in the banking industry. Behind him Colonel Stuaart sat at his desk. The suit he wore was thread worn, as would befit an office clerk rather than the civilian in charge of Constabulary Intelligence.

Colonel Stuaart was no longer on active duty. He had previously worked on staff for the general commanding Division East. Given the extensive knowledge he had acquired in the intelligence field by the time he retired, it had been decided to employ the colonel in a civilian capacity. Outside the Constabulary chain of command, he was free to pursue his duty any way he saw fit. The rest of his office was staffed with active duty members of the Constabulary. For all intents and purposes, they resided outside of the chain of command, answering to him only. Even though Wilfz was assigned to Stuaart, he had no authority over the colonel's men.

"I asked you a question, Major!"

Wilfz could not understand what he had done wrong. His years as a captain, leading in the field, had accustomed him to wielding authority. Lieutenants naturally needed guidance from the officers senior to them. Captains, on the other hand, had proven that their judgment was sound. Wilfz had been a senior captain for several years. To be queried in such a disrespectful manner was uncalled for, no matter the superior position of the questioner. Not a little bit angered, he allowed his mouth free reign before he could stop himself. "I went out for a hot coffee."

"You went to a train station? That's a long way to go just for a drink," Lang seethed. "It's hardly the productive use of time I would expect from a major!"

"I didn't ask to be a major," Wilfz countered, unrepentant. "Bust me to captain and send me back to the field." *Back where I belong.*

"Don't take that tone with me, Major!" Lang shouted.

"We have already discussed this," Stuaart interjected. "That is not possible."

Wilfz stared at Stuaart, prepared to take issue with the retired colonel. The two of them had never discussed Wilfz's desire for a reduction in rank. Stuaart held up a hand warning him to remain silent. With his back to the colonel, Lang had not seen the gesture.

"I have a report from the police about a Constabulary major involved in a gunfight," Lang continued.

"Gunfight? I have not been issued a firearm," Wilfz stated. "Am I being accused of something? I want to see this report."

"Are you denying your involvement in this?"

"Of what am I being accused?"

"Answer my question!"

"Make your accusation!"

"Director," Stuaart regained Lang's attention. "I sent Major Wilfz out to familiarize himself with Bremen. The exercise also serves as his medical rehabilitation. You *do* recall that he is on light duty?"

"Who were those people you were with?" Lang would not drop his line of questioning.

"I don't know." Wilfz shrugged. "I don't know anybody here in Bremen."

He met Lang's stare for several moments, not inclined to give the director satisfaction by looking away first. Colonel Stuaart had ordered Wilfz not to discuss this subject with anyone but Stuaart himself, but it was difficult for him to keep silent … not to tell Lang to ask the colonel about the things he wanted to know.

"This is not over," Lang finally said. "There will be an investigation." He walked to the door, almost pushing Wilfz aside as he left.

Stuaart flashed a hand signal to his lieutenant. The young officer went to the outer door and watched down the passageway as Lang left the area. During the meantime, no one spoke.

"He's out of the complex," the lieutenant reported after a brief while.

"Very good," Stuaart replied. "Let me know if anybody comes."

With that, the colonel closed the door and bade for Wilfz to sit. Stuaart went around the desk and sat in his chair across from him.

"Okay," he said. "What really happened? Start at the beginning."

Wilfz described his arrival at the hotel. He gave his honest appraisal of the members of the delegation—the men of the Celestial Guard were competent, but he had been unsettled that a woman had been sent as envoy. He could see Stuaart echo his feelings of incredulousness. Even if other worlds enjoyed gender parity, the thought of women serving alongside men in the military and sharing the risk of combat was unconscionable to these Holland men. Such was the strength of their cultural upbringing. Stuaart raised his hand to stop Wilfz when he reached the point in the report about what happened when he left the hotel suite.

"You left before getting the word?"

Wilfz nodded.

"Major, do you mean to tell me that you ran like a little boy?"

Wilfz stood up suddenly, the chair scooting back with a squeal. Of any reaction he expected from this retired colonel, a charge of cowardice was not one of them.

"You are free to relieve me," Wilfz said carefully. Sensitive and a bit angry from the Constabulary Director's tirade, he permitted his displeasure to show. "If you want it, you can have my resignation right now."

Stuaart remained silent, merely regarding the major.

"After what happened today, perhaps I should submit it anyway," Wilfz continued in a grating voice.

"And then what? What will you do?"

"I will go to the Free Scouts," Wilfz answered, surprising himself. He had not stopped to consider what he would do if he were to resign from the Constabulary. Until a moment ago, resignation had not been a conscious option. Now he wondered why he had not thought of it before. "Forget this nonsense. I don't know what I'm doing here anyway."

"I'm sorry, Major, but that is not going to happen." Stuaart replied. "Lang disbanded the Free Scouts some weeks ago."

Wilfz sat down in his chair hard, blinking from the impact. "Is he insane? No one knows the territory like they do!"

"There is a method to his madness," Stuaart replied, seeming pleased by the major's reaction.

"Things were so much simpler when I was a captain."

"Unfortunately, as I said before, that is not an option," the colonel intoned. "Things are only going to get worse around here for us."

"Well then, this is as good a time as any," Wilfz motioned to the desk. "I'll write my resignation and get out of your hair. It seems I've caused enough trouble for you."

"That will not save either of us from Lang," Stuaart said. He paused, holding his hand up to prevent Wilfz from speaking. "I may have been critically judgmental in questioning your courage. That was not my intention. I apologize for that."

Considering the colonel's words, Wilfz nodded after a moment. "That does not change the fact that I have no business sneaking around Bremen," he announced. "I don't understand what I am doing here."

"Believe me when I tell you this, Major," Stuaart said. "You are singularly qualified for this."

"Really ..." came Wilfz's dubious response.

"You're not going to like what I have to tell you," Stuaart predicted. "However, you were telling me about your day. Please continue, Major."

With dread growing concerning what was in store for him, Wilfz thought back to what he had already told Stuaart. Remembering where he had stopped, he returned to his story. He related how the delegation had followed him onto the train in Gold Borough. He skipped over much of the train trip, coming to the point that Stuaart had been waiting for. "The asset is in place. You just have to ask," Wilfz quoted the woman's message, his mind dwelling on that unforgettable moment.

"Good. We have that," Stuaart sounded pleased.

"There's more. This is the part of the story that the director was haranguing me about."

Stuaart nodded for Wilfz to continue. Wilfz described the encounter with the two armed men at Iron Borough Station. Following this, he relayed the message that the delegation would be moving.

"Okay. That makes sense." Stuaart nodded again. Wilfz thought that Stuaart should have expressed surprise at that bit of information, perhaps even have asked if the lieutenant had given him directions to their new location. As before in the hotel suite, he felt suspiciously ill informed.

"Things are happening faster than I feared," Stuaart said, adding to Wilfz's ill feeling. "I shouldn't be surprised."

Funny you should say that. You haven't shown surprise so far. The major waited for the colonel to continue.

"It is not an accident that many officers in the Constabulary have been replaced with officers of the Council's own," Stuaart explained. "Many have been relieved on trumped-up accusations and arbitrary charges that are difficult to defend against. They run the gamut of failed inspections, inability to follow regulations, inappropriate conduct, and other sundry allegations like that. Lang and his cronies make up whatever charges it takes to remove undesirable personnel and put in their own."

Wilfz mulled that over as Stuaart continued.

"Some have been killed in so-called training accidents."

Wilfz stared sharply at him. "So-called? You mean they were assassinated?"

"That pilot purposely targeted you," Stuaart confirmed. "I can't prove it, but with the replacements going on right now … we're damned lucky to still have you here."

Wilfz considered the implication for a moment. He felt light headed from the knowledge that a member of the Constabulary had tried to kill him.

Stuaart went on. "As a major with your vast knowledge and experience, you should be on staff in the brigades. Instead, I brought you here to keep you out of the line of fire," he explained. "If you had gone back to a brigade, it would only have been a matter of time before you suffered another 'accident' or were relieved for 'cause.' Unfortunately, it seems that Lang is still trying to find a reason to get you relieved from here. Like it or not, that's proof enough that we need you."

Wilfz slumped back in his chair as the ramifications sank in. The organization that he had served so loyally was trying to eliminate him.

Stuaart opened a drawer and brought out a bottle of Mallory's Orange Label whiskey and a pair of small glasses.

"You look like you could use a drink." Stuaart poured amber liquid into each glass.

Wilfz nursed his drink as Stuaart brought up the issue of the men of his office. Lieutenant Holloway and the sergeants were good men. Reliable and trustworthy, they didn't deserve to be stood against a wall and shot on trumped up charges of treason. "I want to get them out of the capital," he finished.

Get them to First Mountain, Wilfz silently agreed. Up among the peaks and valleys, vehicles were useless beyond the narrow roads.

Lighters would be vulnerable to sniper fire. The only way to get at the men up there was for other men to go in on foot after them. First Mountain Brigade was the best the Constabulary had to offer.

"This is no time to be gallant," Stuaart said, breaking through Wilfz's reverie.

Wilfz could admit that he had been badly shaken by the news of the insurrection. From Stuaart's expression, he could see that the colonel feared Wilfz would do something hasty. That Stuaart was fully cognizant of everything that was going on offended Wilfz's sense of justice. Stuaart had been privy to the information of the insurrection and had not acted on it, not even to file a protest. Not that protesting it would have done any good. The very individuals that Stuaart needed to report to were the very same who were the cause of the wrongdoing. On top of that, his information consisted of suspicion and coincidence. It was an exceeding amount of coincidence to be sure.

Wilfz had not finished his first drink, but still he grabbed the bottle and refilled his glass. He was most contemptuous in the way he tossed it off in one gulp. "What are my orders?" From the satisfied look in Stuaart's face, Wilfz knew his question had not been unexpected.

CHAPTER THREE

Wood Borough, Bremen, Capital City of Holland

"This isn't the man I met today," Monique declared, the report in her hand. Monique was seated at the dinette, her jacket draped inside out over the backrest. After Monique and Cameron had meandered for two hours through the different boroughs of Bremen, Sergeant Van and Guardsman Perez had met them at their new residence, a small apartment. She had asked for the report upon their arrival.

Still stinging from Cameron's earlier criticism, she had reread the report. She paid particular attention to the information about Major Wilfz. Having stated her disbelief, she stared across the room. She had made the comment in the hope of tweaking Lieutenant Cameron. To her surprise, it was Sergeant Van who reacted. He had been unpacking his uniform and spreading the different pieces on the couch. Now he paused, straightened up, and faced her directly. "I believe you are mistaken, ma'am," he said in a low voice. Before Monique could reply, he gathered up the charcoal-colored uniform and left the living room.

"I've heard about it, but this is the first time I've seen it." Cameron's voice was tinged with awe. Monique looked at him in curiosity. He looked back at her, almost smiling. "I've never seen him get angry."

He was angry? Why? Monique looked down at the report in her hands. Sergeant Van had always been imperturbable, a steady influence on the Celestial Guard team. Thinking back on the guard sergeant, she realized that she had only seen his mature, quiet demeanor. When compared to his past conduct, what she had just witnessed was the equivalent to a violent outburst, relatively speaking, of course. She could understand her lieutenant's surprise. She felt a little ashamed of herself.

Her relationship with the rest of the team was different from the relationship she had with their lieutenant. Cameron acted more like her keeper than her protector, almost contemptuous in his criticism of her professionalism regarding their present assignment. On the other hand, the members of his team had initially been distant from her. She had given up her show business career almost a year previously, but her popularity had ensured her lingering fame. She had been careful to compartmentalize the animosity she felt for the team commander and keep it from those he led. In her day-to-day activities, it was as if she were still working with show business professionals. Day in and day out, she spent so much time with them that, like her show business colleagues, they had become like a second family.

Her offense to Sergeant Van had been unintentional. She had not noticed it before, but she could now see that he held for Wilfz a ... a reverence? Monique was unsure of the word she was searching for. Certainly there was respect for the Constabulary officer. When the door guard at the CMO building had saluted Major Wilfz, she had seen the seriousness in the man's face. She had been too far away to hear, but she could tell that the other door guard had objected to the salute. She could not understand why it had been an issue.

She looked at the men in the apartment. It seemed strange to see them in their charcoal-colored uniforms. The men had not worn their uniforms since the delegation left Pearl. At an intellectual level she knew these men were professional soldiers, as was the door guard that had saluted the major. Their uniforms made their identity official. Then there was the major. She knew he was a military officer, but perhaps the long coat he wore took that sense of identity away. *Clothes make the man.*

Like the men, she felt the need to change her clothes. Turning sideways to the dinette table, she started to peel her boots down. They were formfitting, and she liked the way they complemented her legs. Unfortunately, it took effort to pull them on, and they were all the more difficult to get back off. On Pearl, she was rarely alone, so there was always someone to help with her boots. Here on Holland, she was reluctant to ask these men for their assistance. At the moment, they were engaged in readying themselves for more important duties.

Guardsman Gray had spread out pieces of his rifle upon an oilcloth on the floor. The air was sharp with the tang of cleaning solvent as he performed his weapon inspection and cleaning. Guardsman Perez was seated by the front room window, a submachine gun suspended from one shoulder as he looked outdoors through a crack in the blinds. Guardsman Schmidt was in the back of the apartment watching out of the kitchen window.

Monique found herself distracted from her private musings as she looked for her own luggage. The team had reequipped themselves from the gear bags that had been cached away. She knew there had been six bags, one for each of the men and one for her. Only one bag sat unopened against the wall. Seeing no sign of the luggage she had last seen at the hotel, she asked after it.

"The bags were left behind," Cameron explained.

"All of my things are there!" Monique protested. She noticed Perez cringe.

"Van and Perez couldn't very well carry all of that luggage and our gear." Cameron defended the actions of his men. "It would have been incredibly easy for anybody to follow them here."

"Why did we have to leave the hotel anyway? Those men were not after us!"

"Not this time, but someone was suspicious of us enough to attempt to eavesdrop on our meeting with the major. We are the next logical target. I wouldn't be surprised if you are next on their list."

Monique waved back at Cameron dismissively.

"All of my clothes are there—my shoes and expensive underwear!"

"You packed a backup bag, just like the rest of us." Cameron pointed to her bag. "Given our druthers, we all would rather have all of our gear, not just basic necessities. We have only a minimum of our allotted weapons load. We don't have our ballistic vests and helmets, much less everything we *really* need."

Monique stared at her bag, remembering what she had packed in it. The flimsy bag was not sturdy enough to carry anything she would consider decent to wear. Apart from under garments, she had packed only a few wrinkle-resistant outfits and a simple pair of shoes.

With the exception of Cameron, none of the men had looked at Monique during her tirade. Returning her attention to the report on the table, she picked it up and waved it around. "No, but they were able to bring this and the other gear from the hotel."

"It was easy to get that out of the hotel without arousing suspicion," Cameron countered.

Van walked in from the bedroom, the charcoal shirt and trousers he wore adding to his formal demeanor. "Ma'am." He approached her with a small lacquered box in hand. "We couldn't bring much from the hotel, but I thought you would want this."

Monique carefully accepted the box from the sergeant and hugged it to her chest. Tilting her head down, she closed her eyes tightly. "Thank you, Sergeant Van," she choked out in a whisper. "Thank you. Thank you. Thank you."

"A jewelry box," Cameron commented with a shake of his head.

"This is much more than my jewelry." Monique whipped her head around to glare at Cameron. She set the flat box on the table and opened it. Necklaces, rings, and earrings of silver and gold lay tangled carelessly, adorned with modest precious stones. For weeks she had worn them with extravagant abandon. With a shaky hand, she dug beneath them and took out a bar-shaped piece of silver set with a dark stone on one end. She had never worn the pin. The one thing she treasured most was something the team had never seen her wear. "My grandmother gave this to me. I have always kept it with me. It's the only thing I have from home!" Her voice shook, betraying her petulant feelings. Her sharp stare dared Cameron to fight with her. She wanted an excuse to lash out at him. She could see that he wanted to oblige her, but he was holding back. His self-control infuriated her.

"If that is so important to you," he finally spoke, "perhaps you should keep it close to your person so you do not lose it again."

Monique searched his face. His suggestion lacked the anger that she had expected ... no, that she hoped for. She knew he was willing to argue with her. He'd done it before. She could also see that he was making an effort not to react. Silently deliberating for a moment, she looked at the other men. They were not looking at her, not even Van.

I feel like a child, she thought with no little embarrassment. Without another look at the open box on the table, she clutched the pin to her breast and went to her bag by the wall. The soft carpeting yielded under the tread of her bare feet. She said nothing further as she took the bag into the bedroom and quietly closed the door behind her. She heard Cameron speak. "Good work, Sergeant."

She heard nothing else in the apartment after that. Discarding her clothes, she sat on the bed in her underwear. She did not want to put on the dreadful clothes waiting for her in the bag. She delayed doing that as long as possible, staring at the wall in silence as she regained her composure. An hour later, when she'd finally dressed, Monique ventured back to the front room.

She noticed Cameron's inquiring gaze. Compared to her previous attire, what she wore now seemed most sensible for a woman of Holland—a knee-length dress and a simple, button-up sweater. Flat-soled, pull-on shoes completed her ensemble. She had scrubbed her face free of cosmetics, and the image of her reflection still remained fresh in her memory. She was feeling sensitive, aware that he could see the redness of her nose as well as her pale complexion. When she had prepared her backup bag, she hadn't thought to include makeup. "I feel so dowdy," she announced in a subdued voice.

"You look fine, ma'am," Van spoke up. "Perez has prepared rations for you."

"Rations." Monique repeated the term in a flat tone as she looked at the nondescript food. "We passed a restaurant on our way here. We could eat there. Or we could bring the meals back here."

"The less we are seen, the easier it will be to remain in concealment," Cameron said. "I believe we should be thinking about our egress."

Monique perked up, the timbre of her voice rising in inflection. "We're leaving? Are we done, then?"

⊰✺⊱

Copper Borough, Bremen, Capital City of Holland

Sergeant William Meadows' day had been mostly uneventful. He had stood his watch at the main entrance of the Constabulary Management Office with the blue-cuff corporal. The two men rarely spoke to each other. Days before, when they had first met, the corporal had attempted to extol the virtues that accompanied the wearing of the blue cloth. As a senior in rank, it had been simple to rebuff him. Since then the two had rarely exchanged words.

Donning the blue cuff entitled the wearer to extra pay. Where officers wore the coats of blue, the men who chose to follow their doctrine were allowed to sew blue cuffs onto their sleeves. Few sergeants took advantage of the additional accoutrement, but many corporals and troopers accepted it. A provision was that the blue-cuffs attend meetings to learn of additional obligations to Holland and the Constabulary.

Many members of the Constabulary could not understand the need for such indoctrination. At the root of it, the blue coat officers were elevated in stature, and they expected to receive higher esteem than the regular Constabulary officers. Regular officers and their police brethren were trained at Magdeburg. Conversely, the blue coats attended Holland Academy and trained in an associate course to earn their Constabulary commissions. A few regular officers had converted to the "blue cause," a semiderogatory term that was quietly being circulated among the rank and file. This stemmed from the blue coats' undeserved elitist attitude, since they lacked the training and experience of the so-called "ordinary" officers. The captain of the watch was one such blue-coat.

When the watch was over, the corporal wasted no time becoming scarce. While Meadows was getting ready to go home, he was summoned to see the captain of the watch. An order to report at the end of duty was rarely a good sign. The strict expression of the officer of the watch confirmed the ominous nature.

Sergeant Meadows unexpectedly found himself charged with lacking proper respect for authority. The captain of the watch gave him two choices: he could accept a reduction in rank to that of corporal, or he could accept instant reassignment. "Of course, you can fight the charge if you so choose," offered the captain, but the eager gleam in his eyes proved the officer's eagerness for Meadows to entertain such a course of action. Meadows knew he would entail greater punishment should he lose in such a process. There would be no formal proceedings. The blue-coated captain of the watch, as his superior, would serve as judge and jury. The odds were unfavorable against him. The penalty would be greater also, than either of the choices currently before him. He would most likely be reduced to the rank of trooper and perhaps be required to serve jail time as well.

Accepting reassignment was the more attractive option. He would retain his rank of sergeant, and the transfer would get him out of the stifling environment of the blue-infested CMO. After he had apprised the captain of his decision, the captain imperiously told him that he had two days to get his affairs in order before leaving.

Meadows would not need even a single day. When he arrived home, his wife, Honey, could tell by the look on his face that something was wrong. "Will?"

"Do you remember Corporal Sims?"

"Yes, Molly Sims and their son lived two blocks away."

"Yeah, and you remember when he transferred?" Meadows continued.

"What are you talking about?" Honey asked, her voice trembling with uncertainty.

"Molly was going to stay in Bremen. Her parents are still here, and he didn't want to make her live out in the sticks. Especially not with their boy."

"I remember."

"Molly and her son are gone," Meadows said. "Her parents contacted the CMO looking for her. Apparently they were told Molly went to follow Corporal Sims."

"That's what I would have done," Honey said sensibly.

"But she didn't," Meadows reported. "On my way home after I heard that, I stopped by their neighborhood to check it out. The neighbors didn't see them leave."

"What are you saying?"

"They heard a disturbance one night, but no one knows what happened," Meadows explained. "I think someone took Molly and her boy away."

"Why?"

"I think to exert influence over Corporal Sims ... to ensure his cooperation."

"You're scaring me. It's not good to scare a pregnant woman."

"I know, Honey, but you need to be scared." Meadows held her close in his arms. He could feel her shaking. "Something happened today, and I'm next. Honey, I've already decided that they're not going to get you ... or our baby."

"Will ..."

"Honey, listen. You're leaving the city tonight. I'll write a letter for you to take to some friends of mine. They'll take care of you. No one will find you there."

"I can go to my parents'."

"No, that's the first place they'll look. It's better if I get you out of here, alone. No one will pay attention to a single woman. They'll be looking for both of us together, but not you alone."

"But, you ... what will you ...?"

"I'm going to stay behind and look for Molly and her boy."

"Why? Why does it have to be you?"

"Look, I'm already marked," Meadows said. "If you were missing, I know I would want someone to save you."

"Will …"

"Look, I'll be fine," he said. "I have to know that you are safe. I already have kroner set aside to take care of you, but we have to get you out of here now."

"What do you mean, now?"

"I don't think we even have tonight."

CHAPTER FOUR

Wood Borough, Bremen, Capital City of Holland

Colonel Stuaart had come to Wood Borough early in the morning. It was not uncommon for him to take walks before the sun rose above the skyline. He had been following his personal routine for days, alert to any change. There was nothing suspicious about the few passersby he encountered.

Director Lang's threat to investigate the incident involving Major Wilfz had come to naught. In spite of that, things were far from complacent. Sergeant Meadows' desertion two days earlier was just the latest occurrence, another warning sign of trouble to come.

Stuaart had prepared an apartment for the Celestial Empire delegation in case they had to go to ground. He was the only one who knew of it, and this was the root of his care in ensuring that he was not under surveillance. There would be dire consequences should anyone follow him.

The task that had brought the delegation to Holland to set up a flow of information would seem to be too late. Stuaart now had a new mission. He needed to get the delegation safely off of the planet. Should the turncoat members of the Constabulary apprehend the delegation, the penalty to Holland could be war. It was unlikely that the Celestial Empire would permit its citizens and armed forces to be held against their will. Against a similar nation able to protect multiple star systems, armed intervention could result in a standoff. In the case of Holland, having no navy at all, the planet was only a glorified fortress. Their civilization barely occupied a portion of one hemisphere of the planet. All the empire had to do was bring in enough ships to outgun and overwhelm the defenses.

As was usual for the hour, the narrow street was deserted. He had been alone when he took the train, and there was no one following him now. That did not, however, prevent him from exercising caution as he approached the apartment. Stopping at the door, he tapped lightly.

"Yes?" came a muffled reply. "Who is it?"

"I am a friend of Michael Wilfz's," Stuaart replied in a low voice. "Is Cameron home?"

The door cracked open.

"Please come in and close the door behind you." Within the apartment, Sergeant Van backed away from the door, stepping aside from his team's line of fire. Gray and Schmidt knelt on either side of the couch with pistols in hand. Lieutenant Cameron had been soundly asleep on the couch until their caller had knocked on the door. In a reflexive action, his own sidearm was now in his hand and aimed at the door even though he wasn't quite fully awake.

Stuaart slowly entered, pushing the door open as he crossed the threshold. The room was dark, but he could see that the man who had answered the door was holding a pistol at his side, the weapon leveled at him.

Stuaart carefully held his arms away from his body, horizontal to the floor with his palms down and forward. "I trust that your accommodations are satisfactory?"

Nodding, Cameron introduced himself, placing his pistol back in the holster by his head. Wearing an undershirt with his trousers, he sat up and put his feet on the floor. Reaching for his shirt, which was draped over the back of the couch, he dressed himself. "We were expecting contact before now."

"That was the plan," Stuaart confirmed. "Unfortunately, like battle plans, everything fell apart due to circumstance."

At that moment, Monique silently entered the room and took a seat on the couch next to Cameron. Her auburn hair had not been brushed, and she sleepily combed it back from her face with her fingers. It was clear she had just risen from bed. "Introduce me to our guest," she said.

Cameron announced the colonel. Stuaart gave the woman a respectful nod.

"Holland Constabulary, retired," he amended.

"This is Lady …" Cameron paused then repeated himself. "Lady Monique Lewellen."

Stuaart raised his eyebrows at the dirty look Monique gave Cameron. The lieutenant did not respect her, and the use of title had just become an issue.

"I am pleased to meet you," Stuaart said pleasantly, attempting to avoid a contest of personalities. He turned his attention to Cameron. "Lieutenant Cameron, it seems that you came all the way out here to Holland for nothing."

Cameron opened his mouth to reply, but Monique interrupted him. "I have lost all of my things, and I now live in this hovel, and you tell us it is for nothing?" There was no disguising the disgust in her tone. "Perhaps someone would be so kind as to tell me why we are even on this dinky planet?"

"That's enough," Cameron declared.

"Enough? No, it's too much. Admiral Christie, Inspector Genda, and my genius brother Hampton sent us out here … and for what?" Monique gestured around her with both arms. "Nothing! Well, thank you for your hospitality. We'll be leaving now." Monique pushed herself up off of the couch and strode to the bedroom. Finding her way blocked, she stopped just outside the door. "Excuse me, Sergeant Van."

The sergeant stepped out of her way, permitting her to exit the front room.

"I'm sorry about that," Cameron apologized. Stuaart waved a hand.

"No, I understand how you must feel," he said. "My major is unhappy too. He has a right to be. It seems we have already lost control of the Constabulary."

Cameron was speechless.

"You know, I should have expected this," Stuaart said almost whimsically.

"You know, I should have insisted on bringing our ballistic armor," Cameron paraphrased.

The two men looked at each other.

"I cannot stay here long," Stuaart explained. "If I do not stay on schedule with my routine, your safety could become compromised." He paused as if gathering his thoughts. "You need to be ready to move. I won't be able to get you out through the spaceport. That's locked down tight. You'll be arrested if you attempt to leave that way. Instead, we have to get you out from the bowl. Your ship is capable of extracting you, am I correct?"

"Yes, they can fight their way down if they have to and pick us up outside the city."

"That would mean spiking the guns," Stuaart sounded horrified.

Spiking was naval nomenclature for orbital-to-surface gunfire. The guns that protected the land within the bowl-shaped mountains and ridges were vital for the security of the planetary population. To disable the weapons would make the people vulnerable to attack.

"Yes it would, but I imagine that won't happen," Cameron surmised. "The empire wouldn't do something like that to save a mere six lives. No, we'll have to figure out something else."

"You're going to need a guide," Stuaart said. "I'll send Major Wilfz to you. I don't know when I can do that, much less how without giving our plans away. I'm sure someone is keeping an eye on him."

"Perhaps we can coordinate something." Cameron gestured to one of his men. "Perez, you got that?"

Stuaart watched curiously as the charcoal-uniformed guard approached and handed his lieutenant a flat, hand-sized case. Cameron gave it to Stuaart.

"This is a radio. It's off right now. We don't know what Holland has for radio detection, so we haven't been using our own communication."

Stuaart examined the electronic device. There were no actual buttons, but it seemed to have a touch-activated control and status screen. The speaker and microphone were self-evident.

"We will monitor your frequency. We'll get any message you send. You won't have to risk another face-to-face again."

"I'll use this when I have something to tell you," Stuaart said. "We cannot let the opposition get their hands on you. There's no telling what accusations they will make against your empire."

◄❈►

After the colonel had departed, the team settled into their morning routine. Schmidt had prepared breakfast. Monique gave a dismissive sniff as she pushed her meal away to the center of the table. Across from Monique at the dinette, Perez was eating his own breakfast. He looked up absently at her activity while listening to the earpiece of his personal radio.

"I've had to eat this slop for three meals a day," Monique complained.

"If you want variety, skip a meal," Cameron said testily.

Monique straightened up, her eyes flashing in challenge.

"Fine," she said. "I'll let you know when I want to eat again."

"Sir, listen to this," Perez called to Cameron. Removing the lead from his radio, he pressed the message replay command. The device repeated a conversation that had been sent by Stuaart's radio.

"Come with us, Colonel."

"Is there something wrong?"

"We have orders to take you into custody."

"Whose orders are those?"

"The orders come from the director."

"Constabulary Director Lang—that director?"

Perez stopped the replay.

"It sounds like the colonel is getting picked up," he surmised.

"What is his bearing?"

"The signal is strongest from the direction of the train station, but they aren't taking the train. The people with him told him to get in a truck."

"Sergeant Van, we have a mission."

"Sir," Van acknowledged.

"Perez will stay behind with the envoy," Cameron instructed. "The rest of us are going to rescue the colonel."

"No!" Monique's objection came as a surprise.

"If we're going to get out of here, we need the colonel," Cameron insisted.

"You misunderstand me. I'm going with you."

Cameron gave her a level look. "We don't have time for this. You'll only be in the way."

"Yes, I can see. So you will save the colonel and abandon Guardsman Perez and myself. I understand." Monique's feigned tone of sensibility bit with sarcasm.

Before Cameron could offer is rebuttal, Van spoke up. "She has a point. Once we get the colonel, we can't afford to waste time coming back here. We'll have to get going from there."

Cameron silently regarded his sergeant.

"Sir?" Guardsman Perez prompted.

Cameron looked to him next and then his other men. When he did speak, it was a whisper. "Damn."

"Sir?" Van repeated what Perez had asked.

"She has no business going. Our duty is to spirit her away from here, not take her further into danger."

"What is your order, Lieutenant?" Van asked precisely.

"In order to get her out of Bremen, we shouldn't have to take her closer to the guns."

The guardsmen were unhappy with their commanding officer's indecisiveness. Perez looked to Van, worry in his eyes. Gray and Schmidt shared dissatisfied glances.

"Everybody pack up," Cameron decided. "We're not coming back here. We're going to hijack a truck."

"I'm already packed," Monique said. With the others looking on, she peeled open the collar of her dress to show that she had fastened her grandmother's pin to the inside. His attention on her, Cameron just shook his head. He did not see the looks of relief his men exchanged.

❦

The Imperial delegation trotted along the sidewalk in single file. In the fading twilight of morning, no one else was outdoors. They were in a residential area with sidewalks bordering narrow streets. Stone walls built to shoulder height separated the walks from the modest front lawns of homes. Light poles stood upon the curb, widely spaced and connected at the top with power lines. On contemporary worlds such as Pearl, electrical power was transmitted through underground conduits. The use of electrical cables suspended in air only emphasized the outdated architecture of Holland.

Perez was on point, using the signal strength meter on his radio to guide them. The others made a cordon with Monique between them and the wall. The men wore their packs on their backs while Schmidt carried Monique's in one hand and gripped his shoulder-slung submachine gun in the other. Monique had offered to carry her own pack, but the argument was made that she would have enough trouble keeping up without being burdened with a load.

A physically fit woman, Monique made no secret that she was offended by that decision. Following a strict regimen of recreational swimming, she had developed sleek muscle tone and core strength. As she easily kept pace with the men, her legs, bare under her knee-length skirt, flashed pale in the refracted sunlight as it peeked over the city skyline.

Their pace slowed as they approached a T-shaped intersection. The street that made the base of the T was to the right. The group paused while Gray peered around the corner of the wall to scout up the street. It was not straight, but curved to follow a hill and disappeared around the bend. He flashed a hand signal, and the team proceeded across the side street, encircling around Monique as they did so.

The team had just picked up their pace again when Perez reported that the signal strength of the colonel's radio was rapidly getting stronger—an indication that the truck was coming in their direction. Cameron gave the order to fall back to the intersection.

Cameron took Monique by the elbow and marched her several paces along the side street. Shrugging off his pack, he dropped it as he forced the woman down to the walkway next to the wall. Releasing her, he pointed his finger at her. "Sit! Don't move from that spot!"

Monique was wide eyed before the lieutenant's intensity. In the face of his sharp look, she gave a jerky nod. His attention lingered on her as he ordered his men to pile their packs against the wall to provide her with protection. She shrank down behind the small stack, leaning against the cold stone wall. Shivering, she hugged her legs to her chest.

Leaving Monique in concealment, the team members pressed themselves against the wall, crouching down with Sergeant Van at their lead. Lieutenant Cameron issued instructions, telling Van and Schmidt to take the back while he and Perez took the front. Gray would provide cover with his rifle.

As they set out, Van and Schmidt remained ahead of Cameron and Perez against the wall. The order had nothing to do with their order of procession, but how they would attack the truck. Hearing an engine, they knew the truck was close.

"Call it, Van."

Cameron's order recognized that the sergeant was in the best position to order the attack. It also conveyed the trust that the lieutenant had in the guardsman's judgment.

The engine grew louder, slowing at it neared. The truck was stopping at the intersection. Van held his hand up. Behind him, the men readied themselves.

The truck had not stopped yet when Van dropped his hand. Within moments, he and Schmidt had rushed around the corner. Cameron and Perez darted straight forward.

"Don't move!" Cameron shouted at the driver as the truck came to a full stop. Pulling open the driver's door, he stepped back and aimed his submachine gun at the occupants. The driver was dressed in a brown-colored uniform with corporal's insignia on his jacket sleeve and blue bands sewn to his cuffs. A lieutenant in a blue coat was in the passenger seat. Perez ran to the other side and opened that door, his weapon pointed at the officer.

"Keep your hands where we can see them!" Van's orders were directed toward the cargo bed of the vehicle.

He and Schmidt had their submachine guns up to their shoulders, the weapons pointed into the rear of the vehicle. Gray remained back, keeping a lookout around the neighborhood.

The man they had come to rescue, Colonel Stuaart, sat on the bench in the back of the truck. Beside him were carbine-armed troopers, two on each side. Facing him were three more troopers and their sergeant. Unlike the other men, the sergeant was armed with a pistol. All of them had blue cuffs on their jacket sleeves.

A desperate look appeared on the sergeant's face. He reached for his holstered revolver.

"Don't do it!" Van commanded.

The sergeant grabbed the trooper next to him, using him as a shield as he pulled his pistol from the holster. His cuff a blue blur, he brought the weapon up in Van's direction. Schmidt shouted in warning before both he and Van unleashed short, simultaneous bursts of gunfire.

The sergeant fell as he half spun from the impact of the bullets. The trooper he had been holding slumped to the truck bed clutching his arm. The remaining troopers took cover by throwing themselves down, entangling Stuaart among them in the process.

There was a moment of silence, broken only by the groaning of the trooper the sergeant had seized. The lifeless sergeant lay behind him with a look of final surprise on his face.

"Nobody move!" Van ordered, and the men obeyed under his alert glare. He spoke to Stuaart. "Are you all right, Colonel?"

"I'm just pinned down," Stuaart replied.

"We'll take care of that, sir," Van assured him. He raised his voice and addressed the other occupants. "You! Yes, you! Leave your weapon and get down. Now!"

The trooper singled out by Van warily clambered off of the vehicle. Following further directions, he lay facedown on the walk with his arms spread wide and legs crossed at the shins. Leaving the corner, Gray stood over him with his rifle at the ready.

"Help your comrade out!" he yelled to another of the troopers. The indicated trooper grabbed the wounded man and assisted him off of the truck where they joined the first trooper facedown on the walk. The remaining troopers followed one at a time. Very quickly the only occupants remaining in the vehicle were Colonel Stuaart and the shot Constabulary sergeant.

"Colonel, is he dead?" Van asked. The colonel nodded. "Get that revolver out of his hand and, if you would, drag him over this way."

Stuaart pried the handgun from the dead sergeant's grip. Setting it aside, he moved to the man's legs and seized an ankle. He pulled the body awkwardly toward the end of the truck. A discarded carbine clattered as he scooted it out of his way with his foot.

"Okay, we have him," said Van, taking control of the body.

Stuaart sat on the bench as Van and Schmidt hefted the body down to the street.

Cameron and his four men had attacked and subdued nine, two of whom had fallen.

In the meantime, Perez had put the truck's driver and the officer with the other troopers. The blue-coat lieutenant stared at his captors with a surprisingly confident sneer—a very disproportionate sign of confidence since it was the lieutenant and his patrol that had just been captured. He should have been showing anger and shock, not contempt.

"Is it safe now?" Monique spoke up, her voice quavering. She had left her place of concealment and stood at the corner of the wall.

Cameron ignored her. Instead, he addressed the prisoners.

"Take your wounded man and go." Holding his weapon, he pointed it back the way the truck had come from. "Take the body too."

As the Hollanders turned to obey, Guardsman Perez stepped close to Cameron.

"Lieutenant, I'm picking up a signal from the truck. It's not from the colonel's radio."

Van hurried to the cab of the truck and climbed in. Moments later he returned to the team. "There's a radio in the truck. The microphone has been in the on position all this time," he reported. "I just turned it off."

"There must be more personnel on the way," Stuaart spoke up. "They must have been using me as bait to draw you out of hiding."

"Get our gear into the truck! Hurry it up!" Cameron said decisively. Only then did he look to Monique. "Lady Lewellen, get over here!"

Van, Perez, and Schmidt retrieved the packs as Monique obediently went toward the truck, her knees suddenly shaking. "Why am I shaking? It's not *that* cold," she muttered, pulling her jacket tighter around herself.

As the guardsmen returned carrying a pack in each hand, the rumbling of an engine came from past the curve of the street behind them. They turned to look as the sound became louder. Nothing was in sight, but the noise indicated that the vehicle was closing the distance quickly.

"Hurry, Milady!" Van urged as they passed Monique. Reaching the back of the truck, the men quickly tossed their packs in.

Monique looked behind again and watched as a truck came around the bend in the road. Clearly visible in the back was a pedestal-mounted automatic cannon. The gunner had the heavy weapon aimed over the truck cab at them.

"It's a weapons carrier," Stuart announced. He attempted to duck down to the truck bed, but Gray reached up and pulled him out instead. Off balance, both men went sprawling onto the street.

"Everybody get down!" Cameron propped his submachine gun on the wall and sighted his weapon over the corner of the yard toward the new menace. The guardsmen followed his lead. Gray picked himself up, quickly checking his rifle for damage and motioning for the colonel to remain down on the ground. Monique stood where she had stopped at the corner, staring at the heavily armed truck.

Cameron gave the order to fire. Monique covered her ears, but took no other protective action to move from harm's way. As the guardsmen coordinated their aim, their gunfire converged on the truck cab. The windshield disintegrated in front of the driver and he threw himself sideways to take cover in the cab. As he abandoned his control, the truck automatically veered off of the street and struck a lighting pole. The engine immediately died. Some of the gunfire had penetrated through the back window of the cab, striking the cannon gunner. He fell back, unleashing a few rounds before releasing the weapon. He succeeded only in shattering some brickwork on a house across the intersection.

With the truck neutralized, Schmidt looked around. The Constabulary troopers were taking advantage of the attack by attempting to return. Perez being closest to him, he called attention to the potential threat while aiming his weapon at them. The advance quickly turned into a cautious retreat.

At that moment, another truck arrived from the same direction the Celestial Guard team had come. With most of the guardsmen behind the commandeered truck, only Monique was clearly visible to the gunner.

Monique had remained where she had been standing during the first attack. When the second carrier appeared, Cameron shouted for her to take cover, but she merely stood and watched the vehicle come closer. Van was down on one knee next to the captured truck, ready to take the carrier under fire. He heard the lieutenant's order to their ward and saw that the woman had frozen in place.

"Lady, down!" he shouted. He leaped up and took hold of her hand as the cannon began firing. As he violently pulled her around, she gave a screech of surprise. Cannon shells struck the wall nearby, detonating and creating divot-style holes in the stonework. Van pulled Monique after him as hard as he could. She screamed as they fell together. A shower of brick and mortar bits fell onto them, and she screamed again. Van struck the ground first, using his body to cushion Monique's fall. Rolling himself onto her, he ordered her to stay down.

Cameron returned fire against the newest attacker. From where he stood by the back of the truck, he could not see the driver's side of the carrier. The gunner shifted himself sideways out of the lieutenant's line of fire. The sound of clashing of gears from the weapons carrier joined the cacophony of competing gunfire. There was an unpleasant grinding sound, and then the engine quickly revved. The gunner lost his footing on the jerking truck and, not being directly behind his weapon, he fell forward against the truck cab. He pushed himself back to regain his footing and return to his heavy weapon.

Gray had been standing behind their newly acquired truck, his rifle trained on the first weapons carrier. The driver was still hiding in the truck cab and could conceivably man the automatic cannon. With the arrival of the second weapons carrier, Gray quickly reassessed the threat facing his teammates. Turning to face the cannon fire with his rifle at the ready, he moved away from Cameron to the other side of the truck. Seeing the second gunner, he lined up his sight picture and pulled the trigger. Hit by the single round, the gunner quickly sank to his knees, wavering for a moment before collapsing out of view in the back of the truck.

The driver crouched down in his seat, inadvertently stalling the engine. But the engine did not remain silent for long; it quickly restarted, screaming as the driver stomped down on the accelerator without engaging the transmission. Letting up on the accelerator, he clashed the gears and the truck shuddered as it backed away. The rumbling sound from the truck diminished as the vehicle retreated the way it had come.

For the Constabulary troopers, their retreat quickly turned into a complete rout under what seemed to be a fusillade of submachine gunfire. Having lost their backup firepower, Stuaart's former captors scattered and threw themselves over the stone fences. With Schmidt facing them, they had no reason to believe that he was not firing at them.

"Is everybody all right?" Cameron called out.

As each member of the team answered to the affirmative, Gray assisted the colonel to his feet. Van took a careful look around as the first rays of sunlight filtered past the distant roofs at the head of the street. He pushed himself up from Monique, conscious of the shattered stonework underneath the palms his hands. He opened his mouth to speak when something glinted in the sun and caught his eye. Shiny red spatters were spread on the ground near them. Instinctively he looked at himself. Seeing nothing wrong, he looked down at the lady beneath him. Although his voice had failed him, his comrades were alerted by his silence.

Monique was looking up at Van, her eyes wide and her lower lip quivering. She seemed breathless and unable to speak.

"One down!" Van barked out. He lowered his head to hers. "Can you hear me, Lady?"

Her only answer was a shuddering breath.

"I'm going to roll you over, okay?" he warned her as Perez dropped to his knees beside them. His pack in hand, he pulled out a medical bag.

Van moved Monique onto her side to reveal a bright redness welling at the small of her lower back. It was apparent that she had been hit by shrapnel from the explosive shells that had hit the wall. A small pool of crimson had collected on the ground beneath her. Van and Perez shared a look.

"Hold on, hold on, you'll be okay." Van pulled her jacket up, his fingers seeking the blood-soaked hole in her dress. The irregular-shaped hole was not very large. He tore at the hole, making it larger. He looked to Perez. "Compress."

Perez brought out the requested bandage. Ripping open the hermetically sealed wrapper, he pulled out the thick, flat bandage. Attached to the external part of the covering were folded straps for tying the compress to the patient. Rather than trying to wrap it around Monique's waist, he used medical tape to hold the compress over the wound.

"Hurts ..." It took effort for her to utter that word. The woman was hiccupping in shallow sobbing breaths.

Van wordlessly held his hand out for the painkiller. Perez presented one of the single-use hypodermics from the bag.

"Just relax and let this medicine work, Milady." He removed the protective cover from the needle and then pressed the syringe into her back near the compress. "You're going to be okay."

The rest of the men stood around helplessly while Van and Perez worked over the wounded woman. The guardsmen kept careful watch on the homes. Periodically they caught sight of a furtive face spying from a nearby window. Having just witnessed the Celestial Guard team engage the planet's own defense force in combat, it was natural for the locals to see the Celestial Guard as their enemy.

Cameron's sick expression manifested the realization that he had failed to fulfill his duty. In a low voice he berated himself for bringing Monique along on the rescue. If only he had left her at the apartment, the team would now be racing back there to get her.

Cameron's men were not in earshot, but Stuaart silently placed a sympathetic hand on his shoulder.

"Well, that's a blessing," Van said finally. "She's fainted. She won't feel it when we move her."

"Where can we go? She needs a doctor. If we go to the hospital, the authorities will roll us up." Cameron looked to Stuaart for an answer.

"I have a place," Stuaart said. "We can hide there for a while—the truck too, but no doctor. Can't you take care of her?"

"I don't know what hit her, but it's too close to her spine and kidneys. I'd probably kill or cripple her if I tried to get it out myself. We need a real doctor," Van explained.

"Is it safe to move her?" Perez asked.

"We don't have a choice," Cameron snapped. "We can't stay here; the others will be back with reinforcements."

It took Van, Perez, and Schmidt to pick up her prone figure and get her into the back of the truck. Unconscious, Monique whimpered only once.

Silver Borough, Bremen, capital city of Holland

A civilian dual turboprop aircraft taxied toward the threshold of one of the two runways at Bremen Regional Airport. The day was overcast; gray clouds concealed the sky. The wet tarmac reflected the navigation and warning lights of the aircraft. These kinds of aircraft were typical on worlds that lacked access to more sophisticated technology. The general public of Holland could not afford gravity induction engines for small aircraft. Only the government and affluent corporations could afford induction-powered aircraft like lifters. The only aircraft available to the common population were those powered by turbines and internal combustion engines.

The pilot was a company executive named Jerrin Milton. On board with him were his wife, and two sons. For weeks unpleasant rumors had been circulating that certain Bremen residents had vanished unexpectedly. The previous day his best friend had failed to meet with him for lunch. He had questioned their mutual acquaintances, but had been unable to find out what had become of him. His friend's disappearance had galvanized him to action—he had decided to get his family out of the capital.

Upon reaching the runway threshold, he set his brakes and reported his arrival to Flight Control. He prepared for takeoff, increasing the throttle to the engines. He announced that he was commencing takeoff when he was instructed to return to the terminal.

"Holl-Tech Two-One to Flight Control, is there a problem? Our flight plan should be on file."

"Two-One, return to the terminal." The final tone of the voice invited no debate.

He turned to look at his wife. Seated in the copilot seat beside his, she was not a pilot. She looked back, her eyes sharp with concern. He then noticed a lifter—not a commercial ship but the Constabulary version. Flight Control had not warned him of aerial activity over the airport. The lifter crept forward into his view, the nose first. As it circled around his turboprop, he could see that the side door was open, revealing a mounted machinegun. His wife caught her breath, and he turned his head to see what had alarmed her. On his side was another lifter, similarly armed. Neither lifter had deployed their landing spoilers, a clear violation of flight regulations when landing or in low-level flight. Their slow speed was almost a hover, relying on induction engines to remain airborne.

Located at the outskirts of Bremen, the civilian field was separate from the port, where the spaceships landed. The Constabulary had its own field. Their lifters normally didn't have any business here.

Looking at the lifters, the pilot noticed that the gunners had not bothered to point their weapons at his aircraft. It didn't matter. The implied threat was there. It would only take a moment to bring their machineguns to bear and fire at his aircraft and his family riding within. Flight Control repeated the instruction to return as the lifters drifted over the runway in front of the turboprop aircraft.

Milton reduced the throttle. He would not need full power to taxi back to the terminal. He released the brakes and applied the rudder to turn the aircraft around.

"Two-One returning to terminal," Milton responded. He faced his wife and tried to give her a reassuring smile. "This is probably a mistake. I can't believe they would permit us to come to the threshold only to call us back. It doesn't make sense."

The aircraft had barely begun the return when two vehicles approached, a truck and a sedan. The car flashed its headlights on and off repeatedly as it maneuvered to block the airplane. A man in a Constabulary brown field uniform stepped from the car and signaled for the aircraft to stop. When the plane stopped moving, the man pointed to the wing on the pilot's side of the aircraft and made a cutting motion with his hand in front of his neck. Obediently, Milton shut that engine down.

The man from the car approached the aircraft. With no propeller blast to hold the door on that side of the plane shut, the uniformed man opened it easily. Milton turned to look back past his sons to the door but remained in his seat.

"I'm Lieutenant Winwood with Special Services. Sorry to come unannounced, but we have need of your services."

"Look, I'm about to go on a trip ..."

"Yes, we're aware of that, but you are needed now," Winwood said. "I'll have a pilot park your airplane for you."

"I need to see to my family first," Milton protested.

"I'll have my driver take them back home," Winwood persisted. "We really need you now." There was an electric undertone in the kind voice of the lieutenant that seemed to convey that any action would only result in harm to Milton's family.

"Papa?" spoke a tremulous voice from the back of the plane.

That was Milton's oldest little boy. A moment later, his younger son mimicked his brother.

"It's all right," he reassured them in a level voice, turning his face forward. Not seeing the helplessness their father could not conceal, the boys did not get upset, but his wife could see his expression.

On the other hand, Winwood exuded the confidence that came from unfair advantage. He knew there was nothing Milton could do. Winwood had not openly implied consequences; still, Milton's only choice was to cooperate. It was understood that, as long as Milton was docile, the lieutenant would keep his word and have his driver deliver the Milton family safely home.

As his wife vacated the copilot's seat, she leaned over to him and kissed him on the side of his mouth. Milton turned to her and kissed her again. Looking at her one last time, he quickly uttered encouragement in a voice only she could hear. "Everything will be all right. I'll come back. This will be over soon."

His misery was reflected in her expression of resigned disbelief at his words. Then she was gone with his boys, taken away in the sedan.

"Mister Milton, if you would disembark from your aircraft now." Winwood spoke from his position near the doorway. "Don't shut it down. I have a pilot here. He will take over now."

Milton released the buckles on his seat harness and picked himself up. Turning, he squeezed past the pilot's seats and joined the lieutenant on the ground. True to his word, there was a pilot. Also in Constabulary field uniform, his jacket was adorned with a patch depicting a pair of wings on the left breast. The pilot was brusque as he pushed past Milton to board the airplane.

This did not bode well with Milton. Two men stepped to either side of him and one of them directed him to the truck. The gesture brought the band of blue on the jacket sleeve to his attention. Though Winwood was not wearing a blue coat, it was obvious that he was one of the Council Chosen. The lieutenant sneered at the sick look on Milton's face. Upon reaching the rear of the truck, two more men armed with carbines pulled him inside and pointed for him to sit toward the front.

The pilot restarted the second engine on his aircraft, the propeller blades disappearing in a blur as they came up to speed. Winwood was watching from the side of the aircraft, and he snapped off a farewell salute as the plane taxied away.

From where Milton sat, the canvas over the back of the truck prohibited what he could see. He was unable to tell if the plane was going to the hangar or somewhere else. The engine noise fell in volume as it drew away. That Winwood continued to watch the plane implied that he had lied to Milton. The officer exhibited too much interest in an aircraft merely returning to its parking area.

The whine of the turboprop engines suddenly rose to a crescendo.

Milton's plane was leaving the airport, not returning to the hangar. The sound decreased with distance as the aircraft rolled away on takeoff. By the time Winwood had turned and was helped up into the truck, the plane had left the ground. The lieutenant sat down across from Milton as one of the armed men stamped his foot twice on the floor of the truck bed. The engine of the truck started, and the vehicle lurched into motion.

"Now," Winwood said to Milton. "Now we will have a little chat." The courteous officer who had first met the plane was gone. Devoid of expression, Winwood's impersonal manner was almost cold as he regarded Milton.

Looking away, the young executive shook off the chill.

"You may think that I lied about returning your plane to the hangar," Winwood said conversationally. "I actually did that to make a point. As far as anyone here knows, you just flew off with your family."

"You did not send my family back home?" Milton asked.

"I see that you are a quick thinker," Winton commended. "No, but they will be taken to a safe place. How safe they remain will be up to you.

"I know that you were tempted to take off in defiance of Flight Control's instruction. I could see it in your eyes back there. The lifters would have shot your plane up before you could have gotten into your takeoff roll. All of you would have perished in such a futile escape attempt."

Winwood stopped speaking and looked expectantly at Milton. The family man wilted under the stare.

"What do you want of me?" he finally asked.

"All we require is your cooperation," Winwood said simply. "Do as you are told without question, and your lovely wife and handsome boys will remain happy and safe."

The officer's transparent manner conveyed an awful truth.

Winwood and his men had purposely waited for him at the airport. Under the implied threat of gunfire, his family had been taken away from him, confirming the rumors that had provided so much worry. Milton's family would now be used against him to ensure his good conduct. They would keep him under duress, and he would be forced to provide service that would most likely be objectionable.

There was nothing he could do to resist. As the Constabulary was the lawful authority on Holland, fully backed by the governing council, there was no one to whom he could appeal.

CHAPTER FIVE

Iron Borough, Bremen, capital city of Holland

Major Wilfz faced the mirror over the bathroom washbasin, razor in hand, while he shaved the stubble of whiskers from his face. Ever since the eventful encounter with the delegation from the Celestial Empire, Colonel Stuaart had not sent him on any serious errands. The colonel kept silent about his intentions, not even repeating his suspicions regarding the blues.

Even days later, Wilfz had trouble believing the inconceivable information that he had been told. To say that he had been disturbed by that news was an understatement.

Once his face was shorn, he rinsed away the residual soap and dried his skin. He closed his eyes for a moment as he considered that he faced another day of …

To Wilfz, it wasn't even worth the effort to finish the thought. It was another day of nothing. That seemed to be his new purpose in life. Looking at himself in the mirror again, he wondered why he hadn't resigned. There was no real reason for him to stay in the Constabulary. Apart from the Free Scouts, there were plenty of options open to a man with his experience.

He stepped back into the main room. Modestly furnished, it contained a bed and a wall desk with lamp and chair. The hotel where he now resided was reserved for officers attached to the Constabulary

Management Office. Unmarried sergeants and troopers assigned to the CMO resided in various hostelries around Iron Borough while the married men rented or owned homes.

As he reached for his jacket, he heard a key rasp in the lock to his door. He watched curiously as the door opened. It was too early for the scheduled room cleaning. Instead of an employee of the hotel, three officers in blue jackets entered.

"Keep your hands where we can see them, Major!"

The speaking officer, also a major, held a pistol in his hand. Pointed at the floor by his feet, the weapon was a semiautomatic. Wilfz was not familiar with the model. The second officer was a captain. He was armed with a revolver, the standard issue sidearm of the Constabulary. This was pointed straight at Wilfz's head. The last officer, a lieutenant, held wrist binders. It didn't take any imagination to predict who would be wearing the restrictive bracelets.

"Put your hands on your head and turn around," the lieutenant ordered. Loath to turn his back on the pistol trained at him, Wilfz slowly complied. The blue-coat was not gentle as he took hold of one arm and brought it down. Once he had the binder locked around that wrist, he forcibly pulled down the other arm and fettered it. The officer leaned close and growled into Wilfz's ear. "Too bad you didn't put up a fight, traitor."

"I'm not armed," Wilfz replied.

"You don't say," the blue-coat major drawled as the lieutenant turned Wilfz around. "How do you explain this contraband handgun?"

As Wilfz watched, the major pointed the pistol at the wall and fired. The report sounded loud in the small room. Before Wilfz could fully comprehend what was happening, the lieutenant swung into him, his fist striking the side of Wilfz's face. The force of the blow knocked him down. Instinctively he tried to catch himself, but with his arms bound behind him, he fell heavily to the floor. The inside of his mouth stung where his teeth had cut into his cheek.

"Very good, Lieutenant, you just saved our lives with your quick and courageous action." Returning his attention to Wilfz, the blue-coat major continued his narration. "Resisting arrest, collusion with saboteurs, and unauthorized possession of this foreign pistol should be enough to support a charge of treason."

Despite the grogginess from the blow, Wilfz was experiencing clarity of thought. He realized the blue-coat major was explaining everything so the blues could keep their stories straight. He could not help wondering if his resignation would have forestalled this injustice. He was not fully accustomed to the animosity from Constabulary Director Lang, and now he was being falsely accused of illegal weapon possession and other trumped-up charges. Obviously, the trial would be pro forma, not intended to end in Wilfz's favor.

This new reality washed over him like cold water dashed in his face. His freshly shaven face tingled at the thought.

"Get up, traitor!" The lieutenant gripped him under the shoulder and roughly pulled him up.

"Hold onto him. I would hate to see him shot while attempting to escape," the major said dryly. It was clear to Wilfz that this blue-coated officer was not only narrating, but orchestrating the actions of his subordinates. He suspected that if the opportunity should arise, these men would make sure he did not live to see that trial.

❖❖❖

Constabulary Director Lang wasted no time consolidating his control over Holland's law enforcement organization. As soon as he had received word that Colonel Stuaart had taken the train to Wood Borough, he put his plan into action. He issued orders to his officers and waited in his office for their reports of successful completion. With the exception of a few malcontents, matters were proceeding according to plan.

His office had originally been that of the Constabulary General, the single highest-ranking officer of the organization. When the commanding general had passed away from natural causes, it had been the director's responsibility to select his replacement from among the three division generals. It was through this process that the Council of Holland communicated civilian control over the Constabulary. With his banking background, Lang had been singularly qualified to oversee the finances as director as well.

Lang's political leanings had been the real reason he had been appointed director, and the same reason that the position of Constabulary General had not been filled. Instead the director himself had assumed those duties, much to the dismay of the remaining general staff. With so many of the officers of the Council Chosen in service, the staff was powerless to do more than offer token protest. They did not have the support of the officer corps.

The general staff would soon be replaced and the rank of general eliminated. The highest rank would become field colonel, which Lang had recently instituted. Only he could award that rank—and the honor would go only to those obedient to the political will of the council. The units they commanded would be smaller than the ones enjoyed by the generals, thus limiting their overall authority. The lessoning of authority was intended to limit the threat to the Council as well as to Lang himself.

The captain of the watch was the first officer to report. His assignment had been to wait for Colonel Stuaart's day sentry to arrive. Leading a detail of men, the captain was to accompany him to the underground archive. They would use the changing of the sentries to gain admittance inside. The sentries would be relieved of duty pending reassignment. Stuaart's office staff would be apprehended and confined to await the investigation into the colonel's activities.

The relief sentry had failed to show up. Checking the building ledger, the captain saw that Lieutenant Allenby was the duty officer for the archive and had not signed out. He went down to the archive to speak with Allenby, but no one answered the door. Additionally, Stuaart's admin officer, Lieutenant Holloway, had not come in; neither had his sergeants. It was unfortunate for the captain that he had nothing to show for his assignment. Lang became increasingly angry as the details were brought to his attention.

"The door locks only from the inside, correct?"

"Yes, sir, with a steel bar," the captain said with a nod. "The door is still locked."

"Then it's safe to say that someone is still inside."

"The detail is still waiting outside the door in case someone comes out," the captain explained.

"No!"

"Sir?"

"No, I have had enough of this," Lang said, his complexion becoming dark as he lost his temper. "There should be no place in this building that I do not have access to. Get someone to force that door. Blow it, if necessary. Do it now!"

The result was bewildering at first. After blasting the door in, they found no one within. Lang saw for himself that the basement exclusionary area was deserted.

From then, the news got worse. The patrol sent to apprehend Stuaart had been ambushed. Two men were dead, two others wounded. Testimony from the scene indicated that the patrol had managed to wound one of the opposition. Lang briskly ignored the casualty figures. Instead it was the discrepancy concerning the opposition that he brought attention to.

It was a force of ten men in dark gray uniforms that had released Stuaart from custody. Lang asked point blank where the additional men had come from. The lieutenant looked askance at the director.

"Sir?"

"We know that five men and a woman arrived at the port. Those same six people checked into the Central Plaza Hotel. With the exception of the crew of the ship they arrived on, no other off-worlders arrived on-planet. All of the ship's company departed when their ship left planet two days ago." Lang ticked off the facts with his fingers. "Where did the other five men come from?"

The lieutenant was speechless.

"There are only the five of them," Lang continued, "plus Stuaart and the woman. Track them down. Find them. Take them into custody or kill them. We have wasted too much effort on this already." Dismissing the lieutenant, he called out his door, "Now, is there anybody who can tell me about Wilfz?"

Wilfz had been taken from his room. The lieutenant held him by one elbow to propel the captive along the hallway. With his arms bound together at the wrist, it was an effective hold. Under the pretext of guiding, the lieutenant took advantage of every opportunity to bounce the captive against the wall.

"Don't let him hit his head again," the major ordered the lieutenant after one brutal slam. "Once is enough to support the resisting arrest charge. Anything more constitutes torture."

Wilfz chuckled.

"What's so funny, traitor?" the lieutenant slammed him back into the wall.

"You weren't so brave until you tied me up." Wilfz was not really amused by the situation that he found himself in. He was angry, but refused to let these men see it. It was not in his nature to give up. Goading them on was his way of fighting back, but any victory he achieved would be fleeting. He knew there was only one way this would end. There was no doubt that the time remaining in his life could be measured in minutes.

"Shut up!" The lieutenant punched into his back.

"Tough guy," Wilfz breathed out, momentarily breathless.

They had reached the foyer. His captors picked up the pace, walking quickly toward the exit. Wilfz expected to be slammed against the front door, to be used as the means to open it. Instead, the lieutenant kicked the door and threw Wilfz out of the building. He tumbled to a stop, lying face down on the outer walk. Without his coat, he felt the concrete leach the heat from his body instantly.

"That's enough! Leave something for the trial," the major ordered.

"Yeah, what he said," Wilfz sniggered. "You're not man enough to finish the job."

The lieutenant lunged down at the prone major, but the captain grabbed his shoulders from behind and forced him away.

"He's only doing it to make you mad," he said. "He'll get what he's got coming to him, but first we have to interrogate him."

Wilfz laughed. The captain stepped over to him and delivered a swift kick to his ribs. Wilfz explosively exhaled from the force, the kick rolling him onto his side. He curled up defensively, coughing.

"Not so funny now, is it? It really is too bad you're a traitor." The captain leaned over him. "I was looking forward to consigning your family to limbo. It would have been interesting to see what we could make you do."

"Touch my family, I kill you," Wilfz gasped. The captain made to kick him again. Wilfz cringed, immediately dismayed that he could not stop himself. It shamed him to show fear to these men.

"Just pick him up. We have to get him out of here," the major said impatiently, stopping the captain's assault.

Rolling Wilfz onto his stomach, the two officers gripped him by the arms and pulled him to his feet. They marched him down a short set of stairs to the driveway. Two cars were parked curbside. Wilfz was propelled toward the vehicle in front.

"Hold him here," directed the captain. The lieutenant enthusiastically obeyed by folding Wilfz over the rear fender, effectively immobilizing him while the captain opened the door to the backseat.

"We'll take it from here," said a new voice. "Easy with your firearms. We'll take those."

Although startled by the unexpected comment, Wilfz thought he recognized the voice. As he puzzled over which member of the Constabulary it could be, the lieutenant suddenly released him.

"I see you like to hurt people," the voice continued. "Give me a try." A moment later, he heard three strikes in rapid order, followed by the sound of a body sprawling to the walkway.

"Which one of you has the key?"

There was a moment of silence. A second voice spoke up, unfamiliar to Wilfz. "Let's just take them all and we'll empty their pockets later."

"I have it," the blue-coat major quickly admitted, revealing his reluctance to accompany the newcomers.

"Very good, now take a walk. Take your friend with you and don't look back." Again, it was the familiar voice.

Wilfz turned his head back to see what was going on. The major and the captain were helping the lieutenant to his feet. After they began walking along the driveway, the voice addressed him. "Okay, Major, it's your turn. Let's get those cuffs off you."

Wilfz turned his head around the other way to see Van and one of his men. The Celestial Guard sergeant unlocked the wrist binders, releasing Wilfz. The other guardsman watched the retreating bluecoats as he aimed his submachine gun at them.

"Are you okay, sir?"

"Now that I'm not facing a firing squad, I feel wonderful." Wilfz gave a little grin.

"We were afraid they were going to kill you before we could get to you."

Wilfz gave a sour chuckle. "If I had known you guys were going to be here, I wouldn't have made it so hard on myself," he admitted.

"You distracted them so we could get close," the other guardsman spoke.

"Let's get you out of here, sir." Van gestured to the car parked behind his former captor's vehicle. "I've got their keys. They will not be following us."

The two guardsmen led Wilfz to the other car.

❧❀❧

Coal Borough, Bremen, Capital City of Holland

The trip took less than half an hour. The car arrived in the dock area of Coal Borough. From between the buildings adjacent to the road, reflected sunlight glinted from the river. As they drove up to a warehouse, the door slid open just wide enough to permit the car to enter. Wilfz emerged from the car to be greeted by Colonel Stuaart and Lieutenant Cameron.

"You're out of uniform, Major," Stuaart commented.

"The blue-coats arrested me during my shave," Wilfz explained. "Did you know that was going to happen?" He indicated his rescuers, alluding to their timely intervention.

"It was purely coincidental that we were waiting for you," Van answered for the colonel.

"I sent them to bring you here," Stuaart said. "We need a doctor. I remember from your dossier that you have a friend here in Bremen who is a surgeon."

Wilfz looked around the warehouse without responding. Stuaart and Cameron were unhurt. Van and his fellow guardsman obviously had no need for a doctor. The remaining two guardsmen were watching through the windows of the warehouse. The woman was not in sight. "What happened?" he asked, making no attempt to conceal the anger in his voice.

❧❀☙

Monique Lewellen had been sleeping fitfully since she had been brought to the warehouse. She hovered on the cusp of slumber, fully cognizant that she was not quite asleep. Despite the injections that had dulled her senses, her mind continued to replay what had happened earlier in the morning.

It had been her decision to accompany the team to rescue Colonel Stuaart. Intellectually she believed she had understood the risks. As a citizen of the Celestial Empire, she had lived in safety her entire life. A backwater planet like Holland would not escape the consequences should any harm come to her. Imperial citizens enjoyed the protection of a first-class military. Monique had been wearing that confidence like a cloak when she'd gone along for the rescue. It had not occurred to her that she could be hurt. Until this happened, it had been inconceivable that anyone would be arrogant enough to *dare* attack. In this case, these people had to be ignorant of the possibility of reprisal from the empire. The consequence of her decision demonstrated that she had been woefully unprepared emotionally.

She had been surprised by the team's ability to plan and execute an attack on the spur of the moment. Witnessing the whirlwind attack against Stuaart's captors had left her powerless with shock. When the other trucks had showed up, she had merely stood and watched, not unlike a spectator. She remembered staring at the second truck as Sergeant Van pulled her down. The gunner was pointing his weapon directly at her. She saw nothing of the barrel of the weapon, only the dark bore within that seemed to grow in her awareness. When the muzzle flashed, she barely registered Van's shout. She could almost see the blur of spinning projectiles as she listened to them whizz through the air at her.

Monique remembered other details, reliving them over and over. The walkway had been cold against her bare legs as Van rolled onto her. Raising her knees up from the walk to escape that chill had brought a spasm to her back. Surrounded by bits of rubble, she had thought a piece of stone had thumped her in the back. She was aware of numbness, but as the shock of being hit wore off she began to feel the pain. Her chest had been tight, and she'd been unable to breathe. The last thing she remembered was Van mouthing words, but she had not been able to hear him.

The sliding screech of the warehouse door brought welcome relief from the repetitive daydreaming. The room where Monique lay was partially in darkness. It was an office, positioned in the corner of the warehouse. Dim light through the open door illuminated the far wall.

The makeshift mattress on which she lay was a folded canvas cover that the team had removed from the truck. It was not very soft, but it effectively insulated her from the cold concrete floor. Guardsman Gray had provided his charcoal jacket as a pillow. From the musty smell emitted by the blanket, she imagined it had been scrounged from somewhere in the warehouse. Curled on her side, she felt unusually warm, so she kept the blanket low on her shoulders.

From where she lay, Monique could see nothing of the warehouse. She had to rely on what she could hear—the car driving into the building, followed by the warehouse doors sliding shut. Stuaart greeted Major Wilfz who apparently had had his own adventure this morning. The conversation continued with Stuaart's mentioning their need for a doctor. She was surprised to hear the anger in Wilfz's voice as he asked for details.

"Apparently it was a trap," Stuaart said. "When they rescued me, we were attacked by weapons carriers with machine cannon."

"You took a woman into the line of fire? What are you, barbarians?"

"Now see here, Major!" Stuaart objected, but Wilfz interrupted him.

"You were supposed to protect the envoy, not use her for cannon fodder."

Monique expected Cameron to speak up for himself, but was bemused by his silence.

Van apparently felt no compunction to remain silent, which did not surprise her. "It's not the lieutenant's fault," he said. "There were operational concerns. It would have been unwise to divide our force in the face of superior numbers."

"Sergeant, it *is* my fault," Cameron admitted. "I could have left her in the apartment. She would have been fine by herself until our return. It would not have taken that long for us to go back and pick her up."

"I would not have stayed."

Monique's voice sounded weak and tired in her own ears. Even though the conversation had stopped, she feared the men had not heard her. The reflection of light on the far wall darkened as Wilfz appeared in the doorway. He wore a light-colored shirt and green uniform trousers. He looked around for a moment before his gaze fell upon her. She watched the anger fade from his features, to be replaced with gentle composure.

As an actress, Monique recognized the effort it cost Wilfz to control his outward expression. It was a concept that she understood. A controlled countenance made for a calming influence. That Wilfz should make the attempt showed his concern for her. No, it was not an attempt. She could see that he was able to conceal his emotion. Perhaps it was from years of practice from leading men into hazardous situations. She knew from reading his record that he had experienced many of his men getting wounded. With that insight she realized a kinship with the Constabulary major.

He entered the room and knelt down by her. She noticed his eyes take in her bare shoulder just before he looked away. She glanced and noticed the exposed strap of her camisole. With his eyes averted, he reached with a cautious hand and tugged the blanket up to her neck. It was obvious that his action was motivated more by embarrassment than compassion.

"I'm a bit warm," she said, wiping the dampness from her cheek with the flat of her hand.

"It's a fever," Wilfz responded. "You'll catch chill if you don't stay warm."

"It's not their fault," she said, changing the subject. "I'm the one in charge of the delegation." Her words had a slight slur to them.

"Are you in pain?"

"Van gives me a shot when I start to hurt. They take very good care of me."

She stared into his face. This wasn't the man she had met before. He was a different man from the man she'd seen at their first meeting. She wondered at the disparity. Apart from the faint bruising to the side of his face, in what way had he changed since she had last seen him? *It is his eyes*, she decided. There was compassion in those soft brown eyes. She thought she could detect guilt too, as he now realized what had happened to her. Perhaps he felt guilt of association, because her wound had been inflicted by his countrymen. Women were not meant to come to harm. That she was not of his world did not matter. She had become hurt on his planet, and that offended his honor. No, it was more than his honor. It was his sense of justice. The perpetrators were fellow members of the Constabulary, lawfully entrusted with the welfare of civilians.

"You're tired. You should sleep," he said. She watched as his eyes, soft with concern, become hard as he looked out of the office. He gave the blanket one last tug before turning to rise.

Monique reached out of the blanket to catch his hand, uncovering herself once again in the process. "Ah …!" she gasped suddenly. Her spine had twisted as she moved. The hollow feeling in her back burst into a flash of pain.

Wilfz dropped back down to his knees. "Easy," he said carefully. "You shouldn't move like that."

"It's my fault." She blinked away tears of pain. "They told me to stay down but I didn't listen."

Wilfz pulled her blanket back over her again. "Just rest."

"No!" Monique let her head fall against the rolled up jacket. "It's my fault. I gave the order. The team works for me."

"I see." Wilfz was obviously placating her. She could tell that he didn't believe her ... that he was pretending to be convinced. She thought back to when he had first entered the room and realized that he was trying to keep her calm and docile until she could receive medical attention. *Two can play this game.* She closed her eyes and forced herself to relax. Tense from her brief pain spasm, she let her muscles become slack as she sank down into the canvas mattress.

❖❖❖

Wilfz watched as Monique closed her eyes. He was struck by how different she looked now from the previous time he had met her. Her face was pale, lacking the color and vitality he had noticed before. She now exhibited a vulnerability that stirred his sense of protectiveness. Seeing her relax with her head lolling back against her impromptu pillow, he knew that she had succumbed to slumber.

Carefully, he picked himself up and left the office. Out of curiosity, he searched for the jacketless guardsman. He found the individual keeping watch through the windows, a rifle slung over his shoulder. He returned to resume his conversation with Stuaart and Cameron. "How badly is she hurt?"

"She took a piece of shrapnel, not very big," Van answered. As the sergeant described the injury, Wilfz looked at Lieutenant Cameron.

"It's too late to throw blame," Stuaart said in a low voice, responding to the stern look on Wilfz's face. "We have to proceed from here. She needs a doctor. It's as simple as that. That's why Sergeant Van and Guardsman Schmidt were sent to get you."

"I'm not a doctor."

"No, but you know one. If I still had my records, I could have found him myself," Stuaart explained.

"Have you been spying on me and my acquaintances?"

As Stuaart didn't respond to the question, Wilfz didn't pursue the subject. "These guys aren't going to stop, are they?" he asked.

"You've seen how ruthless they are," Stuaart said. "Van told me what happened at the officer's billet."

"Is my family in danger? They taunted me about them."

"I honestly don't know," Stuaart answered. "The way things are starting to happen, they might not have the manpower to deal with that right now. Your folks are in Woodland. Lang will have to pacify Bremen before cutting anybody loose to the countryside. But we need the doctor."

"Oliveiras," Wilfz said. "He owes me a favor. I'll get him, and then I'm leaving."

"Major ..." Stuaart started, but Wilfz interrupted him.

"I need to get my family before they do. I'll set out now."

"That's fine, Major," Stuaart agreed, "but wait until dark. It'll be more covert to meet with him at home."

"As opposed to letting the blues seeing me in broad daylight when I go to the hospital," Wilfz deduced for himself.

"They will be looking for us very hard. You, me, and especially these distinctly uniformed men," Stuaart agreed. "Speaking of which, I thought you said they were dressed as businessmen."

"I have specific orders not to let my people be apprehended for espionage," Cameron volunteered, joining the conversation.

"A technicality after the fact. You did not arrive in uniform," Stuaart contended.

"Let's nitpick this another time," Wilfz said impatiently. He tilted his head toward the office. "She's feverish. She needs medical care."

"I'll check on her," Van said. "I can make up some wet compresses to cool her down."

❄

Director's Office, Constabulary Management Office, Iron Borough, Bremen

The loss of Major Wilfz from Constabulary custody was as unpalatable to Director Lang as Colonel Stuaart's escape. The officers in charge of both failed undertakings, the major and lieutenant, faced the director across his desk. The men expected disciplinary action for their failure to secure the two wanted men and the foreign military force.

"Wilfz might know someone here. Here's a list of his known associates. Find out if any of them is in Bremen. It's entirely likely he will attempt to contact someone for help." Lang handed the list of names to the major and leaned back in his chair. "Perhaps someone can explain to me how it is possible that foreign troops are operating, not just on our planet, but in our capital city?"

The officers braced themselves for a bitter harangue.

"I can understand how they were able to find Stuaart. He was bait, after all, and they slipped through your fingers!" Lang looked at the officers. "How did they know we had arrested Wilfz?"

The officers remained silent, eyeing each other at the rhetorical question.

"What happened to Allenby and Holloway? Where is the rest of Stuaart's staff? Why haven't any of these men been seen? We can't afford to allow any of these men to run loose. They can cause incalculable damage to the Constabulary."

The officers looked at each other. Lang responded to their uneasy glances.

"There's no doubt that those men are in contact with Wilfz. Either he or one of those men may attempt to contact the people on that list. Find out if they are in Bremen. Station men there, out of sight, and wait for them to make contact. We must end this conspiracy before it starts!"

❄

Warehouse, Coal Borough, Bremen

Monique's fever was a symptom that indicated she was fighting infection. Van cleaned her wound again and replaced the bandage with a fresh one. After that he turned to the task of reducing her temperature. For the cooling compresses, he tore a strip of cloth from the hem of her dress, the material being soft and absorbent. Folding it into a pad, he dampened it under cold water from the basin in the restroom that adjoined the office. While Monique lay on her side, Van draped the compress over her forehead from the temple. Mercifully her slumber served as a haven from her suffering; she had not stirred while he worked over her.

✦✧✦

After the discussion, Wilfz went to one side of the warehouse to be by himself, helping himself before he left the others to one of the carbines the team had taken during the ambush. Laying it on a workbench, he field stripped it and cleaned it using kit he had borrowed from Guardsman Gray. The other men observed the practiced way the Constabulary major disassembled the carbine, demonstrating his familiarity with the weapon.

It was customary for a senior officer to carry a revolver, since the officer would be issuing orders and directing the fire of his subordinates. Troopers were equipped with carbines, which had more range and knockdown power than pistols. Fitted with bayonets, carbines made excellent close-combat weapons as well as being psychologically intimidating. The long, sharp blade forced respect from any opponent. Wilfz had always led by example by using the same weapon as his men.

When he finished cleaning the weapon, he collected ammunition magazines, discovering that the twenty-one-capacity boxes held only fifteen rounds each. This was a standard weapon load for sentry duty; fewer rounds kept the magazine springs from maximum compression, since prolonged inactivity with the magazine fully loaded would take the temper out the springs. In the expectation of seeing combat, he selected three magazines, taking ammunition from one to top off the other two.

Despite Wilfz's preparation, the carbine was unsatisfactory. He was unable to adjust the sights. Zeroing the weapon was out of the question while the fugitives remained in hiding. The noise of shooting would attract attention to their place of concealment. If he couldn't find an opportunity to test fire the weapon, accuracy would be an unknown factor when the time came to use it.

❖❖❖

When Colonel Stuaart approached Wilfz at the workbench, the major was in a better mood. The act of readying the carbine had proven therapeutic to improving his temper. With his commandeered weapon laid aside, Wilfz had turned to the other weapons the guardsmen had taken. He was examining one of the semiautomatic pistols that had come from off-world, comparing it to a service revolver that was the standard issue pistol in the Constabulary. Turning his head to the colonel, he held up one of the cartridges he had removed from the semiauto's magazine. "This is one meaty round. It's probably as powerful as the nine-ought-six magnum," he commented, referring to the late sergeant's Constabulary-issue service pistol. "Their pistol is lighter than our revolver. How do they keep the round from blowing it apart?"

Stuaart picked up the pistol and gave it a cursory examination. "Hmm, it *is* light. Some sort of alloy, I would surmise," he said. He put the pistol back down. "We need to talk."

"Yes, we do. What's going on here? What happened to them?"

Stuaart went on to describe the ambush of the Celestial Guard team. When he finished, Wilfz critiqued the battle.

The team had captured the truck carrying Stuaart before the captors could call in reinforcements. The Celestial Guards, with their inferior numbers and short-range weapons, had managed to neutralize the blue-coat troopers. Such teamwork was the result of superior training and experience.

Despite the overwhelming firepower they provided, the two weapons carriers had not been deployed properly. It was clear that the attack had been uncoordinated and ill timed. The use of the machine cannon had obviously been planned for shock value. Had the attack trucks been used properly, they could have picked apart the team at range with impunity.

Sending two trucks of troopers would have been more tactically logical. Had they lined the troopers along the street on both sides, the guardsmen would have been hard pressed to fight their way out. It would have been a shooting gallery. Another scenario would have been to pair a gun truck with a truck of troopers. With the machine cannon as fire support, the guardsmen would have been forced to remain under cover. The troopers could have advanced and taken the team.

In Wilfz's spoken opinion, the Celestial Guardsmen had only one decent rifle between them. The rest of them had submachine guns with short barrels and small bores. Their effective range was relatively short. He granted that the rapid-fire weapons were efficient man stoppers.

"It's a good thing we weren't facing you," Stuaart commented dryly.

Wilfz snorted, uttering the epithet, "Amateurs!" Then he lowered is voice. "We can't count on them being cautious and inept. They'll learn from their mistakes," he predicted.

"We have to get the delegation out of here before the blues wise up." Stuaart went on to estimate the number of troopers that the blues had available, explaining that the men were too thinly spread out. He wanted to get the team out of Bremen while the blues were still trying to accomplish too much, too soon, with too little. "I fear that I have underestimated them." Stuaart picked up the semiautomatic again. "It's my fault everything is happening now. They are reacting to what I was doing. They're not ready, but neither was I."

"If they were not there," Wilfz wondered, "then where are they and what are they doing?"

"If I were to guess, it's because Lieutenant Holloway didn't get my call."

"What do you mean?"

"You could say I was being paranoid. I had long expected that something like this could happen," Stuaart said.

Wilfz remained silent.

"I went off-planet earlier this year. That was right after you got hit," Stuaart explained. "I paid a visit to a Celestial Imperial embassy in the Royal League."

"Why not talk to the league?" Wilfz asked. "They're the closest civilized worlds to Holland. We came from there, once upon a time."

"The league has never shown any interest in Holland. We would have seen their warships before now. The Celestial Empire actually sends patrol ships through here. Given their proactive role in keeping the peace, I felt that they would take the threat to Holland as seriously as I do."

Wilfz grunted, looking around at the imperial citizens who had come in response to that trip.

"Fortunately, they took me very seriously. Admiral Christie met with me at the embassy. He agreed to get help from his government. Their ships have the ability to observe on and around Holland, and they can provide information we need to get the upper hand against Lang." Stuaart waved a hand. "When I returned to Holland, Lang became increasingly strict in managing the Constabulary. Through ex-patriots and allies he had off-planet, he knew I was in the league. For all I know his spies told him what I was doing there. I've tracked his people through the spaceport, but what Lang has them doing I don't know. I worried that Lang might take action against me and my men. His officers show more than normal interest in my activities. I didn't want any of his people pulling rank on my people while I was out of the building."

Wilfz nodded in agreement. Given what had just happened to him that morning, the colonel's paranoia was justified.

"I instituted a telephone protocol," Stuaart went on. "I would call my office to expect my arrival at the CMO. After I arrived at my office, I would call Holloway."

Wilfz waited for the colonel to explain the significance of the protocol.

"When I didn't call this morning, Allenby should have evacuated the basement," Stuaart said. "Holloway would have contacted the rest of my office staff and gone to the rendezvous to meet Allenby and everyone from the basement."

"So you think that's why Lang's people are spread out." Wilfz nodded, giving the colonel a shrewd look. "If that's what you planned, that's really sneaky. I would like to think that you're on our side."

Stuaart stared at the major in response to the left-handed compliment.

⊰✳⊱

Later in the afternoon, Monique opened her eyes. The first thing she saw was her dress, which was spread out over the back of a nearby chair. She could not help but note the damage to it, and her lips quirked when she saw the folded piece of cloth next to it. Whatever had happened, she had slept through it.

She did not move, allowing her mind to take stock while she came to full wakefulness. She no longer felt uncomfortably warm, but her back was stiff. Her mouth was dry and she was thirsty. She lifted her head to find a cup of water on the floor near her pallet within easy reach. A scraping sound echoed in the room as she lifted it with a shaking hand. Willing herself to become steady, she tilted her head sideways and brought the cup to her lips. The ambient temperature of the warehouse kept the water cool, a fact she belatedly realized after empting the cup. Placing it back on the floor, she noticed Wilfz looking in from the door. She gestured for him to enter.

"It looks like Sergeant Van reduced your fever. You look better. How do you feel?" he asked, sitting on the floor near her.

"I'm trying not to think about it right now," she replied wanly. She noticed that he had winced when he sat down. She wondered if her injury would bother her as long as his apparently did. "I'm beginning to question my choice of career change."

"You have a career?"

"You sound surprised."

"Women don't normally have employment until later on."

"'Later on'?"

"After the children are grown," Wilfz said in a matter of fact manner.

"A woman's job is to have and raise children?" she asked tartly. "Using up her useful years taking care of the home?"

Wilfz looked startled by the intensity of her skeptical tone. "Of course, my mother didn't wait that long. She tended the books for my old man and my brothers."

"What do they do? Are they in banking?"

Wilfz remained silent, a guarded look on his face. Monique wondered why her question had unsettled him. After a moment, she ventured another question. "Your mother is a bookkeeper?"

The question snapped the major out of his funk. "She's very bright. When I was younger, it amazed me that she didn't use a calculator. She was very strict when I did my math homework. She required me to correctly solve each problem. Other mothers raise the children before getting work," he said in a matter of fact manner while giving her a measuring look. "You're too young to have grown children."

"I'm not a mother. I don't have children. I'm not even married," Monique explained. "Normally, in my profession women begin work at a very young age. I was working before I was twelve."

"What kind of a job makes you work that young?" Wilfz asked. "Did your family have a farm?"

"I was an actress."

Wilfz nodded, but she could see the bewilderment in his eyes. "What is an actress?"

She stared at him. "You know, a performer who acts." She found herself at a loss to explain. "I was a star, acting in dramas. You do know dramas, don't you?"

Wilfz shook his head negative.

"You have stages here, right?" Monique asked, but Wilfz shook his head again. "I stood in front of people and acted out dramas. I also sang songs. I was a pop star. You know, 'pop' as in 'popular'?" Wilfz shook his head once more.

"Are you serious?" Monique burst out incredulously. Wilfz shrugged at her exasperation, an uncertain smile on his lips.

"If I didn't think it would hurt, I would sing right now." Monique lay her head back down on her jacket-pillow.

"Please, don't."

"I believe this is the first time someone has asked me *not* to sing."

"I meant no discourtesy. I don't want you to hurt yourself."

Monique looked at him and saw the serious look on his face. "I was teasing you." She gave him a smile, but he actually looked uneasy. "Let me guess. You don't tease here on Holland?"

"I've never been teased by a woman before," he said, his posture stiff in what Monique assumed to be a diplomatic manner.

She didn't understand why he was taking exception to her teasing. What was innocent familiarity in her opinion was apparently taboo in his view. She recalled her initial declaration, calling him uptight. She could see the kindness in his regard, realizing that it was his bedside manner. *This is how the man must have visited his wounded,* she thought, *the ones who fell in combat under his command.*

"Dramas. What is a dramas?"

"*Dramas* is plural. A *drama* is a dramatic story—portrayed on the stage or in film. The characters are played by actors." Monique found herself amazed. Everybody knew what a drama was. "What do you have for entertainment here?"

"We read for entertainment," Wilfz answered, and then he ventured a guess of his own. "A drama is a reenactment of a book?"

"Many dramas are based on books," Monique corrected him. "Think of it as people playing roles. I'm an actress. I pretend to be someone else and interact with other actors. Instead of reading a story, you can watch and listen to it as it happens."

"Pretending to be other people—you mean make-believe," Wilfz said as he nodded. "Children play at make-believe."

Uptight and staid, Monique mentally labeled him once more. *If everyone here is like this man, no wonder they don't have an entertainment industry.*

❧❀❧

With the onset of darkness, Wilfz prepared for the expedition that had been planned to pick up Doctor Oliveiras. Removing the magazine, Wilfz worked the action of his carbine, ensuring there was no cartridge in the chamber. He knew the bore was unloaded, but it was second nature to check it again. After letting the bolt close, he inserted the magazine and locked it in place. It would take only a moment to operate the bolt to chamber the first round. This manner of carrying loaded weapons was standard operating procedure in the Constabulary.

Sergeant Van and Guardsman Schmidt would be going with him in the car. With the train stations under observation, Wilfz could not hope to use that method of transport to get to Doctor Oliveiras, much less to return again. He accepted Perez's offer of his Celestial Guard jacket to keep warm, the two men being close in size.

"Once I get Olly, I'm leaving," he told Stuaart. Seeing the colonel about to respond, he continued. "I can't take the chance that the opposition is too busy to hurt my family. I've caused my parents enough trouble. They don't deserve this."

"Major, we need you here," Stuaart insisted.

"I don't even know what I'm doing here," Wilfz said. "I have no business working for you. I don't even have a security clearance."

"Security clearances went out the window when the blues made their move," Stuaart declared. "Damn it, man! What about your duty to Holland?"

"My family is Holland," Wilfz countered.

Stuaart closed his eyes for a moment. "Major, we have a serious problem here, and I need your expertise."

"These Celestial Guards are pretty sharp." Wilfz nodded to the other men. "They can handle it. You don't need me, but my family does."

"Do I have to make it an order?"

"You're retired. Since Lang has declared us renegade, you no longer hold office. Neither one of us can issue orders."

"That's defeatist!" Stuaart accused. "I never considered you to be a field lawyer."

"I'm only one man in Bremen. I don't even know my way around these streets."

"That's a cheap excuse and you know it!"

"You're right, but I'm through talking about it. I can do more at home than I can here."

"At least give me until after tomorrow."

"Why? What's going on?" Wilfz demanded, but Stuaart remained silent. "Security clearance out the window, huh?"

"Give me a day." Stuaart chose to bargain with the intransigent major. "Help us here, and then I'll let you go with my blessing."

"One day," Wilfz finally agreed. "I bring you Olly, and then I'll do whatever it is you need me to do tomorrow; then tomorrow night I'm out of here."

CHAPTER SIX

Thatch Borough, Bremen

"Stop here." From the passenger side of the automobile, Wilfz pointed to a tree-lined parking area at the side of the boulevard. Following his direction, Schmidt steered the car among the other vehicles parked therein. From the backseat, Van kept an alert watch on their surroundings. There was no one in sight.

Disembarking from the car, they remained close to the other parked vehicles. In contrast to the circles of light at the base of the poles, the shadows cast by streetlights were all the more effective in concealing their approach. Wilfz carried his carbine against his side with the muzzle down. The other two men had their customary submachine guns slung over their shoulders, ever watchful and prepared for their use. The darkness provided enough cover to make discernment of the weapons very difficult.

Wilfz had been here one time before, just to see where Doctor Oliveiras lived. The doctor had not only been a former comrade in the Constabulary, but a friend of his parents as well. It had been more the family history than their shared past that had served to hold him back from actually knocking on his door that first time.

Illuminated by a light mounted on a lamppost, narrow stairs rose to an alley-like path that led to the gate that opened onto the dwelling complex. Reluctant to expose them on the lighted area, Wilfz silently motioned for the men to follow him onto the grass. They skirted the steps and walked along the wall. Once they reached the walkway beyond the upper side of the steps, Wilfz looked carefully around. Satisfied they were unobserved, he led the way into the gate to the walkway beyond.

Single- and double-level dwellings lined the walkway, separated from each other by the distance of an arm span. Most were two-family residences, with a few single units interspersed among them. The majority of the doorways were dark, but a few were lit by porch lights.

Van and Schmidt looked carefully into the shadows about them as they followed Wilfz. With the Constabulary major wearing Perez's Celestial Guard jacket, the three men looked similar in the night.

Wilfz stopped at one door, it's porch light turned off. Light leaked past the window shade at the side. He reached up to the light with the intention of removing the lamp, but instead encountered decorative lenses on all facets. The fixture was sealed.

"Watch your eyes. I'm breaking the light," Wilfz murmured, raising up the carbine in both hands and striking the butt of the weapon against the porch light. There was a crunch of metal and glass as he crushed the fixture, followed by a popping sound from the light bulb within.

The principle was a sound one. They did not want the porch light to turn on and illuminate them. The sound of destruction rang out in the quiet living area. The other two men cringed. Having used stealth to avoid attracting attention to get this far, the major had now thrown caution away. Schmidt had turned his head at Wilfz's warning, so when the noise occurred he caught movement out of the corner of his eye. He raised his hand in a signal to Van.

At that moment, Van had reached to Schmidt and touched his shoulder to get his attention. He had heard a whisper just before Wilfz broke the porch light. The two men looked at each other, each understanding that the other had been alerted to something. At the same moment, Wilfz tapped furtively on the door.

The response from inside was quick, the voice sounding gruff and unwelcoming. It was obvious the doctor had heard the breaking of his light fixture.

"What is it?"

"It's Michael," Wilfz answered, "David's son."

❖❖❖

Four men had been waiting outside Doctor Oliveiras' home since dusk. With the report that one of the foreigners had been wounded, the probability was high that Major Wilfz would turn to his friend for help. Operatives in plain clothes had discretely observed the doctor during his hospital rounds, watching every person he came into contact with and maintaining their surveillance until he arrived home. As night settled, uniformed members of the Constabulary took position around the neighborhood. In addition to the four men—two on either side of the doctor's residence—there were two pairs of lookouts posted outside the gates. The lookouts at the south gate reported the arrival of a car and the subsequent surreptitious behavior of the occupants. Alerted, the capture team watched the three armed visitors cautiously approach the door.

"Wait, we have to be sure," the leader whispered into his radio. The electronic device was not standard Holland Constabulary issue. Only select members of the chosen blue's staff were permitted to use them. "Let me figure out which one he is."

The shatter of broken glass sounded from the doorway. This was followed by an urgent knocking, rapid but low in volume. They could barely hear the muffled reply from behind the door. The team had to listen carefully when the center man introduced himself.

"It's Michael Davidson."

The leader of the team sized up the men at the door.

"It's not the one in the middle. As soon as we shoot, grab the man nearest to you. The other men aren't him, those we'll put down," he whispered. He turned to his companion. "Shoot when I shoot. The center one is mine, you get the one on the right."

❧❀❧

"What?"

"It's Michael. Turn off your lights and open the door," Wilfz hissed.

He had barely finished speaking when the shade was pulled aside at the window. Light spilled out, illuminating the three men. Before Wilfz could protest the light, there was a burst of gunfire.

Van dropped to one knee, the sonic snap of bullets whipping over one shoulder from the strobe-like muzzle flashes. Bringing his submachine gun up, he instinctively lined the weapon in his sight and fired a short burst in return.

During the first fusillade, two figures broke cover from between two homes and charged toward Schmidt, but he saw them coming. As he brought them under fire, something fell against the back of his legs, and he staggered to his knees. Rather than try to remain upright, he permitted himself to fall onto his side while maintaining his sight picture. One of his targets had gone down and the other had dashed back. Schmidt snapped off two more rounds as the form vanished back into the darkness. There was no indication whether he had hit the runner.

Reacting to a groan behind him, he rolled onto his other side to take stock of their situation. Van remained in the kneeling position, his weapon still pointed away but looking down at his prone companions.

"The major's hit!" Van looked from the major back to Schmidt. "Take down the door."

Schmidt regained his feet and stepped over Wilfz in preparation to force the door when it opened. "Is that Michael?" whispered the doctor.

"Get him inside!" Van ordered. The two guardsmen gripped the prone major underneath his arms and dragged him through the doorway. He cried out in pain. The sling of his carbine was tangled around his arm, and the weapon clattered along the hard tile floor beneath him.

Van kicked the door shut behind them. He quickly found and hit the light switch to plunge the room into darkness.

"What is this? What is going on? Who are you?"

"Doctor Oliveiras, we need you," Van said urgently.

"I can see that. I'm going to need light for Michael."

"No," Wilfz gasped. "You have to save the lady."

"Michael, it really is you!" Oliveiras looked up at the other men. "I thought I told you to turn the light back on."

"Here," Van held a penlight, illuminating the major. "He got hit in the back. You'll have to stabilize him quickly. We have to get out of here."

"Leave me," Wilfz groaned. "I'm the one they want."

"Shut up! You're hurt," Oliveiras snapped. "Let me get my bag."

Wilfz fumbled with his weapon. "I want to face the door." He grunted with the effort of trying to pull the bolt back on his carbine.

"We're not leaving you, Major," Van declared.

"That is an order, Sergeant."

"With all due respect, you are not in my chain of command."

"This is Holland," Wilfz explained. "As a Constabulary officer, my order is law."

"You cannot even cycle your Mark Ten." Oliveiras had returned with his medical bag.

"Charge my weapon and leave me."

"Leave you? Why?" Oliveiras demanded. "So I can tell David and Karlynn that I left their son to die?"

"We did not come here for me," Wilfz said. "We're here for the lady."

"What is going on around here?" Oliveiras demanded. He was kneeling by Wilfz now, and had opened his bag. "Get that coat off of him."

"We have to hurry," Schmidt urged. He had taken up watch at the window. "If they knew we would come here …"

"They might already be waiting at the car," Van finished for Schmidt as he obeyed the doctor and began to unfasten Wilfz's jacket. Wilfz cried out despite the sergeant's attempt to be gentle.

"Major?" Van asked as he pulled the jacket off.

"He's fainted," Oliveiras observed. "Thank heaven for small mercies. I don't see an exit wound. Okay, roll him back and lift the back of his shirt. We'll do this quick and dirty."

"You've done this before?" Schmidt asked, not looking away from the window.

"I used to patch these guys up when I was in the Constab," Oliveiras admitted. "Just a quick patch for now, but he needs to go to the hospital."

"No hospital," Van said. Still holding the penlight, he pulled up the blood-sodden shirt with his other hand. "That's the first place they'll look for us."

Oliveiras grunted, immersing himself in performing first aid on Wilfz. Red welled up from two entry wounds a hand span apart. With a competence born of experience, he worked at stopping the blood flow with compresses. That he had just witnessed a gunfight was not evident in his steady demeanor.

"Okay, that should do it," Oliveiras declared, wiping his hands on a small towel. "Now, who are you guys?"

"Not here," Van said. "We'll tell you everything, but you have to come with us."

"What has Michael dragged you guys into this time?" Oliveiras asked bitterly.

"More like we dragged him," Van responded.

"Hmm, that's a switch." The doctor shook his head.

"Van, I think you're bleeding," Schmidt indicated the side of the sergeant's neck.

"It's a scratch," Van dismissed the injury. "Doctor, is there a back door?"

"No, the only way out the back is through the bathroom window. It's high and small. We can't carry him out that way."

"Then the only way out is through the front door. We need to move now before those guys regroup."

"Michael cannot be moved."

"If we don't leave now, we'll be cornered here. 'Quick and dirty,' remember?"

"Leave me," Wilfz grated. "Get Olly out of here."

"You're a tough man, Major," Van said.

"I don't feel so tough," Wilfz groaned out. "Charge my weapon and leave me."

"You don't have the strength to raise your carbine, much less shoot the thing," Oliveiras declared.

"They know they hit me. They'll come to look. I'll occupy them while you run," Wilfz argued. "Go save the lady."

"If he's going to die, let it be while I'm saving his life," Oliveiras decided.

❧❄❧

When the team returned to the warehouse, Perez opened the door of the car. In the darkness of the warehouse, it was not immediately apparent that the team had commandeered a different vehicle.

"Help me with the major," Van called to Perez.

"I told you to leave me," Wilfz's pain-wracked voice uttered.

"Where can I operate?" Oliveiras asked as Colonel Stuaart and Lieutenant Cameron hurried to the car.

"What happened?" Stuaart asked.

"They were waiting for us," Van explained. "They took down the major in the first volley, but we beat them back."

"Looks like you took a hit too." Stuaart noted the smear of dried blood.

"Pieces of brick that spalled," Van said, dismissing the wound. "Doctor Oliveiras patched the major so we could move him. We figured they had our car staked out, so we withdrew to the next neighborhood and stole a car from there."

"Leave me! Get the lady out of here while the getting is good," Wilfz slurred angrily. "I'll only slow you down. You should have left me behind. I could have gotten some of them."

"He's delirious. Get him onto a hard surface, preferably a table," Oliveiras instructed, taking charge of Perez and Schmidt. He turned and saw Cameron. "I was told that you have a medical kit. If I can knock him out, you won't have to hold him down."

The doctor followed after the two men who were carrying the wounded major. The table they had found was a workbench, a bit narrow but long enough to lay a man upon it. The lieutenant brought the medical supplies as Oliveiras had asked.

At Oliveiras' order, the men pulled the bench away from the wall. After they draped a tarpaulin over it, they lifted Wilfz and carefully set him facedown onto the covered surface. An agonized grunt escaped through gritted teeth as he made a transparent attempt to conceal the pain.

"I'm going to need one of you guys to stand on the other side to help me," Oliveiras said and then pointed at Van. "Not you. Have your medic clean and bandage that neck. You'll get an infection if it remains untended."

"I'll take care of it," Schmidt volunteered. He looked to Perez. "You're better qualified to help the doctor."

"Don't waste time on me," Wilfz complained. "You're here for the lady, not for me. I'm done for anyway."

Oliveiras leaned down and placed his mouth close to his ear. "Listen, you little jerk," he snarled, "you didn't give up the last time you brought me in on something like this. I'll be damned if I'll let you give up now."

The chastisement only served to ignite Wilfz's temper. "It's my duty to stop bullets. It's my duty to save women. Save her first. Worry about me after that."

"How badly is she hurt? Is she worse than this?" Oliveiras looked at Perez, who shook his head.

"I'm going to need a light," Oliveiras said, "either a big one or a bunch of smaller ones. I'll need to see what I'm doing here. I should be doing this in a hospital ..."

"I gave Sergeant Van an order," Wilfz refused to be silent. "My order is law here on Holland."

"Major Wilfz, you told me yourself that you were no longer in the Constabulary," Stuaart reminded him as he watched the doctor prepare a hypodermic syringe.

"Michael, after what you put me through before, you have a lot of gall to behave this way now," Oliveiras declared.

"Put you through? You owe me, Olly."

"You asked for it. I cannot work on you while you are causing trouble like this." Oliveiras spoke in a mock sad tone. "I hope this hurts you more than it hurts me." He yanked Wilfz's trousers down a bit and jabbed the hypodermic needle into one bottom cheek. As the anesthetic entered his bloodstream, the major gave a surprised grunt of pain.

"I guess it's obvious that we are not the best of friends," Oliveiras said to Stuaart. "More's the pity. He was such a good boy when he was younger."

❖❖❖

Dozing fitfully, Monique was awakened by the commotion of team returning with the doctor. She listened, shocked as she heard the vehemence in Wilfz's voice as he demanded to be left to die. From the urgency with which the doctor issued instructions, she had no doubt that the major had been critically wounded. It hadn't occurred to her that anyone would be hurt in the quest to get her a physician.

To be honest, she had not respected Major Wilfz. The passive manner he had displayed the day they met had not impressed her. She could not reconcile the information in the dossier with the man himself. The report seemed to be no more than fiction to her.

Monique had listened to the conversation Wilfz had with the colonel earlier in the afternoon. They had not tried to keep their discourse quiet. From his comments to Colonel Stuaart, she gathered that the major had done his own family a disservice. Wilfz's manner had been positively fervent.

She reconsidered the private thoughts that occurred when she had spoken to Major Wilfz prior to that. While he discussed his family, his eyes had been unfocused in melancholy as if he were looking within. Had she actually thought this man staid?

She lost track of her thoughts as the drama outside of the office continued. The doctor's gruff and coarse manner, almost vulgar in his treatment of Wilfz, dismayed her. She shivered with the realization that this was the man who had come to treat her.

She couldn't see what was going on from where she lay, but she listened to the doctor's commentary. Having asked for scissors, he was apparently cutting the major's clothing off. He hissed in surprise at one point, and the colonel explained that the major was still recuperating from wounds previously suffered during a training accident.

"He could have taken cover and saved himself," Stuaart said quietly, "but he made sure his radio operator was under cover first."

"There have been a lot of accidents lately," Oliveiras said slowly, "but I get the feeling that there are more than accidents going on here. What is he doing working for you anyway? He's always been a field officer."

"You seem well informed for a retired Constabulary doctor," Stuaart commented.

"I still have friends in service, and we talk," Oliveiras explained. "No one could explain to me why Michael is working for a retired colonel, much less why he was assigned to the intelligence branch."

"The answer is simple," Stuaart explained. "I requested him."

There was a pause. Monique heard the doctor give a grunt of skepticism.

"I knew this day was coming," the colonel continued. "I didn't expect it to be today."

"This is about Michael?"

"I need an officer to rally the Constabulary," Stuaart said. "There are many undecided men in the Constabulary, men serving under undeserving officers and sergeants. Wilfz has served in many brigades. There are many men who would resist or openly break away and join him. Now everything has all gone to hell. Damn!"

"So you want me to patch Michael back together so you can … what?"

"I want to get him off-planet," Stuaart said. "These people here, they need to get off-planet too. I will provide them the means to rendezvous with their ship. And you too, of course."

"Thank you." Oliveiras conveyed more sarcasm than appreciation.

Home, Monique thought. *I'm going home.*

"Despite what you heard here tonight, I'm actually fond of this boy," Oliveiras admitted.

Boy? Monique thought. Wilfz was older than she was, her own age being in the upper twenties.

"I don't want to tell his parents that he died under my care," the doctor went on. "They already hold me responsible for his joining the Constabulary in the first place."

"Really?"

"He was a decent tracker and hunter," Oliveiras said. "So I showed up at his parents' home in uniform while I was on leave. I looked splendid in that dress uniform. Michael was impressionable back then, and he liked the hat, the jacket, and the boots. I can still remember being so proud of myself even though I wasn't a doctor yet. And this kid here almost idolized me. His parents still talk to me, but they haven't completely forgiven me. I guess I can't blame them."

There was silence for a while.

"Well, I'm about ready to start. Go take a walk. There's enough risk of germs from myself and this gentleman here," Oliveiras said. "What's your name?"

"I'm Perez, Doctor."

"Call me Olly," Oliveiras genially corrected. "Okay, Perez. Have you done anything like this before?"

"Not this," Perez acknowledged.

"Well, I watched you sterilize the instruments with the alcohol, so that's something," Oliveiras commended. "Just follow my instructions. Unless something's been nicked inside, it should be pretty straightforward."

Straightforward? For a surgeon maybe. Monique pulled the blanket over her head. Knowing that soon it would be her turn, the thought of listening to the surgery made her queasy. She placed her hands over her ears to block out the doctor's voice and willed herself to go back to sleep. She was still feeling the effects from her last anesthetic injection, so slumber swiftly returned to her.

❧✳❧

Wilfz could hear nothing. He was aware that the blanket felt rough against his bare skin. There was a dull pain between his temples, and his mouth felt dry. He opened his eyes. Morning light filtered dimly through the dirty office windows.

He was lying on his stomach. Without looking around, he realized that he was where the lady had been sleeping. If she was no longer here, then it made sense that he had been left behind.

"They'd better be gone." His voice sounded coarse in his dry throat. He tried to lift his head, but his body proved unwilling to obey him. He let out a low groan as he recalled the events from the previous night. He had been shot in the back—again.

He started to close his eyes when movement caught his attention. A head with tousled auburn hair rose into view. The lady rubbed one bleary eye with a slender hand as she regarded him.

She must have been sleeping on the floor, he realized. "They left you behind too?" His voice was rusty with dryness.

"They're still here," she answered. "It was a long night. They're tired."

"You should have left me," Wilfz growled.

"The wolf is awake." Oliveiras walked into the office and knelt down by his two patients.

"You know better than to call me that," Wilfz whispered angrily.

"Then stop growling like one," Oliveiras said. "How are you feeling?"

"How am I supposed to feel?" Wilfz snapped. "I've been shot up again."

"I wasn't talking to you, ingrate." Oliveiras turned his attention to Monique.

"I'm starting to feel it now," Monique reported.

Wilfz looked at her, seeing the strain of discomfort around her eyes. "She's in pain." He glared at Oliveiras. "You should be taking care of her, not me."

"I'll give you a pill after you eat," the doctor promised Monique.

"She needs more than a pill."

"She doesn't need an overdose or a dependency on painkillers." Oliveiras gave his professional judgment. "Bless these guys, but they had her so doped up it wasn't good for her. It's also a waste. As it is, there's not going to be enough for you."

"Forget me!" Wilfz caught sight of Cameron at the doorway. "Lieutenant, I was given to understand that your responsibility is to protect the envoy. By permitting me to slow you down, you are putting her life in danger."

"This from the former lieutenant who wouldn't give up on frozen corpses in a dale," Oliveiras said.

"That was different! If anyone had still been alive, I could have called in reinforcements," Wilfz gritted. "These men have no support. They lack the manpower and resources to care for two wounded. At least she is ambulatory. Get her out of here."

"Out of the question," Cameron said firmly.

Wilfz glared at the Celestial Guard officer. He took a deep breath to continue his tirade. To his surprise, the woman suddenly intervened.

❈

Monique leaned over and took his face in her hands. The day-old whisker stubble felt sharp against her palms. Wilfz was startled into remaining silent. The woman pressed forward and brought her face to his. She kissed his mouth.

His eyes grew wide, but only for a moment. As if a switch had been thrown, he seemed to lose strength. His head became heavy in her grasp as he relaxed. His eyes closed as he fell into slumber.

Monique lifted her head and gently released the major. She could not understand why she had done as she had. The man lying wounded before her had declared his life forfeit in favor of her own, not only once, but repeatedly. When he had first awakened, she had heard the relief in his voice when he had believed himself to be abandoned.

No one had ever sacrificed himself for her. The concept that a man would willingly die so that she would live was something she had not actually contemplated before. Her surprise was that it only occurred to her now. The guardsmen had always been by her side, but it was only after actually coming under gunfire that she realized that they could have been hurt too.

Harm had already come to one of them. Sergeant Van had been hurt while getting her the doctor. Because of her thoughtlessness, he had been wounded and the major before her had almost died. This had all happened because Monique Lewellen erroneously believed that she knew better than the men assigned to protect her.

Her face felt wet as her vision suddenly blurred. A sob escaped her lungs as she turned her head to Cameron.

"Are you all right?" Oliveiras asked.

"Lieutenant Cameron." Monique raised an arm to him, fingers down as she gestured him closer.

Cameron knelt close to her, but she could barely see him. Her lashes sprayed her tears as she blinked rapidly. Monique gripped his arm, her fingernails digging into his jacket sleeve. She used his weight as an anchor as she pulled herself toward him, bringing herself upright. The blanket fell away to reveal the shirt that one of the guardsmen had given her to wear.

"Be careful," he urged, his voice conveying that he was genuinely afraid for her.

"I'm sorry." She made the attempt to lean forward in a bow. "I didn't understand. I was wrong. I'm so very sorry." She gave a gasp of pain.

"Don't do that!" Oliveiras protested. "You'll hurt yourself."

"I need to apologize to everyone," Monique continued. "Please, let me see them. What I have done to them is unforgivable."

"You're overwrought." Cameron held on to her upper arms.

Despite his firm grip, she was shaking uncontrollably. Her sobbing was turning to hiccups as she began to have difficulty breathing.

"Okay. Okay. Okay," Cameron said in a soothing voice. "Just calm down. It won't do much for their morale to see you like this. Just pull yourself together."

Monique allowed herself to be placated, keeping one hand on Cameron's forearm as she dashed tears from her face with the other. While he eased her back, she did not resist him, but still held his sleeve. "I'm sorry."

"Can you do anything for her?" Cameron asked Oliveiras.

"She needs to rest and conserve her strength," the doctor advised. "As soon as she is calm, send the men in one at a time. She needs the peace of mind. She obviously needs to feel closure."

"I want to see Sergeant Van first," Monique requested, both hands now holding his sleeve.

"Yes. Just relax and calm down." Cameron nodded. "In a while, I'll send him to you."

Monique searched his face, looking for sign that he was telling the truth and was not just appeasing her. Cameron had never lied to her, and the doctor had volunteered his prognosis. Giving a shaky nod, she finally released his sleeve.

❖❖❖

Sergeant Van quietly entered the office and sat down next to Monique. The doctor had been adamant about stopping the painkilling injections. Her pale features were severe with discomfort, but there was no sign of the hysterics she'd given vent to earlier that morning.

He remained silent, watching her sleep. Minutes passed before she slowly opened her eyes, giving a small jolt of surprise upon seeing him. "Sergeant Van," she said without preamble, "it's my fault you were hurt. I'm sorry."

"Lady Lewellen …" Van began, but Monique continued.

"Please, if I hadn't insisted on accompanying you, I would not have been hurt. You would not have had to get the doctor and risk getting killed."

"If you hadn't been there, it could very easily been one of us who got hit instead." Van sounded reasonable. "If that had happened, we would still have had to get Doctor Oliveiras. It is our task to protect you. We volunteered to serve. There is no need for you to feel guilty. If one of us gets hit instead of you, then we have done our job. Your guilt would only serve to insult and cheapen our endeavor and sacrifice."

"I was disrespectful. I disregarded your experience and expertise," Monique admitted. A tear that had tracked down the side of her face during his zealous proclamation dropped onto her shirt. "I held you all in contempt, and for that I am sorry."

"I saw no contempt," Van said. "You gave the lieutenant a hard time, but you were always courteous to the rest of us."

"I treated you all shamefully. I lived like a lady and treated you like servants."

"We are here to serve. There is nothing wrong with conducting yourself as a lady. Any injury you perceive to have given me …" Van paused and then shook his head and made an open gesture with empty hands. "I cannot think of a single instance."

"I can think of several." Monique smiled shyly, using a finger to wipe the dampness from her face.

There was a groan from the beneath the blanket covering Wilfz. Looking over, Van addressed him. "Major."

Monique winced as she rolled over to look at the wounded Hollander. He looked back at her warily. "Was my kiss that unpleasant?" she asked him, her demeanor instantly changing from a repentant woman to that of a coquette. Van looked at her in surprise as she extended a hand to Wilfz's face, touching his cheek for a moment then checking his forehead. "You're a little warm. Would you like some water?" she asked.

Wilfz opened his mouth to speak, but only an unintelligible noise came out. He nodded his assent instead.

"Sergeant, my cup," Monique looked back at Van. "Please."

Monique had been sipping from a cup of water that had been left within easy reach from where she lay. Now that she was tending to Wilfz, she could not reach it. Van picked up the half-empty cup and placed it in her hand.

Wilfz tried to lever his torso up and lift his head, but lacked the strength to do that.

"Hold on, Major, I'll assist you." Van moved around the bedding. With surprising tenderness, the sergeant shifted the wounded man onto his side, holding his head with one hand. When the injured man's head was more or less level, Monique placed the cup to his lips and carefully tipped it toward him.

Wilfz tilted his head forward, trying to tip the cup toward him to allow him to drink faster.

"Don't let him choke," Van warned her.

"I know you're thirsty," Monique soothed Wilfz. "I did the same thing earlier."

Van looked at her in puzzlement. Looking at him, Monique tilted her head in a shrug. She had just lied. From her periodic bouts of nausea, it had been all they could do to get her to have more than a sip at a time until her fever broke.

"There, it's empty," Monique showed him the inside bottom of the cup when he had finished the last of the water.

"More," Wilfz requested, his voice having returned.

"Let me take a look at you first." Oliveiras walked in. "Sergeant, you can set him back down. Thank you both for looking after this guy."

❧❈❧

Monique sat up with the blanket gathered around her waist and watched, sympathetic to Wilfz as he suffered through the indignity of being examined. The doctor checked Wilfz's pulse by holding his wrist and looking at his watch. He then checked his patient's temperature. Taking up his stethoscope and adjusting the earpieces in his ears, the doctor placed the chestpiece against Wilfz's back and listened intently. Whether he wanted to hear the heart or the breathing, Oliveiras did not say.

Monique thought back to the previous evening, when the surgery on Wilfz was over. The guardsmen had begun combing through the warehouse for more bedding material. The pickings had proven to be slim. Monique had risen and left the office, wearing her blanket as a robe. From the doorway she could see the major's lifeless form on the workbench, a pair of work lights suspended over him still shining down upon him. A blanket covered him from the neck down. Bloody scraps of cloth littered the floor around the bench in addition to the clothing that had been cut away.

Doctor Oliveiras and Guardsman Perez sat on the floor against the wall. Monique had been unaware of the passage of time, but the two men must have spent hours working on the major. It had been a long night for all of the men. The others were now looking for a place to lay the wounded man. She did not see Colonel Stuaart. She had looked around and noticed the car that Van had brought back was no longer in the warehouse. The colonel had apparently departed while she had slept.

"Bring him to my bed," she had ordered. At the time, she was inwardly surprised to have heard herself say that.

"Lady, you need to lie down too," Oliveiras had protested.

"I'll sleep on the floor," she responded. It wasn't as if that would be the first time she'd done that.

Guardsman Gray had managed to locate a section of dust-covered composite board. After he cleaned it off with a damp cloth, it made for a better surface to lie on than hard concrete.

When the major had been put to bed, Monique could not help but view his unclad form. Some of the scarring on the back of his thighs was still red, proof that he was still recovering from his previous wounds. She recalled his slight grimace of pain when he had sat by her earlier. Not for the first time she wondered how long she would have to live with her own pain. As for the scar, she had discovered that she was in no way prepared to think about that. After all, she had never expected to become hurt in any way.

"Okay, young lady," Oliveiras voice brought Monique out of her reverie. "Lie back down. You should be resting."

"Why?" she challenged him, looking him straight in the eye. "He has been hurt worse than I."

"Please." Oliveiras gestured for her to lie on her board.

"What is really wrong with me … really wrong? It's more than just a piece of metal, isn't it?" Monique asked. "No one will talk to me about it."

Oliveiras looked at her thoughtfully for several moments before eventually nodding. "Fine, I'll tell you while you lie down."

Monique merely sat where she was. The doctor knelt down and put his hands on her shoulders to guide her down. She resisted until he began to speak. "It could be nothing," he said.

"It's the other than nothing that concerns me," Monique said as she settled down.

"Yes." Oliveiras carefully unwound the blanket from around her and pulled it over her. "I had been concerned that one of your kidneys may have been hit, but you're normal."

"Only my kidney, or is there more?"

"The other worry has also proven unfounded." Oliveiras was obviously trying his best to keep from upsetting the young woman. "You still do not feel any numbness or tingling anywhere, do you?"

"I only have the pain back there," Monique admitted.

"Good, that means no nerve damage."

Monique's lips quirked up at his saying "good" about pain.

"The important thing you must do is relax. Make no unnecessary movement," Oliveiras instructed. "Don't get up any more than you have to. I don't know where that shrapnel is or how close it is to your spinal column."

"That would cripple me, right?" Monique asked bluntly.

Monique had not exactly been uninformed about her condition. She had overheard Van telling Cameron about his fears. He had been reluctant to allow Perez to attempt a risky and sensitive surgery with his limited skill and the rustic facilities available to them. Getting the guardsmen to talk to her about it had been unproductive. Now that it had been confirmed, the issue of having her body defaced with a scar paled in comparison to the real possibility that she might live as a paralyzed invalid. She sagged back and stared away, feeling the blood drain from her face.

"Oh, damn. You didn't just go into shock, did you?" Monique saw the doctor peering into her eyes, the concern apparent in his features.

"No, I'm a lot tougher than people think." She knew the pallor of her face belied her statement.

"Look, you're going to be okay," Oliveiras said. "Just be calm and think positive thoughts. Before you know it, this will be all but a memory."

CHAPTER SEVEN

Coal Borough, Bremen

Driving a delivery truck, Colonel Stuaart returned to the warehouse shortly after noon. It had been snowing all morning, and white slush had collected on the vehicle. Water dripped down the sides of the vehicle and puddled on the dirty floor as the snow melted in the relative warmth of the warehouse.

The guardsmen were naturally curious about the new vehicle, but Stuaart would satisfy that curiosity only after he had seen Wilfz.

"Is he awake?" he asked Doctor Oliveiras. It was obvious about whom he inquired.

"He's just eaten," Oliveiras nodded, "but he's drowsy. I have him hopped up on anesthetics. We're going to need more soon."

"I've already got that arranged," Stuaart explained. "I'm going to talk to him." Knowing Wilfz was likely to resist his plan, the colonel looked at Cameron and waved him over. He would attempt to win over both men at once.

Wilfz lay on his stomach on the bed of tarpaulins, his head turned toward the far wall. Monique Lewellen lay facing him on her side, wrapped in her own blanket.

"Major?" Stuaart asked softly.

Monique twitched, looking over her shoulder at the men.

"Present and accounted for," Wilfz muttered. His tone sounded almost flippant, a sign that the man was amenable. The colonel went over to the desk and pulled the chair over to the prone pair.

"Major, we need to talk," he said, sitting down.

"Should I leave?" Monique asked.

"No, this concerns you as well." Stuaart saw the questioning look on Cameron's face.

There was a low groan as Wilfz lifted his head to turn it toward the visitors.

"I'm getting you out of here tonight," Stuaart announced. "All of you."

"You and what Constabulary?"

Stuaart almost smiled at the old rejoinder. "You're going out with the Celestial Guard."

"That's insane. They cannot take care of the lady and me."

"Doctor Oliveiras will be able to take care of you both."

"Not in that parts van. I doubt it would carry all eight of us."

"No, it's not for everyone." Stuaart shook his head in agreement. "I had to get rid of the car your friend Van commandeered. I think I managed to ditch it before it was reported stolen this morning."

"You're really sneaky, you know that?" Wilfz delivered his observation in a less-than-admiring tone. Monique's eyes widened at the disrespect he was showing to his superior.

"You've already told me that. Unfortunately I'm not sneaky enough," Stuaart conceded, "otherwise all of us would not be in this mess."

Wilfz gave a grunt of agreement, closing his eyes for a moment. When he opened his eyes again, he stared back at the colonel tiredly. "What's the plan?"

"I'll send you all out in a field ambulance."

"That could work," Wilfz admitted thoughtfully.

"Thank you for your vote of confidence," Stuaart said dryly.

"It will work at least for getting out of Bremen," said Wilfz. "It'll take more than a field ambulance to get us out of the bowl. I asked you before—you and what Constabulary?"

"What do you mean about getting out of the bowl?" Monique asked.

Wilfz looked at the woman as if to answer, but his statement was directed at Stuaart. "Correct me if I'm wrong, but you are counting on getting these people back to their ship."

"Not exactly. We arrived by commercial ship. We've already missed its departure," Cameron stated. "The ship that will extract us will be a destroyer."

"Same difference," Wilfz said impatiently. "I doubt they will risk landing in the bowl, unless they plan on taking out the sniper emplacements first."

"No, Major," Cameron responded. "The Imperial Navy has strict orders not to destroy Holland's infrastructure. It is in all of our best interests that Holland remain safe from transgression."

"Well, that makes me feel a little bit better," Wilfz commented. "How about saving us from ourselves? Have you any orders about that?"

Monique spoke up, "Officially, the Celestial Empire recognizes the autonomy of Holland." Her bureaucratic tone came as a surprise to everyone.

"That explains what you *can't* do, but what *can* you do?" The argumentative tone in Wilfz's voice lost strength, and he closed his eyes as he continued speaking. "Any uninvited ship attempting to land in the bowl will be shot down."

"Why can't we just stay clear of the bowl?" Monique asked. "Can't the ship pick us up on the other side of the mountain?"

"There are only a few passes in the mountains. Those will be heavily guarded."

"Then what good will it do to leave Bremen?"

"It will be only a matter of time before the blues capture you in the city. At least out in the bowl you will have a chance to evade captivity." Wilfz's frank appraisal was brutally direct.

Monique brought one hand to her throat as if she were suddenly breathless. "Are we to live on the run now?" she asked. "Are we supposed to hide from men who have demonstrated willingness to shoot first and not ask questions later?" With an angry shake of her head, she leaned forward, hissing in pain as she stretched her body toward Wilfz. "What do you mean, 'you'?" she asked. She placed a hand on his blanket-covered shoulder. "You are coming with us."

Wilfz made a visible effort to focus on her face. The scene would have laughable if the situation had not been so serious.

"Listen," she continued, "this is not *Sergeant Pressman of the Imperial Marines.*" Monique stated the title of a popular drama that had recently aired in the Celestial Empire. She warmed to her subject, changing her voice to imitate a man: "That's it, lads! Save your last bullet for yourselves!"

"What?" Wilfz demanded, incredulous at what he was hearing.

"We won't leave anyone behind!" Monique finished her imitation.

"That's not funny!" Wilfz snapped, shocked.

Cameron stiffened angrily at her conduct. She was mocking the major to his face. He had been about to interject when she followed up with her chastisement. "I know it's not funny." Monique rounded back at Wilfz, unrepentant. "I wasn't laughing when they brought you back last night, and I'm not laughing now."

Like the other men in the room, Wilfz was speechless as a result of her strong emotional outburst. His eyes became soft as he looked back at her. Then he smiled, reminiscent of the first smile he had shown that time on the train. "Yes ...," he acquiesced, his voice trailing off. The smile faded as a quizzical look appeared. "It occurs to me, we've never been introduced. I don't know your name."

His admission came as a surprise. "Well, Michael," she replied, "my name is Monique."

"Hng," Wilfz grunted. "That's unique. Pleased to ..." He closed his eyes and noticeably relaxed with a sigh.

"And then he falls asleep," Monique commented.

"That went surprisingly well," Stuaart said. "I thought he'd put up more of a fight."

"What went surprisingly well?" Cameron asked.

"We need to talk." Stuaart stood and motioned for the lieutenant to follow. "I'll tell you what you need to know. I need your help."

❧❀❧

Iron Borough, Bremen

Sergeant Van led Guardsmen Gray and Schmidt through the alley toward the Division Central vehicle depot. Colonel Stuaart had separated from the group when they had debarked from the delivery truck, driven by Guardsman Perez. Perez was returning to load up the lieutenant, the doctor, and his patients in fulfillment of Stuaart's plan. There had been too much traffic to and from the warehouse. There was no sign that they had attracted attention to that location, but no further chances would be taken. The hiding spot would be abandoned immediately, and the two groups would rendezvous elsewhere.

The guard team was an effective fighting force, but against an entire organization they were too few to be of any assistance in the coming conflict. Nothing would be served if they were killed or captured. It wouldn't matter whether they were alive or dead, the blues would use them as a propaganda tool. In the resulting scandal the Celestial Empire would be open to accusations of subversive activity, legitimizing the punitive policies enacted by the council against suspected collaborators.

No, remaining on Holland was too risky. It would be better to avoid further contact with the blues and deny Lang that propaganda.

The present undertaking was dangerous enough. Just being seen—never mind getting caught—would be enough to justify a charge of espionage, if not sabotage and theft.

Stuaart had managed to convince Lieutenant Cameron to take Wilfz with them. In the view of the empire, Wilfz was a foreign national. The Celestial Guard was under no obligation to take the major off-planet with them, such action not being covered by their mission mandate. The major could do nothing from off-planet, but in his wounded state he was of little help. Given that his recapture would provide the blues with a propaganda coup, it would be best to spirit him off Holland.

The colonel and the lieutenant had agreed that convincing Wilfz to leave Holland would prove to be problematic. He had already declared that he would not abandon his family. There was no denying his resolve. He had, after all, spent his life in defense of his world.

Snow had been falling steadily all day. With the ground of the alley and the paved roadway still retaining the warmth of the past summer season, the slush quickly melted to a shiny sheen. In contrast, the grass and trees were covered in solid white.

The three guardsmen reached the end of the alley. A wide boulevard passed before them. Across the street was a chain-link fence topped with razor wire. Beyond the fence were parked row upon row of snow-covered, armored trucks, parked facing the interior of the depot. The vehicle they had come for was parked at the very end of the row closest to the fence.

The team waited, keeping to the shadows of the alley. They saw no sign of sentries, but remained watchful nonetheless. For this task, Gray was armed with the submachine gun he had borrowed from Perez. His customary rifle would only get in the way.

After several minutes, five successive flashes from a small light came from the gloom. It was the colonel, signaling that it was safe for the guardsmen to commence their part of the plan. The three men quickly crossed the street. Schmidt uncoiled a thin line of cutting cord and approached the fence. Van and Gray faced each other, making a platform with bent knees. Schmidt stood on their thighs with his slush-slick boots. While his comrades held him steady, he used both hands to apply the malleable explosive cord to the razor wire at the top of the fence. When he had firmly attached the end, he trailed the length down and molded it to the chain links alongside the metal post. Once he reached chest level, he dropped down to the ground to finish applying the explosive train. Satisfied it would hold, Schmidt accepted the fused igniter from Gray and attached it to the cord at ground level. "Firing," he hissed.

"Clear," Gray and Van said in unison, stepping away. They were careful not to look at the cord.

"Fire in the hole!" Schmidt pulled the tab, and the timed fuse ignited. He stepped back quickly and covered his face with one arm. A moment later, a flash of pure light lanced up the fence. Molten metal from the links cascaded to the ground in bright sparks, hissing as they dropped into the snow. The tortured link fence snapped and sagged away from the post, the razor wire draping across it. After a silent count, Schmidt uncovered his face to see that part of the fence had collapsed; the other half of the section was still supported by the other post. With gloved hands, he pulled the cut side of the fence away to create a vehicle-sized opening. Looking around, the other two men detected no sign that anybody had noticed their nocturnal activity.

They hurried into the parking area. Schmidt stopped at the rear of their chosen vehicle and tapped a fuel can that was mounted in the rear rack. He was rewarded with a muted noise. "You don't suppose all these trucks have full spare cans?" he quietly wondered.

"Yeah." Van nodded toward the truck parked to the side. "Let's grab a few more if we can."

Gray went to the truck parked ahead of their vehicle. Schmidt returned after checking the truck next to the one they were commandeering. "Empty," he reported.

Gray returned a minute later. "That truck and the one ahead have full spare cans," he confirmed. "Perhaps this column of trucks is for their ready response force."

"Maybe," Van agreed thoughtfully, but Gray wasn't through speaking.

"I was thinking, this truck is big, but with all of us it's going to be cramped."

"There are three of us," Schmidt suggested. "Perhaps each one can take a truck?"

"Let's not be greedy," Van decided. "But I can see us taking two. Two trucks and all the full cans of fuel we can get from the other trucks."

❈

After leaving the Celestial Guardsmen, Colonel Stuaart met up with members of the Constabulary who had been recruited for Free Holland. He had gathered these men as part of his preparation to counter the insurgent threat introduced by Director Lang. He conferred with the officer in charge while they observed the guardsmen.

"Do you think Lang will fall for this?" the lieutenant asked Stuaart, jerking his head at a group of men waiting further in the darkness behind them. The two men watched from concealment near the gate.

"His medical records have already been altered. Even if our guy isn't the one who verifies the body, no one will know the difference."

"I hate doing this."

"I know, Lieutenant. He was a good friend and a good officer." Stuaart nodded. "I can't believe he keeled over like that. Tonight he will help solve two problems."

"We stored his belongings like you ordered."

"Good. Anybody checking up on him at home will think he packed up and ducked out of town. When this is over, see his things get to his brother."

"Yes, sir. What are they doing?" the lieutenant asked. "I thought you said they were just taking the ambulance?"

"That was the plan," Stuaart confirmed.

"They are on our side, right?"

Stuaart did not speak right away, watching as the guardsmen cleaned the snow from the windshields. "What's in the other truck? Is it the other ambulance?" he asked.

"No, sir, that ambulance is at the head of the column. All the other trucks have standard field supply and basic ammunition loads," the lieutenant reported. He fixed the colonel with an unhappy stare as he continued. "Even though nobody knows it's there, it's unattended and completely illegal. It's sure to be caught by the next inventory."

"Unless the inventory happens now, it won't matter," Stuaart judged. He looked at the other man who had accompanied the lieutenant.

Sergeant Meadows had been discovered trying to get into the depot two nights previously. It was fortunate that he had been apprehended by one of the colonel's men. Had the blues captured him, he would have been summarily executed as a looter, not to mention he was already a deserter.

His story was all too typical of the times. After he had been relieved for cause, the sergeant had sent his pregnant wife out of Bremen. Whether it was instinct or something else, it had proven to be wise. After making sure she was safely away, he had returned to find his home occupied by strange men in civilian dress. Most of them were strangers. Among them he recognized the CMO watch officer, the officer who had relieved him of duty.

He'd spent the following days on the streets. He had some money for food, but it would not last indefinitely. He had nothing to spare to rent a place to stay, so he found out-of-the-way places in which to sleep. His bold plan to find Molly Sims and her boy did not seem practicable while he was occupied with survival. He had come to the depot in the vain hope of scrounging something useful, perhaps a forgotten weapon from a vehicle. Having no previous knowledge of the trucks that had secretly been loaded out, finding such items unattended was unlikely, but he had made the attempt anyway.

Back in uniform, but with the insignia of trooper, Meadows now hid in plain sight. He would appear as one of many men assigned to work at the depot; no one would look twice at him. The blue-coat officers preferred to interact with sergeants and corporals. As a mere trooper, he would be snubbed if not completely ignored.

"So what do we do? Let them take off with all that gas and both trucks?"

"This has been one big change of plans. They know nothing of the operation here," Stuaart said. "We'll wait for them to get mounted up.

"Are we clear?"

"It didn't take much to talk the duty officer into staying inside on a cold night like this."

"Good. Remember, when we start, don't hit me."

◅※▻

The three guardsmen had taken turns carrying fuel cans from the other trucks. As one kept an eye open for passersby, the other two loaded the second truck.

"Okay, get the ambulance out of here," Van instructed Schmidt. "We'll pick up the colonel and follow."

Taking a last look around, the men climbed into the vehicles as Sergeant Van went on foot to the boulevard. The field ambulance started easily. Leaving the lights off, Schmidt backed away from the other trucks. At a wave from Van he made a U-turn and drove out through the hole in the fence. As the ambulance drove away, Van motioned for Gray to drive out.

Van looked to where the colonel had signaled to them as the second truck approached the fence. The darkness revealed nothing. As Gray's truck stopped short of the street, the sergeant crossed in front and opened the passenger door.

"Should we wait here or drive there?" Gray asked as Van pulled himself inside.

"We'll go there," Van said, looking past Gray toward where the colonel had gone.

With a nod, Gray put the truck back into gear and started to turn in that direction.

There was a shot, the sound sharp in the crisp air. From the darkness, a figure ran into the lighted area of the street. There was a second shot, and the man, presumably the colonel, fell to the ground. Two more men followed. They stopped quickly when they sighted the truck sticking out of the fence. A moment later, the guardsmen saw muzzle flashes as the men fired upon the truck.

"Get us out of here!" Van ordered. "There's nothing we can do for him."

Gray cursed, but obeyed his sergeant. He turned the steering wheel in the opposite direction and sent the truck racing away.

✢❆✢

"Are you all right, Colonel?" Meadows asked.

Stuaart picked himself up.

"I'm fine," he replied. "You didn't hit them, did you?"

"We aimed at the wall across the street from them," the lieutenant assured him.

"Good. Let's get the rest of that line of trucks out of here," Stuaart ordered. "We're going to need a fuel truck and empty cans to replace those our friends borrowed."

"Yes, sir," the lieutenant said.

"And make sure that Lieutenants Holloway and Allenby and the sergeants go out in the first truck. You gave them the section I asked for?"

"Yes, sir, they're all good men."

"Good," Stuaart repeated. "Get them on their way. Their mission is of vital importance."

Their primary objective was to get Stuaart's office staff out of Bremen. Should the blues capture them, the information they knew about the colonel's activities could compromise the resistance. Getting Major Wilfz's family away from harm was their secondary objective.

In his original plan, Stuaart's men were to hide on Silvertip Mountain. That plan went out the window when the envoy and Wilfz were wounded. The safety of the delegation was paramount, so he had provided Lieutenant Cameron with the chart that had been meant for the men of his office.

"Remind them to make the checkpoint look like desertion, if at all possible. See if we can get Lang to waste manpower looking for his own troops. If we can sow the seeds of discord among Lang's people at the same time …" The addendum gave credence to the accusation of sneakiness that had twice previously been bestowed upon Stuaart.

"Yes sir," the lieutenant said. "Once everyone is out, we'll blow the depot. It'll look like a real firefight. The blues won't know what happened."

❀❀❀

"They shot him down like a dog," Gray said bitterly. The two armored trucks were parked by the delivery truck on a darkened street by a deserted park. The major having been transferred to the field ambulance, Doctor Oliveiras now assisted Monique in beside him.

"Other than that, everything went smoothly," Van said, adding to Gray's testimony. "The colonel must have been discovered by roving sentries. I'm surprised they didn't hit our truck when they took us under fire."

"I think it's obvious that they'll be looking for these two trucks," Cameron figured.

"Maybe not. Schmidt had already driven off when the sentries fired on us," Van said. "Perhaps they don't know to look for two trucks together."

"We were counting on the colonel as a guide," Cameron spoke aloud.

"We still have the major," Van reminded him.

"Okay, let's get this show on the road." Cameron had been watching the transfer. The back door of the field ambulance was closed. "Hopefully we won't have to deal with any roadblocks."

The two trucks sped through the dark streets. Upon reaching the boundary of Bremen, they discovered that indeed there was a roadblock. It was a simple barricade. Seeing no one, Van disembarked from the lead truck to investigate. It was untended, apparently abandoned. On either side of the road were machinegun positions. Tripods had been set up behind a protective slope of sandbags, but no weapons occupied their cradles. Either the machineguns had been taken or they had not been deployed in the first place.

Van could not know that the lieutenant who had previously commanded the checkpoint had reconsidered his personal allegiance.

Director Lang's charge that Major Wilfz was guilty of sedition, declaring him traitor and renegade, was incredibly unbelievable. The major was known for his courage and loyalty, for being a straightforward officer. Director Lang's irrational behavior toward the Constabulary at large did not bode well for the men assigned to the checkpoint. When Stuaart's office staff and their security escort arrived, the lieutenant was more than amenable to their reasoning.

Van moved the barricade post out of the way. When the trucks were safely through, he replaced it. If the guards returned, they would not suspect that someone had driven through their security checkpoint. Once Van rejoined his truck, the fugitive group continued on into the night and disappeared into the swirling snow.

CHAPTER EIGHT

Highway West, Outside of Bremen

Wilfz had been aware of the steady engine rhythm long before he was actually awake. His last memory was Oliveiras giving him an injection to put him to sleep after Lieutenant Cameron and Guardsman Perez had loaded him into the delivery truck. Despite the care the men had taken when they moved him, the pain caused by the move had caused him to break out in a sweat. At first, he had tried to keep quiet, but when they shifted their grip to load him onto the truck, he had cried out involuntarily. That was when Oliveiras had put him out of his misery.

He could tell he was in a different vehicle from before. Above him were three bunks folded against the wall. As he noticed the bunks, he wondered why he was lying on the floor. Why wasn't he lying in a bunk?

His face felt cool, but beneath the field brown blanket, he felt very warm. The blanket felt rough to his bare skin, but he could feel something smooth. It extended up one side and onto his back. As he wakened further, he became conscious of hot air near his shoulder blade as well as some sort of weight.

When he raised his hand to brush his face, he encountered an arm that was not his! It was unusually slender. Puzzled, he probed blindly. It took a few more moments for him to realize that the lady had draped her arm across his back. He turned his head and peered under the blanket. Seeing the top of her head confirmed that she was using his shoulder as a pillow.

"What is this?" he muttered.

"Michael?"

"Olly?" he replied, craning his head around.

"I'm up here," Oliveiras had been sitting in a jump seat at the head of the compartment. Beside him was a door to the driving compartment. The door was open, and Wilfz could see the side of the passenger seat. "Don't move so much."

"Why is she here?"

Oliveiras left his seat and sat on the floor. "Not so loud," the doctor cautioned him. "She needs her rest, too."

"Why is she here?" Wilfz repeated in a lower voice.

"The weather is very cold. You're keeping each other warm," Oliveiras explained. "I took all of the bunk mattresses and set them on the floor. They don't provide much cushioning, but they'll keep you off the cargo floor. No sense in letting the heat leech away."

"How long have I been out?"

"It's morning now."

"Where is everybody?" Wilfz craned his head around again, but he saw no one else with them.

"Two of them are up front," Oliveiras jerked his head toward the driving compartment. "The others are driving point."

"That makes sense." Wilfz put his head back down. "The colonel would know the way."

Oliveiras remained silent for a moment. He gave a small sigh. "Michael," he said carefully, "I have something to tell you, and it's not good."

"I've got gangrene?" Wilfz asked. "Nerve damage?"

"Your colonel is dead."

At first, Wilfz did not react. The words had no meaning—not when he first heard them. The colonel was dead. The colonel had information that Holland needed, that he had withheld. Wilfz had believed that he would eventually learn what the colonel had planned. He had entertained the thought that he could convince the colonel that his place was on Holland, not off-planet with these foreigners. Now that option no longer existed. He would remain ignorant of Stuaart's intentions.

"How?" he asked finally.

"It happened while they were getting the trucks," Oliveiras said.

Wilfz said nothing, but he tucked his head back into the blanket.

"I don't know if you two were close or not ..."

"We weren't close at all," Wilfz blurted. No longer interested in continuing conversation, he closed out the doctor.

Monique was in denial. Their situation had taken a turn for the worse, and she did not want to face it. One man was dead, another critically wounded, and she now lived with the possibility of paralysis. All of that was because she had interfered with Lieutenant Cameron's command. His team had been prepared to obey his order to leave her in the apartment. It wasn't until she'd protested that Sergeant Van had spoken up.

Her sense of guilt had returned, despite the reassuring words of the sergeant and his men. Cameron had also come to her to talk, kindly explaining that she really was not responsible for what had happened. In all concerns diplomatic, she had seniority. In that sense, she commanded the delegation. Once the situation had blown up in their faces, however, it had become Cameron's duty to assume control. He had actually gone to great effort to explain that the fault lay with the opposition and not with her conduct. From their turbulent past together, she had no trouble altering the word to *mis*conduct. In her mind, the only reason the lieutenant was being kind to her was that she had been wounded under his charge. A part of her wanted to take advantage of that, but the guilt she felt would not let her. To avoid those thoughts, she turned her mind to the man with whom she had been placed.

Monique noticed that, without the uniform, the major looked as nondescript as any other Hollander. Like most men here, he was short of stature, but he would be considered common even back on her home world of Pearl. She could not understand why the colonel had held this man in such high esteem.

It was almost noon when the trucks stopped. Except for his breathing, Wilfz had not moved at all, and Monique assumed he was still asleep. She lifted her head in an attempt to find out what was going on, shifting the blanket from over the two of them in the process.

"How are you feeling?"

Monique looked up to see the doctor in his jump seat. "Have you been awake all night?"

"I nodded off a time or two." Oliveiras mimed leaning against a cabinet and sleeping in his seat. "It's not my first time riding in one of these things."

"For some reason, I slept very well." Monique looked down at the major next to her.

"I'm so happy for you," Wilfz muttered, his voice conveying sarcasm.

"My, aren't we snarky."

Oliveiras' eyebrows arched at Monique's delighted comment. At the same time, the major turned his head to look back at her. From the way his bleary eyes widened, she knew he could see into the blanket.

"Good morning, Michael," Monique greeted him brightly.

"Where are your clothes, Eunice?" Wilfz turned his head back the other way, the pallor of his haggard face darkening.

Looking back to Oliveiras, Monique silently mouthed the name *Eunice.* The doctor shrugged in response.

"Doctor's orders," she said aloud, returning her attention to the man beside her. "Clothes inhibit the effective transfer of heat between two people. Direct skin contact is most efficient."

"At least put your underwear on."

"I only have the one set," Monique informed him. "I've been wearing them for days. They need to be washed, and I refuse to wear dirty clothing." She could see only the side of his face from behind him. His embarrassment lent the illusion of health, judging by the mild blaze on his exposed cheek.

One of the doors up front opened. "Go to the other truck." It was Van talking to the men in the driving cabin. "We'll confer here and let everyone know what we're going to do."

A moment later, the rear door opened and Lieutenant Cameron hoisted himself up, kicking the snow from his boots before stepping inside. He was wearing a Constabulary parka, light brown in color, one of many that had been part of the supplies in the ambulance. In his hands was a waterproof canvas case.

The temperature in the field ambulance fell noticeably. Monique pulled the blanket up around both her and Wilfz.

"How are they?" Cameron asked.

"*They* are fine, Lieutenant Cameron," Monique replied with a hint of acid in her voice. She buried her face against the blanket, surprised by her own manner, but not unpleasantly so. After her hysterics the previous day, it was comforting that her old spirit was returning.

"She needs clothes, Lieutenant," Wilfz growled. "Get her some."

"Never mind that," she said. "We don't need any right now."

"Unless there is a toilet on this crate, you'll need to go outside," Wilfz explained to her. "I know that I need to go. It was about time we stopped someplace."

The meeting had to wait while nature called.

Once everything was settled, Wilfz insisted on staying in his own blanket. For the meeting, it was the most logical and convenient arrangement. Lying with his back to the wall, he was able to see the chart that Cameron had had removed from the canvas case. It was spread on the mattresses. Cameron and Van were kneeling to either side. During her call of nature, Monique wore the shirt that she had worn at the warehouse. Now wrapped in a blanket, she sat in Oliveiras' jump seat where she had a view of everything.

Wilfz ran his finger along the road designated as Highway West on the map. At one point it forked toward Sharps Pass.

"There's a camp at the base of Silvertip Mountain," he said. "It's fortified with a gate. The road runs right through it."

"Couldn't we go cross country? Certainly the pass is not the only way to cross the mountain," Monique asked.

"During the warm season, yeah," Wilfz agreed. "Not mounted, though. We'd have to go on foot, but it's too late in the season now. The ridges are too dangerous in the winter. Soon, even the roads will be snowed in. Even if the weather were optimal, there are two wounded to move."

"You say that as if it's an intellectual problem," Monique said.

Cameron's looked up at her sharply, his mouth opening to tell her to remain silent when Wilfz interrupted him. "Everything we do is an intellectual problem." He grinned at her. "It's what we do."

"So how do we get out of the bowl?" Cameron asked, glaring at Monique before returning to the problem at hand. Monique interpreted his stern look at her as an order to be quiet. She rolled her eyes in response.

"We don't," Wilfz admitted. "I don't know what the colonel was thinking. He didn't tell me how he expected to carry this off. I don't recognize some of these markings on this chart."

"You've used maps before," Oliveiras said. "What's different with this one?"

"This chart is standard Holland Survey," Wilfz explained. "All of the topographical features are properly labeled by machine print. That's normal. Someone added these pencil notations. There are what I presume to be tunnel entrances along this mountain range. They might even by mine entrances or bunkers. This one has the letters *HS* above it.

"This has to be important." Wilfz tapped the marking. "It's far enough out of the way that no one will look for it. I just wish I knew what this information is. Where did it come from? Who else knows about this?"

"The colonel told me this is the only map when he gave it to me yesterday," Cameron informed him. "He said that this is so secret, nobody else knows about it."

"I don't like this," Wilfz admitted. "It's strange. How can nobody know?"

"What do we do? We can't get out of the bowl and we can't remain here in the open," Cameron stated.

"We're safe for now under these iron crowns," Wilfz said, referring to the trees that surrounded them. "We can remain parked beneath them during the day."

"That's what the colonel suggested," Cameron admitted, "but we can't stay here for the duration."

"Yeah, so tonight we take this road." Wilfz ran his finger past the fork that led to the pass. Instead of turning toward the mountain road, he indicated a point near the cave entrance labeled *HS*. "Winter is coming and we'll need to bunker down before it gets here. We don't want to drive in snow. Someone will see out tire tracks. If I were running interdiction in the bowl, I would know where all of my units are. I'm sure that's what they'll be doing once the snow starts to stick."

"Well, we need to get somewhere," Oliveiras complained. "I need to get that shrapnel out of her back, but I can't do it here. And she can't be bouncing around in the back of this thing after the operation. She needs time to recuperate."

Wilfz gave a sour chuckle.

Monique was puzzled by his reaction. She felt her face become warm with indignation. The doctor had been talking about her, and the major was laughing at her.

"I didn't have a choice with you, Michael. If I hadn't operated right away, you'd be having a dirt nap right now."

Oliveiras' comment made it clear that Monique had misunderstood the major's ill humor. He wasn't laughing at her. Michael was recuperating on the move.

"Dirt nap?" Monique repeated.

"It means we'd have buried him after he died," Oliveiras enlightened her.

"Olly, you don't need to teach the lady that," Wilfz said.

"Actually, I already figured it out," Monique admitted. "I just never heard it called that before."

"You shouldn't be saying such things around her," Wilfz continued to object.

"Why? Because I am a woman or because I was injured?" Monique asked. "It's too late to lament about that. What's done is done."

Cameron shot a dirty look at her, the anger plain on his features. For a moment, she couldn't understand his displeasure. She was the one who had been hurt, not him. She had been talking about herself. She was about to take umbrage when the lieutenant returned his attention to the major.

She realized then that Cameron had been angry on behalf of Wilfz. The thoughts she had managed to relegate to her subconscious reemerged in full flower—the guilt over the major having been wounded and the colonel getting killed. Rightly Cameron had taken issue over her indelicate comment.

Chastised, Monique kept silent. During the silent exchange between her and the lieutenant, Wilfz examined the map, not noticing their visual exchange. When Monique looked back, she noticed that his finger had wandered across the chart to the township of Iron Grove. She was not familiar with that place, but she did remember the name *Woodland* from Wilfz's dossier. That was his home according to that record, but it was not marked on the map anywhere around his finger. *Is he still thinking of going to his family?*

Holding a pack, Oliveiras brought out a small can. He pulled on a tab to remove the lid then handed it to Monique.

"This ought to put color on your cheeks," he said.

Holding the can in her hand, she examined the contents. The only description that came to mind was congealed cornmeal. She lowered her face for a cautious sniff as Oliveiras gave her a flat wooden spoon.

"Where's mine?" Wilfz asked, looking up at them.

"You've already had color on your cheeks this morning," Oliveiras commented.

Wilfz gave a short chuckle, returning his attention to the chart.

"This map has markings in only one area. To my thinking, the colonel had to be aware that there is no hope of getting out of the bowl by road. The only way out is to follow animal trails, but not with two injured. You guys can't carry us all the way. We have to heal up first.

"What is our timetable?" he asked.

"What do you mean?" Cameron asked.

"How long will your ship hang around before it leaves?"

"Indefinitely," Cameron answered. "There are four destroyers. One will remain on station while the others do whatever it is they do."

"It's going to be a year before we can attempt to get out of the bowl," Wilfz explained.

Monique inhaled unexpectedly, choking on a spoonful of cornmeal. She quickly coughed and spat it back out onto the floor.

"Are you all right?" Oliveiras asked.

"A year?" she asked incredulously, ignoring the doctor.

"We'll have to go over the mountain on foot if we are going to avoid getting captured. It will take at least a year for winter to pass and the snow to melt enough to permit passage." Wilfz nodded to Monique then looked back to Cameron. "Will your destroyer wait that long?"

"They'll stand by until they can pick us up," Cameron said with assurance. He glanced at Monique then spoke in a lower tone. "Or until we're dead."

Monique could not help but hear that disclaimer. Still stunned by Wilfz's estimate of a year, she was further dismayed at the thought of dying.

"How would they know that? Are you in contact?" Wilfz asked.

"We have a radio," Cameron explained. "We sent a message the day we met at the suite to let them know that we were going into hiding. We received a reply, letting us know they heard us. We sent another from the warehouse just as we abandoned it, telling them we're on the run now."

"So you only communicate when you're leaving a location," Wilfz surmised thoughtfully. "No one can track your location if you're already gone."

"It's a burst transmitter. We record the message and then send it at really high speed," Sergeant Van interjected. "It's so fast I doubt your radio here would even detect it."

"But Colonel Stuaart warned us that the opposition may have radio equipment from off-world," Cameron added. "So we have been as careful as possible."

"A year," Monique repeated. "Please tell me that includes the crossing of the mountain too."

"I'm sorry, Eunice." Wilfz looked to Monique.

At a less distressing time, she would have enjoyed the puzzled looks Cameron and Van were giving the major for using the wrong name. At the moment, she quailed inside with the disappointment at what Wilfz was telling her.

She remembered what she'd read in the dossier about Holland's planetary cycle. When she had first read about the seasons, she'd considered the information merely novel trivia. She had not expected to be on the planet long enough to experience such long seasons. Winter would be ten months. Wilfz had just said they would have to wait an additional two months for the snow to melt. That did not count the Mid-Winter's Solstice. Six days long, it marked the period of shortest days and longest nights. He had not said how long it would take for them to cross over the mountain after that. In Monique's opinion, her knowledge of Holland's seasons and culture did not make the bad news any more palatable.

"But the good news is that we don't have to cross the entire mountain range. All we have to do is crest the peaks and get below the other side. Once we get under the guns, your ship can approach safely and pick you up."

Wilfz turned to Cameron. "Will the destroyer come down, or is it carrying small craft? How big is a destroyer anyway?"

"They're pretty big. I think the plan was for the ship to come down for us. It's not unheard of. The Wicked Witch grounded to pick up wounded Imperial marines," Cameron said.

"The destroyers have always been good about supporting the men and women on the ground," Van added.

"You normally allow women to be put into situations like this?" Wilfz looked startled. Monique could imagine that he found that unacceptable to his way of thinking.

"The Wicked Witch is a destroyer?" Oliveiras asked.

"The Witch is her captain," Van explained. "Captain Mai. She's a celebrated legend among the destroyer service."

"We have one of those here. We call him Wolf," Oliveiras said cheerfully.

"You know better than that." Wilfz looked at the doctor, his eyes sharp. Monique saw from his expression that the doctor had gone too far. She noticed her guardsmen had become perfectly still. There was something about the major ... this man ... that she had not noticed before. Needing a shave and wearing only a blanket while lying down, he still managed to convey the power of command. Oliveiras became contrite and said nothing more.

Van broke the silence. "We maintain a listening watch on the half day—half an hour in the morning and again in the evening. It wasn't a problem when we were in town. We were using house current, but out here we're on battery. These vehicles have field generators, but the voltage output isn't the same. Our transformer is not compatible. Perez tells me he can make one from scratch, but without a meter it'll be trial by error. He'd much rather wait until he absolutely has to before risking the charger."

"Perez is an electrician? I thought he was your medic," Wilfz asked, turning his attention from Oliveiras to Van.

"He's more of a technician than a medic," Cameron explained, "but for this mission I had to keep the team small, and our team medic is a woman. The mission parameters excluded females from the guard team."

"Providing we do not send, we have enough juice to last at least a month," Van informed them.

"That's definitely not long enough to last us while we're on the wrong side of the gun line," Wilfz determined. He scrubbed the side of his bristled face with his hand for a moment, making a scratching noise. "Being on the wrong side of our own guns—I never imagined that I would ever say something like that."

"Perez doesn't have a meter?" Cameron suddenly changed topic. "Why doesn't he?"

Van looked at him in puzzlement for a moment. "Ah, you weren't there, sir," he said. "One of Genda's people went through our gear to streamline it. The meter was removed with the rest of the equipment they considered 'inappropriate to the mission.'"

"I would think Perez would have tried to at least sneak that past him," Cameron said whimsically.

"He did, but he was caught at it." Van looked at the ceiling. "After that, it was confiscated. They kept a close eye on us until we shipped out."

"So that was why ..." Cameron murmured.

Monique noticed the major's look of amusement. *I wonder if something like this has happened to him too?*

"I'm going to need my carbine," Wilfz announced.

"I wondered how long it would be before you asked for that thing," Oliveiras spoke up. "Not that you have the strength to hold it, much less use it." Wilfz ignored him.

"Gray has it," Van informed him.

Wilfz nodded. "I really don't like trusting these notes on this chart," he continued, indicating the markings, "but there is no other place to get shelter and still be out of sight from everyone. Once winter sets in, we'll be easy to track down unless we're in shelter. On the up side, it'll be hard for anyone to get at us once we're snowed in."

"Unless they come in by air," Van said thoughtfully.

"So we don't give them reason to drop in on us." Wilfz agreed with the sergeant's assessment. "Winter will give me time to get back on my feet."

"And then?" Cameron prompted.

"And then I will take you over the mountain once the snow melts," Wilfz decided. "I'll get you to your ship and send you home."

"What do you mean?" Oliveiras asked. "You're not going?"

"I'm staying," Wilfz said seriously; then he gave his familiar grin. "You can go. It's a ship with armor. It'll take you where no one will shoot at you anymore."

"That's not funny!" Oliveiras snapped. "You're the one who dragged me out there. We could have been killed."

"Well, this time I'm dragging you out of the line of fire," Wilfz said with less humor. "Don't say I never did anything for you."

"So you're going to go back and get blown away just like the colonel!" Oliveiras accused angrily.

"I've already been blown away," Wilfz said. "Now that they think I'm dead, they won't be looking for me. I can go back."

"What makes you think they believe you're dead?" Oliveiras demanded. "You looked just like those other two when you came to my door."

Wilfz said nothing. Giving a quiet snort, he shrugged.

"Just because you've already been hit doesn't make you invulnerable." Oliveiras warmed up to his tirade. "How many of your young heroes have been wounded, only to die the next time they go back out?"

Wilfz jerked visibly at the verbal onslaught.

"You've had a very good run, *Major*," Oliveiras said, stressing Wilfz's rank. "Every time you went into a fight, you came out unscathed. That's an unusual outcome in a service that stresses leadership from the front."

Oliveiras paused to get his breath. Shocked by the doctor's display, everyone remained silent.

"But now you've got an enemy that's managed to hit you," Oliveiras declared. "Just what do you think you can do?"

"I cannot go and do nothing," Wilfz said quietly. "The colonel wanted my help, but I refused him. I failed to uphold my duty. I placed my personal desires above the needs of Holland. I will not do that again by running away from my home."

Monique contemplated the strange rivalry between the doctor and the major. They seemed to have what she would call a difficult friendship. She remembered the previous interaction between the major and the colonel. The major had been at odds with Stuaart too.

As she thought about the similarity, she remembered the conversation between the doctor and the colonel when the major had returned wounded. The doctor had admitted that he was a friend to Wilfz's family, even though the two men were adversarial at the moment.

"As I live and breathe," Oliveiras said mockingly, "I have lasted this long to see the Wolf admit he was wrong."

Monique was frightened by what happened next.

Wilfz slowly pushed himself up into a seated posture, his back against the folded bunk. His face flushed red with effort, only to quickly pale in spite of the fury evident on his features. "I told you before," he said, carefully pronouncing each syllable, "you are not to call me that. Say whatever you will about me, but never call me that again."

There was an electric undercurrent in his quiet voice. Monique felt a chill run down her spine, a chill that had nothing to do with the cool temperature in the truck. It was obvious that Wilfz was incensed, and his self-control as he concentrated his rage against one man was frightening. He spared no attention to the other occupants of the truck. Van kept his head level with eyes looking upward. Monique could not understand why he did that, but she decided to call it his "socially uncomfortable look." Cameron's spine was stiff and upright. Sitting perfectly still, both men behaved as if they were in the presence of their own superior.

Monique had to admit that she felt the same sensation. She had read about this man, unwilling to believe that what she had read was accurate. The Major Wilfz she first met had failed to meet her personal expectations. She now knew without a doubt that she had been sorely mistaken. This man, naked save for the blanket around him, exuded an aura of command: *You* will *obey*.

As soon as that phrase went through her mind, she looked at Oliveiras to see his reaction. The older man stared down at the major, his own features pinched with anger.

"Very well, boy," Oliveiras said finally.

"Better." Wilfz gave a curt nod and then noticed the others staring at him. "I apologize for my display." He leaned over to lie back down, his arm shaking as he attempted to support himself. Van reached forward to steady him. The major murmured his thanks as he relaxed and pillowed his head on his folded arm.

"We seem to be finished," Cameron commented as he watched the major close his eyes to rest.

"I'll bring the major's carbine when I come back this evening," Van said. Cameron nodded. It seemed to Monique that the two men had become very deferential. No, they were more deferential to the major than normal.

The doctor had called him "boy." On Pearl, to call a grown man a boy was a demeaning practice, unless the name caller was much older than the man so called. That was the case here. The doctor appeared old enough to be Wilfz's father, but even so, why was being called "boy" preferable to being called "wolf"? Despite her curiosity, Monique was still in a state of shock. She could admit to herself that she was more than a little bit intimidated. At the moment, she was unwilling to ask Michael about what had just happened.

After the guardsmen had gone, it had become quiet. Doctor Oliveiras went to the pack. He pulled out a can of cornmeal, the rustling sound thunderous in the still truck. He made to open it but stopped when Wilfz spoke.

"Colonel, you idiot!" he sounded as if he was speaking his thoughts out loud. "You shouldn't have done that. You're supposed to be here, telling us what to do." His voice held a tinge of bitterness and regret. He cleared his voice then continued: "Falling before the guns; scattering like leaves. Their memory may fade, but their deeds shall ever shine."

Monique couldn't tell if Wilfz was singing a song or reciting a poem. His voice had been low, barely above a whisper. She looked at the doctor, seeing that he was staring at the wounded man. She could read the look in his eyes all too well—it was the realization that he had hurt his friend, hurt him badly. Monique intuited that it wasn't so much the use of the nickname, but the irreverent mention of lost comrades in connection with it. Though the doctor had not said so directly, he had implied that, while Wilfz had remained unscathed, those who had followed him in battle had paid for his bravery.

This man had spent his adult life defending his homeland. Monique had only thought of the heroism and courage it took to fight the battles this man had faced. What she had not considered was the cost—not in ammunition expended but in lives lost and futures affected by wounds, both physical and psychological. It was clear that Wilfz felt that debt keenly. Monique considered her use of the word *debt*. A life lost could not be regained; it was much like a debt that could not be repaid. Many had paid with their lives so that Holland could survive.

Oliveiras put the unopened cornmeal back into the pack, apparently not wishing to further disturb Wilfz. Monique still sat in the doctor's seat, her mind momentarily blank when she felt the doctor tug at the can in her hands. She looked down, surprised to see that she had eaten the entire contents. She couldn't remember tasting it at all, such had been her hunger.

"I'm going for a walk," he told her. He pointed at the pack of meal cans. "Give him one of these if you get a chance."

Monique nodded and watched him leave through the rear door. She looked down at the major then looked thoughtfully at the pack for a moment. She considered the doctor's direction and retrieved one of the cans. Mindful of her back, she sat carefully on the floor across from Wilfz and pulled open the can. Wilfz opened his eyes at the noise. "You need to eat," she informed him.

"Eat that yourself. You're the skinny one." Wilfz closed his eyes.

"I didn't think you saw that much," Monique said. *You think I'm skinny?*

"I could feel your ribs."

"I'm sure," she said in an "I know differently" tone, spooning some of the cornmeal out of the can. "Here, tilt your head so I can feed you."

Wilfz gave a little groan and sat up. He reached out of his blanket and took the spoon from her hand. Monique saw that he noticed the shirt she wore and found herself oddly pleased by the way the sides of his mouth quirked. He shifted himself to get his other arm free so he could hold the can, but she stopped him.

"I will hold this for you," she said. "It's still chilly in here."

"I've been colder," the major persisted.

"There's no need for you to get cold now," she replied sensibly. She was surprised to see him eat ravenously after having initially refused the food.

He said nothing to that. The silence, broken only by the scuff of the spoon against the can, only served to embolden her to speak. "I have something to say," she said.

Wilfz paused with the spoon in his mouth.

"I misjudged you," she said.

Wilfz shrugged as he continued to eat.

"I have done you a disservice ..."

"Misjudge, disservice. I have no idea what you are talking about." Wilfz dug into the can with his spoon.

"You seemed so different from the person outlined in your dossier."

He looked at her sharply. "Dossier?"

"I didn't understand. I didn't know you." Monique realized that she was rambling. She had had no trouble expressing her regrets to each member of Cameron's team. Speaking to this man was proving difficult in that she found herself flustered.

"You are new here. I doubt you know anybody," Wilfz said.

Monique realized that he was getting the wrong idea. "I'm trying to apologize to you."

"You said it was doctor's orders."

Monique's mouth clicked shut. *He thinks I'm apologizing for sleeping with him*, she thought. "I'm talking about before, when we first met," she explained. "I didn't take you seriously."

Wilfz ate another spoonful before replying. "No reason you should. We're from different worlds."

Monique was at a loss of words. She watched Wilfz scoop from the can and was surprised when he spoke again.

"I would like to know," he said, bringing the spoon to his mouth, "are all women where you come from as bold as you are?"

The first answer that came to her mind was flippant. She felt compelled to tell him that, compared to other women, she was quite tame. That seemed to be the wrong thing to say, even in jest. "I'm only as bold as I need to be," she replied. "It comes with the work I do."

She watched him eat as she spoke. He seemed to weigh her words as he observed her. She realized that he could somehow discern her thoughts by the reactions she displayed. She hadn't been acting, so anything he saw was the real Monique. It hadn't occurred to her to compose herself before speaking to him, to become mentally prepared as well as visually arranged. She could imagine the view he had of her at that moment. She hadn't seen, much less applied lip rouge and facial blush. She looked pretty much the way anybody would see her when she awoke from a night's sleep.

"You might want to consider your reputation," he said finally. Her hand shook for a moment as he scraped the last of the food from the can.

Did he really say that?

"Are you in pain?"

Monique was startled by his question. She looked askance at him, not trusting herself to speak. The remark about her reputation seemed too personal from a virtual stranger.

"I can see the strain around your eyes," Wilfz explained. "You wouldn't happen to know if the colonel left something to drink. I know I can use something stiff right now."

"Do you mean alcohol? Doctor Oliveiras wouldn't like it."

"I would like something to wash this down with." Wilfz pointed at the can with the spoon.

"I'll give you some water," she said, seeing that he had emptied the can. She carefully took the wooden spoon from his fingers. "I don't know about alcohol. You're shot full of painkillers right now; you shouldn't have that."

"And you. Is he holding back on the painkillers?"

"He doesn't want me to become addicted," Monique said. "It doesn't hurt much."

She could see that Wilfz didn't believe her, but he said nothing. He accepted the cup of water she poured for him.

"More?" she asked as he finished it.

He nodded and handed the cup back. "Please." He finished the second cup with a nod of thanks.

"He cares about you," she said. From the sad look he gave her, she could tell that he knew she meant the doctor.

"I know." He laid his head back down to rest.

❖

Mindful that the woman was watching him, Wilfz tried to relax. He had never been in such close proximity to a woman before, and he was uncomfortable now. His clash with Olly had further unsettled him. Losing his temper in front of the guardsmen, not to mention exposing Eunice to his anger, had embarrassed and deeply shamed him.

Rather than dwell on personality conflicts, the professional Constabulary officer that he was asserted himself, and he took solace in the intellectual exercise he had been presented with. He pondered the reason that the colonel had sent the Celestial Guard team toward the west. In his informed opinion, east would have been better. The eastern mountain range was closer to Bremen. Not only was he familiar with the territory, Wilfz was known there. He could locate many of the camps maintained in the mountains, given his years of prior service in First Mountain Brigade.

As the premier unit of the Constabulary, First Mountain was intentionally kept separate from Bremen to make it difficult for potential attackers to wipe out the ready reaction force. Central Division kept a lifter detachment embedded with the brigade to provide immediate aerial mobility. Not only was the brigade a force to be reckoned with, their isolation provided a barrier against the new punitive politics of Holland.

Wilfz considered the options. Given the few matters the colonel had shared in confidence with the major, it was difficult to presume what the colonel had known. Wilfz was unaware of any so-called "training accidents" or other incidents involving the First Mountain Brigade. He assumed the brigade leadership and chain of command was untouched. Although Stuaart had said nothing about them, it was likely that the major would have been sent to link up with them. At least, before everything fell apart.

Before he had been wounded, Wilfz had been serious about returning to his family. In retrospect he had been derelict in his duty to the Constabulary—the original Constabulary that is—and to Holland. Minutes earlier he had been wishing it was possible to go to Woodland. Even if he could talk Cameron into sending one of the trucks to take him there, he wouldn't make it. Both Woodland and the First Mountain Brigade were logical destinations. The blues would expect him to go there. Colonel Stuaart would have known that and dismissed both options.

To travel out into the flatlands of the bowl would be equally risky. Two trucks would stand out, especially when observed from the air. Pilots were naturally curious, after all. It was logical to assume that the blues would be keeping track of their assets. They would know that these trucks were in the hands of renegade forces.

That left the mountain range to the southwest of Bremen. It wasn't the closest mountain, but it was closer than any other reasonable location—*reasonable* being a relative term, of course. There was still a lot of unsettled land in the bowl. With a stagnant population growth, it hadn't been possible for the people of Holland to outgrow the settlements, much less the capital of Bremen itself.

Wilfz remembered the handwritten markings on the chart. He wished he knew the source of the information. The colonel's secretive nature had done little to reassure him. Lang had been suspicious of him after all. The colonel's promise to Cameron that this was the only information about those tunnels did not make sense. Would they encounter friendly forces there? Would they even be expected? Probably not, given the speed at which everything had occurred. The colonel had to have learned about them from somewhere. Someone else had to know about this.

Could he trust this information? It wouldn't be the first time he'd gone into a situation with little intelligence on the target. The one thing he was always sure of was that there were people waiting to kill him, but that had never stopped him before …

❧❀❧

Monique watched as Wilfz drifted off to sleep. Rather than nap, she listened to the occasional voice she heard from outside. Indirect sunlight filtered from the driving compartment. Looking past the seat, she could see the overhanging tree branches through the windshield. Coated with white, they dripped moisture as the snow melted. The pitter-patter of drops sounded like rain hitting the roof of the ambulance. The light downpour reminded her of summertime on Pearl, and she willingly surrendered to the musings of pleasant times past.

Oliveiras returned after a couple of hours, accompanied by Gray and Schmidt. The guardsmen took off their boots and carefully stepped around Wilfz and Monique to pull the upper bunks down from their stowage position. The doctor looked at Monique meaningfully, pointing at the pack of rations. She nodded with a smile. The doctor then looked to the guardsmen.

"Let me get a couple of mats from beneath these two," Oliveiras offered.

"The canvas is fine," Schmidt said.

"I'm so tired I could sleep on rocks," Gray added.

They set their submachine guns against the wall on the bunks before clambering up. The doctor handed them blankets to drape over themselves; then he took a last look toward the floor. It was not Monique he looked at, but the man beside her. Giving a soft sigh, he turned to squeeze through the door that led to the driving compartment.

"Olly." Wilfz's voice was soft, but it still carried in the quiet truck. Oliveiras stopped to look back. Monique looked to Wilfz as he tried to speak. It was obvious that he was having trouble finding the words he wanted to express.

"Sometimes it's what you don't say that matters," Oliveiras said. "You were right. I do know better, but so do you."

"Yeah," Wilfz replied.

"You didn't have to drag me out there," Oliveiras said.

"You were the closest medic at hand," Wilfz said. Monique gathered that is was a subject the two had repeatedly covered. "The sooner I got you out there, the better were the chances of finding someone alive."

"You should have linked up with your patrol before going out."

"It's just as well that I didn't. They were delayed, as you recall."

"You shouldn't have taken me with you. I was never any match for your forest craft."

"If I found someone alive, I wanted to give them the best chance of staying that way."

"But no one was alive."

"And if I had waited, I would have always wondered if their loss was due to the delay."

"And I almost joined them. I tripped the ambush," Oliveiras said. "I'm not like you. You move like a ghost. I couldn't hear your feet on that ice and snow as you were creeping around."

"If I suspected there was someone waiting, I would have left you under cover in the tree line," Wilfz explained.

"But you were so quiet—as if you expected something to be there."

"Standard operating procedure in the field. Uncle Mac taught me that."

Monique saw that Oliveiras was about to reply to the first part of the sentence, but he quickly shut his mouth at the mention of the uncle. It must have been the family reference that caused the doctor to back down. Instead, the doctor snorted and shook his head in resignation. Somehow Monique got the impression that this argument always ended in a draw.

"The lady said something interesting a while ago." Wilfz changed the subject, surprising both the doctor and Monique. "Apparently the Celestial Guard has a dossier on me. I'm wondering if they have any more information that we can use."

"I wouldn't know about that." Oliveiras shook his head.

"The colonel provided it," Monique said helpfully. "There was a lot of information about Holland and the situation developing here."

"Do you still have it?" Wilfz asked her.

"Have what, the file?" Monique asked.

"Yes, do you have the file?" Wilfz could not conceal his eagerness.

"I don't know," she admitted. "I haven't seen it since we were in the apartment. Lieutenant Cameron or Sergeant Van would know."

"Olly, could you …"

"The lieutenant is sleeping, just like these gentlemen are trying to do." Oliveiras obviously surmised what Wilfz wanted. "Van and … Perez, I think it was … yes, Perez. They are on lookout duty. I think we should leave them alone."

Wilfz gave him a sour look.

"Rest now. Give us all some peace," Oliveiras instructed him.

"Do me a favor and ask them about it later, Olly." Wilfz settled himself down, sparing Monique a glance before closing his eyes.

CHAPTER NINE

Director's Office, Constabulary Management Office, Iron Borough, Bremen

Constabulary Director Lang read the daily report. The previous evening an entire patrol had failed to return from a routine tour in Coal Borough. Over the past few days there had been a gradual but steady loss in manpower. Given the diversity of the units, it was unlikely that the absences were connected to each other. The only common link was that the missing were men of low rank. In the report from the previous day, a trooper from the Central Depot and a corporal from Quick Reaction had reported for duty and then disappeared.

With everything they were trying to accomplish, there were not enough Chosen officers to ride herd on every unit in the Constabulary. Fortunately, keeping a tighter grasp on the resources and equipment was easier for Lang than it was for most. Division Central was under lock and key. Anyone with a thought toward resisting the Council Chosen would accomplish nothing without weapons, supplies, and the conveyances to move them.

Even counting the patrol, the number of deserters was not overly remarkable. On the other hand, they could become a cadre that could be trained to supplement civilian volunteers. Except for the patrol, it was doubtful that any of the other men were together.

To establish an irregular force of resistance fighters, they would have to be organized and equipped with additional weapons and ammunition.

In all likelihood, the missing men were not a threat to the Council, but Lang took nothing for granted. He commissioned a company dedicated to the internal security of the Constabulary. Made up of officers personally chosen by him, their orders were to regard every report as conspiracy.

Colonel Stuaart was a case in point. His association with foreign soldiers from the Celestial Empire had been established when they interfered with the patrol sent to arrest him. The disappearance of Stuaart's personnel at the same time suggested conspiracy.

The captain assigned to apprehend those men had failed in that duty. Using a cutting torch, his team had managed to get through the armored door to the exclusion area, but there had been no sign of Stuaart's men. Since setting the bar to barricade the door was only possible from inside, it was logical that the men had left the security area by another route.

It had taken time, but the mystery of their egress from the underground workplace had finally been solved. One of the captain's men had discovered a secret passage in the storeroom adjacent to the colonel's office. From there, it connected to the maintenance tunnels beneath an office building next to the Constabulary Management Office compound. The Constabulary had lost the opportunity to capture Stuaart's people, but Lang gained access to the intelligence colonel's files.

He suspected that some files had been removed, but those that remained had proved helpful. The ambush outside of Doctor Oliveira's home had been more fortuitous than had been previously realized. The team leader had reported that one of the men in the foreign jackets had identified himself as Davidson. Before having to break off contact from determined counter fire, both the team leader and another survivor testified that Davidson had fallen from severe wounds. Investigators found a substantial blood trail leading into the front room of Oliveira's home. The rest of the team waited for the foreigners to return to their vehicle, but their prey had taken another route, escaping by stealing a neighboring resident's car.

As for Davidson, Lang had no doubt that he was really Major Wilfz, the son of David Wilfz as recorded in his personnel file. The intention had been to capture him alive. A well-publicized show trial would have effectively destroyed the credibility of the old guard of the Constabulary. At the very least, if Wilfz had not died of his wounds, he would be in no condition to cause any trouble in the near future.

The file on Colonel Stuaart had proven less than enlightening. It portrayed a man who'd had a lackluster career, and it shed no light at all as to why he had been chosen to head the intelligence arm of the Constabulary. Lang suspected that Stuaart had removed information from he file that he deemed sensitive, but that mystery no longer mattered given that he was reliably reported dead. Stuaart had attempted to steal a field ambulance, but he had been discovered in the act. In the ensuing firefight, the vehicle had blown up, resulting in catastrophic damage. The medical examiner had confirmed that the body in the wrecked truck was that of the renegade retired colonel. It was easy to figure out why the colonel wanted the medical vehicle. With no reported sighting of the major or his doctor friend, it was clear they were holed up somewhere. It would only be a matter of time before they were found. A wounded man would be difficult to take care of without proper medical equipment and supplies, much less overlook in public should the doctor attempt to move him.

Stuaart's elimination was the only positive news Lang had received. During the previous week, a loyalist insurgent had been shot while resisting arrest. Recently promoted to captain, he had been placed in charge of a company that had been set up to deploy patrols in the boroughs. A sergeant under his command had become suspicious when the captain conducted clandestine meetings with his lieutenants. The sergeant reported him to a trusted Chosen officer. When the lieutenants were interrogated, it was learned that the captain had been planning to rebel with his company.

As a result of that incident, Lang had instituted the loyalty oath and arranged for a ceremony to be held. In the Constabulary, a man's word was his bond—a guarantee of faithfulness and loyalty. It was possible that some men of iniquitous nature gave their word without meaning it, but there were other guarantors for their service.

Lang firmly believed that it was unlikely that subversive loyalists were part of his inner circle. His people had been thoroughly vetted and had been chosen because of illegal activities or unethical behavior they had committed in the past. Having gained that knowledge prior to his appointment as director, Lang used it to ensure their cooperation. Should he become displeased, all he needed to do was let slip a bit of information. In short, Lang's collaborators belonged to him, body and soul. He kept their secrets quiet and enabled them to gain positions of responsibility in the city capital of Bremen.

Some officers and senior enlisted men had not shown up at the ceremony. They were considered deserters, and Lang's investigators were now hunting them down. Of those on hand to take the oath, a few were unwilling to compromise their principles and refused to participate. Of those conscientious objectors, one shot himself with an arresting officer's sidearm, but the others were successfully apprehended. These men were now in confinement awaiting interrogation.

Since the objecting individuals had shown up for the ceremony in the first place, it was suspected that they were not part of the resistance. Nevertheless they would be treated as conspirators, their punishment serving as examples to others contemplating seditious behavior. They were not the only ones facing retribution.

The officer who had allowed his weapon to be taken away had been reassigned to a patrol. Ostensibly, this assignment was an opportunity for him to atone for negligence; however, that alone was not enough to make up for his indiscretion. Such dereliction should have resulted in his execution, but that wasn't conducive for orchestrating the proper mindset of the population. Should the officer concerned be overtly eliminated, the other Chosen officers could turn against the council. Instead, a sniper would be employed, and the blame would be laid on the resistance. That scenario would provide the regime with the benefit of a martyr, which would gain sympathetic support of the people.

❖❀❖

Highway West

Sergeant Van stifled the yawn that threatened to crack his jaw. During the day, he and Guardsman Perez had taken turns up in the cupola of Lieutenant Cameron's truck. Van had shortened the sling on his submachine gun and hung it from his neck to facilitate freedom of movement while he occupied the open hatch. The roof-mounted position rotated and was equipped with a pintle hard point for the mounting of a heavy machinegun. Rather than rotate the cupola during watch, Van twisted his head and body around to keep lookout. The noise from the cupola would disturb Lieutenant Cameron. After giving orders to wake him if something happened, the Celestial Guard officer dozed on a folded tarpaulin in the truck.

The snow had been falling intermittently all day. The dry, rust-colored leaves of the trees shielded the vehicles from the initial fall, but some clumps of snow fell through the branches at odd moments. The roof of the truck around Sergeant Van was splattered with melting slush. To shield his head from falling snow, Van wore a helmet that had come with the vehicle.

Down below, Perez tapped his foot. That was a signal that he was getting sleepy. Van took one last look around and then slipped off of the seat and slithered down to the floor of the truck. Doffing the helmet, he handed it to Perez to wear. The cool air in the truck felt stifling compared to the brisk breeze flowing over the open hatch up above. The men had been awake for two days, and the cool fresh air enabled them remain alert and awake.

As Perez took Van's former perch, the sergeant quietly stepped to the doorway at the front of the passenger compartment. Watching out through the windshield, he did not sit down, as it would take only a moment to drift off to sleep in the cozy environment. The only sound apart from the falling melt was the lieutenant's deep breathing.

With the vehicles parked under the trees out of sight of the road, the team anticipated no problems. It was while they were moving that something was likely to happen. That was the logic behind the duty assignments. Van would have tactical command during the day while the lieutenant slept.

The outdoor light had noticeably dimmed when Cameron awakened to the silent alarm on his wristwatch. Sitting up, he took stock of his surroundings and observed the sergeant facing the door to the driving compartment.

"Status report?" he asked.

Instead of Van, it was Perez who responded.

"I relieved Sergeant Van an hour ago. All quiet out here. Haven't seen or heard anything all day, sir."

Van jerked at the voices, almost falling forward through the doorway. He braced his hand against the front wall to stop himself, his weapon swinging out from his chest. Still holding the wall, he turned and faced the officer.

Cameron's face looked serious as he regarded Van. It was obvious that the sergeant had been sleeping.

"I don't know how you didn't fall down," the officer said quietly, too low for Perez to hear. He picked himself up and approached Van. "You should have woken me if you couldn't stay awake. Damn it, Sergeant. You've been sleeping less than any of us."

"It's my job, sir."

"Your job is to do your job, not fall asleep at the switch.'"

"No excuse, sir. It won't happen again."

"You could have gotten hurt if you had fallen down. Next time, wake me or get someone else. You know better than this, Sergeant."

"With all due respect, you and the others need sleep more than I do," Van said. "We can't have Schmidt and Gray fall asleep at the wheel. We also need you to make the right decisions. It's hard enough to see what is happening in the dark without your judgment being clouded by exhaustion."

"We can't afford to lose any of us," Cameron said. "We're too few as it is to be doing what we're doing."

"So we do it anyway." Perez spoke up above them. The two men looked up. Their voices had risen in volume while they were talking.

"How are you doing, Perez?" Van asked.

"I'll feel better when I can lie down and close my eyes."

"Stay up there while Van gets the others up," Cameron ordered Perez. Then he turned to Van. "I need to talk to Gray and Schmidt about the drive tonight. As for you, Sergeant, get something to eat and go to sleep. I want to know that you'll stay awake tomorrow."

"Yes, sir," Van said.

"Take the major's carbine with you," Cameron pointed at the weapon.

Van complied, giving a fatigued groan as he hefted the carbine. The Holland-made weapon was heavier than a comparable Imperial rifle owing to the obsolescent manufacturing process employed. Rather than metal alloy, the receiver and barrel were made of steel. Dense wood made up the one-piece stock and foregrip rather than the lighter weight composite material he was used to. Contemporary imperial small arms were deceptively sturdy, but there was no mistaking the robustness of the carbine.

Leaving the truck, Van trudged through the ankle-deep snow to the field ambulance. Tapping twice on the rear door, he opened it and boarded the vehicle.

❈

Monique lay with her back to the wall facing Wilfz. Across the compartment, his posture was almost a mirror image of hers. Above them, the guardsmen slept in their bunks. The doctor sat up front in the driving compartment.

Throughout the day Monique had tried to engage Wilfz in conversation, but he had declined to participate. The first time, he pointed up at the slumbering men and held a finger in front of his lips in the universal sign for silence. When she tried to talk to him after that, he merely shook his head. The final time, almost half an hour before, she had started to crawl over to him so they could whisper. His response then was to close his eyes.

At the tapping on the door, Wilfz's eyes opened alertly. Monique watched as Sergeant Van pulled himself into the truck.

"Sergeant," Wilfz greeted him. Monique noticed that he eyed the carbine in Van's hand.

"Major," Van answered. He set the carbine on the butt plate then laid it next to the Constabulary officer. "Chamber empty, safety on, magazine charged."

"What time is it?" Schmidt asked. At the same moment, Gray looked over at the sergeant.

"You look like crap, Van."

Oliveiras and Wilfz spoke in unison.

"There's a lady present," Oliveiras said in objection.

"Don't say things like that in front of her," Wilfz said.

Monique glimpsed the doctor's face as he looked back into the passenger compartment. "Don't worry about me. I was just napping. I heard nothing," she piped up.

"Have a tough day, Sergeant?" Oliveiras asked.

"Long day, Doctor," Van replied. "Thank you for asking."

Oliveiras blinked at the courteousness. Observing his reaction, Monique realized that the sergeant's tired tone could have been construed as sarcasm. From her association with Van, she knew that was not the case.

Van addressed his men. "The lieutenant wants to talk to you before we hit the road. Grab something to eat and take something for him as well."

As the men acknowledged the instructions, Van sat down on the floor, his back to the rear wall of the ambulance. He unslung his submachine gun from around his neck and set it on the floor beside him with a groan. Drawing his feet in, he untied the laces on his boots and pulled the footwear off.

"You shouldn't have sat down," Gray said. "You're not going to be able to get back up."

"Now you tell me." Van almost whispered as he leaned his head back against the wall.

"The major asked me a question," Monique spoke up. "Do we still have that file on Holland?"

"Holland? We're already there," Van murmured with his eyes closed.

Wilfz gave a low chuckle then spoke. "Leave the poor sergeant alone. He's exhausted."

"I'm not looking forward to lifting you up onto the top bunk," Schmidt commented.

"Pull down the middle bunk," Oliveiras said. "Those two on the floor don't need the headroom."

"Use the lower one," Monique pointed at the bunk on her side. "I will be sleeping with the major tonight." She was gratified to see that all of the men were staring at her.

"You stay on your side of the truck," Wilfz countered instantly. "You are not sleeping with me."

"It will get colder tonight," Monique complained. "I'm freezing already."

"Then put on more than that shirt. Olly, give her another blanket."

"She has two," the doctor informed him.

"Let her have three."

"Why are you angry with me?" Monique protested. "I didn't call you by that name you don't seem to like."

"It's not my place to tell you," Wilfz said.

"What do you mean by that?" Monique asked.

"Michael is too much the gentleman," Oliveiras spoke up. "As your personal physician, if I may be so bold?"

"Tell me. I'm not shy," she encouraged him.

"That is precisely the problem, my dear," the doctor said. "Holland women are not quick to share sleeping arrangements with strange men."

"Michael is not strange. There is nothing unusual about him," Monique quipped. "It's not as if I propositioned him. I'm cold, that's all. We are just sharing body heat. As uncomfortable as I am right now, romance is the farthest emotion from my mind."

Monique could not keep the pain out of her last sentence. She noticed the clinical look she received from Oliveiras. Even Wilfz's hard expression softened. There was something in their cultural makeup, apparently something shared by men from all over the world, that made them receptive to a female in distress. She looked at Van and saw the same thing.

"Do you need help with the major?" he volunteered.

Monique wondered at the connection the sergeant had made between the two invalids. It occurred to her a moment later. *He's referring to the call of nature!*

Oliveiras immediately confirmed her deduction. "I've already taken Michael out, so he's good for the night."

"You make it sound like I'm a dog you took out for a walk," Wilfz said peevishly.

Monique opened her mouth, but closed it again without saying anything as Wilfz stared at her. Somehow he knew that she would make the connection between dogs and wolves. It was only logical, and her face colored with the shame of almost inflicting an emotional wound. She watched as the hardness left his eyes and he gave a small shrug.

In the meantime, the other two guardsmen had dismounted from their bunks and pulled their boots on. As they helped themselves to the canned rations, Oliveiras spoke to them. "Ask the lieutenant if we can get some meat," he requested.

"Meat? Are you asking us to hunt?" Schmidt repeated.

"It shouldn't be too hard to hunt something out here." Oliveiras nodded. "These two need to have the protein for proper healing, and these rations don't provide enough."

"We're not going to be able to hunt tonight," Van said. "But I will bring it up to the lieutenant."

"During the day isn't good, either," Wilfz said. "The best time is dusk and dawn, when scavengers are moving. Dusk would probably be better. The trucks will have been stopped all day. Just throw out the bait around an hour before dusk."

"What kind of bait?" Gray asked.

"One of those cans," Wilfz nodded to him. "Pop it open and throw it as far as you can. Just be careful not to get any on you." At that, he gave a knowing grin.

"Why not toss an empty can?" Monique asked.

"Empty cans won't toss as far," Wilfz explained. "Not enough mass." Gray chuckled appreciatively.

"Milady, I think I'll take you up on your offer," Van said weakly. "Could one of you guys unfold the lower rack?"

Wilfz chuckled. Somehow Monique understood the major's humor, that he was not the only man suffering a bout of weakness.

Misery loves company, she thought, a smile just touching her lips and lighting up her eyes. For a brief moment, it seemed that she was not dealing with the ever-present pain in her spine.

❖✳❖

True to her words, Monique felt the chill invade the sanctuary of the truck as night advanced. When Perez arrived, it was as if he were bringing the cold in with him. Monique had remained beneath the lower bunk to allow the guardsmen room to get settled. Perez managed to clamber into the top bunk over Wilfz with the alacrity of youth that seemed to shame Van. Seeing the sergeant's face, her heart went out to him. *They try so hard.*

While the sergeant ate his can of cornmeal, Monique was content to remain underneath his bunk. She was resting her eyes when he forced himself to get up and lie on his bunk. When he sunk into the bunk, his weight pressed down on the canvas and she vacated the suddenly cramped location. Her blankets loosened while she moved. Settling in the center of the compartment, she wiggled as she tugged them back around her.

It was almost completely dark when the trucks resumed their trek once more. The creaking suspension of the truck rocked with the uneven ground as the driver carefully navigated over the ditch running beside the road. When the truck finally reached the smooth pavement, the ride of the vehicle became quieter.

Monique huddled in her two blankets, but the chill sapped the warmth, and her teeth began to click rapidly. Clapping a hand over her mouth, she peered out of her blankets to see if she had disturbed Van. Sure enough, the sergeant was looking at her. She was about to apologize when Wilfz spoke. "You'll break your teeth if you don't stop chattering like that."

"I can't stop it," Monique complained. "I'm freezing." *So much for apologizing, I'm sorry sergeant.*

Wilfz gave a long-suffering groan. "Come here."

He had barely finished those two words when Monique suddenly sat up. *Yes! Thank you, Michael!*

Shrugging off the blankets, she threw them over the blanket covering Wilfz. She didn't bother to unbutton the shirt, but pulled it off over her head. In her eagerness she strained her back; a twinge of pain raced up her spine. Forcing her lips together, she managed to stifle the gasp of pain. The shirt tousled her hair as she extracted her head. Discarding the garment with one hand, she ran her other hand through her hair, using her fingers like a comb. It was an automatic reflex, and she looked over her shoulder to see if she had been seen.

Her head level with Van's, her eyes widened at the sergeant's startled expression. She smiled at him, realizing that it wasn't the first time he had seen her bare back. He had taken care of her before Doctor Oliveiras had arrived, after all. She gave the sergeant a wink, almost diving under the covers to join the major.

She pressed herself against Wilfz. No longer facing her, he had rolled face down after having given her his consent. His skin was cooler to the touch than hers—no surprise since his only covering had been a single blanket. Now with three blankets and two bodies sharing heat, the two of them would have no difficulty warming up.

"Those are sharp!"

"Not so loud. The others are sleeping," Monique quietly admonished. She suddenly remembered what Wilfz had said about her reputation. In spite, she said the first thing that came to mind. "If you're going to comment on a lady's chest, you should say something kind."

Wilfz did not respond. Monique positioned herself more comfortably beside him, embracing him with her head on his back. With the blankets muffling the sound of the truck engine, she surrendered herself to the relative peaceful silence of the compartment.

Monique listened to his heartbeat. She remembered the beating being slower last night when he was sleeping. His heart now raced with embarrassment. That realization reminded her that she had wanted to talk to him. The noise of the engine would cover up any noise she made, provided that she kept her voice low. Thus encouraged, she spoke. "I want to ask you something."

Wilfz said nothing.

"I'll make a deal with you if I can ask you something."

There was still no reply.

"I know you're still awake."

"What, Eunice?"

She didn't think twice about the name he had just called her. At the moment, she was more interested in his nickname Wolf.

"I want to know why you dislike that name." She purposely did not mention the name. From the catch in his breath, she knew Wilfz understood her question. Still silent, he was obviously waiting for the deal. "I give you my word that I will never utter that name in your presence," she gave him her oath, "if you will tell me why."

"If I don't tell you why, then you'll call me 'wolf' incessantly, I suppose," Wilfz grudged.

It was Monique's turn to be speechless. Delivering an ultimatum had not been her intention. "Michael," she finally murmured, "whether you tell me or not, I will honor my promise to you." Out of respect for him, she would keep that unconditional proviso.

Wilfz gave a long sigh.

Monique listened to Wilfz's steady breathing. With her head beneath the blankets, the temperature within the bedding warmed with her exhalations. She allowed herself to relax as she snuggled.

"I was fourteen."

Monique opened her eyes as his voice rumbled through his back. Even though she could see nothing within the blankets, she kept her eyes open as she listened.

"Max, my mother's brother, was a hunter and trapper," Wilfz continued. "I was never interested in staying at home. I wasn't like my brothers. Though I was second oldest, I knew that there was nothing for me to inherit from my father's place."

Monique followed the major's rambling. It was clear that he was trying to get his thoughts in order.

"The old man, my father, didn't understand what I found so interesting outside of the settlement," Wilfz said. "I think he just believed me to be lazy. With the logging and other family business, I guess he was right. It was just boring, uninteresting ..."

He's going somewhere with this, Monique thought.

"My Uncle Max noticed me ducking out," Wilfz went on. "I think my mother might have said something to him. He tracked me one day, just to see what I was doing, I guess. He saw that I had a natural affinity for the outdoors. He went on to show me how to survive in the wild—trap small game ... shoot. Mother never told him to do that, but Father was unhappy with Uncle Max for 'meddling.' He could never understand why grown men would go out like that when there was so much to be done at home."

Monique listened to the tone of Wilfz's voice. She could sense the sorrow and disappointment conveyed within the admission that he was at fault.

"When I was fourteen, we were hit with a bad winter. The cold and snow drove the wildlife out of the mountains and toward the settlements. The wolves followed, and they preyed on the livestock. They were not shy about taking down a human being if they could. Uncle Max talked my mother into letting me go with him to hunt the wolves. The predators were too smart to let us get close to them in snow trucks, so we had to track them on foot. We lost a few trackers doing that, but I didn't know about that until afterward. It was just a great adventure to me then. The two of us, Max and I, brought back a load of pelts.

"Upon our return home, I was so proud of myself. Max explained how well I had done. My mother didn't say anything. She just looked at father. He shook his head and criticized me for sport hunting. He said, 'At least the wolves have a reason to prey. Wolf Wilfz doesn't even have that!'"

So it was Wilfz's father who had first bestowed the wolf moniker on him. The name did not reflect favorable recognition; it had been given in disparagement. The major's matter-of-fact tone made it sound as if he were discussing an event of little import.

Of course it would seem to be of little import. He has had years to think about it and let time dull the pain of disappointment, Monique thought. In his mind, however, the name wolf must be a vile curse. She felt a tear crawl across the bridge of her nose and fall onto Wilfz's back.

"Now you know," Wilfz concluded. "If you don't mind, I'm feeling really sleepy now ..."

Now she knew why he had been so vehement against the name. The name was a reminder of the charge made against him. His own father had accused him of glory hunting, and the nickname was a slur against his own battlefield conduct as well as his conduct with his comrades in arms. She remembered the discussion between Wilfz and Oliveiras. At one time they had fought side-by-side; they were veterans of a firefight. From Wilfz's point of view, such a membership carried credibility. He had entertained their heated discussion, granting the right of his challenger to have difference in opinion. Once the use of the name had entered the conversation, he had become intransigent. It was cruel insult, not modesty, that motivated Wilfz to object to the nickname.

❖❖❖

The trucks were parked in a dale, there being no convenient copse of trees to conceal them. Camouflage netting was draped over the trucks while they sat side by side. Any traffic on the road would not see them where they were below ground level. It was hoped that any lifters flying overhead would not notice them.

Immediately upon waking, Sergeant Van prepared a succinct report for Lieutenant Cameron's signature on a scrap piece of notepaper. Because he had let the Celestial Guard team down by falling asleep, he had written himself up for disciplinary action. When he reported to the lieutenant's truck for sentry duty, he delivered the report to Cameron. The officer merely read it without saying a word before going to sleep.

Van and Perez alternated turns in the cupola of Lieutenant Cameron's truck during the day. Unlike the previous day when the trees sheltered them from view, a section of camouflage net was erected like a tent over the hatch. From their perch on the truck, the men could see out of the dale. The camouflage netting did nothing to prevent the cold air from circulating freely. It was difficult for the men to keep warm as they sat motionless in the open hatch.

Near the end of the day, with sunlight waning, Van roused the lieutenant. He explained his intention to shoot an animal for meat, and the officer gave his consent. Following the major's recommendation, he used an opened meal can for bait and then lay on the ground in wait. The Constabulary parka was not enough protection against the freezing ground. With his pistol close at hand, he waited.

❧❀☙

Monique had been observing Wilfz and Oliveiras all day. The major had been solicitous toward her. When they had woken up together, there had been none of the outrage of the previous morning. The outdoor temperature had fallen more noticeably. After their morning constitutionals, he had not objected when she asked to continue sharing heat. As they lay beneath four blankets, the conditions were barely tolerable.

Oliveiras had also tempered his manner. Apart from medical matters, he said nothing. His eyes seemed thoughtful whenever he looked over at the major. She wondered if he had overheard their conversation the night before.

She thought about what Wilfz had said to her. She wondered if, perhaps, the shared confidence had somehow created a bond between the two of them. Her back to his, she felt him shiver as a draft entered between them. She squirmed to bunch the blanket into the gap behind their shoulders.

There was a sudden gunshot.

Monique twitched and looked at Oliveiras. He leaned from his jump seat to look through the doorway to the driving compartment.

"What time is it?" whispered Wilfz.

Oliveiras glanced back at Wilfz before looking out again. "About five," he said. "Why?"

"Someone just shot you some meat," Wilfz replied. Even though they were not facing each other, Monique could sense that he was smiling.

That supposition was proven moments later when Lieutenant Cameron entered the vehicle from the rear door. "Van just shot something for us to eat," he announced as he seated himself by the door. "He's skinning it now to cook over a fire. That should be safe to do now. I don't think anybody will be passing by here this late in the day."

"I doubt anybody will see the smoke in the dark," Wilfz agreed.

"We're keeping the fire below the rise so the flames won't be visible." Cameron leaned forward, revealing a file. "Van suggested that I bring this to you, Major."

Being closer, Monique scooted herself under the blanket toward Cameron and extended her hand. The lieutenant gave her the file, a look of surprise on his face. She assumed that he was not used to the former actress being so accommodating.

"It's getting too dark now," Wilfz said as he accepted the file from Monique. He placed it on the floor beyond his head. "I'll read it tomorrow. Thank you, Lieutenant."

"He probably thought you'd forgotten," Monique teased Cameron.

Turning his attention to the bunks where his men slept, he spoke. "Gray. Schmidt."

"Awake, sir," Schmidt answered.

"We heard the shot," Gray seconded. "I wonder what he got."

"Probably a lebex," Wilfz volunteered.

"Lebex," Monique repeated carefully. "That's a weasel?"

"More like a rodent. A big one," Gray corrected her. "I'm coming down now."

Monique leaned into Wilfz to provide room for Gray to stand. "A rodent?" She shuddered.

"That fire sounds like a good idea." Gray sat to pull his boots on. "Come on, Schmidt. Let's build a fire."

"I wish I could go there," Monique whined theatrically, a delighted look on her face.

"Bring back something hot," Wilfz said from beneath his huddle of blankets.

❧❀❧

Once the fire had been started, Schmidt relieved Perez on watch. After a brief spell to warm up at the fire, Perez joined Gray in feeding the flames. The flora in the dale where they were parked consisted of dried brush. The thin scrub burned quickly and had to be constantly replenished so Van could cook.

The sergeant tended the lebex meat, which he had arranged on a cast-iron grill attached low on the supports of a four-legged stand. With the legs joined at the top, the cooking rig was a pyramid-shaped frame. The fire was small, but it burned hot and kept the meat sizzling. The aroma wafted around the area, unaffected by the wind blowing across the open ground over the depression concealing them. The two fuel gatherers paused after each delivery to savor the welcome heat.

Perez was rubbing his hands together near the open flame when Lieutenant Cameron joined them. He complimented Van on his shooting.

"Yeah, Van, that shot was easily at the edge of the effective range of your pistol," Perez agreed. "I could see you shaking so much, I almost potted him for you."

"If I had missed with my first shot, you would have had to. I dropped the pistol when I fired, I was so cold," Van confessed. Crossing his arms, he used his fists to pound his biceps. "Man, I'm still stiff."

"That was a clean kill. It died instantly." Perez look around. "It looks like it's my turn." He left the fire as Schmidt approached with more scrub.

From his jacket pocket, Cameron removed the small sheet of folded notepaper that Van had given him that morning. "As far as this is concerned, the time you spent on that cold ground is penance served," he said in a nonchalant voice. Without a word, he held it near to the flames of the fire. The edge curled and turned black and then disappeared into ash. The fire quickly crept across the paper sheet, and the officer dropped it into the fire. "Keep up the good work, Sergeant." With that, the lieutenant gave him a nod and walked away.

❧❁❧

Monique had been dreading the upcoming meal. Gray's comment about the rodent had not made the food sound enticing to her, despite her hunger. The rodents on Pearl were considered vermin ... unfit to eat. That such meat was now considered fit for consumption only emphasized the brutal conditions she was forced to endure.

It was well into dark when Van arrived with the fire-roasted meat. Wilfz gave an appreciative groan. "That smells good," he said.

Van handed the small metal tray to the doctor.

"Perez will bring ours," Van told him.

Oliveiras set the tray down by Wilfz and Monique.

"That looks good," Wilfz said.

"This is rat?" Monique sniffed dismissively.

"Lebex is good meat." Wilfz accepted a fork from the doctor and speared a small piece. Monique closed her eyes as the major put the morsel in his mouth and chewed appreciatively. "This is really good."

"Here," the doctor held a fork to Monique. She shook her head in refusal.

"You can have my share," she offered. "I don't want it."

"Take mine, too, then." Wilfz set his fork down.

"You need to eat that," Oliveiras said.

"Yes, go ahead and eat that," Monique added.

"It wouldn't be right." Wilfz turned his head away and relaxed. He gave the impression of preparing to go to sleep.

"Michael, you really need the protein. You're a wounded man, and you need to heal," Oliveiras said reproachfully.

"Eunice is wounded too," Wilfz replied. "I cannot selfishly care for my own welfare while she remains in distress. What man mistreats a woman? I won't do it."

"He means it," Oliveiras said. Monique saw that he was looking at her. She sighed. "Okay," she said slowly. "I'll try just one piece." She accepted the fork from the doctor and obediently ate the small cut of meat. She repressed the shudder as she imagined the animal that had provided it. "Okay, I ate it," she said.

"Have another bite," Wilfz said.

"What?"

"I already had one. I'll only eat more if you will," Wilfz said.

Monique did not want to admit that she had found the lebex meat succulent. Her ambivalent feelings were not something that she could explain, not even to herself. "If you insist," she gave in. She accepted the second piece. She tried to pretend she was more reluctant than she really was. Looking at the doctor, she noticed a glint in his eye as if he were amused. She looked directly at him, only to have him look away as he openly smiled. She rolled her eyes and picked up Wilfz's fork. "Your turn," she said.

The two paced each other as they shared the tray.

"I enjoy seeing healthy appetites," Oliveiras commented as he watched the two eat.

"She is rather skinny," Wilfz stated.

"This is normal for me," Monique said defensively. Then she raised her voice. "Isn't that right, Sergeant Van?"

She noticed that the sergeant had been content to merely listen. She saw his reluctance as he assumed his customary upward-looking expression. "I wouldn't know about that," he drawled. "I've always been a Venus de la Rosa fan, myself."

Monique suddenly started coughing. Wilfz reached over instinctively and slapped her back beneath the blankets. She gave a final cough and took a shaky breath.

"Are you all right?" Wilfz asked anxiously.

"I don't know which surprises me more," Monique said, giving the major a sidelong glance. "Sergeant Van's choice of actress or the fact that you are voluntarily touching me."

Wilfz's hand was still on her back, but he quickly pulled it away as if he had been burned. He muttered an unintelligible oath and rolled away.

"I hope that was an apology," Oliveiras said.

"It sounded like one to me," Monique said, delighted by Wilfz's extremely embarrassed reaction.

CHAPTER TEN

Highway West

Wilfz was hardly surprised by the dossier when he read it. Much of what he read was common knowledge, especially the history and social dynamics. Noticing how prevalently his own history in the Constabulary was covered, he wondered at Stuaart's strategic thinking. Holland venerated her heroes, but why had the colonel expended so much effort on him? He could understand Eunice's disappointment at their first meeting. She had expected a hero and met the social equivalent of a lebex instead.

"These are Holland Constabulary documents and assessments," declared the doctor after he had also read the file. "How can foreigners come to have these in their possession? I was only in the medical branch of the Constabulary, but I know treason when I see it. Someone gave these people sensitive information!"

"You're right, Olly," Wilfz said absently.

"I've had this uneasy feeling since you guys came to my front door for the sake of their injured lady."

"Who wouldn't be uneasy? We're taking the lady out into the field like this."

"I'm awake. You don't have to talk about me in the third person," Monique murmured, not lifting her head.

"I'm sorry, my dear," Oliveiras apologized. He lowered his voice when he continued. "I'm truly frightened. I never imagined I would ever come to fear my own government. Did you know that training accident wasn't a …?"

"The colonel told me," Wilfz interrupted him. The training accident, which really had not been an accident, was still a subject he would rather not dwell on. He could understand Oliveiras' ire. Having previously been informed about the suspicious circumstances by the colonel, he did not now feel the shock that his old friend was exhibiting now. Wilfz thumbed through the files, more interested in finding information he could use than revisiting the memories of his life.

The rear door swung open and Cameron leaned in. Behind him were the trunks of iron crowns that the trucks had parked beneath.

"We've got movement," he announced as he entered the truck. "It looks like a flight of lighters, low on the deck."

Through the open door, Wilfz could detect the distant whine of gravity glide motors. As he listened, the sound rose in volume as the aircraft drew near. The folder he had been reading slipped from his nerveless fingers. It was as if the accident report he had just perused had summoned the aircraft.

His attention turned inward, and he remembered the training accident that hadn't been a training accident. Since learning the malevolent nature of the attack, he had successfully shunned the memory of that day. That it had been inflicted on purpose was something he could not bear to think about. The sound of the aircraft outside brought back the events of that day in a rush. In his mind's eye he could see the striker diving in its firing run on the slit trench that had served as his observation post.

Although high-velocity weapons were available, most Holland Constabulary attack aircraft carried heavy rotary autocannon. Had the explosive shells struck his position, neither he nor the radio operator would have survived. As it was, the pilot overshot his target, and the rounds missed. Pushing the radioman down before him, Wilfz had dived as the explosives struck the ground. The overflying shrapnel had missed hitting his head and back, but had peppered his legs.

Those projectiles could easily punch through the light armor of the ambulance, and then detonate within the vehicle interior. All of the inhabitants within the confined space would be killed or seriously concussed and wounded.

The aircraft were close now, the high-pitched whistling from muzzle openings and assorted projections clearly audible. That noise had been exactly the same when the striker overflew him during the firing run.

"Major?"

No, the radioman had addressed him as Captain. The two men had landed at the bottom of the trench. It was the radioman who had rendered immediate first aid to the officer, his expression showing the strain from the misguided attack.

"Michael?"

The helmeted face of the radioman metamorphosed into that of Monique, her eyes soft with concern. As he focused on her face, she spoke again. "Michael, Lieutenant Cameron asked you a question."

"The lighters won't be able to detect us under the trees, will they?" Cameron repeated himself, closing the door behind him. The sound from the aircraft dropped audibly.

"Unless they come close to us, they won't observe us under the trees."

"Is there anything we should do?"

"No movement outside of the trucks. Unless they can detect the straight profiles of the trucks, there should be nothing to attract attention to us," Wilfz explained, his voice tense. "Don't operate any electrical devices. Don't even charge a battery or listen to a radio. At close range, they can pick up the electrical activity. Residual heat from the engines can give us away. It's been over an hour or so since we've stopped. In this cold weather, there might not be enough heat to attract their attention unless they're actively looking."

They could hear the gravity engines through the walls.

"If we had thirteens," Wilfz explained, we could use them to knock them down, but they still would be difficult to hit. Especially the strike lighters. The best way to engage them is head on, but at that angle their weapons would be aimed right back at us. That is if they're strike lighters and not assault lighters."

"Strike lighters? Assault lighters? What's the difference?" Monique asked. Cameron gave her a stern look, which she ignored.

"Strike lighters are ground-attack aircraft. We use them to shoot up grounded raiders. Assault lighters carry troopers. If we were to knock one of them down, then we'd have to worry about the survivors on the ground—armed survivors out for our blood." Wilfz turned his attention from Monique to Cameron. "You aren't going to engage them, are you?"

"And attract their attention to us? No, sir." Cameron shook his head. "We don't have thirteens. The biggest guns we have are eights." He nodded toward Wilfz's carbine.

The sound of the flying aircraft changed in pitch. It was obvious that they were not flying directly over them, but had veered away. There was also the sound of rapid cannon fire. Wilfz's eyes narrowed as he listened.

"Are they shooting?" Monique asked.

"Yeah, but it sounds like they're not strafing," Wilfz said thoughtfully.

"They're dogfighting?" Cameron guessed.

"Yeah," Wilfz agreed. "Whoever gets knocked down, I hope they don't crash near us."

"What if the lifter is on our side?" Monique asked.

"Especially if he's one of ours," Wilfz declared. He observed a puzzled look appear on her face ... puzzlement and a frown of disappointment. "What a pitiful situation that I should say something cowardly like that." Guiltily uncomfortable with her disapproval, he looked away, not attempting to conceal his own distaste.

"What? What's wrong?" Monique asked. "Why would you say that?"

"If the enemy crew crashes near here, they'd most likely wait out in the open to be rescued," Cameron stated. "If the crew is on the run like we are, they're going to hide. If the enemy looks for them in the cover around here, we won't escape scrutiny."

"We're going to have to stay put in any case," Wilfz said. "There might be ground forces on the road. We'll need to give them a chance to conduct their search and then leave."

"Can't we help?" Monique asked.

"We cannot escape and evade as easily here as we did in the capital. If we try to link up with the survivors, it will be easier for all of us to get caught," Cameron said.

"That's providing that the survivors are on our side in the first place," Wilfz added. "The risk is too great. Your team is already burdened with two wounded— and one of them a noncombatant." He did not like saying that. In effect, he had chosen to abandon fellow members of the Constabulary. It went against everything he believed in. Holland was his world. He had defended his world against foreign enemies and domestic renegades, always coming to the aid of those on the correct side of the law. In choosing not to come to a fellow combatant's aid, he felt less than a man and not a little bit disloyal.

The sound of the lighters drew away.

Wilfz shook himself, drawing everyone's attention to himself. As the auditory influence lost its grip over him, the memory of the attack faded. "Lieutenant Cameron, tell me about these vehicles." His bold voice conveyed his returning confidence.

"Sir?"

"Where did they come from? How did they come into your custody?"

"Colonel Stuaart helped us steal them from the storage compound."

"You mean Division Central?"

"Yes, sir."

"That's strange."

"What's strange about getting vehicles from a depot?" Monique asked.

"These trucks were fully loaded and fueled up for a reason," Wilfz stated. "If these were just in storage, the equipment would have been removed and fuel would have been siphoned out. This ambulance wouldn't even have a first aid kit, much less all of these supplies." He waved his arm around at the gear around them.

"You did say that we don't have a thirteen?" Wilfz prompted. Cameron nodded in reply. "What do we have?"

"Our only weapons are the ones we brought with us to Holland," Cameron answered. "Those and the weapons we took here. Colonel Stuaart must have had the carbines in mind when he left a case of eight-millimeter carbine ammunition in the ambulance. If we run into trouble, we'll be out of our own ammunition and have to rearm with the indigenous weapons."

"That makes sense," Wilfz agreed.

"Both trucks are fully loaded with rations and emergency supplies. There are also some changes of uniform that I imagine were left for you," Cameron continued. "Many of the trucks at the compound had extra fuel cans, so we took them, too."

Wilfz considered what he had just been told. No weapons had been included in either truck the guardsmen had commandeered, but the field ambulance had been stocked with a case of carbine ammunition. The colonel had obviously prepared the ambulance for them, knowing that the team had the captured weapons from the rescues they performed. However, it was obvious that the other truck had been prepared for someone else. Beyond that detail, Wilfz could not know, since the colonel had not confided in him.

"We will have a supply problem of another sort." Cameron changed the subject. "You might remember that our radio batteries will not last through the winter. Outside of the city grid, our chargers won't work. We have to get where we're going before Perez can fabricate that transformer."

Wilfz thought about that. Bremen was pretty standard at one hundred ten volts through all of the boroughs. The settlements were another matter. Spread throughout the bowl, they relied on their own power generators. The townships that sprang up around the industries used two hundred twenty volts, since that was the current required for the heavy equipment they operated. That equipment was ruggedly built to handle the unreliable fluctuations of poorly maintained generators. The family lumber mill in Woodland needed serious voltage to cut trees apart. Thinking back to the map, he remembered that there were no settlements close to where they were headed.

"Yeah, the Constabulary doesn't rely on local power sources when deployed. All field units have twelve-volt generators." Wilfz fell silent as he thought. "Well, except for the heavy weapons," he amended.

"'Heavy weapons'?" Monique asked.

"Siege guns."

Monique started to repeat when she saw the major's slow grin.

"Field rail guns." Wilfz anticipated her question. By Cameron's sharp look, he could tell the lieutenant obviously did not appreciate her interruption, but Wilfz entertained her curiosity. "They're portable and smaller than the guns in the mountains."

"What would you need a siege gun for?" Monique asked. "Holland is under siege, not sieging."

"*Sieging* is not a word," Cameron said.

"Are you sure?" Monique asked.

"We've always called them 'siege guns', but they're useful for punching holes in raid ships and lobbing anti-personnel shells onto the enemy," Wilfz explained.

"For a world without war, you are certainly warlike," Monique commented. "Hardly the staff officer you tried to pass yourself off to be."

Wilfz was startled for a moment before he remembered their first meeting. He had indeed tried to seem less than he really was.

"Why did you act that way?"

"Pride, I guess," Wilfz shrugged.

"Pride? How is being something else pride?" Monique demanded.

"As I recall, you were not impressed by me." Wilfz smiled. "I didn't want to disgrace myself by trying to justify myself to you. Either you respected me or you didn't."

Monique stared at him. "Now I've heard everything," she said. "The pride of modesty."

❖✵❖

In the air over Highway West

Lieutenant Corbet piloted his assault lighter with two strikers in pursuit. He had taken off from Bremen Air Base, his lighter only partially laden with an assortment of weapons, ammunition, food, and medical supplies. The aircraft had been loaded in the predawn darkness, the supplies having been smuggled into a hangar over the span of a week. He had waited for the air base to be clear of strikers before taking off. The interceptors chasing him had been loitering in the air and had been vectored after him by base flight control. It was an additional measure the Council Chosen employed to enforce the blockade around the Holland capital.

Over the past several days, the situation for the Constabulary at large had become increasingly treacherous. Officers in the field had been recalled for emergency meetings, only to be arrested along the way once they were alone. Cadres of Chosen were immediately sent back to take control by filling the officer billets at company and patrol level. The Constabulary hadn't taken the surprise change of organization passively. As the Council Chosen scrambled to consolidate their power, the original members of the law enforcement service attempted their own counter contingencies. A few officers defied the recall order, choosing instead to take their men into hiding. Of those, most of them had been intercepted by strikers and forced to lay down their arms or be annihilated in the open. Only a fortunate few had been close enough to wild country to disappear into the landscape.

It was one of these patrol-strength units that Lieutenant Corbet was trying to rendezvous with. The supplies that his lighter carried would normally be trucked out of the city proper. With winter coming, it would be almost impossible for loyalist units to maneuver. It would be easy to follow their vehicle tracks on the roads. Anyone not authorized for travel could count on being intercepted and investigated. That was why he had to fly now, before the snow became too deep and the loyalists became immobilized by the necessity to remain concealed.

With everything happening so quickly, the Chosen were not yet organized. It was hoped a single lighter could take advantage of the disorganization and slip out of Bremen. After a quick flight, it could land in the foothills to the east to become a cache. The oncoming winter would discourage any serious ground-based search, and the snow would conceal the airship from aerial observation. With that in mind, it was not necessary for him to have a copilot on a one-way trip. He was alone without a crew.

A fully-loaded-out strike lighter would be sorely pressed to keep up with an empty lighter. He had no idea how much ordnance the strikers carried, but his lighter was barely filled to half capacity. There hadn't been time to fully stockpile the required supplies, and he'd taken off with what was on hand.

His lighter was of the support variant. Meant to transport men and materiel, it was armed with a pair of nose-mounted, forward-firing guns. Swivel hard points were provided to deploy thirteen-millimeter machineguns at the side doors. The after angle of the fuselage allowed the door guns converging fields of fire to the rear. Lacking the swivel guns and the crew to man them, Corbet was effectively defenseless from the rear. His only protection was the proximity indicator telling him the distance the leading striker was from his aircraft.

The flight leader for the strikers ordered him to return to Bremen and land for inspection. Corbet knew the inspection was a pretext. His was on an unauthorized flight, and he would be arrested as soon as he landed. He declined to respond, milking as much time as possible by remaining silent.

His pursuers were proving to be impatient. Rather than waste time repeating demands, the lead striker fired upon him without warning.

Corbet chopped power, permitting the lighter to fall toward the ground. The leading striker overflew him, but immediately corrected for his mistake and nosed toward the sky, barely escaping the fire from the lighter's forward guns. Having skillfully evaded

Corbet's fire, the leader would be endeavoring to return to the chase. The second striker dropped his nose to fire on the renegade craft, but Corbet had already put the lighter in a sharp turn toward the mountains. He wove through the foothills, leading the second striker at tree-top level.

The opposing pilots had excellent reflexes. With the short distance between the aircraft, the constant horizontal and vertical shifting frustrated the striker's pilot from bringing his rotary cannon to bear.

"That's it, guy, follow me!" Corbet encouraged the other pilot under his breath.

He had passed the foothills and raised the nose of the lifter to follow the contours of the mountain range. He watched a stand of trees disintegrate under the rapid fire from the striker behind him. He swerved gracefully, permitting gravity to slow his lifter. With reduced speed, the pursuing striker easily remained within his turn radius. "Good. Pay attention to me."

Lifters did not rely on the flow of air around their wings to provide their lift; instead, they used gravity motors to maintain elevation and speed. Following the terrain in any kind of aircraft at high speed was always a risky maneuver. Clipping a treetop could result in loss of control. Slamming into the side of a ridge would be catastrophically worse, leading to complete destruction. The dangerous activity required the utmost attention to detail and exercise in skill.

Corbet steered back toward the mountain, dipping to follow a valley. With a ridge boxing him in on either side, the only way out for him was upward. That limited the maneuvering options available to the lifter, and the striker pilot would know that.

Corbet piled on the speed, the trees flashing by beneath the lifter as it angled upward. The striker fell back momentarily, opening up the range between the two aircraft. That didn't last long, as Corbet's proximity indicator detected a decrease in range.

"I'm running … chase me!" taunted Corbet. "That's right, follow your instincts."

The striker pulled up, but Corbet didn't give the pilot a chance to capitalize on the maneuver. Cutting power once again, he deployed the spoilers. In horizontal flight, the winglets on the leading edge of the aircraft would serve to provide lift and allow the pilot a modicum of control. When used in an unpowered climb, the landing spoilers became a drag upon the fuselage. The lifter shuddered as it came to a pause in the air and then fell back in an uncontrolled fall. Behind him, something slipped out of the cargo net and clattered about the cabin. "Let it be food and not something explosive," Corbet implored. Then in a louder voice, he announced, "We're going to have a talk later about proper stowage!"

Corbet reapplied power and retracted the spoilers. The aircraft stopped tumbling in the air, its belly to the sky. Corbet rolled the lifter over. Lifters were unlike ordinary winged aircraft. In a stall, an aircraft held aloft by wings could be returned to flight only by a highly trained and skilled pilot. A lifter could be returned to flight from the same sort of stall simply by the application of power.

The striker accelerated, climbing into the sky to take his turn to follow. The lifter lacked the elevation to do anything but run. As for the attack craft, it had all of the room in the sky to turn around and bring its gun to bear. Any maneuvering by the lifter would be nullified by the increased altitude of the pursuer. With the additional firing range, it would be a simple matter for the pilot to make minute corrections against the moving lifter. The high rate of fire of the rotary guns would ensure that enough explosive projectiles would tear the unarmored fuselage of the lifter apart.

Once the striker reached apogee, it began to transition for diving. The flight leader, attempting to rejoin the two embattled aircraft, radioed his warning to remain below the mountain peak. The close maneuvering on the mountain gave the opposing pilot little time for conscious thought. The forced stall and recovery planted the idea that the lifter was trying to dogfight by latching onto the striker's tail. Altitude had always been a striker pilot's ally.

"Too late," Corbet replied to the warning he had heard on the radio. Intent on knocking down the difficult lifter, the striker pursuing him had inadvertently become the target of a different gun.

Under normal circumstances that would not be a concern, but the Chosen had declared a no-fly zone at the higher elevations, enforced by the guns on the mountain peaks. The lighter had managed to fox the striker into the gun arc of the bowl defense system. Corbet had preyed on the striker pilot's instincts.

Because they all had the same transponder codes, there was nothing to differentiate Holland aerial vehicles from each other. The nearest gun performed as programmed, enforcing the no-fly zone with brutal finality. A single round was fired. Designed to engage armored marauding spacecraft, it was more than enough to eliminate the striker. The ballistic impact shattered the aerial vehicle, transforming it into an expanding cloud of incandescent dust.

Corbet did not have time to celebrate his escape. The flight leader was now on the attack. As the two craft flew head to head, the lifter had little chance of escaping the encounter intact. Due to their speed, attacking strikers made very difficult targets. The odds of hitting one increased when the aerial attack craft flew directly toward or away from the gun, albeit the craft still presented a small target nonetheless.

The striker fired, and the lifter shook from the impact of projectile strikes. Corbet pressed his trigger. His twin cannon fired wide of the mark. Without releasing the trigger, he adjusted his aim. The volley of gunfire traveled across the nose of the striker. On Corbet's console, a light died, indicating he was no longer getting a radar signal from the striker. He'd managed to knock out the sensor suite. As he'd been firing single-barreled weapons, as opposed to the striker's rotary cannon with a higher rate of fire, Corbet had not delivered the amount of damage he needed to knock the striker down.

As for his lifter, it was losing power. The whistling noise from the fuselage behind him indicated that air was blowing through the passenger compartment, bringing the temperature down in the flight deck. The striker passed by on the right, its windscreen having been shot opaque. Corbet's gun had not been enough to shoot through the armored glass, but with the sensor suite down and the pilot's vision obscured, the striker would be an easy target for the lifter. Correction: it would have been an easy target for the lifter if it weren't for the battle damage to the lifter.

The striker turned away toward Bremen. With the lifter failing, Corbet had no chance to attempt a pursuit of his own. With the surviving striker abandoning battle, there was no danger that the lifter would be shot down before crash landing. That was only a temporary respite. Once that striker got back to Bremen, additional interceptors would be dispatched, if they weren't already on the way.

The lifter stalled as power continued to fail. The landing foils deployed automatically, providing minimal control as the craft fell from the sky. Corbet did not want to crash into steep, tree-covered slopes. Although the lifter was sturdy enough to survive such an impact, the scar would show up easily among the expanse of standing timber. He had enough altitude to select a clearing, but with Chosen control of the air, locating him would be very simple. Every clearing was bound to be searched.

A valley at the base of the mountains would be good, provided that the ground was uniform and not steep. Camouflage netting would easily conceal the lifter from the most determined search. A systematic ground search covering every square meter of the ground would find it, but given the manpower available, such a search would not be practical. With no witnesses, it might be assumed that the lifter had not crashed but continued on its way.

The main sticking point was to keep the lifter from crashing in the first place.

As the ground rose up to meet the falling lifter, a canyon running parallel to Corbet's flight path appeared, the mouth of which faced the foothills down below. The steep walls were ideal for shielding the bottom from direct observation from anything but a careful search by a hovering aerial vehicle.

The lifter had become nothing more than a glorified glider, losing altitude at a rapid rate as the tree-shrouded mountainside whipped past. Corbet steered at a right angle, the turn costing him precious elevation. The lip of the canyon filled the view of his windscreen. Tree branches whipped at the nose of his aircraft and snagged the spoilers before thumping and scraping against the bottom. The craft bellied over treetops at the canyon edge, the tail of the lifter shuddering with the impact. Corbet turned the lifter to avoid hitting the opposing canyon wall. The tilt of the turn created further loss of lift, shifting the lifter sideways toward the wall he had just barely cleared. The fading sound of air whistling through the compartment was a clue that the lifter was in danger of stalling. Just as it would with a conventional winged aircraft, the loss of velocity would send the lifter into an uncontrolled descent. The aircraft would then behave like a stone being dropped.

Without the engine providing powered assist, the foils responded sluggishly under manual operation. It was an effort to lower the nose to dive the lifter, but the craft increased forward momentum.

A scattering of trees covered the canyon floor with a mix of geological debris made up of boulders and stone outcroppings. A narrow stream meandered through the clutter. The regular shape of a tent appeared for a moment then passed beneath him.

Corbet cursed bitterly. Rather than find a hiding place for his lifter, he had managed to crash land into an encampment.

The tent disappeared to the side as trees seemed to sprout up in front of the aircraft. He could sense a barrier of air from the flat ventral surface of the fuselage being in close proximity to the ground. He pulled the nose up, flaring the lifter on the cushion of air. It appeared he was going to have the soft landing he had striven for.

The lifter struck. The foils crumpled, absorbing the impact before the rest of the lifter careened into the trees. The living wood bent and snapped under the weight of the lifter as it plowed through. There was a *thud* against the bulkhead behind him. Metal screeched against stone at the rear of the fuselage as the lifter finally made contact with the ground.

The seat harness prevented Corbet from being thrown against the control console by the sudden deceleration. The trees had absorbed much of the shock of the crash, but his arms and legs still flew forward from the inertia, his chest squeezed by the seat straps. Then the lifter was motionless.

Coughing from loss of breath, he stared at the windscreen. A maze of broken trees dominated the view. The lifter had come to rest nose down on the ground.

With practiced fingers he shut down the lifter. The engine already having died, the cargo carrying aircraft was silent. There was a crackling snap over his headphones as he turned off the radio. He double-checked to make sure the emergency beacon was deactivated. Without the beacon, the patrol he was sent to meet would not find him. He had gone down too far east to make rendezvous, much less be seen by them going down. At least the opposition would not find him either.

Air no longer blew through the aircraft. Corbet became aware of the smell of burnt insulation as faint tendrils of smoke wafted through the lifter. Likely the grav motor or electrical conduits were fried.

Finishing his shut-down procedure, Corbet now faced getting himself free from his seat. With the lifter sitting on a forward slope, it would be injudicious to quickly unfasten his harness and risk falling onto the panel before him. Bringing his leg up, he braced his knee against the face of the console. The instrument panel elicited a cracking sound as he settled his weight on it.

Pressing a hand to the overhead, he released the harness buckle. The console gave a warning creak as it took all of his weight. Holding onto the harness for support, he shifted sideways, balancing himself as he lowered his other foot beneath the console. Once he had found purchase, he slipped off of the console and moved between his seat and the copilot position. Gripping the seats, he pulled himself up, the deck tread providing his boots with traction as he negotiated the slope of the compartment.

He had to climb over the armored electrical junction box, armored being a relative term. The protection the box gave the electrical contacts inside was proof against shell fragments, but not much else. He sat on the bulkhead behind the copilot's seat. Across the doorway from him rested the wayward piece of cargo that had broken loose during the dogfight—a wooden crate fastened shut with a piece of wire wrapped around it. According to the stenciling on the side, two boxes of eight-millimeter carbine ammunition were contained within.

With his feet dangling through the door, he opened the junction box. Inside were toggle switches, each with an indicator light, some now dark as a result of battle damage. There was also a master breaker switch. He unlatched and moved the breaker, effectively unhooking the emergency battery system from the circuit. With the system completely deactivated, there was no risk of any electrical activity to attract attention.

Not filled to capacity, the cargo compartment appeared spacious. At the far end of the compartment, the motor housing that made up the rear wall was covered with shrapnel holes. A cannon shell had detonated in the motor compartment. Between the housing and himself, cargo nets were anchored along the centerline of the floor. In addition to the supplies settling forward against the netting, he saw a loose strap that had been worn through. That was where the ammunition box had fallen out. Standing on the bulkhead, he made his way up the lifter once more. The lifter creaked around him as the craft settled. The craft had not been designed to park on its nose, and the fuselage settled along new stress points.

Scraping his way up, Corbet reached the left-side portal. Though the door was designed to retract rearward under power, there was also a hand crank for when power was not available. There was also a release handle located beside the entry to be used in case emergency evacuation became necessary. The handle would disengage the rollers from the door and let it fall away. Corbet was reluctant to add a much bigger hole to the fuselage. There were too many shell holes that required sealing already.

Taking the crank handle from the bracket by the door, he pressed it into the crank socket and ensured it was seated. It was a slow difficult process to turn the handle. He had to brace his feet against the tie-downs on the deck when he pushed the crank handle upward then use his weight to pull it back. The door crawled upward against the pull of gravity with agonizing slowness. After several revolutions of the crank, the door had opened about a meter.

Pausing to rest, he went to the opening to get a breath of fresh air. On the ground below, several men watched. Most of them were armed with bolt-action rifles, the muzzles of which suddenly pointed at him when he appeared. They were not in Constabulary uniform, so they were not Free Holland renegades. Their work-worn clothing testified that they were regular citizens.

"Take me to your leader," he called.

❖

Highway West

Monique had difficulty falling asleep. As darkness fell, the residual heat from the day disappeared like a distant memory. Since the trucks were remaining overnight in concealment, the drivers served as sentries. The quietness seemed unnatural as the vehicles sat, unmoving in the dark. There was no comforting rumble from the engines, no vibration from the tires traversing the roadbed, and no sense of motion. Without the engine running, what little heat normally ducted through to the passenger compartment was conspicuous in its absence.

Wilfz's fitfulness contributed to the inconvenience. She could hear his heartbeat speed up as he kept twitching to wakefulness. She hesitated to say anything comforting to him, fearing he would become agitated by some taboo on her part. It felt like hours before she could feel him relax. *Finally!* A warm feeling stole over her consciousness, driving the ever-present chill from her mind. She surrendered to the null state, when conscious thought turned to dreams.

"Fix bayonets!"

Monique opened her eyes at the low mutter. She couldn't tell if she had managed to fall asleep, but she was awake again. *Now what?*

"First section is with me. Second, cover us." His voice was louder now, more emphatic. Monique heard Guardsman Perez and Sergeant Van shift themselves on their bunks above her.

"You! Stop right there!"

"Michael, wake up. You're dreaming." Monique touched the back of his shoulder. She was afraid that he was disturbing her guardsmen's rest. "Wake up. It's only a nightmare."

"Sergeant? Sergeant! The sergeant's been hit!"

"Michael …" Monique didn't get another word out before the major suddenly twisted beside her. She fell back as he took hold of her shoulders.

"We're taking fire! Get down!" he shouted.

Frightened, Monique was paralyzed into inaction. The blanket slipped from their shoulders, cold air circulating freely against their bare skin. She stared up into his face. With his wild expression, he gave every appearance of being awake. She noticed movement above him and saw Van quickly dismount from his bunk. The sergeant seized the major's shoulder to pull him away, but she reached past Wilfz to stay the Celestial Guardsman's advance.

"*Ngăn cản không cho ai làm việc gì!*" She commanded sharply in Vietnamese.

Van obeyed the order to stop.

Her voice appeared to have broken through to Wilfz. He seemed to see her for the first time—and not as the person he had been dreaming about. Carefully, she lowered her arm to his slippery back.

"What …?" his arms shaking, he collapsed on top of her, his face in the crook of her neck.

"It's okay," she said into his ear, her voice low and soothing. "You're safe here. It's just us." Her fingers felt sticky from the wetness she encountered on his back.

Wilfz started to groan, but it ended in a sigh. His previously taut muscles now seemed inert as he relaxed completely.

"Lady Lewellen, are you all right?" Van asked. Oliveiras suddenly appeared, and he quickly shifted Wilfz back to his spot.

"I'm not hurt," she reassured the sergeant. She looked to the doctor. "There's something wrong with Michael. I think he's bleeding."

❖❖❖

Monique had watched as Sergeant Van helped Doctor Oliveiras with the major. Upon completing his examination, the doctor declared that Wilfz had only lost a stitch. The blood loss had been negligible.

Monique had listened as the doctor muttered to himself. He was of the opinion that his friend was suffering from posttraumatic stress. When he finished with Wilfz, he looked straight at Monique. "Remind me to talk to him about physical therapy in the morning."

She nodded slowly.

The commentary over Wilfz's suspected mental distress put his reactions in a new light. He had not attacked Monique, but sought only to protect her. The protests he had uttered made it clear he wasn't afraid for himself; he was expressing his fear for others. When he was wounded the first time, he had made sure his subordinate was safe at the risk of his own life. It was for the sake of a wounded woman that he had been shot the second time. On both occasions, he had been preserving the life of another.

Wilfz groaned only twice during the remainder of the night, bringing Monique to full wakefulness each time. She listened to him carefully until she was assured that he would remain asleep. She was roused when Van and Perez rose at daylight and left the ambulance. As the door closed, the major shifted in his sleep. The cold air in the vehicle encouraged Monique to remain close to him for warmth, but that contentment would not last. Attuned to his heartbeat, she knew he was not really sleeping.

"Michael." Monique moved her head from his back and crept up on him. He lay as usual, on his front side with his head turned away from her. He gave no outward sign of being awake, but she was familiar enough with his breathing pattern to know that he was pretending to sleep.

"Michael," she breathed his name again, this time directly into his ear. "I know you're awake."

"You should have left me behind." His voice was barely above a whisper. Unlike his manner the previous night, he was cognizant and responsive.

"We need you, Michael," she replied quietly. "I am the useless one here. I am the one who should have been left behind. I contribute nothing here."

"You would not be here if you were useless."

"The only reason I am here is that my brother thought I couldn't possibly screw this up. I guess I showed him."

"Your brother is the one who sent you here? He should have his butt kicked."

Monique felt an unexpected sense of loyalty for her brother, Hampton. "He didn't know this was going to happen," she said. "It was supposed to be a simple mission—so simple that I was not really necessary. Lieutenant Cameron could have done it without anyone from the foreign office."

"Then why didn't he?"

"I believe that no one realized that this would happen. Did you know?"

Wilfz gave a quiet snort.

"It would have been better if I had not come here at all," Monique continued. "I complicated things and got you shot too."

"You can't take the blame for that," Wilfz said. "I was already on their hit list. It wasn't the first time they had come after me."

"Maybe things would have been different if we hadn't come at all."

"I would have been locked up instead of riding in this truck."

"We're the reason you're in trouble in the first place."

"I worked for the colonel. Lang was suspicious of him and has no love for me. I'm merely guilty by association."

"You're not making this easy."

"If you wanted easy, you should have left me behind."

"Look, Michael, you're more important than I am. Apart from my previous career, I am nothing. Apart from my linguistic ability,

I have no diplomatic skills. I owe my job to my brother. That is the only reason I am here."

"I'm starting not to like your brother."

"Well, don't … don't not like him because of that."

"Hunh?"

"That did sound confusing, didn't it?" Monique said thoughtfully. "Well, the real reason I wanted to talk to you is to let you know that I'm okay. I understand."

Still facing away from her, Wilfz did not respond right away. When he did speak, it was in a tortured whisper. "I shouldn't have hurt you."

"You didn't hurt me. You kept me safe. I was afraid that you had hurt yourself."

"This is another reason we should not be lying together like this." He lifted his hand, an attempt to bring attention toward their blanketed forms. "You shouldn't be here with me—you're better than this."

"What makes you think I'm better?" Monique asked.

"You're first consort or something like that, I think."

"The first consort? Me?"

Wilfz turned to face her, his eyebrows raised at the surprise in her voice.

"You think I am first consort to the emperor?" she asked.

"You have all these men protecting you."

"No, I'm not the first consort. She's much more beautiful than I am."

"There are women more beautiful than you?"

Monique was fully aware of her appearance at the moment. She wore no makeup, and her hair was disheveled. Her last bath had been done hastily with a washrag the previous morning while Wilfz was out answering the call of nature. The most astounding thing to her was that this man had clearly demonstrated little interest in her, at least as a partner.

"Yes," she said simply. "When we get to Pearl, I will introduce you to some of them."

Wilfz shook his head. "I won't be going with you."

There was a groan from a bunk on Monique's side of the truck. Doctor Oliveiras stretched as he woke up.

"Doctor, is he always this obstinate?" Monique turned her attention to Oliveiras.

"That is between the two of you. I want no part of that."

Monique sighed. "I can't always call you doctor," she mused, "and Olly seems disrespectful. May I call you by your given name?"

Oliveiras gave her an uncertain smile, an unexpected reaction from the older man.

"It's Oliver," Wilfz said quietly.

Oliver Oliveiras? No wonder Michael calls him Olly, Monique thought. She saw the momentary flicker of displeasure with which the doctor favored Wilfz. The expression that he presented to Monique was much kinder. "You may call me Oliver if you wish."

"Thank you, Oliver," Monique said kindly. "At least your middle name can't possibly be Olivier."

Wilfz suddenly sputtered into laughter. Oliveiras gave him a fierce look. Slipping from the bunk, he went through the doorway to sit in the driving compartment. Monique was aghast at her unintentional impertinence. "What parents name their son Oliver Olivier Oliveiras?" she pondered out loud.

"His parents," Wilfz said with a chortle.

"I didn't mean to make him angry," Monique said. "I was trying to be nice."

"He's not angry with you," Wilfz said soberly. He quietly cleared his throat in an attempt to regain his composure. "He's angry with me."

Monique had initially been startled when Wilfz began laughing. Recalling the curious look on Wilfz's face when the lifters had been firing overhead, she found that she was oddly relieved to hear it. It signaled to her that he would be more communicative with her. When he was introspective, she felt as if she was alone and she did not like it.

The rear door opened and Lieutenant Cameron entered. "I heard about last night," he said, his voice gruff with displeasure.

"Doctor Oliveiras said Michael will be fine," Monique offered in Wilfz's defense, seeing the irritation in Cameron's expression.

"What about you?"

"I'm fine," she replied. "He's awake, you know. It's rude to talk about him as if he were not present."

"He's not the one talking about me." Wilfz lifted his head to look at the lieutenant. "I gather that there has been no activity out there since yesterday."

"No, sir," Cameron said, the irritation fading from his features.

"About last night ... I was out of line," Wilfz said. "I must have been out of my head. I couldn't even understand Eunice when she yelled at me."

"I wasn't yelling at you. I was yelling at Sergeant Van. I didn't want him hurting you," Monique said.

"I still didn't understand you," Wilfz said. "I must have been disoriented."

"You may have been disoriented, but you were not crazy," Monique explained. "I wanted to make sure Van did not hurt you, so I commanded him in Vietnamese."

"You commanded Sergeant Van?" Cameron said dubiously.

"*Ngăn cản không cho ai làm việc gì,*" Monique demonstrated. She then asked Cameron if he understood. She looked to see Wilfz's reaction.

"That's what I heard," he confirmed, nodding.

"You know Vietnamese?" Cameron asked.

"Of course I do!" Monique was offended by his incredulous tone. "You didn't think I was just parroting lines in that drama did you?"

"I'm not going to dignify that with an answer," Cameron said.

"I knew it! You're one of those who criticized the show!"

"What are you two talking about?" Wilfz asked, having lost track of the conversation.

"Oh, that's right. You don't have drama here." Monique visibly warmed to the subject. "I played the title role in *My Dear Captain.* My character was the captain of the guard for the crown prince."

"It was unrealistic!" Cameron snorted. "There is no crown prince. The plot was contrived, and the rivalry between the Celestial Guard teams was excessive."

"It's called artistic license," Monique defended. "It was one of my most dramatic roles. You're just mad because I outranked you."

Saying nothing, Cameron merely looked at her. Monique turned to Wilfz. "I was a disgraced Celestial Guard captain who redeemed herself in the final episode. She came back, avoiding interception by her former guard team and saved the crown prince by taking the assassin's bullet herself," Monique explained. She noticed a strange look on the major's face. He seemed to be unsettled. "You see, she had previously had an affair with the crown prince ..."

"No Celestial Guard captain would be that unprofessional!" Cameron burst out, interrupting her. "Such conduct is unthinkable!"

Monique regarded the Celestial Guard lieutenant coolly. When she spoke, her voice lacked the enthusiasm she had expressed only moments before. "I will interpret your revulsion as an expression of your pride for the professionalism in the Celestial Guard," she said slowly, her face warming from the insult she perceived from his interjection. "I will not take your judgment as a personal attack against me."

She glanced at the major, wondering how he had comprehended her explanation. Ruddy just a moment before, he was now suddenly pale. She abandoned her stern visage for one of concern. "Are you all right, Michael?"

"I think I might be sick," Wilfz muttered.

With surprising alacrity, Doctor Oliveiras was out of the driver's compartment and with his two patients within moments.

"Lieutenant, open that door. Let's get some fresh air in here," he instructed. "It's just as cold in here at it is outside anyway."

"I'm okay," Wilfz said, holding a hand to signal Cameron to stop, but the lieutenant opened the door anyway.

The cold breeze that entered the truck compartment quickly put the lie to the doctor's prediction. Attacked by a fit of shivering,

Monique huddled into the blankets. The fresh air also proved Wilfz's protest to be false as color returned to his face.

Monique burrowed further into the blankets, sidling close to Wilfz.

"We really need more blankets," the major said, trying to shift away from the woman. With the wall next to him, it was a futile endeavor.

"Would it bother you this much if you still thought I was the emperor's first consort?" Monique enjoyed Wilfz's reaction, pleased to see the Constabulary officer behave in a familiar manner.

"What did you just say? First consort?" Cameron asked. "What did the two of you do last night?"

❧❀❧

Highway East, Great Barrier Mountains, Holland

Due to operational commitments, cannot comply.

Those six words summed up the response from the First Mountain brigade commander. It had been sent in answer to Director Lang's officer recall. Lang, incensed by what he termed "gross disobedience," demanded the colonel's arrest at once—a task soon proven easier said than done.

A lifter with a brace of strike lifters as escort had been sent. On board the lifter was an officer of a rank commensurate with that of the commanding officer of First Mountain—a situation that would give him the right to confer with the First Mountain officer. At least, that was the announced intention. In reality, Chosen Colonel Raul would relieve the defiant officer of his command. Assisting him would be a detail of security force personnel. Given the exercised professionalism the brigade had repeatedly demonstrated, it was certain they would not tolerate mutinous behavior. Once the new colonel had restored order by enforcing compliance to the director's orders, the brigade would most assuredly support the new commander.

The first step to encourage the old commander to step down was to take away his men's mobility. The Chosen had infiltrated pilots among the lifter detachment crews, posing as mechanics and crew chiefs. On the morning Raul was to arrive, they took off with many of the assigned lifters, effectively isolating and stranding the brigade. There were not enough pilots to take all of the aircraft, so irreplaceable critical parts were taken from the lifters left behind. Since the same part was taken from each abandoned lifter, it was impossible for the brigade to cannibalize some aircraft to make others operational. Those specific spare parts were also stolen from brigade stores, ensuring that the lifters would be unusable.

The complex plan was pathetically naïve. The Chosen had underestimated the determination of the men of First Mountain. The crew and passengers were disarmed and arrested upon landing. The strikers were unable to intervene. Using sniper emplacements, First Mountain sent an ultimatum of three choices: They could land and surrender. They could depart the air space over First Mountain area of operations. Or they could persist and be destroyed.

The strikers retired from the area.

As for Colonel Raul and his entourage, they had been driven to the bottom of the mountain and released on foot. The colonel had in his possession a letter signed by the commanding officer of First Mountain. The message was succinct: First Mountain would not obey unlawful orders; neither would they assist in a coup d'état.

For his failure to implement the director's orders to take command of First Mountain, Colonel Raul was demoted to lieutenant and assigned to a reconnaissance patrol. Adding insult to injury, his patrol was in the vanguard company that was leading the expeditionary convoy back to the mountain.

The convoy had departed Bremen the week before, the vehicles making good time on Highway East. The broad roadway ran straight on a compass bearing across flat plains. The convoy turned off the highway before it dead-ended at a heavy machinery park, and spent another day on narrow paving that wove through ravines. They were deep in the foothills when they came to an unplanned stop.

Field Colonel Bertrand looked forward from the cupola of his command vehicle. He could not see the reason for the halt. For his own safety as convoy commander, he had arranged the convoy so that his combat car was in forward center of the column. Behind his vehicle was the long-range radio car. Individual vehicle radios lacked the range to contact the Constabulary Management Office in Bremen.

Ahead of the convoy, the flat expanse dominated the horizon like a giant wall. Unlike the mountain ranges to the west, the eastern range was most inaccessible due to the flat faces of the cliff-like geography, hence the name Great Barrier Mountains. There was only one way up, at least for an armed force like the convoy, and that was by road.

The majestic plates that made the faces of the mountain had begun as bedrock back in the ancient past. A section of the mountain fell away eons ago during a titanic upheaval, which now made up the foothills. The flat bedrock had become the sheer cliff faces, almost perpendicular to the ground.

The road had been completed over a century before, but given the topography, there was little room for improvement on the ascent. Beginning at the bottom, the road switched back and followed the upper lip of the plates. The road was backstopped by another plate, making it inadvisable to widen into the rock. The fragile strata could cause the entire face to collapse onto the roadway.

A corporal trotted back from the head of the column, kicking up snow with his boots. The stitching that held the blue cuffs to his parka was sloppy in contrast to the stitching that secured the rectangular leather patch on his left breast that was imprinted with the name Wilkinson. Once he was abreast of the truck ahead of the command vehicle, the trooper slowed carefully to keep from skidding on the slippery ground. In his hand was a sheet of paper, the edges trailing gray-colored, all-weather tape. As he approached the command car, the corporal held the paper up. "There's a tree blocking the road. This was taped to it, sir," he reported.

"Hand it here!" the field colonel ordered, leaning over in his cupola.

A look of consternation momentarily appeared on the corporal's face. It would have been easier to hand the paper into the side door to a member of the car crew and have him hand it up through the interior. The flat-topped appearance of the vehicle had only seemed to make it appear squat; the hull was still shoulder high.

He kicked his boot against the tire to knock the snow off the sole then placed his foot on the axle hub of the wheel. Gripping the cargo rack, he was able to climb partway up the side of the vehicle. He switched hands to bring the paper closer to the field colonel. Even stretching, he couldn't get it over to him. Rather than climb out of the cupola, Bertrand operated the vehicle commander's override. There was a yelp of surprise from inside the vehicle as the turret swiveled, bringing the field colonel closer to the forward quarter while directing the gun away from the line of travel. The field colonel leaned down to catch the paper with his fingertips. The corporal's dismount back to the snow was more of a fall than an exercise of grace, and earned him a critical look from the field colonel. He remained standing next to the vehicle and awaited orders.

Bertrand read the paper. Signed by the commanding officer of First Mountain, it declared that further travel beyond where the sign had been posted was prohibited. Bertrand looked up at the imposing plated mountain face that lay ahead. There was no one in sight, nothing to indicate that the brigade had the road under observation.

From his elevated vantage point, the flag of Holland that was draped over the back of one of the leading trucks was in plain view. The brigade would have to be callously disloyal to fire on units bearing their own flag. By disregarding lawful orders from the Constabulary high command, the renegades had to realize that they were in rebellion.

However, this was a force that would be able to defend itself. In addition to Bertrand's combat car company, armored trucks transported Chosen troops and their officers. Additional conventional Constabulary troopers rode in regular trucks. In the van of the column was the reconnaissance car company.

Bertrand looked down at the corporal. "Tell Captain Mainer to advance. We stop for nothing," he ordered the corporal.

"There's a tree in the way, sir," the corporal repeated.

The field colonel stared at the young man. The corporal's audacity in voicing an objection to a senior officer's order was astounding.

"I believe it is customary to assume that removal of the tree is an anticipated part of my order. Did I not say 'we stop for nothing'?"

"Yessir! Rightawaysir!" the corporal's words ran together in staccato. He turned and ran back up the column from where he had come, the sticky snow scattering from his feet.

The column did not begin to move as expected. From his vehicle, Bertrand gave a grunt of dissatisfaction. Only officers had disembarked and were standing in a small group near the barricade, but no men had begun to perform the task of clearing the road. Much as he wanted to call the lead vehicles on the radio, he was under orders not to transmit any communications. The radio would surely be overheard by the forces on the mountain.

He ducked down into the turret and pushed past the loader to get out of the combat car. Mounted on the slanted wall, the side door fell open when he opened it. As he reached the ground, his booted feet skidded on the snow and he almost fell into the ditch. The corporal had not, apparently, been as clumsy as he had appeared to be.

As Bertrand stalked his way carefully up the column, he did not return the looks from the troopers on the vehicles he passed. He should not have to make this trip. The instructions he had given to the corporal should have been enough.

As he neared the lead vehicles, he could hear the officers arguing with each other. One of them, a lieutenant, was most persistent in his desire to lead the vanguard up the mountain. The two captains pointedly ignored him as they debated their own plans. The corporal was first to notice Bertrand. His eyes widened at the field colonel's displeased expression. He stepped back, coming into contact with the fallen tree. The officers turned to face Bertrand as he arrived. "The corporal has been apprised of my desires. I trust that he has relayed my orders to you," said the field colonel. "Or am I mistaken?"

Bertrand's overly formal tone was not lost on the officers. They knew that there would be dire consequences, but they were reluctant to obey the order to proceed. Even the most inexperienced trooper could see that the mountain forces had an excellent line of sight from concealed observation posts to the road where the convoy had come to a halt.

"The tree is not blocking the field," he observed. "Why haven't we gone around it already?"

A captain, but not Mainer, opened his mouth to reply. The field colonel did not give him a chance to explain. "That was not an invitation to speak," he snarled. "I shouldn't have to come up here and kick your tails into gear! You dare call yourselves officers?"

The two captains quickly returned to their vehicles, trailed by their lieutenants—all of the lieutenants save one, the officer who had been ignored by the debating captains.

Lieutenant Raul faced the field colonel. "Give me the recon company! The *captain*," he sneered the rank of his superior, "doesn't have the will to lead it."

"Lieutenants lead patrols," Bertrand replied. He eyed the upstart officer before continuing with a hint of displeasure in his voice. "On this day, that is your assignment. Tomorrow we'll see about your company." In this way he gave his tacit approval.

Raul saluted, but the field colonel had already turned away.

"Wilkinson! Get my car. Bring it here. We're leading!"

The corporal suddenly sprinted toward one of the scout vehicles. Moving across the ditch, Bertrand moved out of the way of the convoy and waited for his command car to reach him.

It did not go unnoticed that the lieutenant took charge. The captain of the reconnaissance company looked askance at the field colonel. Bertrand responded with a level stare.

Lieutenant Raul clambered up the outside of his scout car, his boots finding purchase on the nonskid surface of the front fender. Standard for a small vehicle, there was only room for a two-man crew. Wilkinson sat with his head out of the driver's hatch in front. Behind and higher on the vehicle was the gunner's turret. Two thirteen-millimeter machineguns were mounted on pivots on either side of the small turret. Raul slipped into the open hatch on top and pounded his fist against the top of his cupola. Looking back over his shoulder, he raised his arm to signal his patrol to follow.

Four scout cars, identically equipped to Raul's, pulled forward. The five vehicles drove past Bertrand and crossed over the ditch to bypass the tree barricade. A patrol of troopers, a troop per truck, passed by the field colonel next. He had just turned to look at his vehicle when a dull rumbling sound came from the mountain. The ground trembled as he looked up. Dirt and snow blasted upward in fine geysers along the roadway on the cliff face.

"They mined the road!" someone shouted incredulously.

The rumbling was only the beginning. Beneath the roadway, the rock face began to break apart, slab-sided pieces flaking away and falling. The front of the mountain was disintegrating.

The linear strata of the plates shattered under the explosive pressure. Once a plate tipped, it would lose the support of the plate behind. The center of the plates, weakened by the loss of integrity within, crumbled under the weight remaining on top. The ground shook as the massive pieces thundered to the ground below. Great clouds of dust and snow rose, shrouding the sky in a steady expanse.

First Mountain had not mined the road. They had mined the entire mountain face. They had drilled down behind the plate, and had filled the hole with explosive compound. When it detonated, the explosion totally removed the road along with the cliff face.

Wilkinson immediately applied the brakes, and the scout car skidding in the mud of the ditch. Amazed by the spectacle, the driver of the truck behind failed to see him stop. The truck struck Raul's vehicle, and Wilkinson bit his tongue. He gave a harsh grunt of pain. Lifting his cuff, he experimentally dabbed his tongue on the blue fabric, leaving a red stain.

Staring at the destruction, the field colonel gave no indication that he noticed that the trucks had stopped once more. In contrast to the smooth weathered feature that had formerly adorned the mountain, the cliff now appeared rough and unfinished. When the damp mist of snow wafted over the convoy, Bertrand shook off his reverie and made his way to the radio car. He would report this development to the CMO. The need for communications silence was no longer necessary.

CHAPTER ELEVEN

In an orchard, Highway West

Monique sat against the driving compartment partition. It was midday, the warmest part of the day, but with the rear door open, she received none of the supposed benefits. With the cold invading the interior of the vehicle, she stared nonplussed at the scene before her.

There was no traffic on the road, much less any aerial movement. Cameron was permitting Wilfz to zero his carbine. In their collective judgment, there was minimal risk of discovery. Oliveiras watched the proceedings with disapproval. Firing out of an ambulance was a violation of Constabulary code. The vehicle was supposed to be noncombatant. He had raised that point, but Wilfz had just shaken his head. The moment the colonel had cached the carbine ammunition in the field ambulance, they were already in violation. Wilfz went on to state that the blues would not hesitate to fire on them, ambulance or not.

Facing out the rear door, Wilfz now lay beneath two blankets. His carbine was aimed at an angle from the linear direction in which he lay. His targets were three empty ration cans had been placed off to that side. Monique could not see them from where she sat next to Oliveiras. Swathed in the other two blankets, the woman watched with her hands over her ears.

Wilfz fired, the muzzle flash creating a spot in Monique's vision. The report of the weapon discharge was sharp and loud. The bolt of the carbine cycled automatically, ejecting the empty shell casing up against the inside of the doorway where it bounced back and landed beside Wilfz on his blanket. The heat of firing shimmered off the casing into the cold air. Taking his right hand from the trigger, Wilfz made an adjustment to his rear sight.

He fired again. This time, she heard the bullet punch through metal, followed by the sound of the can bouncing along the soft ground. Wilfz gave a thoughtful grunt as if he were pleased. He fired again, striking another can. Then he fired three more single shots.

"Keep your ears covered. This is going to be noisy," Wilfz announced. Monique saw him move his other hand and wondered what the major had adjusted. Firearms not being her specialty, she knew nothing about the selector switch.

Wilfz shifted the carbine and aimed at a point within Monique's range of view. He fired, releasing the trigger to send a three-round burst down range. Bark flaked from a tree as the impacting rounds penetrated the wood. The ejecting brass ricocheted off the ceiling and fell around Monique. One of the empties landed against her neck, burning her skin like a hot coal. She dislodged the painful piece of metal as Wilfz switched his aim to a second tree and repeated the process and then attacked a third tree.

Monique watched as Wilfz adjusted his weapon again, announcing that he had set the selector to safe. He removed the magazine and then opened the bolt. An unfired round ejected from the chamber, clattering onto the floor beside him.

"My old man would tan my hide if he saw me do that," he remarked.

"Shooting while naked in blankets?" Monique teased.

"Shooting at trees," Oliveiras stated.

"Bullets are hard on saw teeth," Wilfz added. He suddenly huddled into his blankets. "I think I'll clean it after I warm up a bit." Monique realized that he was talking about cleaning the weapon.

"I'll do it," Oliveiras volunteered. Monique was surprised that the doctor would touch a weapon designed to inflict harm on his fellow man.

"Olly? Actually, it's so cold, I'm not too proud to let someone else clean my weapon," Wilfz accepted gratefully while making himself comfortable under cover. "I wish you would give me some clothes."

"*Not* giving you clothes is the only way to make you follow doctor's orders and stay in bed!" Oliveiras declared.

"At least get her dressed then," Wilfz nodded at Monique.

"There are men who would be honored to share these blankets with me," Monique boasted. She was shocked to see expressions of indignation directed at her from both Oliveiras and Wilfz.

"I can't believe you said that," Cameron said from outside the door.

"This is a planet of prudes," Monique snapped petulantly as she scooted down and hid her face in her blankets. "Close that door. That wind is cold in here!"

❄

The guardsmen had been gathered outside the ambulance while the major sighted in his weapon. Given the primitive conditions, they had agreed that the officer had been very methodical while adjusting his sights between shots against the first can. The other two cans had served to confirm the accuracy of his adjustments.

The three-shot bursts had come as a surprise. They were aware that the Constabulary awarded ribbons to the enlisted men for that proficiency, but they had not expected to witness such precise shooting. The Mark Ten carbine as issued to the Constabulary was typical of those provided by Holland Armory. Having examined the weapon, they knew there were only three selector settings: safe, single-shot, and full automatic fire. There were other weapons that provided a setting for three-round burst fire, but apparently the Constabulary did not use them, choosing to rely on training to provide that skill.

The astonishing thing was that Wilfz had barely taken the time to aim when he chose the three trees as his targets. After Van had gone to bury the shot-up cans, he went to inspect the major's marksmanship.

Perez joined him. Standing before one of the trees, he pointed while he spoke. "These bullet holes are chest high."

"Tight pattern too," Van agreed. "They hit dead center."

"I think I know why those carbines are so heavy," Perez went on. "I'm thinking that the eight-millimeter rifle round is too large, so they need the heavy weight to control the carbine when they shoot."

The principle behind the design was obvious—heavy knock-down power and decent accuracy against anything that a trooper might encounter, be it man or beast. In the hands of someone like Wilfz, that weapon was a serious threat.

"That's some pretty good shooting for a man freezing in a blanket," Gray commented.

Nodding, Van took a last look at the holes in the trees before returning to where he had buried the cans. He kicked leaves and snow to better hide the freshly turned dirt. Anybody driving by would not notice that anything had been disturbed. The snow had fallen in patches beneath the trees, so his handiwork was not immediately apparent. As for the holes in the bark, unless someone stopped and looked closely, no one would see them in the mottled shade from the branches.

❈

That evening the trucks returned to the road. Monique was able to fall asleep easily to the drone of tires on the road. Prior to dawn she awoke feeling exceedingly warm. The heat radiated from Wilfz as he slumbered, his skin damp. Reaching over him, she placed her hand over his forehead.

"What is it?" Oliveiras asked in a low voice.

Monique peeked out of the blanket, surprised to see the doctor kneeling by them.

"I think he has a fever," she said.

Oliveiras touched the back of his hand against Wilfz face. "Idiot," he said with a nod of confirmation. "He caught a chill playing with his gun. I knew that was a bad idea."

"Eunice shouldn't have done that," Wilfz muttered.

"I shouldn't have done what?" Monique asked.

Wilfz turned his head with difficulty, but managed to fix her with a cheerless stare. "You shouldn't have been captain of the guard," he said. "It's not the place of women to risk themselves like that. You shouldn't have died."

"He's delirious." Oliveiras shook his head. "I need to get his fever down now."

"And you ..." Wilfz looked at the doctor. "Some crown prince you are ..."

"Help me with him," Oliveiras instructed Monique. "I'm going to roll him over. Just get a hold of his hip and pull him toward you. I'll hold his shoulders and head. She did as she had been told. "Okay, that's it ... yeah," he said when Wilfz was satisfactorily repositioned.

Oliveiras then poured water into a cup. He handed it to Monique. "Give him only a little bit, if he'll take it," he ordered.

Monique looked into the cup; it was less than a third full. *Only a little bit of this?* She slipped her hand beneath Wilfz's head and tilted his face forward. His hair felt warm and damp. "Drink some," she told him, holding the cup to his lips. As he sipped, he tried to tilt the cup more with his lips. She pulled the cup away, remembering the doctor's admonition. He gasped as some of the cold water fell onto his neck.

"*Choe song hamnida,*" she said apologetically.

Wilfz twitched as she finished speaking. "It's you," he said. Monique looked at him, sensing that he was in a moment of clarity.

"Of course it's me," she said. "Who else would I be?"

"You said something again," he said. "Or am I fever dreaming?"

"Was that what?" Oliveiras asked. He had poured water from a canister into a basin and was soaking a cloth in it. "You wouldn't be feeling this way if you hadn't been hanging out the back of the truck."

"You should have given me clothes," Wilfz said.

"If I had done that, then you would have stayed outside and you would be dying now," Oliveiras said. "Pneumonia will kill you if you don't listen to me." He removed the cloth from the water and wrung out the excess moisture from it.

"No, Michael, don't just *listen* to the doctor," Monique said. "Obey him. You'll only exacerbate your condition."

Wilfz closed his eyes. "Don't use words like that. It makes my head hurt," he said.

"Exacerbate?" Monique asked.

"Obey," Wilfz clarified.

In his bunk, Perez started laughing.

"I wish you wouldn't do that," Oliveiras said mournfully. "You're only encouraging him."

"You aren't supposed to be paying attention," Monique spoke up to Perez.

As Doctor Oliveiras placed the damp cloth on Wilfz's forehead, Monique looked at her bunkmate. Despite his fever, he seemed to be in good spirits. Before anybody else could speak, the engine noise changed in pitch as the vehicle slowed. Cameron had chosen their next parking spot.

Monique said nothing more. She put her head down and closed her eyes. She remembered the reproachful look Wilfz had given her the day before. She had spoken of other men wishing to share her bed. *Why did I have to say something like that? Was I trying to get a reaction out of him?* Monique wondered at her temerity. She wouldn't normally make such a boast, yet this man seemed to bring out the coquette in her. That was the last thought she had before she drifted into sleep again.

❧❀❧

Wilfz rested fretfully, having no appetite but drinking all of the water he was given. Doctor Oliveiras and Monique took turns watching over him, periodically refreshing the cool, damp compress. His mind floated feverishly, grappling with the cultural inconsistencies that defined his companions.

Wilfz's surprise at the idea of women serving in the Celestial Guard had been more profound than he realized. From his point of view it was completely unthinkable for women to serve in the Constabulary. There were too few women on Holland to permit such irresponsibility. He found Eunice's casual disregard for her own life sickening. In fact, he had literally been taken sick, judging by the nausea in his stomach, when the actress described throwing herself into harm's way. Women serving alongside men in combat had long been unthinkable to him. How could any world permit their women to undertake such risky assignments?

As he lay not fully asleep, but not quite awake, the imagery of Eunice wearing a Celestial Guard uniform continuously replayed in his mind. Putting herself in the position of human shield, she fell repeatedly, saving someone different each time. The circumstances changed as Wilfz's memories were dredged from his own past. One of his own men had thrown himself in front of the younger Lieutenant Wilfz, but in his fevered recollection it was Eunice who took the fall. The striker attack that had cost him his captaincy …

◄❋►

Monique watched Wilfz suffer in delirium. He had been lucid when he was awake earlier that morning, thus everyone's surprise at the severity of his illness. In slumber he had become restless. She was well aware of his uneasy feelings about women serving in the armed forces. Until now she had dismissed it as male chauvinist overreaction. Observing his current unguarded state, however, she could see that his emotional distress was genuine.

He suddenly twitched, his lashes trembling over closed eyes. "No!" His eyes opened wide as if his own voice had wakened him.

Monique brought her face close to his, but he gave no sign of seeing her.

"Kill me."

"Michael?" Monique extended her slender hand to his damp face.

At her touch, his attention fastened upon her. "Stop doing that."

Monique withdrew her hand. "Stop doing what, Michael?"

"Stop dying for me. Let them kill me."

It took no stretch of the imagination to realize the role she was playing in his nightmare. Staring into his face, Monique realized that he was still dreaming. His eyes were open, but he was not seeing her. His irrational behavior reminded her of the nightmare he'd had before. Fearful he would hurt himself again, she furiously sought a remedy to the situation. She considered patting him on the cheek, but that might incite a violent reaction. She feared anything physical that would cause him to fight back.

Her use of foreign language had snapped him out of his hallucination before when she'd given Van an order in Vietnamese. But there was no doubt that he was dreaming about her guard captain persona, so she dared not use that language. Wilfz would associate it with the Celestial Guard. Contributing to his delusion was the last thing she wished to do.

Nevertheless she was certain his fascination with her linguistic ability was the solution. She would speak in Korean. Yes, she was satisfied that would work.

She took a breath ...

... and words failed her.

She could not think of anything to say.

"No ..." Wilfz groaned, squeezing his eyes shut. The anguish on his face was plain to see. Monique felt uneasy knowing that he had just dreamed her death again.

A phrase came to mind spontaneously. She spoke the Korean words in an undertone, before she realized where they came from: *When you go, I'll still be here.* They were lyrics to a song about the promise of love and hopeful longing. She remembered telling

Wilfz about her singing and his caution when he stopped her from demonstrating for fear of aggravating her back injury.

The words came unbidden to her lips. She did not sing, but spoke with rhythm to the music playing in her mind. When she gave up show business to work for the foreign office, she had left a part of herself behind as well. She realized only at this moment that, without that outlet of self-expression, she was denying her very identity.

She spoke encouragingly to him in a low voice. As she had hoped, the soliloquy proved to be a diversion. He listened with half-lidded eyes as she recited the words to a popular song she liked. After that, she fended off his agitation with another lyrical recital. Song after song she spoke, some that she would never dare sing, given her vocal limitations. Performing for Wilfz gave her a sense of contentment that she had not felt in months.

Wilfz's fever broke later that afternoon. Having been restless all day, he was languid with exhaustion by the time evening arrived.

"That was nice, Lady Lewellen," Gray commented thoughtfully as he and Schmidt rose from the bunks.

Monique felt a flush, seeing he was sincere. She gave a nod in lieu of the bow she would normally bestow after a performance. She had hardly expected an appreciative audience. After Schmidt and Gray left the truck, Monique took the opportunity to engage Wilfz in conversation. "How is this ambulance different from the other truck?" she asked, choosing the first thing that came to mind. Talking about the vehicle they lived in seemed as natural as discussing the weather.

Wilfz looked at her, his brows furrowed as if she were speaking in an incomprehensible manner. Monique opened her mouth to repeat herself, but his response quieted her.

"Why do you want to know something like that?"

Monique paused, momentarily unprepared to answer with a question still on her lips.

"You make it sound like an unusual question."

"You're a woman. Of course it's unusual."

So we're back to this again. "I can't believe you said that," she said.

"That sounds like something the lieutenant would say," Wilfz commented. Monique made no attempt to keep the insulted look from her face. "I can see that you're determined not to discuss this with me," she said.

"I just didn't expect you to ask something like that."

"I suppose you expect me to discuss female subjects," Monique snapped. Fixing him with an indignant glare, she went on with sarcastic enlightenment. "You know, the usual things that women are supposed to occupy themselves: theoretical housekeeping and applied motherhood and childcare."

"Those sound like college courses," he observed.

Monique rewarded him with a sharp look in the hopes of disabusing him from continuing that line of conversation. In her irritation, she had forgotten that this man had just recovered from fever.

"I guess that was wrong." Wilfz admitted uneasily.

The man is patronizing me. Displeased, Monique assumed an icy countenance as she looked at him through narrowed eyes.

Wilfz's eyebrows rose momentarily in response, as if he were shrugging. "They are basically the same truck," he said. That he relented to her will came as a surprise to Monique. She was emboldened by a sense of vindication.

Wilfz continued, pointing up at the hatch in the roof over their heads. "Even that cupola is functional. Install the seat under it and mount a thirteen to the hard point and this truck will operate as the other trucks do."

"But there is no identification on it, no medical sign or anything to tell this is an ambulance," Monique argued. "Isn't there an accord or something against arming hospital vehicles?"

"Even medical personnel are permitted to defend themselves and their patients," Wilfz said simply. "Olly did."

Doctor Oliveiras snorted. Monique realized that this was a reference to the incident that he and Wilfz had shared before.

"Ordinarily, we do not arm ambulances," Oliveiras declared.

"There was a time when we painted white crosses on our medical vehicles," Wilfz continued, ignoring the doctor. "Not in my time, but long before. They would be targeted first, either for the medical supplies or to demoralize our men. Raiders and slavers don't follow any accords that you refer to.

"This is why an armored truck is an armored truck, first and foremost. They're not as tough as combat cars, but they're suitable for most purposes."

"So why don't we have thirteens? What is a thirteen, anyway? Cameron mentioned that before," Monique demanded.

"It's a heavy machinegun," Wilfz said, "called that because the bore is thirteen millimeters across. The correct nomenclature for the weapon is mark three heavy machinegun."

"So how come you don't call it a mark three?"

Wilfz shrugged, not answering. To Monique's surprise, Oliveiras spoke up. "Only a few weapons are referred to by their marks," he said. "The mark ten carbine is an example. It's also referred to as an 'eight,' but the mark seven carbine is also eight millimeter. The seven is the semiautomatic version of the ten. The civilians use the seven for hunting."

"So why don't we have thirteens?" Monique asked again.

"I imagine that the colonel didn't have time to arm these trucks before he was discovered stealing them," Wilfz guessed. "Sergeant Van did very well to abscond with these vehicles, thirteens or no."

Monique set the side of her head on her palm, propping herself on her elbow. "You must have a very low opinion of women, Michael Wilfz." Monique was gratified to see how her comment hit home. The major's face became a mask. She watched him as he visibly sought to keep from speaking, his lips pressing into a hard line. She especially enjoyed the confusion in his eyes. *The prude doesn't realize what he has done wrong,* she thought triumphantly.

Without a word, not even a sigh, Wilfz settled himself down and closed his eyes.

Monique cast a glance at the doctor, facing him directly as she noticed the thoughtful look he gave her.

"It's not his fault," he said softly. "Were it not for his respect for women, he would have answered that charge. Instead, he backed down."

"Olly, don't," Wilfz whispered. To Monique, the simple plea sounded like begging.

"I have always wanted to see you admit you were wrong," Oliveiras claimed, "but I won't sit here and see you falsely accused." He turned his attention back to Monique. "He doesn't deserve that," he said. "Neither do you."

Monique looked at the doctor, wondering what he was trying to say.

"Michael is a typical man of Holland. He was raised to respect women," Oliveiras said. "Men here have always guarded women as preciously commodities. The things Michael has seen and done in the line of duty would not be considered proper conversation with the gentler gender."

"The gentler gender," Monique repeated, trying unsuccessfully to keep the doubt out of her voice.

"Men don't bring up unpleasant subjects in the presence of women." Oliveiras went on like a tolerant schoolmaster, ignoring her jibe. "Life on Holland is precarious enough without subjecting our loved ones to undue stress and worry."

"Undue ..." Monique almost sputtered. "That is the most male chauvinistic drivel I have ever heard! You talk as if women are chattel. Commodities, indeed! You are not protecting women, you are dominating them! Women are not as delicate and fragile as you would make them to be. I'm certainly not!"

"Somebody set her off," a muffled voice sounded from outside. "This time it wasn't me." A moment later, the rear door opened and Cameron looked in. Behind him, Sergeant Van stood uneasily, his eyes, as usual, examining something over the heads of the occupants in the field ambulance.

Even Sergeant Van shows that sense of discretion around me.

Oliveiras ignored the newcomers. "Perhaps you see it that way—men keeping the women ignorant of constant risk and threat against them as domination. To us—to Hollanders—it is a kindness. It is the mercy of ignorance to permit our families to live peacefully."

The doctor's voice did not change, but it was clear that he was lecturing.

"This man here," he indicated Wilfz, "has spent over half of his life protecting us all. To call him chauvinistic for facing the brunt of it and choosing not to speak of it—it's … unconscionable."

"That's the nicest thing I have heard anybody say about me," Wilfz said quietly. Monique noticed the resigned expression on Cameron's face. The lieutenant had that look that said, "What has Monique Lewellen done *this* time?"

"The next time I see your parents, I'll tell them that too," Oliveiras promised Wilfz.

Monique leaned over to Wilfz and stared into his face. Sensing her proximity, he opened his eyes. The impression she received from him was one of shame; the indignity of having his world laid bare. At that moment, she truly understood him.

"So that's why you said you were a staff officer," she said softly. "You cited a lack of war as the reason you could not distinguish yourself, yet you have always been at war."

"We don't have war." Wilfz shook his head. "We battle transgressors and keep the peace."

Monique felt ambivalent. Arguing against what she perceived to be his chauvinism, she now had to accept this new perspective. "Perhaps you are right," she conceded. "Before becoming persona non grata, I actually felt very safe in Bremen. I could actually believe your world had never seen warfare."

She saw his eyes narrow. His thoughts were visible to her. He had to know that she was patronizing him … that she had agreed all too easily.

"I've been known to be right on occasion." He gave her a cautious smile, displaying his previous spirit.

A look passed between them. Monique recognized the unspoken truce. She turned to the guardsmen at the door.

"Are you going to come in or stay out? Michael has only just started feeling better." She fixed them with a stern expression. "We don't want him sick again, so make up your minds so you can close that door!"

CHAPTER TWELVE

Silvertip Mountain, Holland

It had taken only a few more nights of travel to reach their destination. They had spent the first night on the main road and then the rest of that time on an overgrown trail that led through the foothills that lay at the base of the mountain. It was daytime when the trucks began traversing the road that threaded up the mountain. The ground was thicker with snow than it had been in the plains area of the bowl. The unfamiliar and elevated terrain was deemed too dangerous to navigate in darkness. The vehicles drove during the day within the concealment of the trees. By mid afternoon, the trucks stopped in a vale beside the mouth of a cavern. A stand of trees hid the wide opening in the mountainside from the vale entrance. To one side of the cave was a covered vehicle port, large enough to park one of their vehicles within.

With Guardsmen Perez and Gray guarding the field ambulance, Lieutenant Cameron led Sergeant Van and Guardsman Schmidt into the cavern. It wasn't long before they returned and declared the cave to be empty of occupation. The temperature inside the ambulance fell uncomfortably each time the door opened.

"It looks like no one has been up here in years," Cameron explained to the occupants in the ambulance. "That surprises me.

It's very nice inside. Now I understand what *HS* means—it stands for hot springs."

"That means hot water," Monique exclaimed eagerly, the warm vapor from her breath coalescing into the cold mountain air before her face. The mere activity of speech had created a delicious vision.

"Actually, once you get through the door, it's very warm inside." Cameron grinned. "The snow is a bit deep here, so we'll carry you two in by stretcher."

"Lady first," Wilfz said.

"Are you really in that much of a hurry to get me away from you?" Monique asked him.

"You shouldn't be with me in the first place," Wilfz replied obliquely.

Perez and Schmidt carried Monique into the cavern, Oliveiras accompanying them to oversee her transfer. Monique looked around curiously as she was carried beneath the rock overhang. With her eyes blinded from the glare off the snow, the cave at first appeared to be nothing but darkness. The doctor switched on a hand lamp, illuminating the way for the stretcher-bearing guardsmen. Ahead of them was a wall with an open door in the center of it. As they walked the doorway, Schmidt spoke up. "There are electrical lights in here, but there's no power going to them."

"There's probably a generator," Oliveiras commented.

Monique said nothing. After spending days in the back of an ambulance and seeing the outdoors only during their stops, she drank in the new surroundings. As they passed through the door, the cold breeze lost its bite against their exposed skin.

Inside, a table was set against one rocky wall. On the other side of the doorway was an open area. Under the feet of the men came the hollow sound of wood flooring. Oliveiras' light reflected off of the interior ahead of them, casting shadows behind the group. Deeper in the cavern, bunks with lower and upper berths were set up on each side. They were made of quick-connecting metal framework, and there was a mattress with impermeable coverings on each bunk.

"Set her down here," Oliveiras instructed. "I'll wipe the bed down so she'll have a clean place to lie down."

The men obediently lowered the stretcher to the floor.

"Oh, it's cold!" Wilfz's quavering voice sounded as he hobbled in through the door, Sergeant Van supporting him by the shoulder. In his free arm he carried his carbine.

"Don't tell me you walked in here in your bare feet," Oliveiras asked angrily.

"Okay, I won't," Wilfz said with a chuckle in his voice.

"Sergeant, you guys were supposed to carry him here."

"Olly, don't take it out on the good sergeant," Wilfz said as Van helped him to the bunk nearest to the door. "He would have had to hurt me to stop me. It was easier to let me walk." Wilfz sat on the bunk and pulled his feet up into his blanket. "I want my clothes," he declared.

"I want a bath," Monique chimed in. "You said there's a spring here, right? I can wash in hot water for a change?"

"Let's get moved in first," Cameron spoke up.

"I'll see about getting you two cleaned up," Oliveiras said.

"Let her wash. Then you and the men," Wilfz decided, rubbing his wet feet inside his blanket.

"That's going to be a while," Oliveiras said. "You should wash now."

"Officers take care of the men first," Wilfz explained. "You know that, Olly."

"But they're not your men," Monique said.

"It's the principle of the thing," Oliveiras automatically spoke up for Wilfz. "Lieutenant Cameron does call the major 'sir.'"

Wilfz settled on his side with the blanket tucked in around him. He hugged his carbine to himself, the muzzle of the weapon extending past his head. Monique watched as he visibly relaxed. She did not doubt that he quickly fell asleep.

"I can't believe he dropped off so fast." Monique spoke in amazement. A critical frown appeared on her face. "He's sleeping on a dirty mattress."

"That's his prerogative," Oliveiras shrugged. "Let me take a look through the rest of this place and see about your bath."

Oliveiras went deeper into the cavern, taking the light with him. He disappeared around the turn in the cave, the illumination descending indicating that the floor sloped downward. In the meantime the guardsmen brought in the gear. Monique listened to them discuss their new surroundings while they worked. Perez mentioned that he could probably hook one of the truck generators to the cavern electrical system. Schmidt reported that canned goods were stored at the deep end of the cavern. Gray noticed a fuel tank by the vehicle port and would inspect it later. They agreed that someone had obviously taken the effort to set up the cavern for emergency occupation.

◆※◗

"Major Wilfz."

Wilfz was sound asleep when his name was called, the voice seeming to come from far away. Comfortably warm for the first time in recent memory, he was loath to wake up.

"Major, it's Cameron." Wilfz felt a tug at his blanket, the rough fabric scratching his bare skin. He opened his eyes, seeing only a confused blur in the darkness. He didn't move for several moments, waiting for his vision to adjust. He could tell that the space around him was larger than the truck. Wilfz tried to reconcile his present surroundings with his memory.

"Major?"

He noticed Lieutenant Cameron kneeling by the bunk. The officer watched him warily from a distance of an arm span. The major had barely moved since he'd gone to sleep. His arms were still wrapped around his weapon, his head resting against the fore stock. It was obvious that the Celestial Guard officer was unsure how the battle-experienced officer would react upon waking. Wilfz was familiar with the caution. The carbine made an effective club after all.

Wilfz remembered their arrival at tunnel HS—the hot spring. The heated tunnel had been a welcome respite after so many days living in perpetual cold. His wounded body had been exhausted from the constant expenditure of energy necessary to generate warmth. For the first time in recent memory, he had actually slept very well. As the last of the sleep fog cleared his mind, he returned his attention to the patiently waiting Celestial Guard officer. "We're here," he said with a yawn.

"Everybody's washed and waiting on you," Oliveiras called out from the inner cavern.

Wilfz propped his carbine on its butt stock and used it to pull himself up. Once in a sitting position, he shifted his feet to the floor.

"I think we should talk this evening," Cameron said.

"We can talk while I wash." Wilfz nodded toward the inner cavern as he gingerly stood up. He wavered unsteadily. The Celestial Guard officer took him by the arm for support, and Wilfz thanked him.

It was evening, and the only illumination in the cavern came from battery-powered lights. Wilfz counted the number of bunks. There were seven sets of double bunks, more than enough for the present occupants. If a patrol were to encamp here, there wouldn't be enough bunks for them. The cavern could comfortably house a troop, which corroborated with the single-space truck park. He pondered at the impracticality of taking this amount of effort only to create a hiding place for a unit as small as a troop.

He noticed that Gray was standing sentry duty by the door, his rifle slung from his shoulder. Perez and Schmidt had already taken to the bunks and were asleep. Sergeant Van was in the process of getting ready to lie down. He nodded to the sergeant, who returned his nod of greeting.

On the bottom bunk closest to the inner cave he found Monique asleep on her side. With her face to the dim light, Wilfz could see her pinched look of pain. His own back pain had since faded to a momentary throb, flaring up only when he overexerted himself. In his case, that meant the times he had to answer the call of nature. It still humiliated him.

He shuffled with Cameron's assistance past the barrack area. The cavern had a slight bend to the right and dipped downward, the planked floor following smoothly. Lighting had been installed overhead, but the area was dark at the moment due to the lack of electricity. To one side of the cavern was a level platform that served as the kitchen—a long workbench with canned goods stored beneath. Across the ramp from the bench was shelving that held more cans.

The air had steadily become warmer as they progressed. Farther down the ramp, in a wall that extended half a meter above his head but did not reach the ceiling, were two doors. They stood open to reveal a pair of rooms; one was for bathing, the other was a water closet. At the end of the cavern was a wall that sealed the end of the cavern from floor to ceiling. It was inset with a sturdy door that was barricaded closed by means of a beam set on brackets fixed on either side. Wilfz could only imagine what lay further down the cavern.

"I'm glad to see that," Wilfz indicated the water closet. Inside was a bench set over a trough of running water. Inside the room, which was located downstream from the washroom, water was diverted from the channel through the trough. From there, it went into a second channel that disappeared through the wall. "If you don't mind …" said Wilfz, indicating that he should like to use the room.

When he emerged, he was carrying the blanket as well as his weapon. He put the blanket down on the floor then placed the carbine upon it. Going into the washroom, he noted the simple construction. A moveable sluice had been added to the side of the channel. Beneath it was a stool within a sunken stone floor. Downhill was a drain that led beneath the floor of the water closet.

"Not so much a bath as a waterfall," Wilfz surmised, looking at the sluice.

Cameron indicated one of half a dozen towels draped over the washroom wall. "This one might be dry now," he suggested

Wilfz reached into the channel and touched the flowing water with his finger. It was not as hot as he thought it would be. Thinking of the bandage taped to his back, he muttered to himself, "I hope this doesn't wash off." He sat on the stool and pulled the sluice down. Water poured over his head and shoulders.

"I have ears," he said to Cameron. "What's going on?"

"Perez has been trying to build that transformer we talked about before."

"He has wire?"

"There was a spool of communications wire in the command truck."

Unable to do anything else with water in his face, Wilfz raised his eyebrows at the reference to Cameron's truck. The lieutenant apparently noticed, for he promptly explained. "Perez found the wire and telephones. We figure they're for setting up listening posts when your Constabulary sets up camp."

Wilfz nodded in agreement.

"He's been trying his best with what there is at hand. I've been watching him coil wire around a paper construct to make air core windings. If he can't get it to work, come spring the radio will be dead."

"The Constabulary has battery-operated equipment. Do you suppose Perez could get the batteries to work with your radio?" Wilfz suggested.

"He said the same thing," Cameron admitted. "It's a matter of how long those batteries will last. Yours are not rechargeable, so it's an iffy proposition either way. Of course, it might not be necessary ..."

Blinking the water away from his eyes, Wilfz looked at the lieutenant. The man was trying to bring up a new subject. It was clear that the battery issue was just an excuse to bring it up. He remained silent, permitting the Celestial Guard officer to broach it on his own.

"We won't need the transformer if we can get the envoy out," Cameron said. "Can we get over the mountain now?"

"It would be tough going in the best of weather," Wilfz said thoughtfully, "but the lady is in no condition to make the journey. Even if she were carried, it would be too dangerous. With the snow, we couldn't carry her and make the trek over the mountain. Only one force could do that. First Mountain, but they're not here."

"Suppose she has the surgery first?"

"By the time she can travel, winter will be set in. Snow gets deep in the passes. First Mountain is the only unit that would be able to attempt it."

"We're pretty capable ourselves," Cameron said.

Wilfz lifted the sluice to stop the fall of water over his head. Wiping his face clear, he looked at the lieutenant. "Yeah," he nodded in agreement. "Hand me the soap."

He ran his hand over the side of his face. As he accepted the soap, he spoke again. "I really ought to shave this sometime."

"Actually, I believe that was requested, sir."

"Eunice?"

Cameron's look was indecipherable. It wasn't the first time he'd received a funny look whenever he mentioned Lady Lewellen.

"It was the doctor," Cameron answered him after a pause. "He said that your haggard face makes you look older than he is. He doesn't want to feel any older through association than he has to."

"Hunh." Wilfz grunted with a faint smile on his face.

Wilfz felt renewed once he had removed the thick growth of beard from his face. After his wash, it seemed odd not to be freezing. He still marveled at not seeing his exhaled breath after spending seemingly endless days in the back of the ambulance.

Oliveiras arrived, carrying a set of folded clothes.

"I'll examine your back before you put these on," he said.

"I don't see boots," Wilfz observed.

"You won't get them until I deem you are ready," Oliveiras said imperiously. "You'll go right outside, get too tired to come back, and then die of exposure."

Wilfz looked at him skeptically.

"Don't look at me like that," Oliveiras ordered. "You're carrying that rifle with you everywhere you go. I know what you're thinking."

"I need the exercise," Wilfz insisted.

"You need physical therapy," Oliveiras declared. "Your legs shouldn't still be bothering you after all this time."

The doctor inspected Wilfz's back wound and replaced the water-sodden bandage with a fresh one. Wilfz donned the light brown field shirt and trousers. They felt loose, but he carefully cinched the belt. He had discovered that seemingly unrelated movement would pull at the healing wound in his back.

With the carbine cradled in arm, he returned to the living area of the cavern. He noticed some of the gear had been placed by the wall on the landing at the head of the ramp. The packs were Constabulary issue. Curious, he sat by them and crossed his legs. He set his weapon upright on one thigh and let it rest against his shoulder as he pulled a pack toward him.

"Put that thing away and I will feed you," Oliveiras ordered, holding a can of meal. Purposely misunderstanding, Wilfz pressed the pack back where he had found it. Oliveiras sighed. "I meant your carbine."

"The carbine stays with me," Wilfz announced.

"No one is going to find us here," Oliveiras said. "You don't need to be armed all the time in here."

"I know." Wilfz nodded. "Indulge me."

"Indulge you?" Oliveiras sounded incredulous. "What if that thing goes off? A bullet could ricochet in here!"

"Safety on, no round in the chamber." Wilfz sounded reasonable. A sudden motion caught his eye. From where Monique lay, her blanket was suddenly flung aside.

There was a groan as she set her feet on the wooden floor. She was half shrouded in darkness, but Wilfz could still see her squint against the battery-powered light illuminating the common area of the ramp. She stood and carefully padded toward Oliveiras. The doctor looked at her and did not resist as she took the meal can from his hands.

Wilfz observed the fit of Monique's Constabulary field uniform. The trousers were too short, barely covering her calves and showing off her slender ankles. The days in the field ambulance had caused him to forget how tall she was. The shirt fit better, though, and she had not tucked it in; she was wearing it as if it were a jacket.

Monique gave the can to Wilfz. Turning away, she made a big show of yawning into her hands. She padded back to her bunk and lay down.

Wilfz watched her thoughtfully as she sought to get comfortable. She shifted with difficulty until she had satisfactorily arranged herself. Looking up at Oliveiras, Wilfz motioned for the doctor to join him on the floor. Taking the hint, Oliveiras sat down. In a very low voice, Wilfz spoke. "When will you operate on her?"

Oliveiras was silent for a moment, thinking. "We need to have reliable power in here first," the doctor determined. "I will need to bring the equipment in from the ambulance and make sure it works."

"What equipment?"

"Surgical lights, for one. There is also the ultrasound. I will need it to get a good look inside before I start cutting. In order to have that, we need electricity in here."

"We'll get you set up," Wilfz said with certainty.

"What do you mean, 'we'? You can barely drag that rifle around," Oliveiras said. "You are obviously delirious from hunger. Here's a spoon. Eat."

Wilfz accepted the flat wooden implement. Before he opened the ration can, he placed his carbine across his lap, the muzzle pointing to an unoccupied part of the cavern.

"Is there another pair of trousers in her size?" he asked, opening the can.

"I think so. Why?"

Instead of answering, he spooned out some cornmeal and occupied himself with eating. Oliveiras looked at the pack that Wilfz had pushed away, wondering if that had something to do with his question.

"I'm too tired for this. It's been a long day." The doctor stifled a yawn. "Don't stay up too late."

Wilfz nodded to him.

Noting Gray on sentry duty, Wilfz remained awake, busy with a pair of trousers. With a sewing kit from a pack, he cut the trousers at mid leg. On the trousers proper, he completely opened up the inseam. Taking the lower legs he had cut free, he split the seams to make them flat panels. Tailored to fit the human form, the upper part was wider than the lower. Inverting the panels to put the narrow end at the top, he reattached them to the front and back of the trousers and carefully stitched them in place. When he finished, he was surprised to look up and see Van standing in place of Gray.

❖

Monique woke brightly, if not a little lonely in the morning. Rising, she quickly sought out the major.

Wilfz lay on the floor where he had fallen asleep. It was warmer near the hot spring channel, so he had not sought a blanket for warmth. He was lying on his side with his head resting on a half-empty pack. The arm he lay on loosely hugged the pack while his other hand rested on the foregrip of his carbine. Monique knelt before him, her eyes intent on his peaceful face.

In the meantime Sergeant Van had quietly awakened the Celestial Guard team. It did not go unnoticed when Monique began poking experimentally at Wilfz.

"You might want to be careful," Cameron said. "He could get violent if you wake him the wrong way."

"He's never hurt me before," Monique declared. She touched his shoulder again.

"Hng!" Wilfz's guttural utterance was accompanied by an impromptu attempt to push her away. His hand found her trouser-clad knee instead. The woman emitted a surprised gasp and almost jumped at his sudden movement.

"I warned you," Cameron said.

Monique bit off a reply as she felt Wilfz's fingers rub her leg through the fabric of her trousers. A smile replaced her sense of irritability at Cameron's words as she kept her attention on the major. She placed a hand over his.

"It's called a knee," she said playfully. She felt his hand tweak in response. She tried to hold onto him, but he managed to pull his hand free. Looking at his face, it seemed to her that he was too tired to open his eyes. Unerringly, his freed hand found his weapon and he pulled it toward him.

"When did you get to sleep?" she asked. Wilfz did not reply.

"He was still up when I turned over the watch to Van," Gray volunteered.

Monique looked inquiringly at Van.

"He's been asleep for about three hours," the sergeant estimated.

"What was he doing all night?" Oliveiras wandered over as he buttoned up his shirt.

"He was sewing," Van reported.

"Sewing?" Monique asked.

"Many men in the field mend their own clothes," Oliveiras explained.

"What did he do to damage his clothes?" Monique wondered out loud, reaching for a pair of neatly folded trousers. The garment unfurled into a skirt. "Oh! This seems rather suggestive."

"Michael talked to me about this last night," Oliveiras said. "He was concerned about you."

"I'm sure," Monique replied suspiciously. "For a prude, his creation will show a little too much leg!"

"I was trying to keep the hem straight," Michael spoke with a sleepy voice. "The pant legs were too short to make a long hem."

"Why would you do this?" Monique asked, critically examining the skirt as she held it out at arm's length.

"I was thinking about your surgery," he said. "After the operation, you won't want to move too much. It will be hard enough without privacy. I thought a skirt would be easier for you to put on."

He went silent as Monique thought about what he'd said. Before she could reply, he spoke again. "After what we did in the truck, I want to save you from additional humiliation."

Monique examined the stitching as she considered what he meant. He had suffered humiliation when the guardsmen helped him out of the truck when nature called. He had been very grouchy during those times of day. In her view, she felt sorry for the guardsmen. Like Wilfz, she also had to suffer the indignity of being helped out of the truck, but her modesty did not seem to be as extreme as his.

"This stitching is very regular," she observed, turning the garment over in her hands to follow the seams. "You must have spent all night on this."

Wilfz did not answer. Hearing the rhythm of his breathing, she knew he had fallen back to sleep. Monique peered inside to examine the craftsmanship. "I see," she marveled. "The seams were opened from leg to leg."

Reaching to her waist, she unbuckled and removed the belt from her trousers.

"What are you doing? You're going to change your clothes here?" Cameron asked.

She used to change her clothes when it was just the two of them talking, but not in front of the others. She knew that her arrogant lack of modesty was only one of the things about her that annoyed him. She predicted that her intention to disrobe in front of everyone would add to his consternation.

"I want to put this on," Monique raised the skirt over her head and let it slip down around her. Once it was settled around her hips, she stood up to let the loose trousers fall. Stepping out of the discarded garment, she found herself to be the center of attention. She looked down to see her appearance for herself.

The skirt was shorter than she preferred, ending just above her knees. Despite that, the effect was not displeasing, even if she thought so herself. The years she had spent swimming, as well as dancing in rehearsals and before the camera, had given her slender legs a healthy tone.

"We call this a rapid wardrobe change back in the business," she preened, plucking at her new skirt.

"Why is that even necessary?" Oliveiras asked.

"Often we perform on stage before live audiences." Monique made a cautious pirouette, her skirt flaring out a little. "There are times when we have to hurry and get back in front of the audience in another costume."

Monique was insufferably pleased with herself. Comfortably warm for the first time in days, not to mention clean, she was experiencing emotional relief. Now that they were away from the road, the threat of discovery by hostile forces seemed remote. The explanation about her previous career was a result of introspection. The lack of activity while confined in the back of the ambulance had given her time for personal contemplation. For all of that, she felt more nostalgic than regretful.

Monique thought about her playful attempt to wake the major. Once she had learned that he had been awake all night, she desisted, but her manner had been uncommonly relaxed. She felt she was a different woman from the aloof former actress who had initially been assigned to the team—well, maybe not completely different, judging from the occasional verbal sparring she engaged in with Cameron. Her difficult behavior toward him had become the basis of their personal relationship. That habit had become ingrained and, if she really wanted to be honest with herself, it was something she wanted to continue.

Beneath the 'I'm so much better than this' persona she had projected in Bremen was a women who behaved at an almost practical level, which had been demonstrated during the time she had spent cooped up in the truck with these men. Rather than resent the lack of privacy, she had embraced it, using it as an opportunity to become familiar with the men in company with her.

She treated Doctor Oliveiras with the same due diligence that she would bestow on her own father. The older man had become something like the patriarch of the group. At the moment, he was talking to Monique about her hair.

"It'll be a year. No one will see you in that time, except for us, of course," he informed her.

Monique sat facing him. With one hand behind her head, she had gathered her hair and was now worrying at it with her fingers.

"It has become a bit much to handle," she admitted, "as of late, anyway."

"By spring, it'll have grown back," Oliveiras determined.

"I doubt that." She slowly shook her head. "My hair doesn't grow that fast."

"What's going on?" Cameron asked.

"I thought it would be easier on her right now if she were to cut her hair. There would be less bother for her," Oliveiras explained.

"Unless I could get someone to wash it for me," Monique ventured.

Cameron expressed a sour look.

Monique suddenly laughed, raising the back of her hand to her mouth as she pointed at him with her other hand. "You should see your face," she said. "You look as if I had just insulted you."

Oliveiras looked on curiously.

"It was a joke. I'm joking! You must think I'm really vain," she continued with a delighted look. She returned her attention to the doctor. "Yes, please cut my hair."

Her smile faded when she looked back down to Wilfz. She realized that she was more at ease when the major was awake. It had become evident to her during the time she had spent quietly watching him sleep in the ambulance. When he slept, she felt unusually solemn and thoughtful. That was not like her. When he was awake, she delighted in tormenting his sensibilities with her playful manner, rejoicing in the banter.

◄※►

Monique was folding her clothes on a blanket when Wilfz woke up. She had purposely set herself next to the slumbering Constabulary officer. At the moment, they were alone in the cavern while the other men were working outside.

Shifting the carbine onto its butt, Wilfz once again used the weapon to lever himself into a sitting position. Blinking the sleep out of his eyes, he noticed what she was doing. She placed her hands on her lap and regarded him with a fond look. His quizzical expression informed her that he noticed her short hair. She tilted her head sideways to emphasize the view, her cut hair fanning to the side. As she privately had predicted, Wilfz looked away from her face. She couldn't help smiling at his discomfort. He couldn't look at her for the sake of looking at her.

She observed that he was looking at her things. Included were her undergarments. She was not surprised to see him look away, but she was taken aback by his strenuous protest.

"You lied," he accused incredulously. "You said you only had the one set."

"It's not my fault that you believed me." Monique's light tone conveyed her amusement at his reaction.

"You could have worn that and still kept us warm," he said.

"But my way was more fun," she declared.

Wilfz made a grimace, his expression an opinion of her fun. Monique noticed his shift of attention as he looked around.

"They're moving the generator to the little room," she explained. Seeing his puzzlement, she went on. "There's a little room outside that's wired into this place. Sergeant Van said something about fuel stocks with water in it, or something. The only thing the room did not have is an ox generator."

"Aux?" Wilfz repeated. "Auxiliary."

"That's what I said." Monique smiled then sobered as she continued. "Doctor Oliveiras is checking his equipment. Some of it has to come in to warm up before he can use it. He's especially concerned about the ultrasound."

She shivered for a moment, having reservations about the surgical procedure that was planned for her. She had been contemplating what could happen to her during the operation. The exaggerated care that the Celestial Guardians had taken with her, combined with the tentative diagnosis by Oliveiras, only served to reinforce her fear and compound the worry. The piece of shrapnel in her back could shift and cause irreparable damage from an injudicious motion on her part. That was why the ultrasound was so important. The device would be able to tell the doctor where the fragment was. It would minimize the extent of the exploratory surgery and reduce the risk of collateral harm during extraction.

"He's very good," Wilfz said.

Monique gave herself a mental shake, raising an eyebrow in query.

"Olly," he explained. "He's good at what he does."

"I want you to do something for me," Monique blurted.

Wilfz said nothing.

"I want you to be with me when I wake up," she said.

"I'm not going anywhere." Wilfz gave her a reassuring smile.

"I'm serious," she insisted, her gaze unwavering. "I want you by me when I wake up after the surgery."

Even after all the time she had spent with this man, it seemed that he was unaccustomed to looking her in the eyes. Especially in the field ambulance, she had found it difficult to get him to look at her at all. Perhaps the reason was that she had been so bold.

He did not look so uneasy in her presence now that they were both properly dressed. Looking into his face she noticed for the first time that his eyes were brown.

"Please." Monique quietly spoke with entreaty. It was in his power to provide her with peace of mind, if only he would to it.

"I'll be there, right next to you when you awaken," Wilfz conceded to her relief.

"The bunks aren't really that wide." She looked over to the sleeping area to confirm her analysis.

"I'm not sleeping with you anymore."

Wilfz had obviously spoken without conscious thought. Monique made no attempt to conceal the surprised expression on her face. She watched him become contrite in response.

"I meant that I will be at your bedside when you awake."

"I know what you meant," she replied. "I also remember what you told me before."

She could see him trying to figure out what she alluded to. She was remembering his reference to her reputation. He had been afraid of sullying her reputation just because they had shared body heat.

When it came to her personal morals, she was not exactly proud of herself. She had to admit that she liked the idea that someone cared that she maintain a good name for herself … especially someone who had absolutely nothing to gain from it. It was one thing for Cameron and his men to worry about her. It was their responsibility to safeguard her. If she were to attempt to do something shameful, she was reasonably positive that one of them would prevent her. In so doing, they would limit the shame to them by association, of course.

Not that it would stop her from trying. She could admit that she had been a difficult charge in their care. Perhaps that was why she had been so mischievous with Wilfz. The outrageousness helped take her mind off the upcoming surgery. She knew it was a very delicate procedure, and there was no guarantee that the doctor would not inadvertently cripple or kill her. Van had refused to let Perez do it. Though Perez was proven as a good medical assistant, Van knew better than to attempt a risky procedure unless it was absolutely necessary.

Wilfz did not seem to notice that Monique had become quiet with her thoughts for a long moment. "They started the generator," he said.

"I don't hear anything." Monique looked toward the door that led outdoors.

"Feel that?"

"I feel nothing."

"The vibration from the generator." Wilfz pointed at the floor.

Monique touched the blanket she knelt on then moved her hand to the bare wood floor. She shook her head at the major.

"Hngh!" Wilfz tapped on the floor with his knuckles, moving his fist across the surface experimentally. The noise conveyed hollowness until he reached a point in front of him where the tapping noise became sharper and shorter. "I seem to be directly on a joist. The vibration is traveling directly up from the footing."

"Then shouldn't I feel it, too?" She slipped her fingers around the floor. "Oh! I see what you mean."

"It's a small generator. The vibrations only go so far," he surmised.

Fascinated, Monique lay on her side and pressed an ear to the floor. Though she could barely feel it, she could better hear the sound of the rapid cycle of an internal combustion engine through the wood.

"Noise travels through solids easier than through the air," Wilfz explained. Monique already knew that simple fact, but chose not to reply.

The door opened and Oliveiras shuffled into the room, clapping his hands together to get the blood to circulate. He looked toward them.

"What are you doing to her?" he demanded. Monique could understand his puzzlement at seeing Wilfz propped up with his carbine and Monique lying sprawled before him.

"I woke up," said Wilfz.

Oliveiras goggled at Wilfz, seemingly dumbfounded into silence at his answer.

Not wishing to laugh at the physician, Monique reached over and gripped Wilfz's ankle, letting loose a brief giggle at him instead. "He said that the generator is running and I didn't believe him." She released him after giving his leg a squeeze.

"How could you possibly know that?" Oliveiras asked.

"Lucky guess." Wilfz shrugged, eliciting another giggle from Monique.

Behind the doctor Sergeant Van entered. Monique watched as he took in the tableaux. She half expected him to roll his eyes toward the ceiling at the spectacle she was presenting. She was surprised when the sergeant gave a little smile of amusement.

With stamping feet, the rest of the team entered behind the sergeant. It was apparent that they had been doing more than just setting up the generator. From their boots to their knees every guardsman was covered with dirt and snow. The last man to return inside was Lieutenant Cameron. Using his back to close the door, he peeled his gloves off and flexed his fingers experimentally.

Out of the corner of her eye, Monique saw Wilfz give a slight nod. Looking at him, she saw a glimmer of approval in his expression. It was reminiscent of a superior pleased with the conduct of a subordinate. She remembered Wilfz's admonition; an officer saw to the needs of his men first. Cameron had entered the tunnel only after seeing his men go inside for warmth first. She could actually imagine Wilfz getting his hands dirty alongside his own men.

"Digging another cave?" Wilfz asked.

"No, sir." Cameron shook his head. "The vehicle port will only hold one truck. A pretty sweet setup. Someone made a garage and covered it over with earth. They probably wanted to make another on the other side." As the officer spoke, he first pointed to his left then pointed to his right as he went on. "They started with a parking area, but didn't finish. We just widened it so we could park the ambulance under the trees. Unless someone lands on top of us, no one is going to know we're here."

"Once we get warmed up, we'll bring in the doctor's equipment." Van spoke to his guardsmen.

"Warmed up and fed, I would think," Monique piped up. "You were out there a long time. Let me warm some canned broth." Before she could rise, Oliveiras interjected. "Just stay there, my dear," he said kindly. "We can manage."

Alert to the way Oliveiras spoke, in Monique's mind his "we can manage" translated to "don't risk yourself." Her face became stiff as the brightness faded from her expression. She had become sensitive toward any reference to her physical wellbeing.

Wilfz leaned close to her, attracting her attention. Looking to him, she saw the concern in his eyes. He had apparently noticed her change of mood. When he spoke up, his manner was conspiratorial. "The tyrant won't let me have boots."

Monique's lips parted, but she had no words. Wilfz had come to her rescue in the only way he could, as if he was her personal champion.

"Of course not! You would have gone out there and worn yourself out trying to dig in that cold ground," Oliveiras replied.

"The ground hasn't frozen yet," Wilfz declared.

"And in your condition, we would have had to carry you back in. You would be all worn out and feverish," Oliveiras complained. "And you know why? You cannot follow doctor's orders. You are supposed to rest. Instead, you stay up all night and undo all of the good that I've done for you." He turned to Monique. "And you, young lady, I thought you were helping me."

"Me?" Monique chirped in surprise. "What have I done?"

Having witnessed Oliveiras in full-blown anger, Monique could tell that his heart was not in his diatribe against her now. In a moment of insight, she realized that he was taking a gruff tone with her. Rather than acknowledge her weakness, he was treating her as if she were not as delicate as she really was. In short, the man was manipulating her feelings. Under other circumstances, she would feel outrage.

"Leave her out of this." Wilfz's tone was low, almost a whisper.

It could be her theatrical background that enabled her to discern what was going on. It could also be that Wilfz's inexperience around women was blinding him. In either case—perhaps both—she could see that the major was unaware of the doctor's perceived motive.

In any event, she was developing a tangible fondness for the two men.

"You two are a real handful, you know that?" Oliveiras complained. He threw his hands up, signaling a desire to avoid further debate. "Just let me rest. I know you're glad to be out of that truck, but take it easy. Okay?"

While the doctor was talking, Van had gone over to the cavern wall and activated an electrical switch mounted on a joist. Light fixtures mounted on beams over the sleeping area walkway blazed on.

"Well, these work," Cameron spoke up, looking at the fixtures overhead. To Monique, it sounded as if the lieutenant was trying to fill an uncomfortable silence.

"It's dark over here." She made her own contribution to the conversation.

"Different circuit." Van walked over to the common area and operated the switch, de-energizing the lights in the sleeping area. He turned it back on. "Hmm, a three-way switch." He located another switch and turned it on.

The lights over Monique and Wilfz lit up first, followed by the fixtures over the storage area, and then the ones down in the wash area.

Monique lowered her face, blinking in the brighter illumination of the cavern. She gave a moan of dissatisfaction as she viewed herself in the new light.

"Look at this," she gripped the calf of one of her legs. "The tone is gone. It's flabby."

"You've been inactive for a while," Oliveiras said. "It's normal."

"I'm not normal." Monique shook her head, not looking up. "I'm me."

❧�֎❧

Later in the day, after Monique put her things away, she sat across from Wilfz. He was sitting in his customary spot on the floor near the kitchen, the dossier open before him. "This winter is going to be over in a year," he announced. "After I take you over the mountain, I'll never see you guys again. I can't see getting too attached to you."

Wilfz was becoming increasingly distant. Now that they were no longer forced to share close company, it was as if the major was reestablishing his personal space. At least that was how Monique viewed his latest comment.

"Come with us," she urged. "You don't have to stay here. The colonel asked us to take you and the doctor with us."

"This is my home. Olly can go with you. He'll be safer with you than he would be if I dragged him back."

"But you'll be alone … in the mountains … by yourself …" she purposely paused for dramatic effect.

"It won't be the first time. All I need is my eight." He shifted the carbine in his arm for emphasis.

"If you stay alone and find that there's nothing left, what then?" Monique was horrified by the insensitivity of what she was asking him. She had as much as intimated that it was possible his family was gone.

"Then I will be alone," Wilfz said simply. The hard set of his features told Monique that he understood what she had implied. That realization filled her with fear, not for herself but for him.

"I shouldn't have said that." Monique reached over to touch his arm.

"Nothing I haven't already been thinking," he replied dismissively as he glanced at her hand in an absent manner. Even though he claimed to be unaffected, his words did not make her feel better.

Wilfz had been studying the dossier, and he had explained what was puzzling him as he wondered what the opposition hoped to accomplish. Monique listened to his comments as he talked to her while he fingered the documents. When he was finished, she commented that the quest for power for the sake of power was too simplistic. After saying that, she noticed that everyone was looking at her. Admittedly it wasn't something that anyone would have expected her say. She held out a slender arm to Wilfz. "Let me see that," she requested, "the other part that you aren't reading."

The information that Wilfz handed over was primarily background on Holland.

"I seem to remember something about Maitland," she mumbled, thumbing through the pages. "I remember thinking that Genda had been very thorough in compiling this."

"You actually read that?" Cameron asked.

"I read the whole thing once," Monique admitted. "Then I reread parts when you criticized my conclusion. I have since revised my opinion."

When she made that confession, she was looking at Wilfz. Having returned his attention to his research, there was no way the major noticed the significant look she gave him. It was not unusual for Monique and Cameron to exchange sharp words with each other on occasion after all. In this instance, he could not know that he had been the controversial topic that Monique referred to … that she had misjudged him. "What would happen if someone showed up to collect?" she asked.

"It's been hundreds of years. Isn't there a statute of limitation?" Oliveiras objected.

"Many nations have statutes." Monique nodded. "But they can't impose them outside of their boundaries. Not unless there is a treaty, membership, or charter.

"It seems unlikely, but I can't imagine a foreign military invading over an ancient debt."

"We have the Constabulary in case that should happen," Oliveiras said.

"Do you?" Monique asked, her tone suggesting that she questioned his belief.

Oliveiras and Wilfz looked at each other. It was clear they understood her point. The Constabulary that they were on the run from was not the same law enforcement organization that had previously enjoyed their trust.

"Suppose there isn't any objection to foreign receivership from Holland?" Monique continued.

"What would Holland gain from giving up to the foreigners?" Oliveiras asked.

"I think it would depend on what they were giving up," Monique said ambiguously, "and more importantly, who is in control of Holland when that time comes."

Everyone was silent as that idea sank in.

"Too bad we can't communicate off-planet. If we can find out whoever holds the papers, we could stop them," Monique expounded out loud.

"That's not in our purview. It's not our place to interfere with the governing of Holland. That's a civil matter, not a criminal one," Cameron said in clarification. "In any case, it's not our responsibility, no matter what."

"What about what's happening here?" Monique snapped, displeased at being thwarted.

"There's no proof that's any more than an internal matter. The Celestial Empire has no jurisdiction here," Cameron explained.

"What about your jurisdiction? Don't you have jurisdiction as long as your ward is in your sight? That's your mandate, right? Or am I mistaken?"

"That applies only for your protection and in support of your area of *responsibility*." Cameron stressed the last word meaningfully. "You don't have that authority, so the Celestial Guard has no legal standing to support you in that."

Wilfz spoke up. "So that means that, as a representative of Holland, I am the defendant here, not a claimant."

"That's not necessarily so," Oliveiras interjected. "If you'd paid more attention to your history, you'd know that the ninety-nine-year charter has a finite life span. Unless it's renewed, once it expires, it's no longer binding."

"There goes my theory." Monique sighed.

"Not quite," Oliveiras replied. "From what I read in that packet, Maitland and Holland had a separate agreement when they parted ways. As the senior partner, Maitland stipulated that Holland make payments. That contract was still in effect when Maitland was merged into a conglomerate. Holland went out of business before the end of the original charter, but since a second contract was in play at the same time, that one may still have an effect today. Somewhere it's possible that contract still exists."

"If there was a stipulation about breach of contract, such as failure to maintain payments," Monique supposed, "then why didn't the new management come and take possession?"

"I imagine economics," Oliveiras said. "The same reason Maitland departed. It was economically unfeasible to come all the way out here and take issue."

"What would have changed to make it more feasible?"

"Holland has a more diverse economy now," Oliveiras said, "and a stable population that can support commerce."

"In other words, a population that can be subjugated and exploited," Wilfz summarized.

CHAPTER THIRTEEN

The hot spring cavern, Silvertip Mountain

It was quiet in the cavern now. It hadn't been much noisier during the surgery.

Doctor Oliveiras had spent a lot of time working over Monique. He had decided it would be best to operate in the coolest area of the cave, which was right next to the door to the outdoors. Extra lights had been set up over the front doorway, and the interior shutters over the windows had been opened for additional illumination.

Using the ultrasound, he had determined where the invasive pieces were.

With Guardsman Perez' assistance, he had carefully opened up the wound in the woman's back. Exercising great caution, he skillfully cut his way in. As he had feared, the fragments had shifted. In addition to the twisted piece of shrapnel from the explosive cannon shell, sand-like masonry had also been penetrated her flesh.

After the surgery, he announced his certainty that he had removed every bit of foreign matter. His biggest concern was that a nerve in her spine had been bruised. One fragment had been very close, and he was worried that he may have exacerbated the damage in removing it. As if that weren't enough, he was also worried about the septic environment of the cavern. The bare stone overhead was not hermetically sealed. The air was filled with microscopic dust falling unseen from the exposed ceiling and walls. As long as he was able to disinfect the wound properly, the chance of infection was minimal. Still, he gave voice to his displeasure that something in the environment might jeopardize her safety. The only thing the doctor had said regarding Monique's recovery was that they would have to "wait and see." That prognosis was more to himself that to anyone else, much less to Wilfz.

Although ordinarily this would be considered a fairly minor operation, the exaggerated care he had exercised had strained him to his limits. After he had closed her up, the guardsmen had carried her to her bunk to recover. It was all he could do to wash up before he dropped into his own bunk. "I'm getting too old for this," was his last comment.

Wilfz sat on the floor at Monique's bedside. His carbine lay underneath the bunk, never far from his grasp. The other men had found various activities to occupy their time while they waited for the result of the surgery. Perez and Schmidt were rigging the generator to start and stop only when electricity was being used in the cavern. There was concern over the potential waste of fuel from constantly running the engine. Schmidt and Gray stood outside as sentries while the others worked in the generator room. With no lights, sunlight filtered through the windows where Cameron jotted down notes as a record of their activities. He would write a report based on his transcripts when this mission was over. His notations were necessarily brief since the booklet would have to last a Holland winter.

❈

It was to absolute quiet that Monique awoke. She lay on her front, her face turned toward the walkway. Her last memory before she lost consciousness was counting backward from one hundred. Oliveiras had been administering anesthetic gas at the time, and her voice had sounded hollow in the face piece that covered her nose and mouth. She couldn't remember reaching the eighties.

Her head heavy, she looked around with her eyes, but no one was in sight. She tried to use her sluggish arms to lift herself, but her left arm encountered something on her blanket. With a feeble push, she shifted herself sideways to give herself room to get her arm around the obstruction.

She realized her legs were not responding. Lying half on her side, she willed her leg to lever herself over. She felt numb from the waist down; it was as if that part of her body was gone. Suddenly lightheaded, she pressed the side of her face against her pillow. *I don't feel anything.* Doubt filled her mind, driven by panic. *They should have operated sooner. Something shifted, and Oliver cut a nerve getting it out. I'm never going to walk again.* She squeezed her eyes shut and took a deep breath. *No, I have to believe everything is okay,* she thought. *I'm alive. Why can't I feel anything?*

She felt a pinprick of wetness under her eyelids. *Why can't I hear anyone? Am I alone?*

She wanted to turn herself over. Without her legs and with one arm pinned, she wormed her other arm beneath her torso. Shifting her shoulder, she managed to roll her body. Opening her eyes, she blinked twice to shake the tears from her eyelashes. Now on her side, she could see what had been blocking her arm.

Wilfz was next to her. He was asleep. He was sitting on the floor, arms on her mattress, head pillowed on his arms. He had kept promise to her.

"Michael-*ssi,*" she whispered, "*naneun neoreul saranghae.*" *Michael, I love you.* She sounded sleepy in her own ears and realized that she was still under the influence of the anesthetic. She slowly reached over and tenderly ran her fingers through the major's sandy brown hair.

The major twitched. "Eunice," he said.

Why have I never corrected him? Monique wondered with a smile. *Why does he call me that anyway?*

Wilfz's eyes snapped open. He looked up along the bed up to Monique. In the semidarkness of the room, she could still ascertain the brown of his eyes. "You're here," she whispered, letting her hand cup the side of his face.

"How do you feel?" Wilfz asked. He raised his head and Monique released him.

"I ... I don't know," she replied haltingly, her voice dull with grogginess. She could not conceal the trepidation in her voice. "I can't feel anything."

"Olly said everything came out okay." Wilfz spoke in a level tone. "You'll soon be back to your old self."

"He said this to you?"

"I guess he thought I'd see you before he did."

"I can't move my legs."

"Well, you just woke up. You're still full of painkillers."

"Was that how it was for you?"

"Everyone reacts differently to anesthesia. Even the doctors cannot explain why. I'm told they don't know why anesthesia works in the first place." Wilfz slowly grinned. She rewarded him with a tentative smile in return.

She slipped her hand along the blanket and gathered some of the fabric between her thumb and forefinger. She moved her hand to another part of the blanket and tried again.

"I feel so weak," she complained in a low voice. "I can't pinch myself." She moved her hand over to him and touched his hand. "Pinch me."

"Hngh?" Wilfz said in surprise.

"You heard me," Monique said. "I'm not strong enough."

Wilfz looked at her.

"Please."

She tugged his hand over to her blanket-covered thigh. She could feel his touch on her muscle. She gave a slow nod and he gently squeezed. With a look of concentration on her features, she shook her head in denial. She had felt the pressure of his grip, but she did not want to tell him yet. "I can't feel you through the blanket. Maybe if you pinched me directly," she suggested.

Wilfz looked at her, the expression on his face clearly indicating that he thought her idea was indecent.

"It's okay," she encouraged him.

Wilfz reluctantly lifted a portion of the blanket and extended one arm underneath. At his cool touch against her knee, she flinched.

"I'm sorry. My hands are cold," he replied. He pulled his hand back out of her bunk.

"You didn't pinch me," she said in disappointment.

"I didn't have to," Wilfz said. "You could feel my cold hand. You're going to be okay."

"I wanted you to pinch me."

"You also wanted me to believe you couldn't feel me through your blanket. You're having sport with me again."

"You can't blame a girl for being frisky," she replied. "I was just so worried … afraid for so long. I'm just so relieved now." A tear traced over the bridge of her nose and fell to the pillow.

"Just rest," Wilfz encouraged her. "Give the anesthesia time to wear off."

"You're not leaving, are you?" Monique asked quickly, her hand seeking his.

"Olly won't let me go outside." Wilfz smiled at her.

"Sit with me," she gestured to the side of the bunk. "It's more comfortable than the floor."

"You won't give up, will you? I'm not going to sleep with you."

"Michael, I've become accustomed to your presence. I'll be able to relax with you next to me," Monique entreated him. "I won't do anything to make you uncomfortable. I promise."

Wilfz shook his head.

"I would rather sleep this off," Monique continued. "I'll go crazy if I have to lie here waiting for the numbness to wear off."

Wilfz looked away. Monique noticed that Cameron was watching them. Dismissing him, she returned her attention to Wilfz. "Do this for me. Let me have this moment of peace." Monique gripped his hand firmly. "Please, I'm begging you."

"No." Wilfz looked at her sharply. "Women should never beg."

Monique almost flinched at the chastisement. Before she could speak again, he shifted himself to stand up. "Just this one time," he said.

From their previous time together, Monique was coming to understand this man's thoughts. He had become angry not because of what she had said but over the thought that a woman would debase herself. She wanted to believe that there was more to his feelings than that she was just a woman. She wanted to be the only woman.

That thought had barely occurred to her when Wilfz carefully lay on his side with his back to her. Leaning toward him, she draped her arm over his torso.

"*Kamsahamnida,*" she murmured.

"I don't know what you're saying, but it's very pleasant," Wilfz mumbled conversationally.

Monique was satisfied to remain silent. There would be plenty of time to tell him about the Korean language.

❧❀❧

When Monique awoke the second time, Wilfz had returned to his place next to her on the floor. That he would move while she was asleep did not surprise her. She saw that the others had since returned to the cavern during her slumber.

Remembering the numbness, she tried to determine if her legs had feeling in them. Dismay welled up again at the memory of her helplessness, but the heavy feeling was gone. She could tell her toes were uncomfortable with restlessness. She curled them, encouraging her circulation to flow. She felt the rasp of the rough blanket against her feet. With that minor victory, she experimentally moved a leg.

"Lady Lewellen?"

Wonder of wonders. Cameron called me that as if he meant it.

She reeled as she gingerly swung her legs to the floor. She could imagine her drawn and wan appearance.

"How do you feel?" Oliveiras approached. Wilfz moved aside to make room for the doctor.

"I can feel my legs!" she said with relief. She spoke again with a sense of urgency. "I have to go."

"We'll carry you," Oliveiras beckoned to Perez.

"I want to walk."

"You're still shaky. Let us help," Oliveiras said. He and Perez took her under her arms and escorted her to the end of the cavern. As they left, she heard Wilfz pull his carbine from beneath her bunk.

As Monique returned to the main room, she followed the inside curve of the cavern and used the wall to steady herself, but otherwise she walked unassisted. Ready to catch her if she should stumble, Perez and Oliveiras followed close behind her. Her skirted legs trembled with each step. Wilfz made a noise in his throat and turned away, but not before she saw the shimmering in his eyes.

"I walked all the way back," Monique boasted triumphantly.

"Okay, that's good. You can sit down now," Oliveiras urged her nervously. "I don't want you to fall down."

"When I get back to bed," she replied. "It's only a few meters more."

She stepped toward her bunk. With one hand on the wall, she took a step. As she took her hand away, she glanced at Wilfz. Seeing him looking at her, she looked away and placed her hand back on the wall.

"Lady," Perez reached to her.

Monique refused with a shake of her head. "I can do it," she insisted quietly. At the same moment, her legs shook.

Before she realized it, Wilfz had come to her aid. With his carbine cradled in his left arm, he offered his right hand to Monique. It was clear that he was offering her a choice—either walk across the cave on her own or take his hand.

"I'm not an invalid," she said. She looked away, hiding her face from him. She was unable to hide the little smile from Oliveiras. The doctor gave her a sharp look. *That's right, I* wanted *him to come get me*, she thought triumphantly.

"No, we're ambulatory now," Wilfz agreed with her. She faced him and saw his easy grin. Softness in his eyes conveyed a warmth she'd never seen from him before. Somehow she knew that he'd never looked at anyone else that way. Inexplicably her knees became weak. She placed her hand in his.

"Yes, *we* are," she agreed.

EPILOGUE

Office Q, Celestial Guard Headquarters, Pearl

Inspector-Major Genda entered the reception to her office. Her civilian secretary inclined her head to the other occupant in the room.

"Ah, Guardsman Tuarez, you're early. Come with me." Genda indicated her office. She looked to her secretary. "Thank you, Miss Connolly."

"You're welcome, Captain Genda."

Shakira Tuarez had a shocked look on her dusky face from the disrespect that had been given the inspector-major. Genda stopped instantly, expressing a look of consternation.

"I keep forgetting you're married," she said. "Maybe if you brought in a picture of your husband and put it on your desk."

The secretary shifted a framed picture across her desk. Genda waved a hand of acknowledgement. That suggestion had been made the previous week.

"I'll figure it out, Mrs. Reynolds, I really will. Thank you," Genda looked back to Tuarez and beckoned her to follow.

"Major." Mrs. Reynolds held up a small box.

"You have it. Good." Genda accepted it from her and led the guardsman into her office.

Guardsman Tuarez had never been to Major Genda's office, much less any major's office. As she passed Mrs. Reynolds, the secretary gave her a pleasant smile before returning to her work.

Tuarez had been one of the team members who had been excluded due to gender when Lieutenant Cameron had taken the rest of the team to Holland. It was supposed to have been a brief mission, but he and her team members were now overdue. Meanwhile, Captain Williams had deployed on assignment with the other team, leaving what remained of Cameron's team on Pearl.

"She's been married two months. One would think I would remember that by now. Close the door and have a seat," Genda said in an absentminded manner, gesturing to Tuarez. The inspector-major walked around her desk and sat down, placing to one side the box her secretary had given to her. She watched as Tuarez looked around the office. The room had very little character, furnished only with the obligatory desk and chairs.

Most officers filled their offices with pictures, awards, and other mementoes that represented a life of service and experience. The lack of that display in Genda's office served to emphasize her commitment to maintaining her privacy. It was only in her private quarters that anyone would have an inkling of the things that were important in her life, and only those few whom she counted as friends had ever seen the painting that prominently dominated one wall of her sitting room. A meter wide and half a meter high, it commemorated a naval battle over the spaceport on the planet Rendezvous. The imperial destroyer D577 had dueled three privateer corvettes. Tram Ahn Mai, known to her acquaintances as Tam, had been newly commissioned as the destroyer's commanding officer at that time. The title of the painting, *Rendezvous on the Deck,* was engraved on a brass plaque that was mounted on the frame. It was decidedly a double entendre. Genda had purchased the painting as a remembrance. She had been on Rendezvous at that time and remained friends with Tam.

The only other furniture in Genda's office was the low bookshelf beneath the window behind her desk. Visitors would note that there were no books on the shelves—fastidiously empty much like her desk top—but on top was a framed picture of the emperor and the first consort. Only a few visitors actually recognized the royal couple, since pictures normally posted in government buildings displayed the pair in colorful robes of office. In Genda's picture Min-kyung wore a fashionable jacket and knee-length skirt. Slightly shorter than her husband, she stood beside him against a garden backdrop, her arm looped through his. The informality of the dress, pose, and setting suggested to uninformed visitors that this couple might be family or friends of Genda.

As Tuarez took a seat, the major spoke. "In the absence of Captain Williams and Lieutenant Cameron, it has fallen to me to tell you that you will be replacing Sergeant Flynn."

Tuarez looked at the major in surprise.

"Sergeant Flynn is transferring. She recommended you to take her place."

"I knew she was leaving. I thought someone would transfer in to replace her."

"Your advancement is pending approval by your captain. In the meantime you will be acting sergeant," Genda explained. "You will have all of the privileges and responsibilities of your new rank; you just won't be paid for it yet. You'll get your back pay once Captain Williams returns."

Genda opened a drawer in her desk and pulled out a sheet of paper. She passed it across the desk to Tuarez. "This is your authorization," she said. "An entry has already been noted in your personnel file, but this will give you something to look at. Perhaps you might like to frame it."

At the word *frame*, Tuarez glanced briefly behind Genda.

Genda slid the box that Mrs. Reynolds had given her across the desk. "You might want to put these on, Sergeant Tuarez."

The new sergeant opened the box to see metal collar tabs depicting her rank. She removed one of the tabs and tilted her head in an attempt to look at her own collar.

"I don't know about you," Genda commented, getting up and walking around to face Tuarez, "but I've never been able to see my own neck without a mirror. Let me help you with that." She took the tab from Tuarez's fingers and attended to the younger woman. There were two layers of fabric on the upright collar, the gap accessible from the top. Slipping the fastener down between the layers, she pressed the tab against the outside of the collar, pushing the pin behind the tab through the fabric to the fastener.

As Genda critically inspected her handiwork, the women heard two taps on the door. The door opened before Genda could answer. The flash in her eyes clearly demonstrated that she was not pleased by the interruption.

"Lieutenant Lewis is here from Admiral Christie's office," Mrs. Reynolds announced.

At the mention of the admiral, Genda gave a quick nod. "Give us a moment to get the sergeant squared away then send him in," she said.

"I'll send *her* in," Mrs. Reynolds emphasized.

"It's not necessary, Major," Tuarez said. "I can do this later."

"Sergeant, a word of advice," Genda said. "You are in the Celestial Guard. When you're alone in quarters, you can let your uniform slide. However, in the eyes of others there is no excuse for sloppiness or improper insignia. That is especially true in front of the navy. They are sticklers for proper decorum. Remember that."

"Yes, Major."

"Besides, I want you here," Genda went on. "There might be news of your team."

Moments later, Lieutenant Lewis entered the office. The officer was in shipboard work uniform. Over her left shirt pocket was a black rectangle on which a silver arrowhead was superimposed pointing toward her left, denoting the wearer as a member of the destroyer force of the Imperial Navy. The lack of a hat was also a clue. Members in destroyer service were traditionally exempt from wearing headgear.

"I was led to believe you were from Admiral Christie's office." Genda spoke without preamble.

"I just came from reporting there." Lewis gave an unabashed grin. "The admiral asked me to come see you. I figured you would be more willing to see me if I dropped his name rather than my own."

"I see." Genda quirked an eyebrow. "I gather you are from Captain Quinlin's flight?"

"Yes, ma'am. I'm tactical officer for D530."

"Tell me, how are our people?"

"According to their last communiqué, they've gone to ground." Lewis held out an information clip. "Here are all of the messages they sent, our acknowledgements, and the scans we took of Holland. The admiral told me to answer any questions you have." She looked at the sergeant meaningfully as she finished.

Genda introduced Tuarez. "She is one of Lieutenant Cameron's people."

Lewis gave the sergeant a nod then looked to Genda. "Yes, ma'am, as I said, your team went into hiding. The skipper—destroyer leader Captain Quinlan—allowed the 638 to make a ballistic pass to gather electronic intel. From the radio chatter on the ground, it's clear they're shifting units all over the place down there. It's more like they are establishing garrisons than sending out search teams to go after your people. The 638 got so close they could tell that Holland's First Mountain Brigade was filtering away from their mountain bases."

"Can we get my team back?" Tuarez asked.

"If we could find your team, we could get them out. Even with their short signals, we know where they transmitted from. They signaled from a different borough each time, so we assume they're on the move. Right now we don't know exactly where they are."

"What's a borough?"

"They're like precincts or wards. The capital of Holland is subdivided into boroughs. Each borough is administered by a member of Holland's governing council," Genda answered, and then she looked to Lewis. "It would seem that my team remained in Bremen."

"That's what we figured," Lewis said. "After we take out the guns, we can use the destroyers to provide ground support while the marines land and extract your team. Holland does not have infantry armor or tanks, but they do have combat cars and mobile artillery. From what I've seen, they are no match for us."

"You've been thinking about this, Lieutenant," Genda commented.

"When we're on station, we have a lot of time to think." Lewis grinned. "It helps us to know as much as possible about the location. If we see action, get hit, and go down, we need to know as much as possible about what's down there and who we will face."

"So there is a plan?" Tuarez asked.

"Holland has no orbital defenses, and their suborbital system is antiquated. With no navy to interfere, we've been able to get quite close without being detected. We've managed to map their ground defenses. We were able to see them during maintenance cycles so we're sure we know where most, if not all, of their guns are. When we go in, we can knock out any we missed on the attack run."

"We cannot take any overt action to recover our people," Genda replied. "Taking out the planet's entire defensive infrastructure is unacceptable. For the lives of only six imperial citizens, such an extreme measure cannot be justified."

"We've done it before," Lewis declared in reaction to Genda's formality.

Genda nodded. "Yes, against hostile outposts. If Holland were a haven for hostile forces, that decisive action would be warranted. However, Holland has civilization. To remove their defenses would be exposing them to great danger."

"They are not hostile now?" Tuarez pondered cynically.

"We do not know what happened to our people down there. In the worst-case scenario, they will be considered spies and prosecuted accordingly. Under those circumstances attacking Holland would create an interstellar incident. It would be different if we were facing a declared enemy in battle, but that is not the case here. The only option is for our people to travel to a location where we can extract them without having to face Holland's main line of defense."

"I can understand leaving them to their own devices," Tuarez said. "The Celestial Guard element, I mean. But the envoy is civilian. We can't abandon her there."

"That's a risk of foreign service," Genda said. "She volunteered for that posting. As much as it is our responsibility to bring our people home, we cannot put an innocent population at risk. No matter what their government is doing, the innocent must not get caught in the middle. We can't get a lander into the city proper, never mind a destroyer. Then there is the additional damage from the fighting while making the recovery." She paused as if to make her decision final. "No, it'll be enough of an interstellar incident if they parade our uniformed personnel through their streets at bayonet point."

"I thought your people were undercover," Lewis said.

"I gave them specific orders to get into uniform if things turned sour," Genda admitted. "I don't want them executed for espionage. Lieutenant Cameron's team was not sent for covert intelligence gathering. I was trying to keep everything above board."

"I fail to see the difference," Lewis opined.

"That was my argument when Admiral Christie talked me into this," Genda admitted sourly.

"If they are in uniform now, the hostiles don't have them," Lewis said. "We would've picked up mention of the capture of imperial armed forces."

Genda visibly considered what the naval officer had just said.

"The 530 will be on Pearl for a week," Lewis continued. "We're picking up mail and consumables for the rest of our flight."

"And the rest of the flight is on station around Holland?" Genda inquired.

"Just the skipper right now," Lewis shook her head. "We leave only one destroyer on station. The others are out trolling deep space."

"Trolling?" Tuarez asked.

"Anti-piracy patrol," Genda replied. "A destroyer sits with machinery powered down, watching with passive sensors only. No one can tell she is there. Pirates do that, too, waiting for legitimate shipping to arrive so they can ambush them. The destroyers catch the predatory ships when they power up to attack."

"You know a lot about destroyers," Lewis observed.

"I have a friend."

Tuarez looked at Lewis shrewdly.

"Any more questions before I let you go, Sergeant?" Genda asked.

"Can I go with them when they go back?" Tuarez asked impulsively. "If they can put me on the ground, I'd like to try and locate my team."

Genda regarded the new sergeant silently. Lewis smiled condescendingly, earning a look of irritation from Genda.

"I already have one unit on the ground. I'd rather not put another unit down and complicate the effort by having to pull them both out."

"I'm not volunteering my team," Tuarez said, "just me."

Lewis shook her head, getting another look from Genda.

"I understand that, but the answer is still no," Genda said. "The navy and the marines are trained to do this. It's their job. They have done this before."

"I should be with them. They're my team."

"You are Celestial Guard. Your will is to do the bidding of our emperor," Genda said, her tone not unkind.

At Genda's mention of the emperor, Tuarez looked past her to the picture on the bookcase. Her eyes widened.

"It took you long enough," Genda commented. Tuarez flushed with embarrassment, obviously even further distracted because Genda had caught her looking at the picture.

Lewis looked from one woman to the other, eyebrows furrowed in puzzlement.

"Well, Sergeant Tuarez, if that's all?" Genda waited for the sergeant to respond.

"I can't think of a thing, ma'am."

"Then report back to your team. I suspect Sergeant Flynn will help you celebrate your promotion before she transfers." Genda then spoke in a slightly higher voice. "Miss Connolly?"

The door opened and the secretary entered. The married woman gave no sign that she had noticed the major's gaff.

"Yes, Major Genda?" Mrs. Reynolds said, giving Tuarez a little smile that confirmed Genda's admonition: *Not in front of the navy.*

"Mrs. Reynolds, is the car ready?" Genda asked.

"Yes, Major," she answered.

"Good." Genda looked to Tuarez. "That will take you to your celebratory dinner. That will be all, Sergeant."

Once Mrs. Reynolds escorted Tuarez out of the office, Lewis and Genda were alone. Genda spoke first. "Sergeant Tuarez is the senior representative of what remains of Lieutenant Cameron's team."

Lewis looked at the major curiously.

"In lieu of the fact that her officers were not available, I entertained her questions." Genda's ire waned as she explained, the destroyer officer listening politely. "When she volunteered to go to Holland, I was tempted to let her. If I were of a different mind, I probably would have given my consent."

Lewis nodded in understanding.

"I doubt if it should be necessary, but I would appreciate it if you kept an eye out for Sergeant Tuarez," Genda said. "It wouldn't be good for her if she were to sneak aboard your ship. I'd hate to take away those tabs I just pinned on her."

"Of course, Inspector-Major."